DANEGELD

THE PRICE

As he pulled back, she smiled up at him, and this time the smile was strong. She could see it in his eyes. She pulled the shirt from his breeches and over his head. His fingers worked at her girdle while she touched the scars on his shoulder in the firelight. She traced the vessel that fed the muscle of his biceps, the ligament that bound his shoulder. She had stitched them together once. Now there was skin so soft, so smooth....

Then he had her naked in the firelight. She straddled the rough leather of his breeches and felt the hardness in his loins. Her hands moved over the ridged muscles of his back, as he held her buttocks with both hands and drank her in with his eyes. She ran her fingers over the planes of his chest. Her face buried in his neck, she kissed his satin skin. His scent would haunt her all her days. His groan vibrated in his chest. It was not one of pain.

Sitting up, she pulled the leather strips from her braids as his hands explored her ribs, cupped her breasts, touched her nipples. She shook out her hair. It floated about her head in wavy red clouds the color of fire. She could see the one streak of white smoke. Fire without, fire within, she thought, and turned the focus of her hands back to Karn.

Suddenly he stiffened. He gripped her shoulders and his eyes grew truly fierce.

"Is this Danegeld, Britta?' She didn't understand. He almost shook her. "Do you give your body as the price to make the magic go away? Would any man do for you tonight?"

Pain crumpled her face for an instant. That was part of it. But telling that would hurt him. And it was not the whole truth. "I have wanted this for a long tune." That, at least, was true.

Other books by Susan Squires:

NO MORE LIES
THE ONLY ONE (Anthology)
DANELAW
BODY ELECTRIC
SACRAMENT

SUSAN SQUIRES

DANEGELD

Montlake
Romance

Text copyright © 2001 by Susan Squires
All rights reserved.
Printed in the United States of America.

Published by Montlake Romance
P.O. Box 400818
Las Vegas, NV 89140

ISBN-13: 9781477837313
ISBN-10: 1477837310

To Claire Carmichael for teaching me how to be professional; to Sonndra and Jim for their unfailing contributions in the critique group; to Julie Castiglia for believing enough to want to sell it; to Chris Keeslar for taking a chance; and to Harry, for informing every hero and making the writing possible.

This title was previously published by Dorchester Publishing; this version has been reproduced from the Dorchester book archive files.

Prologue

Witch or saint—which? Wicce or sancte? Even now I do not know. The gods know. Or the one God knows. Everyone around me is sure, though no one quite agrees. Yet to me, the only true witness to the miracles, that sureness is denied.

I thought that my divine connections were lost long before the Northmen began their terrible assault upon our village. Of that I was certain. The magic had been stolen from me even before I knew the true power of its fire in my veins.

But he who by all rights should have sealed it away from me forever brought it back to me, gift and curse, to change the course of my life, the course of history.

Even after he was gone the magic stayed, weakening as the hoarfrost touched my hair and winter chilled my bones. Weakened, but not gone.

Men sing our story in the sagas of two lands, rhyming from father to son, but they only know our deeds, his and mine—not what they cost us. They cannot know the courage those deeds required, or the fear, the hopeless uncertainty that brought them forth.

No one knows, even yet, that the world we forged between

9

us will last down through the ages, different because we lived it joined. But I know. I have seen it in the fire.

Here then is the saga, not as it is sung, but as I would sing it.

Chapter One

Britta could never pity them. Not anymore. She clutched her cloak about her. The wind off the North Sea, cold in the October dawn, struck a damp chill to her bones that echoed the hard, cold core of her. She kept her gaze fastened on the distant band of Saxons on the gray beach and bent again to the oars of her small boat. The creak of wood against wood joined the cries of the gulls to pierce the rush of wind in her ears.

The villagers stood expectantly beneath the stone church that loomed on the cliffs. They must have seen her, for several of them pointed. She could not yet make out who they were. She knew only that they would be needy. There must be a hundred souls in the village of Dunford now, and of course there were Offa's men in the faesten up the river. Offa. The scratch of his beard, the stench of his warm breath, the rough hands, all drenched her senses. She scraped the rough ends of the oars through her palms and sucked in the fecund smell of salt and seaweed until she could banish the memory.

Remember the reason you come here. She swallowed deliberately. If any were truly ill today, payment for her herb-craft might be an iron pot for stews, for lesser cures a new awl or a flitch of bacon. The healing of her herbs was all the magic she would ever have, now.

The water pulled against her strokes as the seabirds wheeled above in the biting air. It was less than a mile from her island refuge to the shore of the mainland, but the way was dread-long. If she had not needed what the villagers could give, they might keep their fluxes and their poxes and be welcome to them. But her island could not be everything to her, though it gave her the protection of its evil name. Deofric Eoland. *Devil Island.* It was called that because of the horns of sand that made its tiny harbor. No god-fearing man dared set foot upon its shores. Which suited Britta well. She only wished she never had to leave its sanctuary.

At least the village had been spared the fury of the Vikings. The faesten up the river protected them. But which was worse, the suffering inflicted by strangers or that inflicted by one's own kind? When Offa came from the west, burning and pillaging, everyone had suffered, not just Britta. Still, ruled by a strong thegn like Offa, the village had enjoyed five years of peace.

She put up her oars, and two of the men stepped into the surf to pull her boat into the sand. She had tight hold of herself as she stopped to gather the small pots of her herbs, her worts. Looking up, she crisply ordered the villagers to form a line and ready their payments.

Karn squinted up into the sun to watch the snapping canvas fall. "Look to the ropes," he shouted as his men hauled against the wind to reel in the striped sail of the dragon ship. Kara pushed his sun-streaked hair away from his face and looked out past the ornately carved prow to where two hundred Danish ships surged on the choppy water. The signal from the lead vessel was clear: raid the little stone church they could see on a rise at the shore.

"Why does he send us?" Sveinn muttered. He had been Karn's second in command since Constantinople. The hard lines of his face resolved themselves into a frown.

Karn himself had proposed these small raids along the shore in Anglia to discourage the Saxon thegns from leaving their lands unprotected to join their Centish brothers to the south. But Ivar the Boneless and his brother Halfdan, sons of Ragnar Lothbrok, usually sent unblooded youths on these easy missions, not hardened warriors like Kara and his men. Kara twisted at the leather that wrapped his wrist. "Ulf is behind this," he growled under his breath.

"His influence grows," Sveinn agreed. "Perhaps Ivar has forgotten that it was you who organized the siege that broke Rouen."

Kara surveyed the small island between the fleet and the shore. It had good protection for landing, with two spits of sand that arched out around a cove like horns, much like the island they had used so effectively off Napoli. "Signal them to put in to the island," he barked.

"The bold brothers will not like the delay." Sveinn watched a signal flag cut the crisp air.

"Ivar must say why he sends us, why we must risk our share of plunder to raid this paltry church."

"Or the Danegeld the towns may pay." Sveinn's eyes lit in anticipation.

"Yes, these Saxons always try to buy off what they most fear." Kara braced himself against the creaking, wet wood of the deck as the dragon changed course. "It never works for long."

"The brutes don't seem to notice." Sveinn laughed.

Karn frowned. All that Saxon silver, plundered or paid, would not buy for him what a fourth son was denied in Denmark—a place, land of his own. Once, such things had not mattered to an unruly youth with too much fire in his blood. He had been eager to leave his homeland. His father had been glad to see him go, having tired of helping him out of one scrape after another. Kara had not been home in years. His parents were probably dead. His brother likely farmed the family land.

Now the best he could hope for was that Danish scalds

would sing his name as they told of the brave deeds he had done in the days when he went viking. Once he'd thought that would be enough, but today discontent plucked at his heart. He did not know what he wanted, but he could not share his doubts with Sveinn. Danish warriors were not allowed doubt.

Karn watched Ivar's ship turn toward the island. Much glory would be denied him if he missed the battle in Cent because he was sent to raid some tiny church. Uneasiness crept over him as he stared out at the dark, forested hump of the little island looming before his vessel's dragon prow. He might regret questioning his orders. That they had been given at all was a bad omen. Somehow, something had begun to go wrong.

It was a long morning for Britta. Decoctions of bergamot for the fluxes, garlic poultices for infected wounds. She gave endless instructions. The wounds were the worst. For those— she had to touch the flesh. But when the wrongness of the wounds called, she could not refuse.

She came at last to Henewulf, who waited patiently. She opened the untidy bandage on his arm and saw a ragged cut. "What was it?"

"A meat hook," he answered stolidly.

She turned to her bundle for some gut and her needle. She always felt uneasy around Henewulf. She had given him herbs once, because his wife Syffa was barren. It had been a gesture only, to stop their pleadings. Syffa was too old to bear. Still, less than three months later, the woman was swelling, and in nine months the babe was hale and healthy. Henewulf would never believe Britta's herbs had not produced his son. His gratitude was a bond she'd never sought.

"Wicce, have you seen my Edgar of late?" The grizzled warrior grunted as she pulled a needle through the hairy flesh of his forearm. "He is the image of his mother."

Britta pressed her lips together and continued to work.

"Withal he is a brave lad and can already lift my sword."

Henewulf paused to chew his lip as her sewing continued. "You can be proud of your work, Wicce."

"That was not my work. I have told you that," Britta muttered.

Henewulf was silent until the last knot was tied and the gut cut with Britta's prize possession, an eight-inch hollow-core knife. "Syffa agrees. She says Jesu works through you."

Britta bound the wound with a linen strip. "Think what you will," she said. "Now be off with you and keep the bandage clean."

Henewulf rose until he towered over Britta. "You dismiss your gift, but I cannot." He gestured to a bundle of fresh wool, too valuable a payment for her simple stitchery.

She bit back her protest. If his gratitude ended in a new cloak for winter, what did she care that it was misplaced? She turned away. Looking about, Britta saw Wynn. The peasant woman held a tiny baby that looked like a dried berry, no longer able even to cry. Britta studied the babe's face as Henewulf stalked away. Her vision blurred in a familiar way. A blackness hung around the tiny bundle. She shook her head to clear it. The presence of death always made her gorge rise. She pushed a wisp of the red-gold hair escaping from her braid behind one ear. "I cannot treat your babe, Wynn."

"But you are her hope, my hope," the woman cried.

Britta steeled herself. No herbs would cure this child, and if she tried and failed, the faith of the village in her skills would be poisoned. "If you are Christian, go to your new church and pray to your God to save your child, for I cannot."

"I have prayed until my knees are raw, and still she wanes." The woman looked down at her listless little bundle.

"Then she meets her maker soon," Britta said tightly. "You should prepare."

"Weave me one of the old spells," the woman beseeched, plucking at Britta's sleeve.

Britta shook her head. She hadn't believed in salvation for a long time. "My prayers no longer reach the gods, or the one God." She turned away as tears welled in the woman's bloodshot eyes. "You will have other babes." A wail rose behind her, but Britta blocked it out.

Hurrying to her things, Britta ignored the midmorning sun as she covered her tiny pots with leather and tied them with string. The others had left the beach without another word. Just as she'd wanted. She heaved her hoard into her boat and pushed it out into the water. Once she had put some distance between herself and the shore, Britta ground her fists into the small of her back and caught her breath. She felt much older than her twenty years. The smell of the sea rose up in all its salty fecundity around her. Her eyes followed the gulls as they wheeled on the updrafts, above.

Something had changed. She felt dizzy and distant from herself. Looking back, on the shore she saw Wynn, still sitting on a giant log washed up last winter, rocking her bundle and weeping.

The babe is dead, Britta thought. I felt it go. Once she would have gone back to Wynn, to hold the woman as she wept until Britta could take the tiny body from her and the two could bury it on the cliffs above the beach together. But that was before Offa and his men had ripped her magic from her, before the world had revealed itself for what it was. She calmed her breathing, pressing down the old rage and the fear. Now she dared not let in another's pain lest it remind her of her own and sap her will to trade with the world at all. Her vision blurred. It must be the wind stinging her eyes.

She filled her lungs with sea air and bent to her oars. The dark hump of her island danced on the waves. It was only a mile from shore, but suddenly it seemed a long way back.

Britta threw open the door of her small single-room house to let out the smell of smoke hanging in the rafters. The huge black dog that slept at the foot of her bed box rose and stretched as she opened the wicker shutters to the light. Fends, the Wolf Who Would Devour the World, she thought wryly, or at least an entire rabbit last night, bones and all. Your fierce looks go very well with my island.

He did not act fierce. He nosed at her hand and leaped about.

Britta unbuckled her girdle, woven in geometric patterns of red, deep green, and ochre, from about her waist. The trefoil silver brooches at her shoulders had been her mother's. She unfastened them and pulled her grass-green tunic over her head. She undid the tiny leather buckles at her wrists that kept the sleeves of her white linen shift tight. Then she unwrapped the many loops of thin leather from her ankles and balanced against Fenris to remove her worn leather shoes. Eager to bathe, she laid out her soap, an antler comb, and a fresh shift. It was always thus after returning from the mainland.

Hungry, she grabbed a hunk of bread and cut a bit of cheese from the wheel hanging high on the wall, out of the dog's reach. With a cup of water from the bucket by the door, her fast was simply broken. The cheese she shared with Fenris. He sniffed fastidiously before he took it.

"I can thank that poor rabbit for your manners, my fine friend," she scolded fondly.

Clad only in her shift, she exited her dwelling and started across the meadow toward the spring. When first she'd come to the island she had scrubbed her skin raw every day, as though she could ever feel clean again. Now, the ritual had become a comfort. After her bath there was much to do. It was an auspicious day for gathering certain herbs: coltsfoot in the clay by the spring, garlic in the sandy soil under the south cliff where it was sunny, comfrey in the shady forest loam and marigolds. The island was blessed with mushrooms and kelp, sea salt, yarrow, and tiny pink valerian flowers all summer long.

Fenris darted into the clearing, capering about the lathe she used to carve her cups and bowls, in front of the woodpile got by the sweat of her brow. Simple work could soothe one's soul. If she had learned anything by living alone for so long, it was that. How long had it been—five turns of the season? Her regret had become like a pebble grown shiny with rubbing until it was beautiful, separate entirely from the rough lump of the original. She rubbed the pebble again, felt the familiar stab of pain, different now, duller.

She followed the rivulet to the shady pool overlooking the east beach. Before she soiled it with soap, she stared into the water. At first she could see only her reflection, her mother's green eyes, her father's red hair and his light dusting of freckles upon her nose. She was a confusion of Saxon and Celt, of her mother's belief in magic and her father's devout Christianity. Both and neither.

Abruptly, she stirred the water. Her reflection shimmered away into a thousand shards of light. Underneath, a fan of precious stime appeared, waving gently in the shadowy depths. Britta breathed deep and quoted the Nine-Herb Charm her mother had taught her to increase its potency.

> *"This herb is called Stime, it grew on a stone,*
> *It resists poison. It fights pain.*
> *This is the herb that strove with the worm:*
> *This has power against poison, power against infection,*
> *This has power against the foe who fares through the*
> *land!"*

Slowly she eased her hand into the chilly water. Just in case, she also used the words her father had given her. "Release to me, in the name of He Who Gave His Life for Us All, your healing gift," she commanded, and tore the plant from its rocky nest. Then she stripped off her shift and stepped into the cold water. Fenris barked from the edge of the pool and raced off into the bracken.

Britta washed as quickly as she could. Nakedness always made her feel vulnerable. She rubbed the lump of harsh soap over her breasts, too heavy for her slight figure, then heaved herself up to sit on the rock wall she had built to create the pool. As she soaped her hair, she glanced down at the cove below. Four dreaded dragon ships floated there.

Vikings! Her heart stuttered. She was close enough to see the fierce expressions of the dragons, the intricate geometric carving on the prows of each sleek ship. The vessels were sinuous evil, fast and supple in the water. They rocked gently now at anchor, bright shields in many colors lining their sides, their striped sails furled. Barbarian beasts strode the decks. Metal glinted in leather and fur. Had they seen her? She slipped off of the wall, back into the water, covering her breasts. They might have come ashore! Her mind darted about until it recalled Fenris.

By the gods! Even now, he might be capering up to greet those scourges from the North. He would find only a spear or an ax for his trouble. And the presence of a dog on this seemingly deserted island might send them looking for its owner.

"Fenris," she whispered fiercely. He would never hear her. If he did, then her voice might reach other ears as well. Frantically, she looked about, but her furry companion was nowhere to be seen. There was only the soughing of wind in the oaks and the communal chattering of starlings. She grabbed her shift and pulled it over her dripping body as she rose from the pool. She had never felt so naked. "Fenris," she called, a little louder.

From bush to bush she crept, crouching and calling softly. Now, from behind a clump of guelder rose, she could see almost a dozen of the Norse brutes standing just under the jutting rocks she called the Teeth of Fafnir, the Serpent Who Circled the World.

She had never seen actual Vikings before. Some were dressed in chain mail with pointed leather helmets whose metal nosepieces made them look like strange and terrifying animals. Huge men they were, with blond hair, or light brown. Several carried round shields, painted in yellow and black, and axes or swords. One wielded a huge hammer. They were ready for war.

Behind her, Britta heard the skittering of leaves. She whirled, expecting enemies. Instead, Fenris came loping down the hill, oblivious to danger. She knelt with open arms. He threw himself at her, all tongue and the smell of warm, fur.

19

"Fenris," she sobbed and buried her face in his coat. They would meet their fate together.

Slowly she began thinking again. This little island could not be the Vikings' destination. She scanned the horizon and saw, faint and small, hundreds of the dreaded ships, a flotilla of destruction. The village of Dunford was not worth so many ships; they had to have another goal. She got up, drawn to know more.

Across the wooded slope she zigzagged, pulling Fenris with her, her fingers buried in his fur. She worked around to where she could observe the intruders but still use the undergrowth of the oak wood for cover. Three Vikings stood and one knelt, talking earnestly while the others, like an honor guard, circled them at a respectful distance. Her glance roved quickly over two grizzled warriors whose sword hilts glinted with jeweled bosses and the one with a white-blond beard and drooping mustaches who squatted to draw in the sand. It came to rest on the profile of the only Viking who didn't wear a helmet. He was taller than the others, and powerfully built. A long mane of unruly hair streaked with blond framed his face and his sandy beard was close-cropped.

Fenris caught the scent of the intruders and barked a sharp challenge. Britta started and squeezed the dog's muzzle as he struggled to break free. Had the Vikings heard? The big one turned up to the woods above the rocks where she and Fenris hid. Britta ducked her head, but she could not tear her eyes away. His face was angular and hard, just as she imagined a Viking's would be. But even from here she could see his soft, full lips. What was a Viking doing with lips like those? The contrast was fascinating. He scowled as he searched the shadows with slitted eyes.

He would surely see them! Then the kneeling man claimed his attention. He turned back to the circle. Faintly, she could hear his angry voice, a deep rumble of authority. Intensity shone in his face. She could practically feel the vitality radiating from him. Here was a man capable of anything. Exactly, she told herself. He was Viking, capable of any barbaric act.

The crouching warrior with the drooping blond mustaches said something that sounded sympathetic. The giant shoved his sword into the sand and nodded as he growled assent. The crouching one rose then and turned away. Only Britta saw his sneering smile. The long-haired giant grew silent and grim. The men broke apart quickly and returned to the waiting ships.

Britta clutched Fenris to her and watched as the sinister, sleek galleys left—all except the one where the long-haired Viking strode the deck. A squarish cargo vessel joined his ship, sailing closer as the fleet in the distance moved south. The cargo ship seemed to indicate the Vikings' plan to pillage Dunford. Squat and evil, it rode low in the water, borne down with cattle and crates.

Britta was puzzled. One raiding ship could take the village but not challenge its protectors in the faesten less than a mile up the river. It would be a slaughter when Offa and his crew came charging down upon these three score Vikings. The invaders must not know about the faesten.

But before Offa's men could mobilize, these Vikings would do their worst to the village. For a moment Britta considered a dash in her boat to warn Dunford's villagers, but the thought of her tiny vessel encountering the Viking ship on the open sea made her shudder. Besides, what did she owe those people? They had not helped in her time of need.

She looped her girdle around Fenris's neck and pulled him down the path leading back to her house by way of the north beach, looking behind her at every third step. That was how she saw the Viking ship round the point of the island, its giant striped sail belled out with the wind, its oarsmen pulling fast toward shore. She dashed across the stony strand, dragging Fenris, and flung herself behind some hulking boulders. Had they seen her? Suspense froze her heart as surely as the Ice Giants from the Old Religion. Though she was close enough to hear their shouted war songs and see their fierce faces as they pulled their oars, the Vikings slid swiftly by without a glance toward shore. The longhaired Viking stood in the prow, his cloak whipped by the wind. That must be what a Norse god looked like, she thought through her fear. But he wasn't a god. He was a dead man. Offa would see to that.

But first Dunford would face the scourge of the Northmen.

Karn paced the deck of the dragon ship in a dark fury. Ulf had done his work well. Sveinn put a steadying hand on his shoulder. Karn broke his stride and looked into his old friend's eyes. They were smiling.

"Aye," Sveinn chuckled. " 'Tis a prize beneath us."

"Did you hear him?" Karn snarled. "He said he understood why we would not want to try and take the church! What could I do but prove our valor?"

"It will soon be done, and we will be speeding south to join the others," Sveinn agreed.

Karn turned away as two of his men came close to tie off one rope of the sail. He did not want the others to hear his anger.

He worked his way through the bustle to the prow, and Sveinn followed. "Ulf dared to reassure me that the church is unprotected and easily taken!" Karn could still hear the man's sympathetic condescension. He kicked a coiled rope fiercely out of his path, then abruptly leaned against the rail above to steady himself.

"Well," Sveinn temporized, "he would know."

Ulf had been through this way with a small scouting party early in the year. Slowly, Karn breathed himself to calm, then clapped his friend on the back and smiled ruefully. "Angry thoughts are fruitless old women. They will bear no issue." He looked to the sails as his men gathered them in. "Lay your backs into the oars, brothers," he yelled. Then he strode down the deck of the ship.

The dragon leapt ahead like a living animal, unfurling a green wake behind it. Only the shush of the water and the creak of the great oars broke the silence as they bore down upon the village. As they advanced, Karn fingered Hemglad, Mail-biter. His sword was carved with interlacing serpents on the hilt and inlaid with carbuncles at their eyes, but the weapon would know no true glory today; this would not be a true battle. Still, Hemglad would sing the blood song today as it had so well on the Frankish shore this summer. Around him his men's eyes began to gleam in anticipation. Even so small a challenge raised their blood.

On the shore, several villagers had spotted them. The men pointed toward the advancing ship in horror, then scattered to warn their kith. Karn broke into a battle chant and his men took it up, their voices echoing over the waves.

He bellowed the order to reverse the oars. The shallow-bellied dragon lurched to a halt just outside the surf line. Karn turned his head up and gave a battle cry. His men's answering shout rumbled into the salty air of the autumn noon. Then the Danir were over the side in a flurry of limbs. Burdened with iron, they slogged through the surf. Now they were most vulnerable, but the villagers only ran shrieking in disarray. Several dashed back up the gorge formed by the river. Karn and his men splashed into the surf and toiled through the sand up the beach.

"Into the village," Karn yelled. "And you five,"—here he pointed to Sveinn and several around him—"to the church with me before they hide the chalices." As he made his way through the village, he hacked casually at any who crossed his path. A boy of perhaps fourteen appeared with a pitch-fork, but he was not quick enough and fell with a startled look to Karn's sword.

Ahead, the bell in the church's small tower began to toll in a sonorous rhythm. Was this hamlet rich enough to boast a bell? That boded well for silver altarpieces. The tolling almost drowned the shrieks and screams around them. But its warning was too late.

A knot of about ten Saxon villagers had appeared with swords and shields. "Make quick work of them," he shouted to his men. Their opponents held swords or axes, some of decent quality. Indeed, several had hardened leather breastplates and greaves. Did this village have warriors in it? With a collective cry, the Northmen rushed at them, and the Saxons were soon lying in their own blood. Karn spun to lead the attack on the church.

The wooden doors were bolted shut, the church's windows high, narrow slits in the flint tower. From its sling at his side Karn swung up his ax. Great splinters of wood from the doors showered around his thundering blows. "It is I, Karn, son of Gunnar, who demands entrance," he whispered to himself, but it was not a whisper. He was shouting. The bell drowned all with reverberating sound. At last the door revealed its bolt. Karn shoved in his sword and lifted the latch.

In the beam of light from the burst portal, Karn saw the altar, two gleaming golden candlesticks, a gilt and jeweled cross. Yes, by Thor! Someone had endowed this church very well, for all it was small. He strode forward, panting, Hemglad quiet in his hand. "Stop that bell," he ordered. In the shadowy tower to the left, the priest heaved on the bell rope.

Karn moved to the altar and swept the cross and the gold candlesticks into his cloak. Turning, he saw Sveinn bearing down on the priest. The cleric left off pulling the rope, but the tolling continued overhead. Slowly, the priest smiled and fingered the beads about his neck, hung with the symbol of his crucified god. He smiled as though he knew some secret the Danir did not. Karn saw Sveinn's anger at that smile. The rage spurted from his friend like the sea through a blowhole in the rocks. A scream of rage tore through his throat.

"No!" Karn yelled, but it was too late. Sveinn clove the priest from shoulder to breastbone, raising a bloody fountain that splattered the stones of the tower. Slowly, the cleric toppled to the side. His smile never faltered. Karn took a ragged breath and strode over to stand behind Sveinn, who still shook with anger and the thrill of the kill. "Why murder the priest? He was no threat." Killing one who served the gods, even a strange god, always seemed an unnecessary risk. Sighing, Karn bent and tore the beads of amber and jet from the bloody wreck of the holy man's body. "So much for the strength of your god, priest." The last tolling of the bell hung in the still air.

"And so much for your smile," Sveinn added in a growl and spat on the stone floor.

Exiting the dim quiet of the church, Karn and his five Danir rushed down the small rise into the village once more, through fallen villagers, noisy chickens, and squealing pigs. Several houses were burning wildly. His men chased survivors through the roiling smoke. They were everywhere, going through the larger halls for tapestries or hacking armbands and bracelets from the fallen. He had not expected much from a village such as this, but then, there had been ten men with weapons. That many warriors in a village this size made him uneasy.

There was another form of wealth here as well. Already some women were being dragged, screaming, into one of the animal pens. The Danir would take whatever men had not been slaughtered, too. There was a brisk market for northern slaves in the lands around the sea far to the south, as well as at home in Denmark.

"Take the swine and chickens to the ship," Karn shouted as he strode through the smoke. Some moved to do his bidding, but most were gathering plunder, their shields and helmets discarded. Sveinn had cornered a comely wench by one of the larger halls and was taking her where she stood, her wails and struggles ignored. At home, if she had been a virgin, deflowering her would be punishable by death. Here, there were no rules except those of the strong.

Karn himself was in no mood to prolong this visit with rapine. He looked around. He did not like this village. It had to do with the bell tolling out over the countryside and too many men with weapons. It had to do with Ulf's condescension.

Karn felt his gut recoil. Something was wrong here. "Get to the Dragon," he shouted over the din. They needed the safety of their ship. Several looked up and nodded, but most were oblivious. They were scattered around the village. Too scattered. Karn pushed Sveinn off his victim. "Gather up the men," Karn hissed. "Now!"

He did not wait to see his order obeyed. He strode across the village, kicking men off struggling village women, pushing others down toward the beach. How had he let his men dissolve into such disorder? Complacency, he thought grimly.

Suddenly, Karn sensed movement above. His gaze jerked up to the cliffs around the village. Hordes of Saxon warriors, well armed, plunged down the sheer side of the ravine. His men were outnumbered three or four to one, Karn guessed. "Look up!" he shouted even as he spun to check the way back to the beach. Saxons were there, too. They streamed down to close off escape.

So be it. Karn picked up a discarded shield and drew out Hemglad. A scream of bloodlust rose from the Saxons' throats as the first poured into the village. Now his band would find the honorable struggle against insurmountable odds all Norsemen craved. His good fortune suffused him, but he knew he must steady his men when they first saw the odds.

"Valkyrie sing!" he shouted, settling his shield. "Tonight we are victorious or we toast the gods in Valhalla." Around the village, the Danir scrambled for their weapons as their foes closed in. "Form your squares," he yelled above the din. "Work back to the boats."

Where they could band together his men stood their ground, shields facing outward, swords and axes spiking out like some strange prickly beast. But those who were late joining their comrades, who had strayed too far afield, were already being overwhelmed.

Karn stepped forward as the first Saxon reached him. It was a young hothead, his beard hardly full. Karn cut him down with a single blow. The impact shuddered up his sword arm. As Harald and a son of Vair struggled forward to stand beside him, trying to form a square, a new enemy landed a blow across Karn's shield. He stuck his sword up under the man's arm to pierce his heart. Another square formed around Sveinn off to Karn's left.

Karn hacked about him now in a flurry of parries and thrusts. Hemglad grew slippery with bright blood. He felt someone bump him. Another of the Vairsson brothers had stepped up to a place in the square, but the boy had not had time to find a shield. Without it, he would not last long.

Saxons swarmed everywhere. Vairsson fell quickly. In the gap he left, a Saxon sword found Karn's sword-arm shoulder before he could cut its owner down. He paid no attention to the blood seeping over the dull metal of his mail shirt, but he knew that soon Hemglad would grow heavy. He slashed about him and struggled east toward the beach. If any Danir were standing at the end of the day they would be standing on their ship.

In the melee, Karn's senses shrank to the smell of sweat and blood, the clang of clashing metal, the grunts of effort, the screams of triumph and pain. Dust and smoke rose around him, a fog made opaque by the sun. He scrambled and pushed and shoved his sword forward, sweat rolling into his eyes. Time meant nothing. He had always fought. He would always fight.

At some point, his sword arm flagged. He felt the odds against survival rise. Then he did the unthinkable without even thinking. He let Hemglad fall. With one movement he switched his shield to his left hand and swung his ax up from its sling into his right, just in time to hack at the head of an enemy. Now he would do, at least for a while.

The band of Northmen around him yelled his name as they struck at their foes, but their progress toward the beach was bought with blood. One of the square fell to his knees and watched, startled, as his life spurted out where his arm had been. When no new jarl stepped into his place, Karn knew their numbers had dwindled. He looked for Sveinn's square and could not see it. The enemy pressed around him thickly. He felt metal gore his hip and he hacked off the hand that held it.

Karn labored for breath. Still he wielded his great ax with

the might of his father, the might of his gods, in his arm. He felt the man at his back waver and fall. He put up his shield and turned his head. It was Harald. He killed a Saxon from his knees, his sword thrusting up under his foe's shield. Karn reached back with his ax still in hand to drag the man up. As he turned, he felt a great blow to his head. From a distance, he heard his helmet crack, felt his knees turn to water. It was the same black water into which he was falling, and there were no Valkyries there.

Chapter Two

Britta clenched her fists as she watched from her island; Plumes of smoke were spiraling up from the village. She had run west to a place where she could see the shore, and she could imagine what was happening. The screams of the women had been her own screams once. She could feel the death throes of the priest. They always killed the priest. She would not think of that. But Offa's men would shortly begin avenging that death with more of the same. She wanted to take joy in the coming revenge, but she could not. The agony of death, the pain of those who lived came shrieking across the water to her, a wail of need.

Leave me be! she thought desperately. But the villagers' need rumbled in the pit of her stomach and lurked at the edges of her mind. Let them soak in the stew of their own making! If it weren't Vikings, it would be neighboring Saxons. The smoke rising from the village grew. Britta wiped the tears from her cheeks. She was safe on her island. That was what was important.

After what seemed like hours, Saxon warriors appeared, and sailed out to the Viking ship. They set the dragon afire and left several men to plunder the cargo vessel. In all the activity, Britta almost missed the small boat that wound its way around the burning hulk, but there it was. Two men were rowing for the island. She leapt to her feet. Who would dare come to Deofric? Should she hide? If any came ashore and lived to tell the tale, her island would not protect her anymore.

As the dinghy came closer, she could see Henewulf, whose arm she had bound up only this morning, sitting in the prow as his companion rowed. He looked frightened. His eyes roved over the island rising behind her. The rower stopped and let the tiny boat drift.

"Wicce," Henewulf called over the noise of the waves on the shore.

Warily, Britta stepped forward. "What do you want?"

"You and your wort-cunning are wanted for the wounded."

Britta shook her head. "It's too dangerous," she shouted, even as the call of the wounded tugged at her gut. She could not name the danger to Henewulf. He knew what she meant.

"You will be safe with Rolf and me," he called back. The boat drifted in slightly. Rolf stroked with his oars to keep it in place. He was trembling.

Britta shook her head again. "Get someone else."

"There is no one else," Henewulf shouted. "You must tell the other women what to do."

"My island will protect me if you try to come ashore," she warned. They must go away now. The calling of the village's wounded grew more insistent by the minute.

"Offa has heard of your powers," Henewulf called. "I must bring you, Deofric or no." He motioned to Rolf to move toward shore. "Won't you trust me?"

Britta almost moaned, the tugging in her belly wrenched her gut so. She couldn't think. Henewulf mustn't come ashore. He wouldn't leave. But what if he left and yet she could not resist the calling of the wounded? Better to go with Henewulf than to end in going by herself.

"Wait," she shouted. "Come no farther. I do not want your

deaths on my conscience." Rolf was only too glad to put up his oars. She gulped for air as the pain in her stomach eased. "Do you swear by Thor and Woden that you will protect me, even with your life, even from Offa himself?"

"By Thor's Hammer and Woden's one eye, I swear, Wicce," Henewulf called. They were so close now that he hardly had to shout.

"Then stay you there while I get my herbs. I will use my own boat."

"As long as you come, Wicce."

Britta turned up toward the house, dread welling into her mouth like bile.

Britta's senses recoiled as she picked her way among the dead and dying in the detritus of battle. Groans and cries filled the air. Horses whinnied, high and frightened from the smell of blood and smoke. Saxon warriors screamed their victory songs as they picked their way among the dead and dying, taking back Saxon plunder from the Vikings with interest due. The afternoon sun was warm. Britta knew the tang of blood would soon turn to pungent rot.

She was not for Viking succor today. They would die gurgling in their own blood. Henewulf pointed to a Saxon trying to sit up, a savage trough hacked from thigh to knee.

Britta knelt beside him. "I need bandages and splints," she said hoarsely, "and water."

Henewulf grabbed a man who was gleefully spearing surviving Vikings and sent him up to the village for every flaxen shirt he could find. "And have some women bring water," he added.

Britta dragged herself through a sea of torn flesh and broken bones. The dull pain of touching each wound made her ill. Henewulf and Rolf stood above her as she worked, going from one Saxon to another, tending only those who might yet profit from her herb-lore. She ignored their words of gratitude. She only worked for the wounds.

After a while, the young warrior returned with three women who said they knew how to dress injuries, but Britta was appalled to find that they did not intend to wash the wounds before they bound them. She showed them how to soap and scrub the injuries in spite of their patients' screams, and passed around pots of cleansing herbs like yarrow and burdock to rub into each. The four women tore the flaxen shirts into bandages, then Britta taught Henewulf and Rolf to pull the broken bones into place and splint the limbs.

Around her, soldiers hauled bodies this way and that. Viking carcasses were piled down by the beach to be burned before the pestilence of rotting flesh could infect the village. The limbs of the Saxon dead were composed for burial near the church, for Christians. If they were still of the Old Religion, troughs were dug where their belongings could be interred with them for the trip to the other side. Women wailed over corpses and children wandered large-eyed after them.

Britta willed herself numb as she pulled the bandage taut around a poultice she had laid on a Saxon's shoulder wound. She stood and picked her way over perhaps a dozen Saxon bodies that would not rise again, looking for another who might use her skills.

With a shock of recognition, she saw, at the center of this whorl of death, the face of the blond Viking god-man who had stood upon the deck of his ship in the midday sun, filled with life. He still gripped his ax. His helmet was split by the blow that had felled him. Blood soaked everything. But his face was peaceful, soft in the midst of all this death. What a waste of manhood. In spite of herself, she knelt beside him and turned his head toward her.

To her surprise, a groan escaped his lips and his lashes fluttered on his dirt and blood-smudged cheeks. He was alive! Not for long, she reminded herself. He was Viking, after all.

Henewulf and Rolf both yelped in astonishment when they saw the man at Britta's feet. "Here is the devil who led the heathen horde," Henewulf shouted to any who would listen.

"I never saw a better fighter," one named Badenoth muttered.

Britta looked around at the hacked flesh that surrounded the Viking and closed her eyes briefly. Was that a thing to praise? She lifted the broken helmet from his head, automatically searching his body for wounds. She could not tell what was Saxon blood and what Danish.

Several others made their way toward the commotion. The Viking's eyes opened, but he seemed not to know where he was or what was happening. "Did you see him at the end?" one Saxon asked as he approached. "He fought like ten men, though he stood almost alone."

Another drew his sword. "He should have died in battle, honorably. Now he dies like a slave and shall not sit in Valhalla." A second drew his sword, and a third.

"Wait," Henewulf barked to the circle around the Viking. The bloodied steel of their great swords glinted in the last rays of the sun as it sank behind the gorge wall to the west. "He deserves death from his equal. Offa should be the one to kill him." There were nods of agreement, perhaps of relief.

"I agree," came a booming voice from behind them. Britta started violently. Dread threatened to overwhelm her senses. She had not seen the man for more than five years, but she would never forget that voice. She turned and saw Offa's forked beard looming above her. The man who had stolen her magic had aged. His cruelty was carved more deeply in his face, his eyes almost opaque gray with hardness, yet there was nothing in his visage that had not always been there and that would not always be etched in Britta's memory.

Though she was riveted in terror, he did not seem to even notice her. His avaricious eyes were only for the Viking at her knees. "I have a use for this one," Offa said, his lip curling.

Britta looked to Henewulf. Even he seemed to draw away from the terrible glint in his thegn's eyes. The others stood back in uneasy awe.

"Bind him and take him up to the faesten," Offa ordered. His smile made Britta queasy. She trembled and shrank back. Then, as she thought he might move on, Offa's eyes roved over her red-gold hair and she saw a dreadful recognition there. The smile that was not really a smile reappeared.

"So, girl," he drawled. "You answered my invitation."

Britta couldn't speak. She only put her hand to her mouth.

Henewulf answered for her. "How could she not, my thegn?"

Offa's eyes jerked over her. "I have waited overlong to make it. Bring her up to the faesten and let her continue her work there."

"I can attest to her magic," Henewulf said eagerly. "She can be useful to you."

Offa looked thoughtfully at Britta, until she was near to shrieking with disgust. "A true healer could enhance my power," he agreed. His gray eyes darkened, as though a cloud passed over the ruffled waters of a wintery lake. Britta shivered.

Offa's attention moved to a pair of men dragging Viking bodies toward the beach. "Light the pyre," he yelled as he strode away, "or we'll never get the bodies burned!"

Britta collapsed to the ground. She had dreaded the day she would again see those eyes, those sneering lips, for five years.

One of the men tossed her some leather thongs. "Bind his hands," he ordered. He turned the Viking over with one toe.

She had to get away from here. She had to get back to her island. She rose unsteadily and began to stumble toward the beach. Henewulf grabbed her and turned her gently to face him.

"No, Wicce, not yet," he said. His eyes had pity in them. He stooped and handed her the thongs. "You hate Offa. But he is loyal to those who serve him. Your skill will protect you."

Britta's glance darted about his face. Then she quieted. Henewulf was right. The thegn didn't care about her. He had not sought her out in all these years. She was one of a hundred women or a thousand to him. All he cared about was her wort-craft. She nodded.

"Steady, girl." Henewulf smiled.

She knelt and grabbed the Viking's hands. They were square and strong, slippery now with blood. She jerked the thongs tight, bringing a groan from the man. No more than he deserved. Badenoth and Henewulf dragged him toward the cart filled with wounded.

"This Viking scum can't ride with valiant Saxon warriors," a narrow-faced man cried. He nursed a wounded arm against his chest. Britta climbed up to the back edge of the cart.

Henewulf surveyed the Viking critically. "No choice. He can't walk."

The man with a wound in one arm pushed a tangle of rope out from behind him somewhere. "Then drag him behind," he growled.

Henewulf picked up the rope and shook it out with his good arm. "And have him dead by the time you reach the faesten? Offa would have something to say to that." Henewulf knotted the rope about the Viking's neck and tossed the other end around the post at the back corner of the cart. Then he hauled on the rope while Badenoth shoved the Viking into the cart beside Britta.

Henewulf patted Britta's knee. "I'll be up later to look out for you. You'll have plenty to do until then." The cart lurched slowly off as he turned away.

Britta's attention was drawn to the Viking at her side as one of the Saxons spit on him. The wounded man turned his head away, but he had not the strength to wipe the saliva from his cheek.

"Such as he should share space with the victorious?" the spitter asked.

"I'd rip his throat with my dirk except that I would deprive Offa of his fun," another complained. Britta glanced at him. He wore a crudely carved cross on a leather thong at his neck, but he had forgotten those Christian words *for-giveness* and *kindness.*

The cart lurched up the track to the faesten. The driver broke into a victory chant, joined by the guard striding behind the cart and the Christian at her side.

> *"Mighty are our Saxons swords,*
> *Mighty are our thews.*
> *And if you choose to cross those swords*
> *Then it is death you choose."*

When her work was done tonight, Britta promised herself she would race out of the faesten and back to her boat. She tried to let that thought sustain her, but her eyes returned to the wounded Viking of their own will. She shook herself. It didn't matter what Offa had planned for him. What was a bit more pain to a lump of flesh soon to be dead? Pain shrieked up around her from thousand wounds. She turned her eyes back to the road behind her. At least the Viking would keep Offa busy, she told herself.

Britta raised up from her aching knees and drew her hand across her brow, lightheaded. She looked around dumbly at the darkened yard of wounded men laid out inside the palisades of the faesten among the halls and barracks. The fires here and there about the central open space lit the scene with flickering unreality. She drew her cloak about her against the damp fingers of sea air combing through the twilight.

Henewulf came striding across the yard. "You have done well today, Wicce," he said gruffly. "Your mother would be proud."

It seemed too much effort to tell Henewulf that her mother had never been proud of her. She was glad to see him, though. She knelt to gather up her knife, her pots of herbs and unguents.

"Henewulf, I would have words with you," a voice behind her called. Britta started, then, to still the pounding in her throat, she reminded herself that this man only wanted her wort-craft.

Offa and his second in command, Raedwald, stalked up. Britta bent her gaze to her pots.

"The Viking horde has sailed past to the south," Raedwald announced breathlessly.

"They must be for Cent," Henewulf added.

"Do you think Wessex will pay again to save Cent?" Raedwald asked.

Out of the corner of her eye, Britta saw Offa shake his head. "He has paid for three years. His coffers must be empty. Cent will make a stand."

"That means Cent falls to Viking rule," Henewulf grunted.

"And Anglia is in their vise," Offa agreed. "The brutes control all to the north. With Cent to the south in their clutches, they will look next to Anglia."

"But where will they strike, and when? And how many can they bring against us?" Henewulf asked. "I'd give a bearing ewe to know their plans."

"Our good King Edmund would give more than that," Raedwald observed. His gaze jerked up to Offa and he pounded his fist into his palm. "By Thor's hammer, so that is your scheme! The Viking leader will know!"

"As I have been thinking." Offa spoke so low that Britta could hardly hear.

"Think you that he will tell you?" Henewulf shook his head. "You may do your worst and you will but kill him slower, I should guess. He will never betray his own."

"Will you bet your bearing ewe? Raedwald," Offa continued, "send a messenger to Edmund with news and a promise of information. Tell him to gather his thegns."

Henewulf raised his brows. "With this knowledge, you will win the king's favor."

Offa snorted. "I care not for Edmund. The thegns of Anglia grow tired of following a king who cares more for the workings of his bowels than the workings of a kingdom. I intend to give them a better choice. Let them see what a strong arm and a strong heart can do against invaders." He glanced around the compound. "Bring that scald from Northumbria. He speaks the cursed Viking tongue. We will have what we want from this man, won't we, Raedwald?"

Britta could see Raedwald's conflicting emotions chase across his face. He was excited and nervous in turns. "Just as you broke the traitor Braedel…"

Britta's stomach clenched as Offa noticed her. She looked away and busied herself with her pots, though they rattled in her shaking hands.

"Healer." Britta could not look at him. His voice laughed at her fear. "Bind up the Viking's wounds. But simply keep him from bleeding to death." As he turned to go, Britta let out the breath she had been holding. But then he stopped and turned back to her. "I will have need of a woman tonight, after I finish with the Dane," he announced. He bent to her. "If you please me, I will keep you by me. Your father had great power." His breath was an intimate promise in her ear.

Britta felt rather than heard him stride away. She looked up at Henewulf with tears of accusation in her eyes. "You said you would protect me."

The warrior gave a guilty start and looked down at her. "It is a great thing to be Offa's woman. Your power of healing attracts him."

"It is not a great thing for me."

"I will do what I can to distract him," he said grimly.

Britta had no faith in such a slender plan. She would take matters into her own hands.

Karn waited a long time in the dim hall with only pain and shame for company. That and his thirst. He lay naked and bound, the only sign now that he was Dane a small medallion around his neck stamped with the Hammer of Thor. But that god had deserted him this day. Breath rasped through his parched throat. Had he fought so many battles with fire in his heart just to die basely in this rude hall? Had the Norns always planned to weave the thread of his life into this fate?

He need not even bother praying for death. Who among the gods would answer?

Ulf had brought him to this, he realized. Ulf had known about the fortress up the river from the church. If only the man were here, that he could gut him in payment for the Danir who'd died today, in payment for his own shame. But he was not like to see Ulf this side of Hel's frozen domain.

Frigid air blasted into the hall as the door opened on twilight. Men wandered in, their drinking horns held high. Women brought bowls of steaming food.

Several Saxons broke away from the loud jesting and victorious laughter to cluster around Karn. He resolved to provoke them into killing him quickly. He kicked out at the nearest of the three. The man lurched back, clutching his shin. Which brought laughter from the others. When he had recovered enough to be angry, he lunged at Karn with his knife. For a moment, Karn thought he had won, but the Saxon's comrades pulled him back and took his weapon, still laughing.

A slender girl pushed her way past the men. Her hair was like a gleaming torch. She knelt beside him and motioned his tormentors away. Her eyes were green as she looked into his face. They were filled with secrets he could not name. He could not pull his eyes away. She looked startled and pulled her gaze away from his face to his body. Her small hands reached out for him, slowly, as if in a dream. As she touched his wounds, a shock shot through him. It wasn't pain exactly. Her eyes jerked back to his face, as though drawn there against her will.

Each stared at the other, paralyzed, for several moments. She had felt the shock of the touch, too. Finally she shook her head and rocked back on her heels. Taking some bandages from a basket, she made a pad. He saw her hesitate, then muster her resolve as she pressed it to his shoulder and bound it tight She dressed his hip, then turned his head to look at the bruise on his temple. Gingerly, she pressed her fingers around the lump. The ache there leaked away. At last she rose and, with one more backward glance, turned and left the hall.

Karn found the whole ritual more frightening than all the rest. Why had they sent a healer? They must want to be sure he didn't bleed to death before they could exact their revenge.

A huge man with a great forked beard strode into the hall. Men rushed to fill a drinking horn edged with wrought silver. This must be the leader of this serpents' den. There was much toasting, raucous laughter, blustery talk. They were recounting their version of the battle, Karn realized with disgust. No Danish scalds would ever sing of this dire day.

His wounds began to throb with greater intensity as the room warmed, even as the sky outside the doorway deepened into night. The smoke from the fire hung in the rafters, wafting over to fill his senses. These Saxon builders did not even put smoke holes in their halls. They were little more than beasts, he thought muzzily. The brutish voices and the laughter whirled into a wall of sound. The bright kirtles of the women who served the food spun before his eyes.

Karn started awake as a foot prodded his belly. There were only eight or nine Saxons left in the hall, including Fork-beard and a scald, strumming a gut-stringed lyre. They filled their drinking horns from bulging leather sacks of mead. Slowly, they wandered, one by one, over to him. He gathered himself. He must give over shame and fear. He must have room only for the fact that he was Karn, a Dane, son of Gunnar, a warrior. His heart beat in his breast. *Serve me well, heart, as you have served me in battle these many times, since my battle now begins.*

An old woman named Cuthrun braided Britta's hair in one of the smaller houses. All Britta could think about was escape. If she didn't, they would take her to Offa's private hall, and the terror she thought she had put behind her five years ago would begin all over again. But how could she slip away? There were too many eyes upon her, not only those of the women in the hut but there were two warriors stationed outside the door.

Through the open door, she saw two men coming up from the feasting hall, wavering on their feet. They carried leather sacks of mead to her guards. Cursing their assignment, her guards addressed the proffered mead with a will. Their grumbling resolved itself into words over the crackle of the fire where they clustered.

"I, for one, will have no part of Offa's brand of torture," one complained.

" 'Tis unnatural," another muttered. "No matter that he's Viking scum."

"What harm? It's not as though they don't wench with the best of us before and after."

"I'd draw and quarter the Dane and be done with it, if it were up to me."

"He'd never get the information he wants."

"Information or no, I don't hold with it," the first concluded emphatically.

"Then you will never sit at his side," the other guard snarled. "Offa never fully trusts those who do not join him. I'd join him if he asked, that's sure."

The two from the hall shook their heads and stumbled off into the night, leaving the guards to mutter into their mead.

Britta was puzzled. What did they mean? Why should they not join in the torture? Had she not saved the Viking for that purpose? His eyes in the firelight of the hall had been ice blue and confused. She pushed down the shame that she and Offa should be allied in anything. The remembered shock of touching his flesh washed over her, so different than when she healed Dunford's villagers.

"What do they mean, unnatural?" But even as she asked Cuthrun, she knew. The jolt of realization hit her like a blow. Gods! Could it be that Offa would exert his power over the Viking in the same brutal way he had done with her? Her heart went out to the man, before she pulled it back.

"What Offa wants from you is natural enough, girl," the

old woman said decisively. "He is one of the most powerful eorls in Anglia. He does you honor by it."

Britta knew she would find a way to kill herself first. If only Cuthrun hadn't taken her knife. Her eyes strayed to where it lay on the table, then came to rest on her bundle of herb pots just inside the door. She gulped a sharp breath. There might be a way.

"Let me serve the warriors," she begged. Cuthrun nodded absently. Britta took a skin of mead and set it on the bench outside, next to her bundle. As she filled their drinking horns from the sack, she let her cloak fall forward, around the bundle of pots. A pinch of flakes made from dried valerian root she stirred in each. It was done. Her eyes lowered, she offered the guards the horns. Inside she was crowing. With humble mien, she filled Cuthrun's cup as well.

Cuthrun patted her shoulder approvingly. "You are a good girl, Britta, worthy of your mother. You will find favor with Offa."

Britta handed her the cup and murmured, "Thank you." Not while I live, she thought. When she had served the other women, she sat on the bench beside the doorway.

Out of the shadows, Henewulf materialized. Relief sighed through her. Henewulf would help her get away. Britta waited anxiously as he hailed the guards and came to her for mead. She poured him an undoctored horn. His hand shook as he downed it at a gulp.

"I wouldn't worry," he said in an undertone.

Britta stared up at him. "You wouldn't worry?"

"He will be too drunk by the time he is done to have aught to do with you tonight."

"And what if he isn't?" she whispered fiercely. "Can't you get me out of here?"

"Later; there are still too many stirring now."

"That might be too late!"

Henewulf only patted her shoulder and went to return his borrowed mead-horn to the guards. Before she knew it, he had melted back into the darkness. She couldn't count on him. He didn't understand what was at stake here.

*   *   *

For a long while, the Saxons just looked at Karn, whispering together. Why didn't they fall on him and do their worst? It felt as though they were mustering their nerve. Spineless dogs!

Fork-beard pressed to the center and stood looming over Karn. Sweat glazed his face. He hauled Karn up by the rope around his neck as the others drew up a table. Fork-beard dragged him onto it. Karn's chest pressed against the rough wooden planks. He could hardly get his breath for the pain in his ribs. They roped each wrist to the table legs. No one laughed now. He could feel them behind him. *I am Karn. Son of Gunnar. Dane and warrior. I am Karn.*

They wrenched his feet apart and tied his ankles to the remaining stout legs of the table. Rough hands pulled at his buttocks. Even more shocking, a thumb pried into him. He bucked with all his strength against the table. The one who held his leash jerked it down so that his cheek banged against the table, but the thumb continued its probing.

"I will have my revenge for this," Karn croaked with as much force as he could muster. The horrible impotence of those words only savaged his soul the more.

A scald stood in front of him. "Tell plans for Anglia," he said in broken Danish. "Where will Danir land and when? How many will they bring?"

Karn knew, of course. He had planned the assault. "You can go hang yourselves," he muttered through clenched teeth.

The scald shook his head nervously. "You don't understand, Viking. They will continue," he stuttered. "You will tell. If not tonight, then other nights. There will be no death. They will keep you as slave…" He trailed off. "You can trade for a clean death."

Karn's mind skittered over a vision of such a future. He dared not dwell on it. He could not betray his comrades. Instead he bucked against the hands on his backside. "Save your words," he gasped.

Fork-beard barked a question at the scald, who shook his

head almost sadly. Fork-beard jerked his head at the door and the scald scurried away. No one now could understand Karn. He could not be tempted to tell these savages anything, no matter what they did. They began a fearful chanting, as though to raise their courage. He had a good idea what they meant to do. He was just not sure he could bear it.

Chapter Three

Britta sat in the dark on the hard bench in front of the hall and tried to master her breathing. She could not trust Henewulf. If her potion took effect before Offa called for her, she might yet hide herself. But how to get out of the faesten?

Screams raked the quiet and cut through her feverish plans. She started up, nerves quivering. They were screams of rage as much as pain, draining slowly away to mere anguish. She drew her knees into her chest. The sound was different altogether than the screams of men felled in battle, the shrieks of pain from the wounded. But it was familiar.

Tears leaked from her eyes. She covered her ears, but screams and chanting and finally a roar of approval leaked through her fingers. The strange chant began again, more grunts than words, repeated even as the screams died away. She huddled there in the night, sharing the rage, the fear, the shame and despair that must be coursing through the Viking. The guards next to her laughed and muttered, but even they seemed nervous in the face of those screams.

Men wandered one by one out of the hall down by the gate. Offa would surely call for her soon. Britta chanced a look into the hut, and saw that the women had retired to their beds. Still, she must wait until she was sure. At last, the nodding guards began to snore. Moving quietly, she stepped to the table and retrieved her knife. The air was oppressive with smoke and stale breath. Then she was out the door. She forced herself not to run until she couldn't stand it anymore and fled around the back of a hall to her left. Panting, half-sobbing, she leaned against the rough-hewn boards. Offa might come out of the hall at any moment.

The safest place to be was behind that hall. From building to building she rushed, until she lost track of where she was. She peered around a corner just as Offa staggered out of the door of the hall she was leaning against. His forked beard silhouetted against the stars, he turned his head up and raised high his drinking horn. She gasped and ducked back behind the corner.

"Wicce," he shouted drunkenly at the heavens. His cry arced up into a laugh that rocked the night. It echoed about Britta as the thegn staggered off toward the back of the huge yard and the largest of the private halls. Britta shrank down as he stumbled past. "Wicce, I want you and your powers," he called again. He had not seen her.

Her gaze flicked frantically over the yard at the wounded and the dead in the center of the circle of buildings, at the horses milling in their pen, and at Offa, stumbling up the hill. Dawn was only a few hours away. She was trapped here, unless she could think of a way to get past the sentry. There was no way over the palisades. God of my father, she prayed, show me how to get out…and could you show me quickly?

No answer echoed in her brain. She leaned against the wooden planks of the hall. The Viking was probably still inside. Offa had gotten what he wanted. She would have told Offa anything he wanted five years ago if she thought it would have stopped him. The Viking must be truly courageous. She remembered the shock of touching his wounds, so different than touching the others.

In spite of herself, she turned to the door of the hall. There was no time for this, a voice inside shrieked. Offa had killed him, no doubt in some horrible way she did not want to see.

But she couldn't help herself. She raised the bolt and crept inside. A few coals yet glowed in the sand of the firebox. She meant to look around for the Viking, but it was the firebox that held her gaze. The coals glowed brighter, pulsing, until they grew so bright she had to close her eyes against them. What would make coals flare up like that? As she opened her eyes, the orange-red flames before her leapt to impossible heights. Higher and higher they burned until they filled her head with dancing brightness. Thundering into the roof, they licked at her consciousness and filled her vision until no darkness remained anywhere. Flames that could eat the world, they were, but she was not afraid. She watched them, entranced by their brilliance, all thought of Offa, of the Viking, of her need to escape, now banished. A flame inside her matched the flames around her. It gorged on fuel laid up for years. She felt a union with that fire. It completed her, as though she had never known what it was to be whole before.

Then the fire that burned—or didn't burn—before her, changed somehow, and she was seeing another fire, one she knew was far away from the tiny coals in a Saxon hall. This one raged about her. The evil crackling of its progress through the trees filled her ears. It was a threat to her and all she knew and loved. She was running and Fenris was there, but not only Fenris. The Viking was there and she had to save herself and her dog, and she had to save the Viking, too. He was important to her. She could feel that, as important to save as Fenris. Only she couldn't see through the smoke, and she knew in that moment that the fire would catch her and Fenris and the Dane.

She gasped as the world shuddered back into place. Her head shook convulsively as she fell to her knees. The embers of the tiny firebox glowed dully. They were small and real. She felt light-headed, and realized she was panting. No wall of flame surrounded her.

What was that? she asked herself. It had been a vision, surely. A vision of the future? The terrible urgency of the need to save herself and Fenris and the Viking still reverberated through her. Why had the Viking been in that vision? Was he in her future? Was he so important to her? Moreover, how could she be having visions?

She looked around the hall, still dazed. The Viking lay like a discarded rag by a table in the center, naked except for her poor excuse for bandages. His face was covered by hair matted with blood, his limbs sprawled awkwardly. Shreds of rope bound his ankles and wrists, and one was knotted about his neck. A small medallion at his throat glinted in the dying firelight.

The vision almost stifled her as she moved through the darkness toward him. If the vision was true, he was not dead. She held her breath. As she drew closer, she saw a fresh wound in his side, oozing blood into a pool on the floor. She knelt beside him. If Offa had wanted to kill him, he would have centered the blow just under the breastbone. She reached out a hand, ghostly in the darkness, to touch the glinting medallion that had failed to protect the Viking. It was the Hammer of Thor surrounded by knotted snakes. *Gods never protect you.* As she touched the medallion, the blood in the Viking's throat beat at her fingers, weak and erratic but shocking nonetheless. He was alive! At least that much of the vision was true.

But could he stay that way? She scanned his body. He had been beaten. She pushed the matted hair from his face. It was almost peaceful. Opening one swollen eyelid, she saw a whole eye there. She pulled down his chin and saw a whole tongue. No, mutilation had not been Offa's plan. With quaking hands she reached out and pulled the Viking over onto his belly. His back was bruised and gouged. There were shallow cuts across his buttocks and smeared gore everywhere. Horrified, she realized what they had done, using the blood to ease their work.

They should have killed you, Viking. Perhaps he would have escaped into death, if she had not stopped his bleeding.

She owed him for that. And then there was the vision…

A way out of the fortress flashed through her mind. Would it work? It almost didn't matter. It was what she had to do, and she needed the Viking for her plan.

There was little time. She darted out the door and over to the livestock pen, directly across from the feasting hall. The horses moved restlessly around her as she crawled in through the crude fence. Taking a rope halter from the gate, she grabbed the first nose she could reach, pulled it down over her shoulder, and slipped the halter over the snorting head. The gate creaked much too loudly as she led her prize over to one of the carts that had carried the wounded.

It took her long moments to hitch up the horse. Offa had disappeared inside his hall. Even now he might realize she wasn't there. She pulled the horse and cart behind the nearest building.

Glancing up toward Offa's lair, she saw him appear in the doorway. He was looking for her! Britta took a deep breath. I still have time, while he searches, she told herself. As Offa started into a neighboring barracks, she darted back into the Viking's hall. Now all depended on him. She could not drag so large a man. She rolled him over and slapped his face.

"Wake up, Viking," she whispered hoarsely. Nothing happened. She called again and slapped him harder, several times. At last, with a low groan, the eye that was not swollen shut cracked open. She reached for a sack of mead and squirted some directly into his mouth. He gasped and choked, but it seemed to revive him.

"If you want to get out of here," she said, knowing he couldn't understand, "you have to help." She pulled him up and knelt beside him. Dragging his arm over her shoulder, she shoved upward with her thighs. They both groaned as she managed to push erect. Panting, she continued talking, hoping to keep him conscious. "Walk, you barbarian beast," she muttered. He did, after a fashion. They staggered, she half-dragging him, out the door into the sea air of the night.

Offa was talking to Henewulf in front of his hall. The latter pointed up toward a hut at the far rear of the compound. As soon as Offa turned away, Britta heaved the Viking into a better position and stumbled toward the cart. She backed him up against the wooden bed and let him fall into it, then lifted his legs in and piled coarse feed sacking over him. Making soft whoa-ing sounds to the restless horse, she scrambled up into the seat. One cluck and they were off.

Britta shivered inside her cloak as she drove the cart slowly toward the closed gate and its sentry. Her will was fierce within her. Offa would not have her while there was yet breath in her body. And he wouldn't have the Viking either. She dared not look behind her. She dared not drive faster. She must trust to Henewulf to distract the thegn. She drew the hood of her cloak forward.

"You there," she called out. The sentry jerked to wakefulness and glanced about him nervously. "Do you sleep at your post, man?"

"What do you want, wench?" he barked as he regained his senses.

"What do you think? Open your gate. I have one last load of Christian dead who deserve to lie in the church tonight." Her boldness surprised her.

" 'Tis too late," the sentry complained. "Wait until dawn."

"Perhaps if I tell Offa why I have failed to obey his express order," Britta shot back, "he will spare me." The sentry leapt down from his platform and came around to check her cargo.

"I see only one," he said suspiciously. "There are fifty dead to fill your cart."

She almost panicked. Instead, she managed a sigh. "Have you never obeyed an order with half a heart when it must be near dawn and your back is breaking?"

The sentry chuckled. "Aye."

Britta held her breath as he lifted the bar, swung wide the gates.

"Don't come back until morning," the sentry warned.

She did not turn to look, but the gate creaked shut behind her. She sucked the night air into her lungs and clucked the horse to a trot. Surely Offa would hear the gate. Surely he would send his men thundering after her.

As the cart careened, bumping, down the gorge, Britta saw strange looming shadows everywhere. Each looked like an angry Offa before it resolved into a bush or boulder. What would she do if he pursued her? She snapped the reins over the horse's back. It trotted even faster down the rutted road.

Her heart was pounding so, she couldn't think. Offa must be convinced the Viking was dead or he would never stop searching for him. That meant a substitute body. She pulled the horse up at the edge of the deserted village and leapt to the ground. The stench of the Viking pyre at the beach assaulted her nose, even from here. Some part of her asked if she was crazy, even as another part continued preparation. A smile came to her face. She liked the thought of robbing Offa of the Viking. In some ways, it was like taking back what she had given up to him long ago.

Something else she had given up might be back. She hardly dared hope that magic was possible for her again. If it was, what could she do but heed its call?

She staggered through the village, peering into each hut. Two children, a woman. She was frantic. In the third hut a male body was laid out in grave clothes. He was young but not too heavily muscled. Could he pass for the Viking leader? He would have to. She stripped him and dragged him out the door. He was much lighter than the Viking but a struggle nonetheless. Groaning with effort, she got him into the cart, his naked limbs splayed over the feed sacks. She ripped the small medallion from the Viking's throat and transferred it to the young Saxon.

There was no time to do more. At any moment, Offa or his henchmen might come galloping down the road. She scrambled back up to the driver's seat and drove down to the pyre. Sharp shards of Viking bones and the rounded shape of skulls glowed in the flames. She slowed the horse and closed her eyes to master her rising gorge. Would this horrible fire yield another, even more fearful vision? But the flames remained flames, awful as they were. She took a deep breath and drove directly up to the men who stood sentinel.

"Who goes there?" one called sharply, rising to his feet.

"An escort to the dead on Offa's errand," she called back. She did not recognize them. That was good. One of the men went around to the back of the cart. She clasped her hands to keep them from trembling. "One for the churchyard, one for burning."

"Is this the devil warrior who led the hordes today?" one asked, peering into the back.

"Aye, so they say."

"Let's to it," the other guard said, "while we still have enough flame."

"You'll need more wood," the other ordered. "These Viking scum are hard to burn." They dragged the Saxon out and carried him to the pyre. Several others heaped chunks of wood on the grisly pile. Britta held her breath, fearful both of discovery and of another vision.

"What's this?" the guard asked, dropping the body. Britta's heart stuttered. The warrior picked up the Viking medallion from the dead Saxon's chest and tore it from his neck. He tied the leather round his own neck and nodded to his companions. Two of the Saxons swung the body back and forth a time or two and heaved it high onto the burning heap. Britta followed it up with her eyes. Showers of sparks cascaded into the night and were lost. Ashes whispered away on the brisk breeze from the sea. But no wall of orange-red flame leapt around her.

The soldiers watched the flames lick at the body. Britta turned her horse unnoticed along the beach. She spared only an instant of regret for the Saxon. Whether he was Christian or he followed the Old Religion, he would view his immolation on this pyre as a desecration.

When she came to the bushes where Henewulf had drawn her boat up this afternoon she hauled on the reins. The horse snorted and reared. She jumped down and pretended to check his feet for stones while she scanned the church above. There were no watchers she could see, so she rolled the Viking out into the wormwood bushes. Then she drove up to the church and left the horse to graze in the churchyard while she hurried back to the beach.

She had almost done it. Tomorrow when Offa went to look for his Viking, he would find him gone. He would question the sentry, who would know only that one cart had been driven down to the church late. If he questioned the pyre tenders, he would find that the Viking was dead when he arrived and that they had burned him. If anyone looked for the wicce, they would find she had escaped back to her island rather than submit to Offa. And Offa would find solace with other women, younger and more comely than she.

She roused her Viking booty and half-dragged him into her boat. Its drunken prow lifted in the onrushing tide. Then, wet to her knees, she climbed in behind him. It was a mile to her island and safety. With the energy of fear receding, she felt like the walking dead. It was stupid and dangerous to take the Viking to her island. But she couldn't help it. It was not pity for what he would endure at Offa's hands, she told herself. It was not retribution against Offa for what he had taken from her. It was the vision. There might be magic in her life again, against all odds. And the vision told her she must take the Viking with her. With luck, she would not regret obeying. She reached for her oars as the boat rose on the swell of the incoming surf.

Offa pushed past the men who stood in a knotted circle outside the hall and gritted his teeth. His head was bad this morning. The precise events of last night were fuzzy, at least the part after they had raped the Viking. The boy sent to tell him the bad news hovered nervously in the background. What did they mean, the Viking was gone? He had barred the door from the outside himself. That Viking had been in no shape to escape. His men averted their eyes as he strode into the shadowed hall. The wooden floor was still smeared with a dark stain and smelled of blood. There was no sign of the Viking. Offa turned to the men behind him. "I don't believe it," he barked. He surveyed the crowd through narrowed eyes. They had had as riotous a night as he. Even in early afternoon they were not yet themselves. "Have you searched the faesten?"

"We continue to search." Badenoth hesitated.

"I had not finished with him," Offa roared, in spite of the effect it had on his head.

"Perhaps he died in the night and one of the women prepares the body even now for drawing and quartering." Badenoth looked around to no avail for another spokesman.

Offa did not trust himself to reply, but strode back past them into sunshine that was much too bright for his eyes. Maybe Badenoth was right. "Let me know when they find him." Then he turned. He had other unfinished business. "Send the red-haired girl to my hall."

Henewulf cleared his throat. "She was in your hall. Didn't you find her?"

Offa couldn't quite remember, but it would never do to admit it. "Of course I found her."

"And skewered her royally." Raedwald grinned.

Offa smiled in return, just to allay any doubts on that point.

"Likely she has gone back to her island," Henewulf said.

"Who let her go?" Offa looked hard at Henewulf as the men exchanged uneasy glances. "Did no one see her?" He fairly shouted.

They shook their heads. They did not understand his ire. Offa remembered her father's eyes, the light fading in them as he pulled his sword from the priest's belly. He shook his head, and the memory was replaced with the pain that rattled in his skull. He had forgotten all about her until Henewulf had begun bragging of her healing powers. "I will need a healer if we are to go into battle against the Vikings. Go fetch her off her island."

"She will not come, Lord," Henewulf said. "She came yesterday only for the wounded."

"Then go get her by force," Offa snapped.

A murmur of shocked protest swelled in the smoky room. "We can't go get her on Deofric," Badenoth protested, almost in spite of himself.

"Any man who sets foot on that isle comes back a change-ling, if he comes back at all," a voice from the rear quavered. There were nods of agreement around the room and nervous gestures of fear. Offa saw many cross themselves repeatedly. "Don't you remember Cerdic?" someone added.

Everyone remembered that tale, though they had it from their grandmothers, and their grandmothers had it from their own granddams. Cerdic's boat had spring a leak and he'd put in to Deofric for the night. When he made it to shore next morning, naught was left of his mind. He died a few months later, a pathetic derelict. He could not even say what he saw there. Of course, Offa thought with disgust, that was much better for keeping up the myth of Deofric. But as Offa surveyed the room, he grew cautious. His men might have followed him to Christianity, but that had not changed the old traditions overmuch. If he challenged their beliefs, he would lose. Nor did he want the reputation of a changeling if he went to the island to get the girl himself.

"If you can but wait, my lord," Raedwald coaxed. "She comes to shore every fortnight or so to heal in return for supplies. You may have her then...."

Offa grimaced. There was no choice but to wait. "Find the Viking. He cannot be far."

Britta woke in the late morning to the chorusing of birds. She stared into the dim recesses of the thatched roof where bundles of herbs hung to dry. A vague sense of expectation filled her, though she couldn't name its source. Was today the day she went to treat the villagers?

The blissful numbness evaporated in a burst of realization. She sat bolt upright, startling Fenris, who jerked to his feet and barked at the Viking. There he was, lying on her storage platform. The entire horror of yesterday washed over her, the dreadful remnants of battle, the terror of Offa's threat, the strange vision in the fire, and the last bone-weary task of coaxing and dragging the wounded Dane up to her hut as the eastern sky paled over the sea, Fenris barking madly.

In God's name, what had she done? She had saved a Viking marauder because of some vision born of fatigue and fear? What a fool! She had brought a Norseman into her very house.

And a man he was. She could see that clearly from here. Her hasty dressing on his latest wound and the torn and dirty bandages on the others were the only coverings on his body. She shuddered and turned away. But she felt his wounds calling her weakly, the way wounds always called. She glanced back. His skin was sun-bronzed, as befitted a man of the sea, except for a pale strip across his loins. His chest and belly were covered with a dusting of hair and also with a fearful set of bruises, mottled with crusts of dried blood. His beard was clipped short. His matted hair was streaked with blond, as she remembered. He was a man and he was Viking, and therefore he was an enemy twice over. She had hauled the enemy inside her own small faesten, all out of a stupid belief that he might be important in her life.

Important? He was probably already dead. She threw back the furs and stood, still wearing yesterday's bloodstained kirtle. She went to touch his throat, wondering whether she had hauled him all this way just to labor over digging a grave. His pulse thrummed weakly against her fingers. She sucked in her breath. The vision in Offa's hall seemed bent on coming true. But already it seemed distant. Was that confused memory of flame really a vision at all?

Some part of her was busy taking inventory. She would clean the wounds with plantain. Then she'd need an astringent to stop the bleeding; that would be yarrow. Finally, poultices of wormwood root and vervain for the fever that would no doubt set in. Stime could prevent the wounds from festering. There was nothing for his broken ribs but binding.

She knew what to do. But she made no move to start the work. She had never tried to heal so much destruction. Her energy, her skill would be wasted on one so likely to die. She dreaded the touching that must come. Surely the vision had been no more than a hallucination. Let him die; that was the sensible thing to do. He was going to anyway. Wasn't there a beginning of the black aura around him? She strained to see. But there wasn't, not yet.

She sighed and knew she couldn't escape trying. Maybe it was because of their shared experience with Offa. Maybe it was just the calling of the flesh. Maybe it was her hallucination. Whatever it was, Britta had to decide. She decided she would try to help him.

Soon the water boiled, the gut was laid out in strings, the needle and the awl were near to hand. Fenris was banished from the hut. Britta's treasured hollow-core knife cut the bandages to reveal the Viking's swollen gashes filled with thick gouts of congealing blood. Here and there old scars peeked through the smeared gore. He had been in many battles, but no wounds had been as bad as these. She rubbed a coarse cloth with the soap she used for her bath and began to wash him.

The touch of his flesh shocked her as she knew it would, but it wasn't exactly horrible. She simply felt the wrongness of his wounds. Her fingers probed, deciding how best to make the flesh right. If her touch was sensitive enough, if she listened hard enough, the flesh would tell her what to do. How had she ever thought to let him die?

The world fell away. She had attention only for the wounds, the flesh, the longing for wholeness when she touched him. Why had she never felt this soothing lightness when she touched the villagers' wounds? With a start she realized that, smeared with his blood, her fingers feeling for lightness as she worked, she touched him in ways more intimate than any other woman ever would. As she worked the wound in his shoulder, the terrible gouge in from his hip, she pulled muscle and sinew together. Her tiny stitches closed the skin. She pierced the flesh with her needle just as she would sew a kirtle, except that this fabric bled.

Finally, she got her courage up and looked at that place where Offa had done his worst. She took a finger full of yarrow unguent and, holding her breath, spread it where she could. She owed him that. If he was torn, this could be the wound that killed him.

Now, for the blow to his head. She pulled open his eyelids. His eyes still startled her. Their blue told stories of icy
skies and summer seas. But his pupils did not contract with
the light. That was bad. She touched the bruise on his temple
willingly, this time, and found no dent in the skull. It soothed
her, that touch. As she watched, his pupils contracted. That
was better.

Finally, she could do no more. She sat back and looked
around her, dazed. The sun was sinking into evening. She
must rise and light the lamp soon. Where had the time gone?
Her dread had disappeared. After the first shocking touch of
flesh, she had felt only a desire for wholeness, his and hers.
She pushed back the wisps of hair clinging damply to her
forehead. She had done the best she could. It was now his
job to heal.

Karn opened his eyes. At least he thought they were open.
He was in a place of dark and pain. He could hear someone
moaning. He must be in the underworld of the Christ cult,
for he saw a glint of coals. The underworld of the Danir was
freezing cold, guarded by the Goddess Hel. Those *were* coals
he saw, weren't they? His eyes swam as he tried to turn his
head to look at them. The moaning grew louder. Those must
be the cries of the tormented. He could not remember the
journey to the underworld. Had he not died in battle? But
then he would be feasting with Valkyrie. He could not think
because he had great thirst.

Someone else was here. The dim vision of a woman
loomed over him, her hair red flame about her face. Was it
she who groaned? He had seen her, somewhere, before. Her
hand, grotesquely large, reached for him. He tried to tell her
to go away, but though his lips were moving, he could hear
no words, only the moaning filled with pain. Pain like his
own. With each breath the pain washed over him. Her hand
moved under his neck and lifted his head. Her lips moved.
Ghastly, echoing words he could not understand issued forth.
He felt a cup press at his mouth and pungent liquid came

pouring through his lips. When he choked, anguish shot through his body. Blackness pushed in at the sides of his vision. The cup and the face receded, leaving only darkness and the pain. Something harsh scraped his skin, a weight pressed on his forehead, forcing him down into the blackness. The pain broke over him in waves, fluxing and ebbing until he felt far away, floating on the sea of agony, and knew no more.

Offa stared resentfully at the blackened pile of bone and ashes. They had searched everywhere for the Viking, in the faesten, in the woods, up and down the shore. For two days they had searched. There was now only one place he could be hiding.

He turned to Raedwald. "Find me who tended this pyre." If the Viking had been burned here, his fine source of information was gone. He savored the rage that churned in his gut. He would know who had done this thing.

The two guardsman who inched forward did not look like conspirators. They looked like frightened rabbits. No doubt it was fear had held their tongues during the days of the search.

Offa turned only his head. "Did you burn my Viking on this pyre?" he asked softly.

The two looked at each other, and slowly both sank to their knees in silent supplication. "She said you had done with him," one stammered. "She said you ordered."

"And you did not question?" he roared.

Henewulf laid a restraining hand on his arm. "We know not this body was the Viking."

But Offa's attention was captured by one of the quivering guards. He stalked up to the man and ripped a small medallion from his throat. "Where did you get this, man?"

"From the body she brought," the man pleaded. "No use to let it burn."

Offa handed it to Raedwald, who examined the wrought Hammer of Thor and the twined snakes and nodded solemnly. "It is the Viking's." He looked up at the clouds blowing in from the sea. "So he is dead." He brought his head down, to fix the guards in a stare. "Now let us speak of the woman who brought him."

Chapter Four

Karn opened his eyes, expecting darkness and agony. The pain was still there, but this time brightness stabbed his eyes. He closed them and drifted. At last he tried again. His eyes hurt. Breathing hurt worse. Slowly he recognized the brightness as a window. The dimness above him was the underside of a thatched roof. Weeds hung from it. With great effort he turned his head.

He was in a small wooden house. No one appeared to be home. The wicker shutters opened to streaming light, and a fire with a cooking pot over it crackled. He lay on a wooden shelf about four feet wide and two feet off the plank floor. There was a bed box lined with furs on the opposite side of the hut and, next to one of the windows, a loom hung with circular weights. He was not in Hel. Someone must have taken him to Denmark. He wondered vaguely who was taking care of him. Why was he not at his father's house? This hut was poor. Smoke from the cook fire hung in the rafters. Could that tiny fire overwhelm the smoke hole?

Karn felt his world shift. This house had no smoke hole! Thor, that meant he was in some Saxon hut, not safe in

Denmark. His chest heaved as he fought for breath. Memories came back half-formed and sporadic. Wounded, he remembered that, and a dark hall...fear. Had he escaped? There was a cart. But this was a Saxon hut and he was in terrible danger. He was sure of that.

Well, he was not beaten yet. They thought him too weak to need guards. He pressed the pain down. There might be little time until they returned. Stiffly, he pushed off the fur that covered him and dragged the upper half of his body to the edge of the platform. A groan escaped him as he rolled onto his side. He did not trust himself to sit up without fainting, but he managed to get his leg over the edge. If he could get to the floor, he might crawl out the open door.

That was when he discovered that his left leg was not his to command, nor his sword arm. He fought back panic as he realized what that meant and rolled off the shelf. The world darkened as pain shot through him in multicolored flashes. It took all his concentration to keep from vomiting. Grimacing, he reached out with his good arm and pushed with his good leg. Slowly, he inched along the rough floor, sweat dripping into his eyes. He dragged his body out into the grass. Its blades scraped against his chest and belly. Hide. He had to hide himself.

Britta toiled up the path from the spring with her buckets of water, Fenris capering at her side. "I feel good, too, friend," she told him. She had bathed in the pool, and the autumn sunshine warmed her hair and shoulders. Her fresh linen under-dress was covered with a kirtle dyed blue with precious woad. It felt good to be out of the house, where she had watched and worked over the Viking for so long. She had thought he would die, even up to yesterday. Then his fever broke. He would soon regain consciousness. She could feel the urge toward life in him. Conflicted, Britta sighed. How much easier for her if he had died.

As she and Fenris entered the meadow in front of her hut, she stopped, appalled. The Viking crawled laboriously across the clearing. Was he trying to escape? She ducked out of the yoke. Fenris loped forward to sniff at their suddenly mobile guest. He growled warily. As Britta ran forward she saw the smear of blood on the grass in the Dane's wake.

"You fool!" she shouted, standing over him. "If Offa can't kill you, you'll finish the job yourself?" She rolled him roughly onto his back. His naked body streamed sweat. Her carefully tied bandages were skewed and torn. The dark bruises and the black bands of cuts stood out lividly against his skin. "If you think I'm going to let you crawl off into the bushes to die after all my effort, think again," she shouted.

The Viking blinked at her with his very blue eyes and put up his good hand, as if he thought she would strike him. As well he might! What a stupid, pointless gesture, and made at such cost! His chest heaved with his effort. She stood over him, shaking with rage, until she saw his protective arm waver and collapse, his eyes lose focus and roll into unconsciousness.

All the rage went out of her in a rush. Of course he was trying to escape. Of course he thought she would strike him. They were enemies. If he was stronger, he would be trying to kill her. His wounds were whispering to her again. If he had torn all the carefully sewn sinew around his hip joint, she would...what? She turned away, feeling small and empty.

She rolled him onto a blanket and dragged him back into the house. "I should leave you on the floor for the drafts to seep into you, Viking," she grunted, breathless, as she put her shoulder into his belly and heaved him onto the pallet.

Opening all the wicker shutters to let in the most light possible, she repaired her stitchery, cleaning and re-cleaning the wounds. Fenris, who normally lay asleep in the sunshine at this time of the afternoon, sat panting at her side. She would have to tie the Viking up now. "And hope the knots hold," she muttered. "Eh, Fenris? Else I am murdered in my sleep."

She wrapped his gouged wrists and ankles with strips of

cloth to protect them. Then she took several lengths of stout rope and tied one around his neck to a supporting timber and one around the ankle of his good leg to the timber at the other end of the pallet. After some consideration, she tied the wrist of his good arm to the same post as his ankle, but more loosely. His hand could lie at his side, but he couldn't raise it very far. That would keep him from working at the knots, but allow her to roll him and tend him.

She spent the rest of the afternoon and the short twilight spinning Henewulf's fine new wool into thread for weaving, her body locked in the soothing rhythm of the spinning ritual. Her right hand rolled the spindle on her thigh while her left hand fed the hungry shaft with just the right tension. Her eyes strayed frequently to the Viking. His flesh looked so vulnerable bound by her bandages and her coarse hemp rope. She remembered him standing at the prow of his ship, the light of the sparking water flickering across his form, making him resemble a god. Would he ever again feel as invincible as he must have felt that day? She was torn inside by the dreadful courage it had taken for him to crawl into the yard and by the fear in his ice-blue eyes. She knew that fear. Today he did not seem a Viking beast, but a man who had felt what she did. That drew her to him as she had not been drawn to a man before. Stop! she ordered herself, more than once. You tread on thin ice. But then her thoughts would stray to the intimacy of healing him, and the feelings that had roused, and she would glance again to the pallet where he lay.

Finally, she rose abruptly and got her dinner. Fenris went out to range the island like the nocturnal predator he was. Britta shook her braids loose and ran her carved antler comb through them until her hair lay in red waves over her shoulders. Without knowing how she came there, she found herself standing over the Viking. His face was healing, resolving itself into the features she had seen on the deck of his ship. Almost against her will, she sat beside him. For a long time she worked at the mats in his hair with her comb, turning his head this way and that until it ran free through the streaked blond locks. Tomorrow she would wash them. When finally she turned to her own bed of furs, the Viking looked almost human once again.

Karn opened his eyes. It was light. He was very thirsty. His lips felt cracked and huge. Screeching pain in places he could not name threatened to envelop him again. At first he could think only of the next breath, the next surge of pain. After a while, he got a firmer grip on himself. He turned his head. A girl stood with her back toward him as she stirred a pot over the cook fire. She was slim, with long, gold-red hair braided in a thick plait with colored leather in the Saxon style. Where had he seen red hair? As she turned, the curve of full breasts pressed against her clothing. Her overdress was clean, the linen of her shift very white. She was not a slave. What was she doing in this poor hut?

He didn't know. The only thing he knew for certain was that he must escape. He was in Saxon hands. Raising his head, he peered down at his body. The house was warm with the fire and the afternoon sun. He was naked, except for bandages and a cloth pressed to his groin. Someone had tied him to the timbers of the house with heavy ropes and awkward knots. He tugged at the bonds on his wrist. Poor knots or no, there would be no escaping until he was stronger.

In contrast, the knots that secured his bandages were tidy and expert. He could smell the herbs in the poultices. These Saxon dogs seemed to have gone to much trouble to keep him alive. A whisper of panic soughed through his mind.

The girl turned and stared straight at him with something like dread in her eyes. With a dull shock, he remembered her. She was the woman who had bound his wounds to keep him alive before...before what he could not quite recall. They must have tortured him. She had come to where he suffered, a dark place. She had touched him. He would always remember that touch.

She put away her dread and stepped determinedly toward him. First, she tugged firmly on the awkward rope knots.

Had she tied them? They looked like a woman's knots. What man would trust her with that task? Then she sat beside him and, with her lips severely pressed together, checked his bandages. Karn groaned and flinched away as she disturbed the wound in his shoulder. She paid no attention, but picked up one of a line of small clay pots at his feet and scooped out two fingers full of yellow, oily paste. He recoiled as she tried to put it on his shoulder, and she spoke sharply to him. There was no mistaking the intent of those words.

But her touch did not match her harsh voice. It was gentle and the ointment was cool. Breathing hard against the bandages that bound his chest and ribs, he held himself still as she applied it to other wounds. He stared at the barbarian trefoil brooches that held the shoulder straps of her kirtle. Good Danish women wore oval brooches. These brooches echoed from a dream where he was crippled, *haltr,* crawling across a meadow. Was it a dream?

She rose and crossed to a large earthen jar. She ladled some rancid-looking liquid into a cup, then sat beside him and lifted his head. The foul brew reeked as she held the cup to his lips and tried to make him drink. Thirsty as he was, he wasn't drinking that. He jerked away. She spoke angrily, no doubt commanding him. Well, Karn was not made to obey a Saxon order! She would learn that here and now. He pressed his parched lips together and stared in defiance. Her own eyes snapped in return. She let his head fall to the boards. Waves of nausea left him gasping as his head hit the platform. Dimly he saw her throw the cup aside as she strode out the door.

Good! Men rotted from drinking water that smelled. Any fool knew that.

She had gone to get her man. They would begin again with whatever they had done to him. A horrible dream he'd had during his delirium threatened him. He could not quite remember it, but the fear it left behind gnawed at him. He screwed his eyes shut and meant to shout his defiance. The croak that emerged startled him, hoarse, inhuman—and worse, weak.

With difficulty, he mastered himself. He dared not despair or he would have no strength for the return of the Saxons. If only his brother-friends, victorious without doubt by now, would return to conquer Anglia, he might yet find allies in this place. How he longed to see the great head of Bjorn the Bear-Hearted push in at the door, or Jael or Thurmak. Did they wonder that he and his band had not joined them? He fidgeted on the platform, the pallet now moist with his sweat. The hemp scraped against his damp skin. His thirst became unbearable as his rapid, shallow breathing raked in through his lips and out.

After a long time, a great black wolf trotted comfortably into the house through the open doorway. He recognized it from his dream of a meadow outside the hut. It nosed forward, its great head level with Karn's own, its ears pricked forward and its feathered tail gently waving. Its cold nose brushed his sweating cheek, sniffing. It was a dog, not a wolf. The mistake was natural, it looked so fierce. He hardly noticed when the woman came in behind it.

"Fenris," she called clearly and then descended into Saxon gibberish. Karn was stunned by the familiarity of that word. The creature turned and gamboled over to her for petting. Fenris, son of Loki, brother of Fafnir, the Serpent Who Circled the World. Fenris, the Wolf destined to destroy Asgard. That was the dog's name.

The woman stared at him in disgust for a long moment. At least she had not brought her Saxon men. He stared back, sweating and breathing fiercely through his cracked lips. If he was free, if he was stronger, he could kill her with a single blow. He held on to that thought.

At last she stalked over to the large jar with the foul-smelling water in it once again. Again she ladled out a cup of the evil brew and approached his pallet looking determined. But this time she hesitated. He heard her sigh. Her shoulders relaxed. She pursed her lips and studied him warily. After a moment she held out the cup and raised her brows. Karn tried to calm his breathing. Speaking low and gently, she approached as though he was a wild animal and sat beside him. He could not think anymore. She nodded reassurance as she lifted his head. Cradled against her breast, he could smell her, sweet and clean, like one of the herbs that scented the room. Lavender; that was what she smelled like. She wanted him to drink her potion. It must be some kind of trick. This might be the only thing he could deny her.

Then the red-haired woman did a most surprising thing. Instead of pressing the cup to his lips to force him, she sipped herself and put it down. She meant to tell him that it wasn't poisoned. Looking into his eyes, she touched her fingers to her tongue. He could feel her breasts rise and fall. Then she touched her wet fingers to his lips, gently, rubbing the moisture from her own mouth into his. He meant to jerk away, but her fingers were smooth against his cracked and swollen lips, the wetness tantalizing. He was exhausted. What did he care if the concoction killed him? He should welcome death. She pushed the damp strands of hair from his forehead and smiled. Then she raised the cup cautiously to his lips. Again her brows lifted in offering.

He drank. The liquid washed over his dry mouth like lukewarm life. The taste wasn't so bad, really. It was like a bitter tea. It soothed his thirst, and he gulped it down regardless of the consequence. She smiled and withdrew it, leaving him searching for more. Now she laid him down and got another ladle from a bucket by the door.

"Water," she said, as she held the cup. That must be the Saxon word for vaather. His anger flashed to think that vaather had been so close while he suffered. Of course, if she had given him it he would never have drunk her foul brew. Was that so important to her? She held him up to drink, then laid him back.

It was over. He had submitted. His thoughts drifted onto painful ground. It was not a dream that he was haltr. That was why she tied only one hand, one leg. If he managed to kill this woman and avoid her men, even if he got back to Denmark, his life was gone. He, Karn, son of Gunnar, best of Ivar's warriors, was a warrior no longer. Scalds sing his praises? He would be reviled by all he knew as half a man, a cripple who had survived his men, denied by the Valkyrie.

In the middle of these horrid visions of his future, he noticed that the pain had receded. It was definitely easier to breathe. His wounds seemed to throb rather than shrieking for attention. A lassitude eased over him, relaxing muscles he had not realized were clenched against the pain. It was the cursed tea! She had given him some recipe to ease his pain. He rolled his head to where he could watch her hanging more weeds to dry. He closed his eyes slowly and felt that sweet surcease of pain increase. Why did she spare him? He understood her binding up his wounds as she had in the hall; the Saxons would want Urn alive to torture him further. But he did not understand why she soothed his pain.

Even as he thought this, she loomed over him and wiped his forehead with a damp cloth. She raised her eyebrows and nodded. She said a word, "Better?" He did not need to understand it to know what it meant. He nodded, still wary. She chuckled at him and turned her attention to his body. He was acutely aware that he was naked and bound, with no weapon, not even a knife, and that an enemy woman was rubbing a cloth all over his body, even his genitals.

When she was done, she ladled out some wonderfiil-smelling stew and held him up to eat it. He managed to swallow several mouthfuls before he felt too weak to take more. He shook his head as she lifted the spoon again, and this time she did not insist. As the woman took the bowl, she examined him critically. Then she went and got another cup full of the bitter tea. "Valerian," she said clearly, holding up the cup. This time he drank obediently until she took it away. Had he tested his will against hers by refusing to let her help him? It seemed so.

A more important question occurred to him. Where had the Saxon men been all day? He had seen no one outside the open door. His mind drifted when he could not answer himself. The lamplight flickered eerily over the woman as she sewed on a bench in the corner. She was always doing something, even this late. Was it late? He couldn't think....

*　　*　　*

Britta watched the Viking drift into sleep as the valerian took hold. She had been so angry with him. It took almost an hour, walking down by the beach, before she'd realized how vulnerable he must feel. The honor of resistance was all he had left. Yet, without her anger to protect her when she returned and held him to drink, the feel of his body against hers confused her.

She refused to think about that. When he was ready, she would take him to shore and leave him to fend for himself, before he had regained full strength but not when he was so weak that she would be killing him to abandon him. Three weeks was her best guess—maybe a month.

In preparation, her needle worked to make him clothing, a flaxen shirt, deer hide breeches. She couldn't feel right about abandoning him, naked and crippled, in his enemy's country. Not when he didn't even speak the language. She silenced the voice inside her that was about to protest. Well, perhaps she could fashion a crutch. She needed to get him up and walking about soon in any case, lest his lungs fill or he get sores from lying on the hard pallet.

Her thoughts returned to her vision as her glance drifted toward the Viking. She put down the shirt she was working on and stood above him. It was a hallucination, no more. She tried to remember the emotion that washed over her as it had first flashed through her brain. Fear, fear of the fire, but fear for this Viking, too. She shook her head to clear it. The vision couldn't be real.

What if it was? She began to pace the hut. It couldn't be the magic working in her again. That required the purity of a virgin. Her mother had said it a thousand times. Lord knew, she wasn't a virgin. Was it from her father's God? Did He give visions to the impure?

She pulled her father's Bible from the shelf above her bed. The book was a treasure, like her hollow-core knife, but she had not read it in a long time. The act of caring for the leather and brass that bound it was always a trial. Every time she took down the Bible, there was always the danger of remembering that other horrible time. She put the heavy volume, wrapped in oilskin against the damp, on the small table under her lamp. Could it explain what she had seen in the fire? Her father had always thought it could explain all. Pulling back the stiff cloth, she touched the gleaming brass, the supple, glowing leather.

She tried to skirt the past as she always did, but the memory came washing over her. She turned her face to the rafters, gasping for control, but she could find none.

In the winter gloaming five years ago, when they had first come to Dunford, Offa and his men had been drunk, all of them. After they had done their worst, Offa had staggered off. His men had stumbled out to plunder silver armbands or livestock. Others nodded in exhaustion. Britta had tried to still her trembling, but it was not from cold that she shivered. She raised herself to one elbow and looked around like a hunted animal. Furtively, she gathered her torn kirtle about her and heaved herself to her feet, ignoring the pain and the blood that ran down her thighs. She had lost her shoes somewhere and her girdle was gone. She wavered on her feet as she darted out the door and looked around for sanctuary. She couldn't bear it if Offa made good his threat to keep her for his use. At the thought, a whimper escaped her throat.

The church. The church was sanctuary. The rough wooden hall, hardly different than the thegn hall or the larger houses, stood on the rise like an inviolable fortress.

Behind her, a guttural voice called, "You, wench! Where do you think you are going?"

Britta reeled up the hill. She glanced behind to see a drunken warrior poke his companion. She must move faster. The wet between her legs, half her blood and half their foul secretions, made her want to vomit. Their first heavy footsteps thundered behind her on the hardened earth.

"Get back here," she heard one of them call. She concentrated on the doors of the church above. The frozen earth tore at her bare feet. She stumbled, then pressed on. She had to reach the church. Her persecutors would not dare their unholy deeds on holy ground. And her father wouldn't let them drag her out. He and his God would protect her.

She thanked the gods for her youth and her fear, which kept her stumbling on long after she thought she could not drag her feet another step. She pulled open the doors, never barred against invaders, and stumbled in. The nave was lit only by candles at the tiny wooden altar and by the twilight behind her. Pungently burning tallow and the dry, musty scent of the wood stung her nostrils. At the altar, two men turned startled eyes toward the explosive intrusion.

Britta stopped, horror seeping up around her.

One man was her father, his light blue eyes calm under his thatch of pale red hair, his cassock knotted with rough rope. The other face was burned in her memory. *Offa.*

"What, done with your duties?" The Saxon thegn asked her, a light in his eyes she knew too well.

The men behind her teetered into the doorway, uncertain. She did not answer, but looked past Offa to her father and let her prayer shine out through eyes brimming with unshed tears. A thousand thoughts flashed through her. Her father had never acknowledged her. But everyone knew. From where else could the look of the Celt about her have come? And he had always singled her out. She could thank him for her ability to read and her knowledge of Christian lore. He took special pains to teach her, though she was a girl. She took special pains to learn. Now he would save her from this evil beast with the forked beard.

"Come, child." Her father's calm voice, with its Irish accent, settled like a lilting mantle of protection around her. She stumbled forward toward his outstretched arm and nestled in against his side, her sobs breaking against his ribs. This was all the acknowledgment she needed.

"The Lord frowns on killing and raping innocent villagers, Offa," her father said, his priestly aura of command gathered about him. "You and your men had best control your sinful urges, else your acts will damn you for eternity. Now, get these beasts out of the Lord's house." He gestured contemptuously at the men panting in the doorway. They slipped back into the night.

Offa turned his narrow eyes back to her father. Though her sire was tall and could look Offa in the eye, he was dwarfed by the devil in his heavy armor. Britta remembered how frail her own body had felt struggling under that hardened leather. "To return to my offer, monk," the devil said. Here he looked from one pale red head to another, then raised his eyes speculatively to the priest again. He gave a chuckle. "You will be allowed to stay on as a second to Father Sebastian if you are baptized in the True Church. I will ask the Abbess of Ely to proclaim you."

"I will never support the dogma of Rome. The Irish church serves these people. They worship simply, in the true ways." Britta's terror retreated in the face of her father's certainty.

"Rome is the church of Peter, my church," Offa snarled. "Priests who serve here do as I command."

"I am commanded by God," her father said simply. He looked at Offa with curiosity. "You support the Church of Rome, yet you do not believe in Christ, do you, my son?"

Offa calmly drew his sword. "So be it."

Call on your God, Father, Britta thought, and clutched him tighter. Bring down fire and brimstone. I know what these beasts can do. Her father patted her hand to reassure her.

Then Offa, with a single thrust, ran her father through. It happened so suddenly, without fanfare, without sound, that Britta thought she might have imagined it. She looked up to her father's face, aghast, but it was still calm and sure. Only the shocking metal blade, visible now on both sides of his cassock, proclaimed what had transpired. Offa grasped his sword in both hands and jerked it free. Her father's hold on her relaxed. He put his other hand to his belly.

"God forgives you," he murmured to Offa. Blood welled from his lips. His next words came as a gurgle. "I forgive you." Then he collapsed to the ground.

Britta didn't bend to catch him. She simply stared, betrayed. He had taken refuge in death while she still lived.

"Where were You?" she whispered to her father's God. "Why didn't You save him?"

Offa stood like a stone, his squinting eyes staring at her father. He looked as shocked as she. Slowly the questions in his face turned to anger. He shook his head, as though to clear it, then barked a laugh that sounded false and grabbed her arm. She thought he would try to excuse what he had done before his God, but he only grinned in a horrible, knowing way and yanked her to the door. It didn't matter. The church had never proven a sanctuary anyway.

Chapter Five

Britta shuddered. What use, to relive the horror? Five years should callus over the blistered emotions. Yet the memories could still surprise her. The awful truth was that the death of her father was not the worst. Offa was not the worst. She still could not think about the other.

It had been three days before she had found a way to escape Offa again. She'd stolen a boat and somehow rowed to Deofric Eoland. Had what happened been a punishment from her father's God for wanting magic? Or was it just an accident, with no meaning for anyone but her? After that day she'd no longer read the Bible. The words inscribed upon the heavy vellum pages seemed silly.

But now, as the gloaming settled in around the hut, darkening faster with a storm off the North Sea, she took the Bible from her storage shelf. She needed answers about the vision. In the light of the lamp, as the thunder began to rumble in the distance, she unwrapped the oilcloth, ran her hands over the leather, traced the embossed letters. Holy Bible. Perhaps it was made holy by the years of work to copy it as much as by the words written within. Her father had once taught her how to let God speak to her through the book, a kind of prayer. She propped it on her lap, the binding on her knees. Then she took several deep breaths. "Speak to me, God, through your words and the words of your Son." She let the book fall open. It split near the back cover in the Epistle of John.

She began to translate the Latin slowly. " 'Whoso hath this world's good, and seeth his brother have need, and shutteth up his bowels of compassion from him, how dwelleth the love of God in him?' " Oh, that was rich! Had she not satisfied need? Had she not been giving succor to the village for years? Yet had not the love of God been denied her? Had she not suffered and been exiled? She wanted to scream again the betrayal she felt as she'd watched her father die.

Britta looked out into the darkness beyond the doorway, clutching the book to her chest. The wind had begun to howl around the hut. The words promised the love of God if you had compassion. They lied.

But no. Was that what they said? Slowly, she read the passage again. It wasn't about receiving the love of God. It was about having a love for others like God's own love inside you. Her mind danced over the meaning before she pulled it back, startled.

She never felt compassion for those she healed; at least she'd tried not to. Her glance strayed toward the Viking, and she thought about Wynn's baby. Oh, maybe she had felt sorry for Henewulf because he wouldn't believe that his Syffa was barren. But that was not the same. The sympathy she had felt for the Viking was not compassion. More like recognition, really.

She snapped the book shut and leapt off her stool to return it to her shelf. There were no answers to the source or purpose of her vision here.

Offa sprawled over a wooden bench and squeezed the mead sack so the honeyed liquid arced into his drinking horn. Somewhere the woman who had robbed him of the Viking was probably chuckling. Offa poured the sweet wine down his throat as though he could erase his angry thoughts by drinking them away. He and Raedwald had taken over a quiet corner warmed by the firebox in the larger hall. The scald sang at the other end, his voice clear and soft, his lyre music melancholy.

Offa held up his drinking horn to Raedwald. "To life eternal," he toasted.

Raedwald looked at him curiously, his mouth hidden by the drooping gray mustaches of which he was so proud. "Your dedication to the Roman religion increases, my friend."

"Perhaps," Offa sighed. He saw again the eyes of the priest he had killed.

Raedwald downed his own mead and called for meat. "I know it provides a way to control the people as the Irish monks never did. Once I thought that was why you supported it."

Offa shrugged. "It was."

Raedwald shook his head and eyed Offa. "Have you become a true believer?"

Offa considered. This was an important question, one that had been growing in him. "I found a man once who was stronger than I was, though I killed him easily," he said, after a moment. He stared into the fire. "He forgave me. His words gave him power over me. They have hung about me these years like a millstone around my neck. I think now he had power because he was sure of life eternal. That is what the new religion gives, Raedwald. I want that power."

Raedwald took a haunch of roast pig proffered by a serving woman and set it on the bench between them. "If you are Christian, so will I be. But the old religion offers life eternal, too."

"No, it doesn't," Offa replied with a ferocity that surprised even himself. "Warriors drink with the Valkyrie, but even the gods know they will die at Ragnorok."

"I see your point," Raedwald agreed as he twisted a piece of succulent pork from the haunch with his teeth. "But Ragnorok is far enough away for me."

77

"I want sureness," Offa muttered. "No one will have the upper hand of me."

"Still, Christians value obedience, meekness…'Thou shalt not kill'? I don't think this religion fits you, my friend," Raedwald said through the meat in his mouth.

Offa grimaced. "That is meant to tempt the peasants. It does not apply to us. And you have missed one important teaching. One can atone for sins and still have life eternal, no matter what you have done. That is why I build stone churches. I atone, then before I die, I repent. My ascent to heaven is assured." Offa smiled, as much to himself as Raedwald.

"You build churches as atonement in advance because you plan to sin?" Raedwald asked. He had stopped eating and was staring up at his thegn.

"Yes, and because they last." Unable to sit, Offa rose and paced in front of the firebox. "My namesake king built a dike a hundred miles long to keep the Celts out of Mercia. Offa's Dike. Men know him, though all his kith are gone. Stone is another way to live forever."

"Your church at Felixstowe will be completed soon."

"They raise the tower even now. I am having the bell cast in Eork."

Raedwald nodded and wiped the grease from his beard. Offa saw the speculation in his eyes as he looked up. "That man who forgave you…was he the red-haired wicce's father?"

"Aye," Offa muttered. "She saw it all."

"Well, you made her sorry. We all did, as I remember."

"I thought that was enough. I forgot about her. But now I wonder if she has some of her father's strength. Henewulf swears by her healing." Offa watched the flames lick at the chunks of elm wood. "Her powers must be bent to my service."

"Else she is like her father, too, above you."

Offa turned fiercely on Raedwald, sloshing his mead over the fire until it hissed in protest. "No one is above me, Raedwald. Not now that I know the Christian secret."

"Except whoever stole the Viking." Raedwald raised his brows. "We'd better find her."

The next morning, Britta stood at the Viking's side with valerian as his pain prodded him toward consciousness. He blinked awake and she held him up to drink. Then she drew back his fur and pulled the rag at his groin from under him. When she came back from washing it outside, he was red-faced and turned his head away. Well, if he was well enough to be embarrassed, he was well enough to use a bowl. She took up a bowl and poked his arm to get his attention. Holding up the bowl, she named it, "Bolla," using the simplest word she could think of. Then she placed it between his legs and raised her brows. He grunted assent hastily. "Bolla," she repeated, and put it on the shelf at his feet. If he got the idea, he would ask for it.

Now, embarrassed or no, she washed him, being careful around the seeping wounds snaking blackly over his flesh. Her stitches made them look like caterpillars crawling about him. The bruises on his ribs were mottled stains of red and purple, as though he had been careless eating mulberries. His embarrassment as she washed him only made her own awareness of his body more acute. The bulges of the muscles in his shoulders and his biceps were sinuous under her hands. The ribbed cords of his abdomen were hard, in contrast to the softness of his nipples, the nape of his neck, his lips. How could such an adamantine warrior have skin so fine?

He turned his head away as she scrubbed his genitals. She pressed down a feeling she couldn't name. Was it excitement? Not exactly. With a fresh rag, she tended his face. His black eye receded into yellow, his lips were less swollen, and several raw places on his cheekbones had scabbed over. Not a pretty sight, but he was healing, much faster than she imagined.

"Now, we turn you over." Her grunt of effort was joined by his of pain as he rolled onto his injured hip. She cleansed his damaged back and stitched buttocks carefully. Britta took a deep breath. If he hadn't liked her washing his genitals, he would really object to what was coming next. He might hurt himself, or her, trying to defend himself. She checked his ropes. Then she took another a dollop of the stime unguent. Her courage almost failed her as she put a hand on his arm and leaned over him. She showed him the thick greenish-yellow paste and touched his buttocks, as if to ask permission. He looked puzzled.

Then she saw the realization creep into his eyes. A blackness seeped up and engulfed him. He looked shocked, then terribly ashamed. Perhaps he had not understood that she knew. Perhaps the wayward memory of those who had sustained a blow to the head had not yet told him what Offa did to him in that hall. She could see him remembering now. He breathed heavily as his eyes flickered and blinked. Finally, he turned his face away and ground it into the pallet fiercely. It was the most assent she could expect.

She moved her hand to his hip slowly, talking soothing nonsense. Carefully she did what she had to do, spreading the unguent on his other wound. She had got used to this process, since she had done it several times, but he was not. By the time she was finished, quick as she was, she could feel him trembling. She pulled up the fur and left him to recover his composure. What if she had tried to force him, like he was a beast, like she had done with the valerian the first time yesterday? A wisp of remorse wafted about her before she could banish it.

Later, when she pulled him onto his back to feed him some soup, he would not meet her eyes as she held his head in the crook of one elbow. He accepted only a single mouthful before he turned his head away. He was feeling what she had felt in those first dark days after the terrible time. He retreated into sleep for most of the day. She woke him to turn him twice, and watched his eyes suffuse in self-hatred as soon as awareness hit him.

That afternoon she was weaving sturdy wool for a cloak when she was startled by a deep voice saying the word, "Bolla." She turned abruptly. There had been a tone of command in his voice, but now he cocked his head nervously and asked the word as a question. "Bolla?" Leave it to the necessities of life to bring his mind away from Offa's dreadful deeds, even for a moment. She pulled back his fur and put the bowl in the free hand of his bad shoulder.

"Don't think I am going to untie you," she said as she turned away, folding her arms across her chest. "You'll have to manage with that hand if you want to be independent." She heard him grunt as he tried to position the bowl and almost turned back to help. But she wouldn't want help if the situation were reversed. Of course, it never would be. A Viking marauder would kill a Saxon woman before he stooped to help her. She didn't need help, anyway. She heard the urine hit the bowl. Well, he had some control of his hand at least. She turned around as he was trying to reach for his furs. Briskly, she took the bowl and pulled his cover up.

When she came back inside from dumping the bowl, he surprised her again. "Vaather?" he asked. What did he want? She could see him think again. "Water?" he asked clearly. He looked apologetic and licked his lips. Well, he certainly learned quickly. She got a cup of water and held his head to drink.

When he was done, he looked at her speculatively with those blue eyes. *"Ek jata skuldarstothum,"* he said, and nodded his head very formally. He looked to see if she understood.

"Oh," she said, startled. "Thanks to you." Then, unsure how she had made this leap, she repeated *"Thonc to thu?"*

"Ja, thonc to thu," he said, as though he'd meant to say just that.

Britta couldn't help but give a little watchful smile as she laid him back down. His free hand made a small gesture toward his chest. "Karn," he said carefully.

Karn. It sounded strong and unforgiving. Her brows drew together in dismay.

The Viking gestured toward her, inquiring.

"Britta," she whispered. How could a name sound so vulnerable?

The Viking nodded. "Britta," he repeated. His voice rumbled out of his sandy beard. Britta was suddenly afraid, as though he had power over her now that he knew her name. And he, was he not less of a beast, now that he was named? She rushed back to her weaving.

"The men don't know the woman who gave them the body," Badenoth ventured, glancing at the others for support. "She wore a cloak."

"She said it was on your orders that he was to be burned," Henewulf corroborated.

Offa cut off the useless words. "Have you found the woman?"

"They all deny they took the Viking," a man named Elther said with authority.

"Of course they all deny it," Offa shouted. "What would you expect?"

"What are we to do if the women deny it and the men don't know?" Henewulf asked.

Why couldn't these fools understand? Offa could not let this go. His belly churned just as it had when the Irish monk forgave him. It was even worse that it was a woman who had flouted him. The men were all saying that the Viking was probably dead anyway, that it was only someone mistakenly taking care of the carcass. He knew better.

"Let's be more persuasive," he said, as if talking to children. "I want answers by sunset!" The men milled about and seemed almost to wander out the door, as though they were uncertain how or even whether to do his bidding. Offa felt the rage within him rising. All this caused by one woman. He would have her hide when he found out who it was. And he would find out.

Karn spent more time awake now, though he still craved the Saxon woman's foul valerian tea when the pain from his wounds was on him. Ever since he had realized that the awful dream had not been a dream at all, his spirit vacillated between a shame that sapped all will and a fierce desire to escape before the shame could begin again, to kill as many Saxons as he could along the way.

That was why he had tried to make an ally of the woman. At first he'd wanted only to kill her and escape. He watched for his time and wondered how long it would be before he had the strength to untie his bindings and creep in the night to the knife she used at her cook pot. Then, slowly, the lesson of his first attempt to escape revealed itself. He needed the woman and her herbs to make him strong enough to get away. He would wait to kill her. But he dared not wait too long. Sooner or later she would give him over to her men.

Why she had not done so already was a puzzle that tested the limits of his mind. He had seen no one at all besides the woman and her dog. He remembered vaguely that the woman had half-dragged him up a hill alone. Why? She despised him as her enemy. He had seen her look of disgust too many times. Yet she tended him carefully. She must be under Fork-beard's orders.

One thing Karn knew: He wasn't safe until he was back on a Viking ship. No life awaited him, of course. He was haltr, now, crippled. His body would tell all that he had survived the shame of his defeat. He would be fit only for begging. No wife, no land, no fame. No Dane would count one who was haltr as a man. Even if his friends Jael and Thurmak and Bjorn walked through the door this moment, still would they scorn him. At least no one would know his other shame—no one but him, and he would remember it each day of his life. Not much of a life. But it was the only hope he had left.

He tried to change the direction of his thoughts and pictured what was happening now in Cent. The Danes would leave a puppet king, while Halfdan and his forces sailed north to conquer Eork. Ivar might already be on his way to winter in Anglia, gathering horses and supplies, until Halfdan joined him. In spring, the last battle for the great island would commence. And there would be a Danish king here before the summer.

Karn spent hours planning his escape to keep the despair at bay. He needed a crutch and he must learn or remember more of the Saxon language. With some more knowledge he might simply pass for foreign. If he could steal a boat, he might make it up the coast to Norse Northumbria, or south to Cent, where he was sure his friends would soon hold sway. He vowed to regain his strength. Only today he had sat up. Small triumph, he thought grimly.

He found the dog a comfort. It was a Saxon dog, of course. Yet it had a familiar name, Fenris. He called it sometimes when the woman was not about. When he called, it would lift its head or cock its ears at the sound of its name. Sometimes it came to visit him on his shelf. The small caress of its sniffing nose was a solace.

The house was empty now. Perhaps the woman called Britta was down bathing. There must be a pool nearby, for she came in sometimes with wet hair, smelling of Frankish lavender. She bathed more than anyone he had ever seen. She wiped him down every day as well, and she had soaped his hair twice. Now she had been gone a long time and it was growing dark.

With great effort, he pushed himself into a sitting position, twisting so that he might rest his weight off his lacerated backside onto his good hip. Just as he had settled himself, the dog skidded into the house through the open door, heralding her approach. He bounced over happily. Karn managed to move his left hand enough to scratch him under the chin. "Fenris, old boy," he muttered. "Where is your mistress?" He wondered whether she would smell like lavender.

She came in, practically crowing victory, brandishing an axe in one hand and the branch of a tree in the other. Karn had eyes only for the axe. It was a lumbering axe, of course. It had little in common with the finely honed blade and wrought handle of his own lost weapon. But it was an axe. She leaned it by the door and held the branch aloft.

"Crutch," she said. He saw what she meant. The branch smelled of green wood and running sap, perhaps two inches in diameter, but it had an awkward Y at one end. Though it was trimmed badly, it was just what he needed. "Crutch," he repeated with suppressed excitement. Another ingredient for his escape. She put it in his good hand, still tied to the post. He caressed the smooth bark of the branch. Freedom, it breathed.

As quickly as it came, the excitement left him beached and dry. Poor fool, he heard a voice inside sneering. You are eager for this crutch? Good. It will be your partner for life, a symbol of your shame. The smile died upon his lips, the eager words of thanks turned to sand in his mouth. He screwed his eyes shut as despair welled up like deep and silent water over his head. He pushed the crutch away and slumped back against the post as it clattered to the floor. The woman's face fell, then hardened against him. She tossed the branch against the wall with the axe.

The axe. He tried to focus on the axe through his black despair. He was used to wielding an axe in his right hand. If he could strap a shield to his useless arm...he would be killed instantly by any warrior he knew. He closed his eyes and slumped awkwardly onto his pallet. Best he learn the woman's language so he might beg her to cleave his heart in two with that axe.

Britta pushed herself about the hut, seething. After all the pains she had taken to find just the right elm bough with a straight shaft, or near enough, and a fork that would support him, and one long enough to boot; after all that, he had spurned her gift without so much as a thank-you. And she knew he knew the words for that! See if she took pains for him again! As soon as his wounds were half-healed, she would dump him on the nearest shore and never give him another thought. She glanced over and saw him eyeing the axe. Jesu! How could she have brought an axe inside where he could see it? Did she want to be murdered in her sleep? Already she slept with her knife. Striding outside, she hid the axe under the woodpile behind the house.

When she returned to the hut, she refused to look at him. She gathered her bowl and her spoon. The Viking need not wait for any food she would give him. Fenris watched her curiously, as if her strange behavior was inexplicable but interesting. "Don't take his side," she muttered. "You've gotten much too friendly with him lately." She glanced over at the Viking. She refused to call him by name in her mind. His eyes were clenched together as though he was in pain. Not true. She had given him valerian before she left on her senseless quest for a crutch.

Not physical pain. She glanced back at the crutch, leaning against the door. Abruptly, she saw it as he did, a symbol of what he had lost, and the anger seeped out of her. What a fearful future it foretold. The dreadful days following her own encounter with Offa still haunted her. *Encounter? Let's call it what it was after five years.* After Offa and several of his thegns besides raped her repeatedly over the course of days, she had wanted to die. She didn't know to this day how she had rowed to Deofric, what had made her carve out some remnant of a life. It might have been her anger. At least she had not been a cripple, as he was. She had a livelihood, of sorts, in her wort-craft, her herbs. What did he have, who was a warrior, however despicable? The crutch must shout to him that there was nothing left of what he had been.

Britta sighed and ladled out a bowl of soup. She could not give him back the prowess he had lost, but she would teach him some Saxon words and force him somehow to use the crutch, whether he would or no. She sat down beside him as he turned to glare angrily at her. "All right, try to eat," she commanded, putting the bowl in his lap.

He pushed the bowl to the floor. Soup spilled across the boards, startling Fenris from his place by the bed box. Britta glared at the Viking for one moment, her anger sloshing over her again. Then she slapped him, so hard his head snapped.

"Barbarian beast," she shouted as she leapt to her feet to stand over him. "Can't you see I'm trying to help you, whether you deserve it or not?" She stood with her fists on her hips, shaking. "Ooooooohhh! You make me angry," she cried. She had half a mind to hold his nose and pour the soup down his throat! He couldn't stop her. Wouldn't she just like to do that!

The Viking was as angry as she was. He glared at her, his blue eyes flashing. He muttered one word, under his breath. *"Bikkja!"* She didn't have to understand his language to know what he meant. Curse him and all his bestial kind! What right had he to call her that? Just because he faced despair? Just because she had commanded him to eat instead of offering the food? Just because she had hit him…? A little crease made itself felt between her brows. It was his fault she had been rough with him. He had been ungrateful, first about the crutch and then about the food.

He chewed his lip as he stared at her, then glanced away. She went back to the fire, not wanting to meet his eyes either. It *was* his fault. It was. As she knelt by the fire, her braid fell over her shoulder, glowing red in the firelight. Her cursed red hair…She sighed. It had always been a sign of her temper. God's breath! Once her anger had saved her from despair. Now it intruded on her best intentions. How many times had her father chided her for her lack of self-control? Behind her, Fenris licked the soup from the floor, undeterred by her anger. He carefully avoided the cabbage and lapped at the bits of rabbit meat she had used for flavor.

Silently, she picked up the bowl and again filled it with soup. Taking a huge breath, she rose and turned back to the Viking. He looked drawn and pale. The lines of pain in his face were probably etched there for life. This time she offered the bowl from a safe distance. After a moment, he nodded brusquely. She set the bowl in his lap. While he ate, his attention fixed intently upon the bowl, she got out the shirt and breeches she had made and the deer hide that would provide his boots, and set them at his feet. He watched her covertly as he slurped his meal.

"Karn." He looked up at the sound of his name. It was the first time she had used it. "You will need these. *Thu nied thes"* she repeated carefully. She pointed to the leather and her feet. *"Sho."* Then gestured to the breeches and the shirt, *"Brec and hemethe."* Then she pointed to her mouth, *"Seax-*

isc werd." Finally, she shrugged her question, opening her hands.

"Thonc to thu," he said. She saw apology in his eyes, though he did not smile.

She nodded slowly. "Tomorrow. *Tomergen."*

Offa knew what he would hear. They gathered in the hall where they had celebrated victory over the Viking horde. The smoky fire and the oil lamps cast the faces of the gathered men in a flickering glow. Offa sighed and tried to remember his feeling of triumph. That victory seemed hollow now that he had been denied the information from the Viking, almost as hollow as his victory over the witch's father. The nagging feeling of incompleteness fueled a spark of rage. He motioned to the small knot of his loyal seconds at the door.

Henewulf stepped forward. "We do not know who took the body, my Lord Offa."

"Then you have failed to be diligent enough," Offa barked. The warriors around him exchanged glances. Even Raedwald looked uneasy. This was what came of letting the sins of the disobedient go unpunished. His rage rose closer to the surface.

"Cuthrun took responsibility for the other women," Badenoth said.

"I am sure she suffered the consequences of your failure." Offa knew the answer.

"She is dead," Henewulf said curtly, "swearing none of the women had done this deed."

"Did the devil take the body, then?" Offa's words were edged with frustration.

"Perhaps," Raedwald interrupted before the others could reply.

All eyes turned toward the man with the long gray mustaches and the cold eyes. Offa frowned. It was unlike Raedwald to make jokes about something so close to Offa's heart.

"Hear me out." Raedwald's glance raked the hall. "What if Cuthrun was right?" His gaze came at last to Offa. "What if it was the witch from Deofric who stole him from you?"

Offa wondered that he had not thought of it before. His two obsessions twisted into one.

"A devil of sorts, since she lives on Deofric," Badenoth agreed.

"Set a watch," Offa muttered. His voice was tight with rage even in his own ears. "I want to know the minute she comes to shore."

Chapter Six

Britta opened her eyes slowly. The coals cast an eerie glow over Karn's sleeping face across the room. He looked so peaceful, his features softened in sleep. Slowly, she pushed back her furs and rose. She wasn't cold. The air was warm and close in the little hut. He must be warm too, because there were no furs covering him. Hadn't she pulled up his furs before she went to her bed box? He was naked. But she wasn't afraid of his nakedness as she had been that first morning. Slowly, she walked toward him, hand outstretched. It wasn't his wounds that called this time. Still, she wanted to touch him. It seemed to hurt, deep in a place she couldn't name, she wanted to touch him so much. As she drew closer, she could see that his wounds were healed. His skin was smooth, no scars, no seeping holes. He was a golden god again, as he had been the day she first saw him. Not golden, though, but flaming red in the light from the coals. Burning. She seemed to be burning, too. Her hand drew close to his flesh, trembling. She knelt beside him. As her hand touched his chest a shock went through her, right down, past her stomach, to some place between her thighs. It made her feel whole, alive. Between her thighs? His eyes opened, blue like the sea at midnight. Between her thighs! Fear wound up around her spine. That place brought only pain and fear. He grabbed her hand and held it as surely as he held her gaze. Trapped! His member swelled before her eyes, grotesque. She struggled away. But between her thighs a feeling rose that said she shouldn't struggle. No! She couldn't give in to that feeling!

Britta sat up in bed, gasping, and threw her furs from her. Fenris leapt to his feet, startled. Sweat beaded on her forehead, trickled between her breasts. Across from her, Karn slept the sleep of the exhausted, covered in furs. His eyelids fluttered, but he did not wake. It took some moments for her to steady her breathing. What dream was this? It must have been a dream. She ran her hands through her hair. It had been awful. But not at first. At first the touching had been as healing as when she had corrected the wrongness in his wounds. Jesu, protect me from the demons that inhabit dreams, she thought. She shoved herself into the corner of her bed box. The chill air struck her, turning her sweat to ice. Fenris circled once, accusingly, and settled into a tightly curled ball with a protesting groan. Britta stared at the Viking. Better to get this man out of her house as soon as possible, she thought. She gathered her furs about her.

Britta cut a piece of cheese for herself and Karn, and one for Fenris into the bargain. The morning sun seeped through the wicker shutters in a stippled pattern across the floor of the hut. Karn struggled up to sit on his own. He was making a remarkable recovery. Good, the better that he should leave this place. The echoes of her dream still trembled above the firebox. She tightened her rope knots before handing him his wedge of cheese. He glared at her.

"Well, how do I know you will behave?" she justified, though she knew he couldn't understand. "Use your right hand. You should work that shoulder anyway."

He had to lean down to take the cheese from a hand that could grasp now but was connected to an arm that worked from the elbow down only. She stuck the knife into the fire's smoldering coals and shut the dream away. It was not his fault. Dreams were dreams. The truth was, she had grown used to him being in her hut. She had to admit she liked someone to talk to besides Fenris, even though he couldn't understand much. And if the feel of his flesh under her hands had become…what? Uncomfortable? Confusing? That would soon be at an end. She sat beside him, untied the bandages, and removed her poultices. They had done what work they could. She did not give him any valerian, as was her wont when he woke. It was time to start weaning him. He glanced to the large jar next to the loom.

She shook her head. "No valerian," she muttered.

He pressed his lips together over his anger. They were almost back to normal, except for the two scabs that marked the splits.

She rolled her eyes. "You can't take it forever," she protested. Then she shrugged and turned back to his wounds. "You'll have to put up with some pain."

She pressed at his wounds gingerly. The one in his belly still seeped, but the ones at his shoulder and hip had drawn together into puffy closure around her stitches much faster than she would have thought possible. She went to the coals and drew out her knife, wiping its fiercely wicked blade clean of ashes. She would be rid of her unwelcome guest soon at the rate he was healing. Her life would return to normal. Dared she go to the mainland? She and Fenris did not have enough jerked venison for winter, or cheese, for that matter. Offa would have forgotten all about her, she told herself. His had been a need of the moment and she had been at hand. Had she not been going to shore for nigh on five years? In all that time Offa had not molested her. She had not even seen him. Grip yourself, she chided. In a few days they would go to the shore.

She sat down next to the Viking, forcing her eyes to look only at his wounds. When he flinched away as she raised the knife, she started and looked up into blue eyes wide with alarm.

"No, no," she soothed and ran her finger lightly along the stitches in his shoulder. He peered down his nose. "These can come out now." She brought her eight-inch blade slowly up to his shoulder and steadied him with a hand on his chest. His flesh sent tingles up her arm and she repressed a shudder. The curling hairs were intimate against her open palm. It would not be like her dream. She wouldn't let it. Trying to ignore the heat of his chest against her hand, she inserted the tip of her blade under each stitch and cut the gut all along the winding wound. She plucked each out by the knotted side, firmly and quickly. Glancing up, she saw his attention riveted not by her blade but by her hand on his chest. She jerked it away. Back to the stitches.

All the stitches broke under her knife except the ones around the place in his side that still seeped. The feel of his thigh under her hand as she worked the wound at his hip made her irritable. She couldn't think why. Maybe she felt bad about her failure. Her awkward repairs would not make him new, and the gouge that ran from hip to groin might have taken something else he treasured. Pray to the gods that she would never know for sure.

When she was done, she presented the crutch he had spurned last night and dared him to refuse it. He grasped it with the only hand that was free and looked at her expectantly.

Gods! She had not thought this through. He would not be able to use his crutch with several limbs still tied to her posts. She would have to untie him. He knew it, too. He spoke, something unintelligible, and nodded reassuringly. She took a deep breath, casting about for alternatives. There were none. She didn't have it in her to abandon him before he could walk. She sighed and hung her knife on a peg above the firebox, then returned to untie his knots. "Don't think you've won," she warned. "You still need my help." He dragged his bad leg to hang over the edge of the shelf as she steadied his bare shoulders. Her heart beat loudly as she sat beside him and put her shoulder under his bad one. It was taking a terrible chance to be so near when he was free.

She glanced fearfully into his face. A fierce and eager little smile shone there. His eyes were bright as he nodded encouragement. He wanted this. Did that mean she was safe for now? She pulled his bad arm around her neck. The closeness of his body got in the way of the fear she should be feeling. She took a breath and counted to three. On three, he heaved himself up as she lifted.

Their effort was almost over before it began. His knees buckled and she staggered with his weight. But she righted herself and he managed to get his legs under him. He pulled the crutch in under his good shoulder and leaned into it. Britta unwound his arm from her neck. He balanced there, his face gone gray. She did not need to urge him, though. He took a step forward with his good side and then convulsively moved his crutch, dragging one foot after him. After three or four laborious, tottering steps, even his good leg buckled. He cursed and would have gone down if Britta had not darted in to support him.

His face registered disgust and intense disappointment. "But you did well," she encouraged as she half-dragged him back to his shelf. "There will be other times."

He sank onto his pallet with a small groan of protest.

Fists on her hips, she stared at him as the muttered curses flowed between his gritted teeth. "Enough," she commanded. Then, as an afterthought, "Bolla?" He nodded wearily, and she handed it to him. It must seem a long way toward independence now.

The messenger who came into Offa's hall had ridden hard. His boots were mud-splashed and his horse sweaty and blowing. Offa could see that he wanted to deliver his message immediately, so he refused to allow it. First the man must have rest and brush the dirt from his leathers, then drink the ceremonial horn of mead. The scald from the north sang a song of welcome as the men stamped their feet.

Offa himself was distracted. The wicce from the island, that traitorous wench, had still not come to shore where he could get at her. It was hard to concentrate on guests. And this was one, Offa knew, whose message would not be welcome just now. At last Offa nodded toward the messenger. The man leapt to his feet and came forward eagerly. "You have news?" Offa asked.

"I have a command," the messenger announced, "from Edmund, King of all Anglia."

Offa smiled. He knew very well whom the man represented. But Edmund had not been quite grateful enough to Offa for his help in taming the wild Suthfolc thegns when they had been scheming with Mercia against the Anglian throne. "What is Edmund's *request?*" he asked slowly and deliberately.

The messenger's face darkened, but he bowed his head. "Cent has fallen to the Viking horde of those two hellbegotten brothers, Halfdan and Ivar the Boneless, sons of Ragnar Lothbrok. King Boroghed has surrendered."

Offa's thegns were thunderstruck. Their murmuring protest swelled around the hall. "He paid the Danegeld, didn't he? That's not surrender," Badenoth protested.

Offa and Raedwald exchanged glances. They knew better.

"He surrendered," the messenger repeated. "Cent is theirs."

Offa made a motion for silence around the hall and drew himself forward on his bench to stare at the messenger. It should have been his lot to tell Edmund what the plans of the Viking raiding fleet were to be. That victory had been denied him.

"Edmund gathers his forces at Thetford for a war council in a fortnight. He prepares to defend Anglia, come spring," the messenger reported. "He orders you to meet him there."

Heads nodded around the hall. This was probably the one thing to which all thegns in Anglia could bind their will in unison at this moment.

"What about Danegeld?" Raedwald asked. "Will Edmund try to buy peace?"

"That you must ask Edmund." The messenger shrugged.

Offa slapped the trestle table with the flat of his hand. "Bide here tonight," he commanded the messenger. "Tell

Edmund it pleases us to be in Thetford a fortnight hence."

That meant that he had very little time to finish his business with the red-haired witch.

Karn pushed himself up on his crutch irritably and dragged himself toward the door. He was angry with Britta. She was gone off somewhere, no doubt to collect more of her weeds. *"Wyrts,"* she called them. Or maybe she was fishing. *"Fiscoth."* He had so absorbed himself in trying to learn Saxon words that he could not turn off his translations. Fire, *"fyr."* Soup, *"broth."* Wound, *"wund."* Some words were like to words in his own tongue, others nothing alike. He was good at languages. Songs and stories from each place he had raided rang in his head. He remembered some Saxon from the slaves his father held in Denmark, too. Now he and Britta could carry on a simple speech of sorts, accompanied by much signing.

The wind blew across the dooryard, telling of winter to come. He stomped to the woodpile around the side of the hut, leaning heavily on his crutch. That must be where she had hidden the axe after she had seen his fascination with it. He had asked after it. He had that little self-control, and she obligingly taught him its name, *"aecs."* But it had never reappeared. She slept with her knife, too. "Seax." He liked the Danish word better. "Knife," he whispered, defiant.

The fact that she slept with her knife made him angry, too. As angry as when she had tried to tie him up again after he had walked those first few steps. Why, she didn't even tie up her dog! Did she think a Danish warrior had less honor than a dog? In the end she had left him free. But she slept with her knife and the axe was gone. She didn't trust him. She must think her body so enticing that he could not keep his hands from defiling her. He snorted to himself. She should see the voluptuous women he had taken in his time. That one in Constantinople made three of her for beauty.

More likely, she thought he would kill her.

He had thought of little else at first. He had to give her that. Then he had waited to kill her until she could heal him.

Now he realized that he owed her his life. She had taken him away from where Fork-beard was, and she apparently had no intention of betraying him, else she would have done it long ago. His life might not be worth much, but she had taken much trouble over it. He was not sure why. But Danes understood debt.

Still, he was in Saxon lands, and therefore Saxons must be about somewhere. He remembered a hill, a cart. But where he was, he had no idea.

Karn made his way around the woodpile. He could see no axe here. Frustrated, he pulled down first one chunk of oak and then another with his good hand until there was an untidy pile at his feet. He could not stop, but heaved down wood faster and faster until he lost his balance and toppled over into the dust of the yard.

His eyes clenched against the morning sun as he lay there panting. Both opened and closed at his will now. Even his scabs were gone. But the torment inside was not gone. He couldn't shake his feeling of impotence for very long, though he knew, in his saner moments, that he had made better progress than he should have expected. Progress toward what? Even if he escaped this land, he had only life as a pitiable cripple ahead of him. Once he'd thought he was weary of going viking. Now he could think of nothing finer than striding the deck of a proud dragon ship, with the lust for victory strong in his heart.

His dreams had been tormenting him too. Perhaps that was why he'd grown so ill-tempered. Every night, it seemed, his sleep danced with visions of himself as whole, strong. He strode a ship's deck, or climbed some foreign battlement. And always she was there. Sometimes she was a black-haired, green-eyed beauty in a harem, squealing in anticipation of him ravaging her. He liked that one, at least until he woke and knew that his days of ravaging harems were long gone. Sometimes she was a Danish girl, rich in her own right, a prize his father was proud he had won. Last night had been the worst. She was herself, in her own hut. She had touched him, smiling, and he'd been made whole. More whole, stronger than he had ever been. As he lay in the dooryard, he could still feel that rightness cascading over him. His eyes blurred. In his dream, he had reached for her, tenderly, almost afraid to feel the soft down of her cheek against his callused palm. Her green eyes had glowed up at him, trusting, and his loins had roused themselves, and she had opened her lips, red and full, and…

Karn pushed himself up roughly, blinking into the harsh light of the sun. *Best put dreams away, fool. They are not for you, with any woman.* Who would want a haltr man? And she, did she not despise him? Did she not mistrust him? Was that not why she had hidden her axe?

The wind brought the smell of the sea to his nostrils as he sat on the packed earth. He was still near the sea. If he listened, he could hear the waves. Ship, *"scip."* Sea, *"sae."* Abruptly, he pushed himself up. He might not be able to find the cursed axe. But he could surely, as Loki was a trickster, know where he was. If he could reach the sea, he might be able to make out where along the coast she had taken him. He was a seafaring man, after all, and the coves and promontories of the land were guideposts, burned in his memory.

He rolled over, got his good leg under him, and pulled himself to standing with the crutch. He tried to hear from where the roar of the waves came. That was confusing. Paths led away from the clearing in several directions, too. At last he struck out straight away from the door, to the north by the look of the sun, and dragged his disobedient leg after him into the trees. The roar of the waves grew louder. The path led down. He could smell the salt in the air, the stink of seaweed on the shore. If the water sounded closest to the north, he must be on the curve of an inlet. The journey wasn't far. A couple of hundred yards. But it seemed a quest to test even the gods. By the time he came out on the cliff he was drenched in sweat, his shirt clinging to his body and his wounds crying for peace.

All effort was rewarded when he saw the gray North Sea heaving below him. He wavered there, his eyes closed and his face turned into the freshening breeze that would fill a striped, square sail. The tantalizing scent of freedom floated up from the water. His hair blew back from his face and the breeze cooled his body.

When he opened his eyes, what he saw as he looked north startled him. The long coast disappeared into haze. But it was too far away. He could not be on the curve of any inlet. He peered down to his left, where the cliff sloped down to a beach. There was the path up which he and Britta had struggled, but the beach curved back behind him until it disappeared.

The truth struck him like the blow of an enemy. He knew exactly where he was. He was on that island where they had come ashore to parlay before the attack. That little empty island. Only it wasn't empty. Probably hadn't been empty then. She was here. She lived here.

Why had she not told him where he was? He would have felt safer knowing there was a mile of water between himself and his tormentors. She could have drawn the map of an island in the sand of the dooryard. Thor knew he had asked often enough. The anger of his weakness rose in him again. Was it too much to ask for the comfort of knowing where he stood?

He had his breath back now, but he felt light-headed and apart from himself. Better get back up the slope to the house before he lost his strength entirely. His anger at her fueled his effort as he toiled up into the trees. He dared not stop to rest. She would find him lying on the path like a beached whale. He would give her no chance to despise him.

As if summoned by his thoughts, he saw her running down the path toward him. Her blue kirtle and her shining red hair seemed too bright to be real. He pulled himself forward with his crutch. She looked angry. He stumbled and almost went over before he lurched against the trunk of a tree and steadied himself. Well, he was angry, too.

She grabbed his waist, tucked her shoulder under his, and tugged his free wrist over her shoulder, all the while berating him. The feel of her against him only increased the trembling of his legs.

"Why did you not tell me where I am?" he gasped in Danish as she half-hauled him up the path. "Safe across a mile of water from the cursed Saxons?" He didn't care that she didn't understand him. "And what about an axe or a knife?" he accused, drowning out her protests. "A man needs a weapon to be whole, even you must understand that!"

She had a weapon. Her knife was stuck right there in her girdle. Almost within reach of his hand, though it was his bad hand. How he longed to hold that knife!

Karn's head grew too clear, with that clearness that comes sometimes when the body's strength is almost gone. As she dragged him into the dooryard, he used his last remaining strength to pull back against her. He grabbed the knife hilt from her girdle as he slid away.

She knew immediately what he had done. She twisted away and stood staring.

Karn fingered the hilt of the knife with something like ecstasy, though he knew he couldn't lift his arm for a killing blow. It was a comfort just to hold it. His gaze caressed the finely molded horn hilt. If he could escape this island, he would take this knife with him. He glanced to where Britta stood, stricken with fear, about to run.

Loki take her! She thought he meant her harm. Stupid woman! What kind of man did she think him, to return all her care with murder?

Karn let his head drop. He just wanted a weapon. As though that would make him a man again. Clearness now evaporated into confusion. He threw the knife in the dirt at her feet with a grunt. Let her have the knife. Let her think the worst of him.

Karn did not even look at her. He turned in the dooryard toward the house, weak and torn in body and spirit. She made no move to help him. He made it to the door, leaned against the timber, then laboriously hitched up his crutch to the floor of the house and dragged himself in.

* * *

Raedwald and Offa stayed late in the hall, long after the orders were given to prepare for departure, long after the messenger and the thegns had gone to their beds. By agreement unspoken they sought to prolong this moment of anticipation, this beginning of a great war. There had been many horns of mead this night, but now the mead was done, the lamps turned down, the fire no more than a flicker in its box.

"There is but one thing that I regret." Offa twined the two ends of his beard absently.

"I can guess what that is." Raedwald put his boots up on one of the skewed trestle tables.

"You think you know my mind?" Offa asked sharply.

His second chuckled. "You have not finished with that wicce who stole the Viking leader. I know your mind very well, Offa."

"A dangerous talent, Raedwald," Offa grumbled. "I shall have to watch my back."

"When have you ever failed to watch your back?" Raedwald grinned.

"I can't go to Thetford knowing she is out there, thinking that she bested me."

"I doubt she'll come to shore before we go."

"No," Offa mused. "I must go to her. There is no choice."

"The men must never know. They'll think you have been exchanged for a devil."

Offa hefted his boots up onto the table with Raedwald's. "I'll slip away just at dusk, after the fishing boats are in and the villagers are at their dinner."

"Then we'll both go," Raedwald said, draining the last from his horn of mead. "Unless you want to keep the sport to yourself."

"No," Offa said through gritted teeth. "Come along."

Britta was irate with herself for letting Karn get the knife away from her. Yet he had not threatened her with it. She had been afraid of him. How long had she lived in fear, fear of Offa, fear that her magic had been denied her, fear of the

Viking? Fear had become the sovereign of her life. This morning she couldn't bear it any longer. So she gave the knife to Karn to cut up their breakfast and turned her back on him.

She liked to think she could best her fear in that one action, but things were never that clean. She was stiff and trembling as she waited for what would happen behind her. When the tension grew too much, she whirled to find him dividing the cheese wheel and fending off an eager Fenris.

When he looked up he was laughing at her—not with his mouth, but unmistakably with his eyes. He held the haft of the knife out in exaggerated politeness and lifted his brows, and she could not help the smile that curved her lips in spite of all attempts to banish it. Fenris used that opportunity to steal the largest piece of cheese and dash for the door. Her smile bubbled over into laughter. That would serve Karn right to mock her.

Karn shook his head. "Bad dog," he said clearly in Saxon. *"Yfael hund."*

All day she was relaxed as she went about her work. Not dulled, the way she had tried to be for so long, but easy... ready, almost. Ready for tomorrow, when good things might just happen. She sang at her loom and hummed as she tended her garden. Now, as she came in with an armload of savory through the late afternoon glow, she looked forward to how tasty it would make yesterday's stew.

When Fenris started barking furiously, some little distance down the hill, she thought he must have cornered something for his own dinner. But the barking didn't stop. And they were deep, angry barks. Britta turned in the doorway, unsettled. The last time Fenris had barked like that was the night she had brought Karn up from the beach. He had been certain Karn was an intruder.

Her eyes widened in horror. She glanced into the hut. Karn was putting the finishing touches on a pair of boots. But he stopped stock still, his awl frozen in midair. The moment stretched as their eyes met. Then she burst into furious activity.

She raced to Karn and pulled him up, grabbing the crutch that leaned on a nearby timber and shoving it under his arm. "Maybe it's nothing," she whispered frantically. Was it Vikings, more of Karn's friends come to avenge their slain brethren? Or were these intruders Saxon?

Fends's barks grew closer. How could she get Karn out of sight before they appeared in her yard, whoever they were? She scurried to the back window and threw open the wicker shutters. Motioning frantically, she drew over the stool. If he was moving as quickly as he could, it was yet too slow. As Karn stepped up, Fenris galloped into the clearing.

"Out!" she whispered, frenzied, and shoved Karn up through the opening. Britta heard his grunt as he hit the grass outside. Fenris dashed up to show Britta his outrage. She leaned out the window and threw the crutch. "Into the trees," she hissed at Karn. "Go!" She slapped the shutter closed and whirled as Fenris darted out the door again, renewing his protest.

Britta was panting. That would never do. She stilled her breathing just as two men entered the clearing. One was Offa. Her stomach dropped and her throat seemed to close. She and Karn were done for, both of them.

Offa grinned as the red-haired wicce came out of her house. She had not even tried to hide, in spite of the dog's warning. Offa thought they might have had to chase her down all over the island once the advantage of surprise was gone. But here she was, as bold as you please. Well, she wouldn't be bold for long. He could feel his loins harden in anticipation. He motioned Raedwald to stop. "Wicce," he called. "You stole something from me."

The girl had her back to the doorpost. She looked frightened. "You can steal something only from its owner." Her voice shook a little.

She hadn't bothered to deny she stole that Viking's body. "Stop your words," he said roughly, his anger rising along with his anticipation. He strode forward and wound his fist in her braid until her head bent back, and he could see the fear in her eyes.

At that moment he heard a warning growl, and the dog launched himself for his free arm. Offa yelped in pain and tried to shake him off. Jaws clamped through to flesh even through his leather jerkin. That was his sword arm!

Raedwald stepped up to save him and laid a furious blow to the dog's head with his fist.

The dog squealed and fell limp to the ground. "Fenris," the girl cried and tried to wriggle away. A black cloud boiled up out of nowhere overhead.

Karn knelt in the long grass at the rear of Britta's house and listened. She would be safe as long as these intruders did not know about him. After all, they must be Saxon, just as she was. But he heard Fenris's squeal of pain and her own cries and knew he was wrong.

He glanced only once toward the trees and escape as he pushed himself up on his crutch. He was not much, but he was all she had. It was time to pay his debt. He staggered toward the corner of the house. There he saw the axe handle, just visible under a pile of wood chips. So that was where she had hidden it. Thor had sent it in his moment of need. He shook it free, wood chips flying, and switched his crutch to his bad shoulder. Then he swung up the axe, hefting its weight. He was weak and he had no shield, but he would have to do.

When he rounded the corner, he saw that there were two enemies. One had Britta by the hair. The dog lay still off to one side. They must have sensed his movement, for they swung around.

It was Fork-beard who held Britta. Time stopped. Rage warred in his breast with shame and doubt. Here was the object of his nightmares. This man knew him, had taken his inmost soul and shaken it like a dog shakes a rat and then discarded it. Numbly he noted that intensely black clouds were boiling up at a furious pace behind the house, like no storm he had ever seen. Lightning forked angrily.

The Saxons seemed as shocked as he was. They had not expected him. Karn let his body take over for his mind. He would not last long in the face of their weapons. He lunged forward awkwardly, his cry of attack welling in his throat. Britta shouted his name, in warning or in protest, and tried to twist away from Fork-beard.

Karn swung his axe upward at the nearest Saxon. Too bad it wasn't Fork-beard, but he would have to hack his way through this one for his revenge. He thought for a moment he would cleave that Saxon like a wishbone between his legs, but the devil managed to get his sword in the way and deflect the blow. A gash opened up on his thigh that colored his breeches with blood. "Yes!" Karn yelled. A tree crashed in the forest somewhere. The Saxon raised his sword with a shriek of anger. Karn prepared to fight for his life and Britta's.

Fork-beard shouted something to the other Saxon, and the man checked his blow. Fork-beard grinned. He spoke slowly. Karn understood. "Take him alive," Fork-beard said.

Britta was angry, so angry she could have spit fire, just like the lightning cracking nearer now, above them. Karn was a fool! He could not possibly help her, and she could see in his face that he knew it. But he was here anyway, to kill Offa or die trying. He probably didn't care which. She cared. Offa would never let them go, now that he knew that Karn was alive.

"Get back!" she shouted at him. She was feeling very strange, her gut in turmoil like the roiling blackness above. She imagined what their future would be, rape and torture, death. Why should these evil men be able to wreak such pain whenever their whim demanded it? She was furious. That fury blew through her head like the wind that rose now into a gale. The elements whirled around her.

Karn lunged. Raedwald bled. A tree fell in the forest somewhere, then another. The crashes seemed to be coming closer. They sounded like the footsteps of some giant beast stalking down upon her house and the bloody scene about to be enacted here. Her fear was gone now, though. She saw Raedwald push Karn's axe aside and lunge in for hand-to-hand combat. Karn went to his knees, parrying a blow to his head, and dropped his axe.

"No," she said calmly, in rhythm to the horrible crashing of the trees, coming nearer and nearer as they marched across the island amid the first fierce spatters of rain. "No, no, no."

She was totally empty now, yet she was very full. She stood frozen, her eyes rolled up toward the heavens. The wind outside mirrored the gale inside her. The others were looking to the heavens, too. She was strong now with wind and thunder and trees. She turned her gaze on Offa calmly. His fear at what he saw there shone back at her.

"No," she shouted, and the voice of the storm spoke through her mouth. It echoed across the clearing. Offa let go of her braid as though he burned and made the sign against the evil eye.

He and Raedwald spun to face the crashing trees as they stalked closer to the clearing. Britta smiled, and it was as though her face was rock or earth, splitting in savage glee. They thought they were safe in the clearing, these evil ones. Britta stretched her arms into the heavens, drunk with the force within her, and turned her head toward the pelting rain as she screamed with the wind. A wrenching sound tore through the noise of the wind. A huge and ancient pine at the east edge of the clearing teetered. Offa and Raedwald yelled something she could not hear.

Britta was still, arms raised. Offa and Raedwald began to move. Slowly the tree ripped up its own roots and arced toward them. Fear coiled in their eyes as they churned their legs to run. The great bole of the tree bounced upon the earth, setting it to tremble. The massive branches brushed Britta's kirtle. She was enveloped in the fog of dust it raised even in the spattering rain.

Through the boughs, Britta could see Raedwald and Offa turn back toward the giant tree, now covering the place where they had stood moments ago, shocked. They were separated from Fenris and Karn and Britta herself by a barrier of fear even greater than the chest-high trunk. Britta turned her face back to the heavens and felt the fullness within her bubble up into a screeching laugh, as all about her roared.

When she turned her eyes toward earth again, Offa and Raedwald were gone.

Karn shook his head to clear it as he watched Britta stand among the branches of the great tree in the pelting rain. His body felt leaden. Revenge was denied him, and he had not even been granted the solace of dying in the attempt. His head rang with the thunder. A storm that could heave down such a mighty trees must surely go on forever, but in a few moments the savage rain stopped abruptly and the wind died. Britta seemed not to notice him. She wavered only a foot or so from the giant trunk. The clouds boiled again in fierce retreat, leaving the limpid dusk.

Karn's breath came raggedly. What kind of storm was this? The image of Britta, arms raised, howling in ecstasy, would be forever burned on his brain. Fork-beard and his crony had fled without another blow. They, too, had been unnerved by the sudden churning of the elements.

Well, one of them had to move. He crawled to his abandoned crutch and used it to push himself up. All his wounds protested. Britta seemed to see him for the first time and turned eyes large and curiously empty upon him. He hesitated only a moment before he put a hand on her shoulder and told her it would be all right in a mixture of Saxon and Dane. He was about to gather her into his one good arm when she came to herself and looked anxiously around.

"Fenris," she muttered as she staggered over to stand above the limp body. Karn gritted his teeth and braced for what she would find. But to his amazement the dog lifted his head.

"Fenris," she cried and knelt to gather him in her arms. She picked through his fur to look for blood. Apparently he had only been stunned. After a moment he shook himself and stumbled to his feet. Britta rose, looked at Karn, and suddenly began crying. Her clothes were soaked, her braid dripping, her cheeks now streaked with tears.

"What was this?" Karn asked in broken Saxon.

Britta wiped her eyes and sniffed. "Offa will think it was the island."

He looked around at the huge tree in the dooryard and saw again Britta, her arms raised in triumph as she laughed. "Was it the island?"

For a long moment she stared at him, her eyes welling. Then she said softly, "No." Abruptly, she turned and stumbled into the house.

Karn pulled Fenris, who had come to stand weakly at his knee, along after him as he followed.

When he got inside, Britta was stretched on her bed, dead asleep.

Britta woke to sun coming in through the open door. Karn was up, kicking the fire into life from a precarious perch and putting on a pot of water. Her eyes moved lazily over his shaggy, light-streaked mane of hair. She could see his muscles moving under the flaxen shirt, the leather breeches. She liked looking at him. Fenris lay panting in a square of sun. It slowly dawned on her that she had an enormous headache. As she tried to lift her head, she groaned aloud and sank back to her furs.

"Bad head?" Karn asked.

"Very bad," she whispered.

"Tea help?" He hitched himself over to her and gestured to the herbs hanging above him.

"Yes. Some chamomile, I think." She pointed.

Karn yanked the bundle down. He crumbled leaves into her wooden cup, then dipped it full of hot water from the steaming pot, swirling it to soak the herb. She watched him move about the room, her mind lulled into a haze of comfort. She had never thought to have the Viking care for her as she had cared for him. She heaved herself up painfully to accept the cup from his outstretched hand.

Karn drew up the stool and sat next to her as she sipped the tea. He said nothing, just watched her as she closed her eyes and let the hot liquid melt the throbbing in her head.

"Britta," he said finally, bringing her out of steaming comfort. "We speak words now."

She drew her gaze up to him. His eyes were so blue. She had never gotten used to that. Why did he look worried? She smiled. "More words, Karn? What do you want to talk about?"

His eyes narrowed warily. "The storm," he said softly.

Britta felt her stomach drop out from under her as the memories came flooding back. She, she had caused that storm last night, and the falling of the tree, maybe many trees. She had caused it, or God had worked through her, or—or what she did not know. But she was frightened, terribly frightened. She reached out instinctively to get a hold on anything and found Karn stretching out his hand. She clutched at him as he gathered her into his good side.

Was this the magic she had craved? Was it God's power loosed by reading her father's Bible? Either way, it was not what she had imagined. This was overwhelming, uncontrollable, leaving nothing of her in its wake. But it had been wonderful, too. She had abandoned herself to it willingly and she would do it again, just to be filled like that to overflowing. That was the most frightening thing of all. She began to cry great heaving sobs into Karn's chest as he held her.

Slowly her sobs subsided, and she realized Fenris nosed at her knee and the Viking was rubbing her shoulders and making soft shushing sounds. She could smell soap and, beneath, his own peculiar scent, which now pervaded her life. She would recognize that scent forever.

Was she a fool, throwing herself defenseless into the arms of a Norse marauder? She pulled away awkwardly and rose without looking at him, relieved that he let her go without a struggle. She leaned against a timber as she caught her breath and put her arms around it, still needing support but not willing to get it from him. Fenris followed her and she knelt to clutch at his neck gratefully. At least she still had her dog. He had almost been torn from her last night.

"Why do you fear?" Karn asked after a moment.

Britta shook her head convulsively. "I fear what happened last night. I did that, I think."

"Yes," he agreed. "You did that."

The sobs tightened her throat again and threatened her sanity. "But don't you see?" she moaned. "I don't know what it was. I can't control it. I might have killed us all. What did I do?" She knew he couldn't understand that torrent of words, but frantic questions welled up that couldn't be answered and wouldn't stop. How could you have the magic if you weren't a virgin? What she had seen in the fire must have been a vision after all. Maybe the storm was not magic, but some distorted evil. Her mind whirled.

Karn twisted full toward her on his stool. "I know this thing," he said firmly.

Britta's treadmill of thoughts stopped abruptly and she raised her eyes. "You do?"

"You are...no, you were," he corrected himself slowly, "berserker."

"Berserker," she repeated. "What is that?"

He hesitated. "Many men"—he made a slashing motion. "What is this word?"

"Battle," she Supplied.

"Not many times, sometimes in battle, the gods give a man strength of wolf or..." He struggled silently for the word, then loomed and growled.

"Bear?" She asked. "Beorn?"

Karn nodded. *"Bjorn.* It is the same in my tongue. Then man *is* wolf, *is* bjorn. You were in battle, Britta. You *were* tree and wind. Berserker."

"Not a thing to be proud of," she murmured. He didn't understand. "Not a good thing."

Karn stood with fierce effort and grabbed his crutch. "Berserker is good. A gift from Thor, only to few, only sometimes."

Britta sighed. "I wanted something gentle." Fine. She was

something called berserker. At least he wasn't afraid of her. He hadn't made the sign against evil once, not even last night, and he, at least, had an explanation. That was more than she had. She didn't quite believe in anything so Viking as this berserker idea. But she felt calmer. She looked up at him, still standing there.

"Maybe you are right," she murmured.

He nodded, and she thought she saw his eyes smile, just at the corners. She might have been wrong. He pushed past her with effort and went to stand in the doorway. Fenris trotted after him hopefully. "He come again," Karn muttered.

"He will come again," she corrected automatically. "You mean Offa?"

"Two-beards?" Karn asked.

Britta nodded. "Offa."

"Offa," Karn repeated slowly. She could not see his face from where she stood.

"He is too frightened," she said to reassure herself as well as Karn.

Karn shook his head. "He will come. He sees me not dead. He knows you help me."

"Not dead is alive," Britta said absently as she thought.

Karn turned back to look at her, accusing.

"All right," she said. "I agree. He will come."

"We must go."

"Go?" Britta asked. "What do you mean, go?"

"Go from the island."

Britta stared at him. "I can't leave Deofric." Her gaze darted about the house. "Where would I go?" She felt her voice rising. "This island has protected me...." She trailed off.

"Can you raise the wind again?" Karn asked.

"I don't know," she almost shouted, then began to stride about the hut. "I don't even know how I did it. If it was me..." Already it seemed unreal.

Karn was silent.

At last her steps slowed. She stood trembling, her breath coming in ragged jerks as she realized what that meant. She had never been farther from her home than a few miles around Dunford. Who knew how far she would have to go to escape Offa? Cast out from her garden, a woman alone, she was likely to fall prey to the first man who could get past her dagger. But Karn was right. There was no choice.

"Gods protect me," she whispered. Her island no longer could.

Chapter Seven

The days were short now. The church bell tower tolled five times and it was truly dark as Offa and Raedwald pushed the boat out into the surf against a stiff wind that foretold a storm. Offa was not sure Raedwald would be much use to him. He had lost some blood from that Viking devil's axe, though Offa had bound it and the blow had not cut too deep. Still, Offa needed him. He dared not think of going to that isle at night alone, though the righteousness of his God went with him. Neither could he let this obsession go. The memory of he and Raedwald scurrying down the path to the beach still filled him with shame. But she would not have the final stroke. They were locked in a death struggle, but he still might win. He had made a plan.

Dripping seawater, Offa leaped into the boat and pulled Raedwald in after him. He wished he could take all his men back to hunt this witch and her Viking down. But it was a test of his men's devotion he would lose. So he hadn't asked.

Offa knew that if he did not go tonight, his courage might fail him by morning. He could not let a red-haired girl best him as her father had, power or no. Here was a challenge to his manhood he could not refuse, no matter the risk. Lunging for the oars, he put his back into his strokes. His rage at seeing that Viking, alive and wielding an axe, filled his breast and banished fear.

He glanced back at Raedwald, who held the bundle of supplies for tonight's dire work. Offa hoped his own face did not look as white, as drawn. He grunted as he rowed.

"The odds are mighty against us. The gods side with the Viking and the witch." Raedwald had retreated to the Old Religion. It was what he knew best.

"It falls to us to set the world straight again." The fire of Offa's righteousness burned in him as he peered into the night, looking for the dark hump of the island. "The devil works in her," Offa said through gritted teeth. "How else could she live on Deofric all these years? My God demands that the island be cleansed. My honor demands retribution for her defiance."

The moon was a wan sliver and the sea was black as Offa rowed their tiny craft toward the blacker blot on the night that was Deofric. "We will purify the world, my friend," Offa said, more to himself than to Raedwald.

"Or die in the attempt," his second muttered.

Britta sat heavily and tipped the stool back against the wall. She didn't have the strength for another trip down to the boat on the north beach. Her sanctuary had been violated. She stewed all afternoon over where to go. She had snapped at Karn more than once. She needed another place that engendered fear in all breasts like Deofric had. Where? Where was another such place?

Karn pushed himself up from where he had been tying a bundle together with twine and collapsed upon his own pallet. Britta peered at him in the lamplight. His shirt was wet over his belly wound. That was hardly surprising. It was miraculous he was alive at all, more so that he was up and moving about in little more than a fortnight. She pushed herself up wearily and took a lamp over to stand above him. His face was sweating and gray, his features drawn. "I knew you were doing too much," she complained. "Now look what you've done."

She pulled up his shirt to examine his belly. "Sorry," he murmured. It oozed a pinkish-brown fluid she didn't like at all. She unwrapped the bundle that held her small containers of herbs. That and her Bible and some cold food for the night was all that was left here, besides their cloaks. She pressed a fingerful of stime unguent into the wound.

"We go tonight," he urged.

"We go nowhere tonight," she corrected as she got flat bread and cheese from her pack. "We are both too tired and there is a storm brewing. Haven't you heard the wind?"

"Britta," he began.

"Look at you. You are too weak." He looked disgusted with himself, ashamed. She softened. "You push yourself too hard." Then, as much to reassure herself as him, "Offa would never return to Deofric at night with a storm coming on." She handed him his cold stew as he cursed under his breath. "Rest and eat. We will go at first light and be up the coast by nightfall."

Part of the plan she did not share with him. He would not make it far in his condition. Who knew where she would have to go to get beyond Offa's reach? One could not go traveling about the countryside in the company of a Viking. She watched him as he ate, his features softened by the fire-light. No, by tomorrow night she would have abandoned him.

Offa and Raedwald scrambled ashore on the flat beach at the eastern end of the island, farthest from the shore, where the wind blew in off the North Sea.

Offa took the precious bundle from his henchman, who shivered as he limped up the beach. Offa did not think his friend was cold. His own neck prickled with the feeling that made one turn suddenly to see if they were being watched. She is on the north face of the island, he reassured himself, deep in the secure sleep of the devil's own. She had better be, or their lives might well be forfeit.

He turned his face into the rising storm. The wind would be their friend tonight, not hers. It had been a dry summer, too. That was good. Jesu, be with me, he prayed. Hold back the rain. He motioned to Raedwald to follow as he scrambled up the bluff and into the dry November grass between the trees. He knelt under a huge oak with long, sere blades of grass licking about its base and opened the bundle. Raedwald caught the flints he tossed and limped off to the north.

Offa ripped a bunch of the larger grasses out by the roots to lay in a carefully constructed cone. At the base of this stack he piled some of the smaller, curling dead grass that lived under the longer blades. The flints felt rough and deadly in his hands.

Die now, you witch! He struck the first satisfying sparks into the tinder. *I send you back to the hell from which you came.* Again and again the flints clicked and scraped until sparks leapt into the night and arced onto the grass in showers. At last he stooped and breathed gently into the tiny pile. A telltale plume of smoke rose in the darkness, followed by a flicker. He lay on all the twigs within his reach.

Offa rose and stepped back. This would purify her evil. Her charred bones would be burned clean. Another light flashed off to the north, where Raedwald had done his job as well. The wind from the sea caressed the flames and ran them up the trunk of the great tree he had chosen. He knelt to add larger sticks. Several trees must catch and spread the flames through the sparse canopy to their fellows. Offa hurried off to the south to set the next blaze of his revenge.

Britta woke to the smell of smoke. Not the acrid little smell always left over from her cookfire, but real smoke, the kind that clogged her lungs. Fenris poked her insistently. She lunged up in the dark and began to cough. A snapping sound crackled above a dull roar outside. Red-orange light flickered in at the wicker shutters and made the swirling smoke in the room glow. Terror shook her like a rag. The great fire she had seen in the flames of the hut where Karn was tortured had been a vision of Deofric burning. Gods, why hadn't she guessed? In the vision she had felt the fire's victory. Her stomach heaved. She scrambled across the floor to Karn.

"Karn," she shouted over the growing roar. She shook his shoulder. "Karn!"

His eyes snapped open, wild in response to her urgency. Then coughing took him, too.

"Come," she hissed. "Fire."

"*Fyr*," he gasped, reaching for his crutch. "Offa."

She gathered up their two bundles. Karn was right. This was Offa's doing.

Hunched over under the swirling smoke, she lurched to the door. Fenris whined behind her. Kara grabbed their cloaks. "Hurry," she yelled.

The door opened on the Christian hell. A blast of heat assaulted her. The eastern side of the clearing was alive with flame. It clawed up the trees with frightening intensity. Britta was stunned for a moment. The whole island was burning. Wind rushed before the fire as it devoured the air. Smoke swirled like fog, obscuring the edges of the clearing. It was exactly like her vision.

Their one chance was to get down to the boat. But her steps slowed.

"Go," Karn yelled.

"No. They'll watch the boat." Whirling, she scanned the trees behind the house. There were only moments until the more difficult trail down to the south beach was cut off entirely. She ran around to the back of the house.

Karn limped after her. She did not have to call Fenris. He was never more than inches from her knee. But it was too late. The south trail was already engulfed. A pine tree close to the house went up like a torch. Its sap showered sparks out over them. Horrified, she watched a little flaming brand course over their heads, land, and bloom in the grass. They would be trapped in this inferno at any moment.

"The trail is gone," she shouted. Her thatch roof flickered into devilish life.

Karn gestured off into the trees to the right. "Go there," he shouted and picked up the axe where it leaned against the corner of the house. She lunged into the woods right in front of the jagged runners of ravenous flame. Fear fueled her staggering steps as she crashed through the undergrowth and caromed off trees. It was perhaps fifty yards before her panic spent itself in running. She spun around. Karn was nowhere to be seen in the swirling smoke. The fire had poked out a long finger into the dry leaves among the trees between them.

"Karn!" she shouted. Her voice was lost in the roar of the flames. How could she have left him? She plunged back around the pillar of flame, Fenris in her wake. "Karn!" Her throat was raw from smoke, her face singed with heat. She turned along the fire line to her right, unsure where she was. This hellish world changed from moment to moment.

A shadow loomed out of the glowing smoke. "Karn," she screamed.

"Britta!" She could not miss the look of relief in his face. She started to help him, but he shook his head. "Go!" he gasped as he struggled forward on his crutch.

Flames crackled all around them. The line of flame had got longer. She could not see the end of it off to her right. She hesitated, feeling panic rise again.

Karn gestured to a smoking point directly ahead and started forward into the fire. Was he crazy? But as she peered ahead, she could see green boughs. Could they push their way through before being charred to ash? Karn disappeared into the smoke. She was about to plunge after him when she remembered Fenris. The dog did not have boots. Jesu! Fenris yipped nervously.

She groaned. "All right, my friend." She lifted him up, grunting with the effort. She keened a high wail and dashed awkwardly ahead with her burden, passing Karn. The smoking black grasses were hot under her feet. Coals glowed everywhere.

Beyond the charred remains of several bushes, forest rose around them again. She let Fenris fall. He twisted up and shook himself, outraged at this attack on his dignity. The flames crackled angrily to her left. Karn's boots smoked as he came out of the thick haze.

Britta turned and strode away from the flames coming up on the left and pushed toward the spine of the island. Resolutely, she kept Karn at her side, no matter that she wanted to run. His chest heaved. He was smeared with soot and sweat. He wouldn't last long. Her vision at the faesten told her that perhaps none of them would.

The tiny escape party slowed as Karn lost strength. The flames seemed to go faster as they angled uphill. Acrid smoke and heat seared their lungs. Britta put her arm around Karn's waist and half-dragged him along. The path began to descend. They struggled on until she lost track of where they were. All at once her heaving lungs inhaled damp air like a newborn babe its first breath. They pushed through tendrils of smoke now tattered by wind until they came out at the tumbled rocks that faced south, high above the waves. Those waves could protect them from the fire at their backs.

Black water was laced with white as far out as she could see. The North Sea was alive with the fury of the coming winter. The wind whistled in her ears. Britta didn't care about the storm. She wanted to feel the salt spray that broke so angrily against the rocks.

"Come on," she yelled to Karn and shoved herself down from rock to rock. Fenris gamboled after her, barking.

Halfway down, Britta looked back up to see Karn outlined in the flames, panting and staring at the slippery rocks. He would never make it with a crutch and such uncertain limbs. Even now the flames pushed at him from behind. She glanced down the beach to the west. Wasn't there a bank of scree here somewhere? She waved him left.

"You can get down over here," she yelled and scrambled over the rocks in that direction. He made his way laboriously along the low cliff edge, the flames chasing him as they made their way from one end of the island to the other.

The fan of scree started perhaps four feet from the top of the bank. Karn fell to his knees at the edge of the bank, the flames at his back, the wind tearing at his hair. He sat. Then, holding the axe and his crutch out away from him, he pushed himself off, bounced onto the scree in a flurry of dust, and scrambled to right himself as he slid down the bank.

Britta waded into the loose gravel and pulled him to his feet, choking in the dust he raised. He made no protest as she took his axe and slung it over her shoulder with her bundles. They stumbled into the surf.

The animals of the island scurried down toward the beach. Hares and rodents squealed, a badger, a fox. A hawk screeched its outrage. There was no hunting. Even Fenris, bedraggled and wet, let his prowess go untested. The entire island struggled for life.

"Don't you faint on me," she ordered Karn. The water was up to their knees. She recognized the pattern of huge rocks that hid her second boat. Offa could not know about this one. Karn sagged against a boulder as she scurried up to the boat's hiding place and began dragging it over the rocks. It was not much, of course, a leaky little thing she kept in reserve. Could it hold the cargo she had planned for it tonight in these rough seas?

She pulled its prow into the surf beside Karn, threw in her bundles and the axe, and motioned Fenris inside. He knew his place and took it in the bow, curling his damp tail around him, his tongue lolling in the reddish light from the flames above.

She waded out far enough so the stern was afloat and beckoned to Karn. She could hardly hold the boat as it struggled in the surf. He threw his crutch in and she took her place beside him as another wave soaked them. They pushed the prow up and over the next huge wave. Karn lost his footing as the water came up to his chest, and he went under. Britta felt for him frantically in the black and icy water until he came bobbing to the surface, spewing water and cursing.

"Hang on," she shouted to Karn. The boat lifted on its own this time, thank the gods, and rode the swell. "Jump with the next wave," she screamed as she pulled at his soaked shirt with frozen fingers. Fenris scrambled to keep his balance as the boat tilted precariously.

They had drifted out a few feet more on the wave. Britta suddenly found no sand under her feet. She bobbed in the water as the wave hit and submerged her. Flailing frantically upward, she could not find the boat. Then a hand clawed at her braid and clutched her kirtle. It was Karn, heaving her up. She grabbed the side of the boat. It tipped dangerously. He let her go and leaned to the far side. Britta hauled herself, her clothes heavy with seawater, up over the side.

"Britta," Karn shouted. He pounded her back and she spit up water. "Britta speak," he commanded, his own voice taut with fatigue. It started to rain.

She rolled over onto her back. "I can't," she complained. Relief glowed in his face. She blinked against the hissing rain as her breath came back to her.

Karn, his own chest heaving, lay back in the stern. Fenris crouched between his legs. There were perhaps four inches of water in the boat. It rode low, struggling through the troughs and careening drunkenly over the crests of the waves. She scrabbled inside one of their bundles for the bowls she knew were there. Karn roused himself as she raised a bowl in triumph.

He did not have to be told what to do. He took the bowl in his good hand and began to bail as fast as he could. Britta bent to the oars and put her back into her strokes. The boat pulled out beyond the breakers. When she was perhaps a hundred yards from shore, she put up her oars, panting. Karn raised himself up on the stern to look back at the island inferno.

"We will not lie with Hel tonight," he shouted over the din of the waves.

He might be premature. There was still the sea.

Together they watched the island burn as they tried to regain their breath and the boat rose and fell on the angry swells. The rain came harder now, yet the fire raged. Britta was numb. By morning her island would be a smoking ruin. The oaks might survive. The animals that made it to the shore would live. Someday it might be renewed. But now there was only desolation.

She shivered as she watched the flames. With the shiver, her eyes blurred and the fire seemed to burn ever higher, until all was a dancing tapestry of orange and yellow. The real world slipped away, just as it had in the hall where Karn had suffered. She heard herself moan in protest or anticipation as the flames consumed her mind.

It wasn't her island that burned. It was a more personal flame. The fire licked up around her from piled faggots. Heat seared her lungs. Through the flames she could see many people cheering and shouting. She was in danger! But she couldn't move. She was bound, bound to a huge stake. The flames leapt higher about her as she realized with a shock that she was witnessing her own death, in flames and pain. She opened her mouth to scream, but the flames had swallowed all the air. She couldn't breathe, couldn't scream. All she could see was fire.

As suddenly as the vision took her, it was gone. The wet wood of the oars appeared under her knuckles. Rain slanted sideways with the wind. The smell of salt air replaced the smell of burning wood and suffocating smoke. Karn gripped her shoulder, shaking her.

"Britta, what?" he shouted over the elements.

She gasped a sob, her tears released. "I saw this fire, Karn, before it happened." She, too, had to shout. "I saw it in the fire of Offa's hall the night I brought you to the island, only I didn't know then what I saw. I felt we would die here." She stared out at the blaze consuming the last of Deofric, now assaulted by the rain. "Just now I saw another fire. A fire where *I* died." She looked up into his face, expecting disbelief or fear.

"The gods' gifts can be hard," he said, his face inches from hers. "You have the sight."

She moaned a protest through her sobs. "I don't want it." He squeezed her shoulder. "What is happening to me?" Her voice rose to a wail.

He lifted his hand to her hair and ran it around to the back of her neck. His hand was steady. "We are in a boat. We must get to land."

Britta took a shuddering breath and picked up the oars. He was right. Time for death by fire later. First she must face the sea.

Offa and Raedwald sat in their boat watching the island burn, even after it began to rain. They had broken the witch's boat into splinters, so they knew she had met her death here tonight. The satiation of victory took them, and they lounged against their vessel's wooden sides, reliving their triumph.

At last the flames raced down the hill to the west beach. The rain had stopped, but the seas were heavy. Still, they waited. Near dawn, the flames turned in upon themselves and died down to licking fingers on the charred slopes.

Raedwald clapped Offa on the shoulder. "Your witch has met her maker, my friend."

Offa nodded silently and picked up the oars. He was sorry that he had to give up the Viking and his information to gain revenge on the witch. He would have liked to face her down and make her suffer more personally for her crimes. Still, both had suffered, though he wasn't there to see it. He wanted her to know who killed her.

He began rowing toward the shore. She was wicce. She had known before she died. He was certain of it.

Britta couldn't row anymore. Even will could not animate her muscles. She could go no farther. Karn seemed unconscious. Fenris was restless. She turned toward shore.

She spotted a little cove through the graying night. Far away, she could make out the white of surf each time they crested the swells. To her left some huge rocks loomed, betrayed by their plumes of spray. In the wind and spitting rain, she was blind, the heaving beast of water under her oblivious to their tiny bobbing craft.

Britta's oars, in raw hands, tried vainly to guide the sodden boat as the huge waves began to crest and dash it toward the beach. Things were moving too fast. Ahead there were two lines of crashing waves. With a rush of fear she realized what that meant. The closest fringe of white, less regular, must be crashing on rocks. Even as she stuck her oar deep in the water to try to turn the boat, she knew it was too late. The power of the water ripped the oar from her trembling grasp like a twig, and the boat dipped drunkenly into a trough, almost sideways.

"Karn," she shouted into the wind as she knew what must happen next. The boat slammed into the swell of the next wave. The rocks were upon them. Britta reached for one of their sodden bundles as the right side of the boat lifted. She clung to the edge of the boat, almost vertical above her as Fenris toppled into the churning water and Karn grabbed for purchase.

For a long moment she thought the boat might right itself as it had a hundred times that night. But that was impossible without its prow turned into the waves. The boat came toppling over on them. She saw Karn's look of dull surprise as he was tossed into the water. She was flung out and away. The dark water closed in above her head.

The next minutes were as hours. She struggled to the surface, gasping for air, and looked for the others. She had no chance to swim. The waves simply crashed over her, pushing her down and forward. She saw Karn floundering once, just before she was thrown onto the smooth, flat rocks that barely broke the surface, deadly and deceiving. She pulled herself onto their crazy, jutting planes, gasping, as the waves continued to batter her. With a start, she realized she still held her bundle in one frozen claw. She tottered to her feet on the slippery surface and began to scream for Fenris and Karn like a madwoman, her voice lost in the night. Another huge roller swept her off her feet. Her head hit the shiny surface of the stone before the blackness of rock and water spread to overwhelm her.

Chapter Eight

Britta stirred, muddled with sleep, remembering vaguely the fluttery feeling in her stomach when she had wakened in the gray light, sputtering with sand, and couldn't find Karn. All urgency was gone now, replaced by a dreamy lassitude. His warmth against her side reassured her. She was so grateful to be alive, she even welcomed the dawning aches and pains in her body.

Light leaked through her lashes. She curled against Karn's side, where he lay propped against a huge log feathered by the surf. Waves roared, pounding through the sand beneath her. Seagulls squealed above them. She knew Fenris was somewhere close. He had been sleeping nearby in the first hours of dawn. Karn must still sleep, too. Her head rose and fell with his regular breathing. Her stiffness told her that she had been sleeping in this position for hours.

After a time, Karn's body against hers began to disturb her languor. She could feel his ribs, where her arm was flung across his chest. His breath warmed her cheek. His thigh under hers was hot. This is dangerous, she thought slowly, but could find no will to move. She turned her face up to his, fascinated by the bits of sand on his cheek. As she watched, his thick fringe of lashes fluttered. He stirred. From her own dreamy distance, she felt his arm come about her and his head drop to her shoulder. He turned into her. His thighs captured one of hers. She should feel smothered, afraid, she thought, but all she knew was the thumping of his heart, matched by the throbbing pulse in her own veins. Blood to blood, calling. Breast to breast, breathing. She closed her eyes and listened to that pulse gain urgency.

When she opened her eyes, she found him looking down at her. His eyes were no longer blue glaciers. They smoldered like skies on the muggiest day of summer, the kind of skies that made you sweat and want to lie naked on the grass in the dappled shade. He bent his head and let his lips lightly brush her hair and then her forehead. She was dissolving, into what she did not know, as his lips found hers. How soft, how tender his lips were. The tip of his tongue just licked her lips, the outside first, and then, so startling, the inside. It made her shiver.

Her hands moved over his back, feeling the muscles under his shirt. She knew his body intimately. She had felt his skin, his ribs, the flesh of him before. Now touching him was different. His lips and tongue caressed her mouth. She was engulfed.

At first she hardly noticed the rising hardness between his legs. Then she could not help but notice as his arms tightened and moved down toward her buttocks, pressing her against him. His hardness sent a thrill of fear circling somewhere about her spine. But there was also a glowing wetness between her legs that spoke of lightness. Suddenly fear seemed like too much effort. She wanted to enjoy this moment of pure sensation. Then his hardness softened. His kisses grew more urgent. He pressed his lips against hers roughly.

The overwhelming sense of body that had captured her crumbled instantly. Memories of Offa and the others, their coarse hands, the pain, and how they had laughed as she sobbed and writhed, flooded her. She gasped and scrambled up, panting. Karn reached out and caught her hand as he struggled to his knees. He pulled her into his body almost desperately. She could hardly breathe, he gripped her so tightly. He ground his lips into hers as she fought to free herself. His other hand squeezed her breast. She wouldn't let this happen again, not while there was breath in her body. She bit his mouth and tasted blood. His grip loosened as he grunted in surprise. She twisted free and hit him, as hard as she could. His head snapped to the side.

He let her go as though she were a blade fresh from the smith's fire and struggled back. He held his hands away, palms out, like foreign objects, as he stared at her, wide-eyed.

"Leave me alone!" she hissed. Then, more brokenly, "How dare you? How *dare* you?" until the question faded into an appalled whisper.

Shame suffused his face. His eyes would not meet hers. "Be not afraid," he choked. "I can do nothing to you." It was painful to look at him.

Britta felt a trembling start in her hands and move up her arms. "What?"

"You want me to speak it?" He turned on her, fierce with self-hatred. "I am no man, Britta. No man! I am *haltr*. Warrior no more. You Saxons took my manhood." The last tumbled out in hissed agony. "I am nothing, not a grain of sand."

It took Britta a moment to register, through the filter of her own demons, what he meant. He meant he could not make good on the need she had first felt in him. Felt in herself. Was that how it happened, that feeling of being lost in your body, both bodies? For a moment...

Britta jerked herself back to the present, horrified. She had almost destroyed whatever magic had been rising in her. She would not lose her magic twice! For once, her terrible memories had served a purpose. If magic had returned to one no longer virgin, it was because of the penance she'd paid for five long years, or perhaps because she had been an unwilling victim to Offa's touch. No one would have said she was unwilling who could have looked into her heart a moment ago! Could even unconsummated lust have jeopardized her magic?

Her gaze turned slowly outward to Karn. His memories had not served him so well. His eyes were screwed shut, his brow furrowed. Panting, low grunts leaked from clenched lips. *He thinks he has lost who he is.* She had felt that once. It occurred to her that he'd grown rough only when he thought his body had failed him. The need emanating from him drew her. Hesitantly, she touched his shoulder. "Grieve not, Karn," she whispered. "The gods ask patience of you."

"The gods take my manhood," he shouted at the sky. His words trembled in the wind and the surf and were lost. "No woman wants a haltr man who cannot give her babes," he whispered as he subsided into a frightening calm. His eyes went dead, even as she watched.

"Karn," she began, thinking frantically, "I have felt what you feel, but I learned to live."

He wasn't listening. "Karn is gone," he muttered. "No Karn. Only a worm that crawls on the earth." His voice drained away. His eyes glazed over, focused somewhere near her waist. Even as she cast about wildly, wondering how to spark his eyes again, he reached for her. With a cry, she started backward. But it was the knife in her girdle he grabbed and with his good arm pushed her away. She landed in the sand and hitched herself up on one elbow, eyes widening. He held her eight-inch knife in both hands, pointed in toward his belly and up. Jesu, she thought, he knows just how to find his heart. He was not looking at her at all anymore, only at the blade.

"No use for me," he muttered. "Not warrior. Not even man."

"Karn," she said, as calmly as she could. "That is no honorable way to die." Already, her words must make their way through a haze of death to reach him.

"I have no honor," he said without emotion, his eyes only for the glinting knife. "No honor," he repeated. "My warrior friends are gone ahead. I am left, haltr, half-man."

"You can find life again," she said breathlessly. "Maybe

not a warrior's life, but that of a farmer, or a wood carver. Are there not other ways of life than that of a warrior?"

He did not bother to answer, but changed his grip on the hilt of her knife. His eyes were almost gray, they were so flat.

There was no way that she could deflect that knife with words. She got to her knees slowly. He took no notice. "You have no courage!" she said desperately.

He nodded slowly. His gaze had retreated inward entirely now. "I have enough."

Britta saw it coming. His grip tightened. His eyes narrowed. She launched herself toward him in a spray of sand even as he jerked the knife toward his body. She pushed the knife out and away from him. His keening cry of protest echoed in the wind off the sea. The knife came snapping back to his breast, streaked with blood. She clutched at his hands, pulling the knife back, prying his fingers up as she grunted with effort. The weapon flashed between them. She leaned first this way and then that, trying to find leverage.

Karn was still weak, thank the gods. She wrested the knife from his grasp and threw it over the log. He stared at its arc as she examined him frantically for wounds. His mind was still fogged with death. He was not back yet from the brink. But she had saved him. The knife had not pierced his belly, though his shirt was ripped. His gaze, still dead, drifted slowly toward her face.

"Karn," she whispered, panting, "don't kill yourself, not yet." Her tears welled. She knew. She knew how he felt. How could she find a way to tell him that? She looked down to see her own hand dripping blood. There was a shallow cut along her forearm.

"No," Karn protested quietly. It was a general negation with no particular object. He was still empty of anything but the will to die.

Britta pulled him down to sit against the giant log. He collapsed, head hanging. She put her arm around him. "I understand. You do not know how much I understand. But give it time."

"No," he said again, louder. The pain was there in his voice again. He was back from the brink. "No!" he screamed at the heavens. All the pain, all the agony of what he had forfeited to Offa echoed and drifted into the wind. He clutched her fiercely and ground his face into her shoulder. This time she did not struggle away. She held him, running her bloody hand through his hair. His body began to shake. That frightened her. A man like Karn did not shed tears. But then, he had just killed himself in all but deed. The need that cried to her was new, not like that of wounds, yet like in some way. How could she heal him?

He needed to feel like a man again. He needed a woman to lie with him, to be patient with him, until his hatred of himself and his shame turned into another kind of fierceness and he spent himself in satisfying it. But it couldn't be her. It would be too frightening, too much like Offa. She could never do it. Besides, to lie with him was to lose her magic, sure.

There was only one thing she could think of to do, and she knew what it would cost her.

"There is a reason I know how you feel," she whispered into the hair that smelled like Karn and no other. She took a breath and gathered what she had of herself. "Offa raped me, too." There, she had said it aloud, as she had not said it since the day it happened. "I was fifteen," she continued. He did not move his head from her shoulder. She couldn't see his face. Then she couldn't see anything. The memory washed over her with her words.

"Teach me," Britta pleaded, tossing back her red-blond braids and sitting on her heels. "Teach me as the Witch of the Fens taught you."

Her mother craned her neck around to glower at her. "I *am* teaching you, child, if you would learn your lesson." She turned back to her cauldron, steaming in the winter chill.

Britta surveyed the worts and herbs spread before her on the hardened earth in front of their small house, biting her fingernails. Everything had changed. She was fifteen, late to start. Yet she had no choice but to wait for her mother to teach her. She looked around the village; no more than fifteen houses and a thegn hall, and the little wood church. It was filled with people she had known all her life. The cackle of chickens, the grunts of pigs, the cries of rowdy children filled the air; familiar sounds and yet wholly new. Everything had changed.

"What do you do for a swarm of bees?" her mother tested.

Britta sighed and recited. "Cast gravel over the swarm and say:

> *"Stay, victorious women, sink to earth!*
> *Never fly wild to the wood.*
> *Be as mindful of my good*
> *As each man is of food and home."*

"You have a good memory, Britta, if you would apply it."

Britta gathered her courage. She understood her mother's bitterness. The fact of Britta's birth had stolen her mother's magic. Britta felt all the guilt her mother constantly reminded her of, but she just couldn't wait. "Mother, I want to learn more than how to keep bees from swarming away to the wood." Her mother's back stiffened. But she had to press on. "I might have it, Mother, the magic. It might have come to me through you."

Her mother turned, such pain in her eyes and such hostility that Britta took in a sharp breath. "So I might give you what bringing you into the world cost me forever?" her mother almost hissed. "He who stripped me of my virgin power would laugh at what I have come to."

Britta trembled, but she wouldn't back down. She couldn't. Not anymore. "But, Mother," she whispered, "it would be yours, in a way, if you taught me. As I am part of you."

Her mother gave an impatient gesture. "Have I not told you a thousand times? You are not of the pure line. Your blood is mixed. The power cannot come to you."

Britta swallowed hard. "Something happened yesterday."

Her mother jerked her head back. Before Britta knew it, her mother knelt on the ground in front of her. Her hands hovered like birds' just inches from Britta's shoulders, not touching her. "What happened?" Her voice was a hoarse whisper.

Britta was more frightened by her mother's intensity than she had been by the bird yesterday. "My plover, it was my plover," she gulped.

"Yes, yes," her mother prodded. "The one with the broken wing."

"I touched its wing. I wanted it to be able to fly again." Britta looked into her mother's green eyes, so like her own. "And it did. It flew away. A broken wing can't heal in a day, can it?"

"What did you feel," her mother whispered, "when you touched it?"

"I felt…" Britta hesitated. "I felt whole."

Her mother's hands unclasped themselves and went to her cheeks. She nodded. After a moment she rose, a strange look in her eyes—of betrayal, certainly, but maybe of acceptance, too. Instinctively Britta reached up her hand, though she knew her mother did not like to touch.

She never knew whether her mother would have answered that touch. Shouts came from the western end of the village. Something desperate sounded in those shouts. The men who ran into the village were followed hard by horses and warriors, thundering down the gorge. Even as they watched, two of the villagers fell under the swords of the attackers.

Britta had time only to glimpse chain mail and hardened leather, conical helmets and flowing beards. The village erupted in chaos as everyone scrambled away after weapons or hiding places, children or livestock. Her mother shoved her into the lean-to off their hut as she took her knife from her girdle and turned to the fray. Britta hid among the broken looms and bales. The air was thick with the oily smell of unwashed wool. All she could see through the slits between the boards was confusion. All around her a cacophony of screams and raucous shouting reverberated. She clapped her hands over her ears to keep herself from screaming, too.

At last she saw her mother dragged, stumbling, by her beautiful chestnut hair into the open area by a huge man with a forked beard. Britta was helpless to save her. She was no match for these huge men. She gripped her elbows tightly, small grunts of terror escaping her lips. She couldn't hear all they were saying. Someone called the fork-bearded man Offa. He was the one who started ripping at her mother's clothes. Her mother fought like a demon but there were too many. Britta moaned. If only her own birth had not robbed her mother of magic! It was Britta's fault that her mother could not defend herself.

Glimpsed through the circle of cheering men, she could only half see what happened. But she knew that they were violating her mother, all of them. Britta pressed her cheek into the rough boards of the shed and wondered whether she could look away. But she couldn't. She couldn't even blink. Her eyes felt dry, in spite of the tears spilling down her cheeks.

The one called Offa stepped into the circle and drew his sword. Two others held her mother's legs. She saw it all in shades of gray and brown. There on the cold winter ground, the fork-bearded beast took his sword and thrust it to the hilt between her mother's legs. The only color was the blood that welled up out of her mother's mouth, the gushing blood around the awful sword as the devil drew it out. Her mother's shriek circled up into the sky, accusing the gods. A strange black pool pulsed around her, and Britta knew instinctively what it meant: death.

She scrambled from the shed and ran out into the circle of grass and mud, oblivious to her danger. She had to stop that black halo. She had to touch her mother, make it right, make all the things right between them. She pushed the first huge man aside, wailing like a banshee. Throwing herself down, she gathered her mother in her arms until the black nimbus enveloped them both. Her mother's eyes stared flatly at the unrelenting gray sky. Britta felt a shriek rising inside her. Like the bird, she shouted silently to whatever would listen. Like the bird!

There was no answer, but she felt a fullness growing and the black halo began to fade.

A great hand grasped her arm. She saw the laugh spurt out between the forked beard, though she could not hear it. He pulled her away from her mother. Britta screamed in rage and tore at the hands that held her. She bit and clawed until the beast shook her loose and she fell to the ground. On her hands and knees over her mother, she looked into the green eyes so like her own. They were dead. The black halo puffed out, obscuring her mother entirely, and was gone.

"No!" Britta screamed. "Mother, no!"

Hands again grasped her shoulders and turned her roughly around. She found herself staring into the face with the forked beard. The eyes were narrow and sharp, maybe gray, the face cut in severe lines, the skin marked with scars from the pustules of youth.

"A mother and child reunion, eh, Offa?" one in the circle behind her called.

Offa's grip on her arms tightened. "No need for her to end like her dam. We'll want to keep a tender piece like this one about for a while."

Britta looked up at Offa and knew that there might be fates worse than her mother's.

Britta stared at Karn without really seeing him. "After they killed her, Offa raped me and let others do the same." Her voice held no emotion, because all the emotion was still trapped inside her, seething. "I sought sanctuary in my father's church." She took a shuddering breath. "But Offa killed him, too. I thought his God would protect us. But He didn't."

Karn sat back. He looked like he wanted to say something but didn't.

She shook her head, remembering the feel of nothingness. "I ran to my island, where no one dared follow. I lived with shame, with anger. I hated myself and everyone else. But I lived."

She watched all those emotions roil in Karn's blue eyes. How could words comfort him? At last he rose to his feet. "The gods are harsh, Britta."

Fenris trotted up from his wanderings, her knife in his mouth, and he nosed her hand tentatively. She pulled at his ears. What to do next? "You will not try to kill yourself again?"

He stared out at the pounding surf. "No." Rising, he limped away without looking at her.

It was afternoon when she came up the beach toward the log where Karn sat slumped. She had found her other bundle, the one with her father's bible, still wrapped in its oilskin. There were a few pots of herbs unbroken, but no food. She had even found Karn's crutch, lying among the driftwood. The axe was gone, of course. It lay at the bottom of the sea.

Last night's vision rolled through her brain uncontrolled. Was her own death to be the payment for the magic she had tried so hard to preserve? Would she pay it tomorrow or when she was sixty? Did it make a difference? She couldn't give up the chance of realizing her mother's lost dream, her own dream. It was the only way she could be whole, the only way she could pay for what she had stolen. What did it matter how much she paid to lift that debt?

But Karn would continue to put the magic in jeopardy. She had wanted him today. Strange, but part of her still wanted him. Now, when he was a danger to her, it should be easy to leave him. But all she could think of was the smell of his chest when he held her and called her berserker. He, a Viking, whom she had once rated as no more than a beast, had tried to comfort her when no one had comforted her for years, perhaps ever. She thought of her hands on his flesh, on his wounds—wounds that were her own. And she couldn't leave him.

It made her angry, as though it was his fault that she could not do the easy thing. What would she do with a Viking in

135

tow? And where could she go to be safe? She almost ran to the bundle and the cloak she had laid out to dry. Only when she had retied the bundle and shouldered the wet cloak did she look back toward the giant log.

He did not call to her. He did not wave. He only looked. She stalked back up the beach.

"You go now, Britta," he said. There was no accusation in his eyes. They were only dull.

"Don't you tell me what to do, Viking," she snapped. "I'll do just as I please."

His face told her there was no hope for him and she had best leave.

"The boat is gone," she said brusquely. "A few herb pots managed to miss the rocks. I have my father's Bible, but we have no food. I think there is a village just inland from here. We'd best get going if we want to eat. You keep your mouth shut and let me do the talking."

She picked up her bundle and called Fenris. Karn would come. He had no choice. Neither had she. But she was stupid for taking him along, and she knew it.

Chapter Nine

Britta touched Karn's shoulder to call a halt and whistled for Fenris. Across a meadow and up a little rise, the modest halls of a small village clustered next to a stream in the failing light. Smoke from their fires rose and drifted south, taken by the rising wind off the North Sea. Britta tried to still her riotous pulse. These would not be villagers who knew her and left her alone. She had not the reputation of Deofric to protect her.

"You are mute. Remember that," she warned.

"Britta, no," Karn growled. "Danger here."

"We can't survive on a few late blackberries and charred leaves. You can barely stand." He looked away in shame. She turned up to the village and put away the churning thoughts that had been tormenting her. "Let us hope there is one among them who needs my skills."

Children skittered between the rude halls. Lathe poles arched into the air among the scattered shavings, though this late in the day no one worked them. Goats bleated some-where and chickens scratched in the central yard. She grabbed Fenris by the ruff, lest he make himself unpopular before she had a chance to announce herself. He was no doubt as hungry as she.

A woman appeared and herded the chickens in for the night. When she saw Britta and Karn she called out a nervous halloo, probably to warn the others. Several men came out of the main hall, and another woman, her loom weights still in her hand, poked her head out of a smaller house. Britta saw a clumsy bandage on one of the men's hand.

"Hello," Britta called, her voice not as steady as she would have liked.

"What is your business?" the largest man asked. Britta realized her shift was torn, her kirtle stained. Karn looked a ragged brigand. Only his crutch saved him from being threatening.

"I am a healer. I know the wort-craft," she returned. "I will trade my knowledge for bread and meat, if you have a need." She hadn't needed to sound so respectful in a long time.

Several of the men began to finger knives. One had an axe. They eyed Karn nervously, and some peered around to see if there were others.

She leapt into the gap. "This is my…my slave. He does not speak." The men glanced at one another. "It is just we two, I promise you, and we are hungry." Britta tried to make them sound safe and weak. But if they were no threat, could they not be taken as slaves themselves? "I see one, at least, can use my skills." She gestured toward the man with the dirty bandage.

At that moment, a young woman came out of one of the older huts, dug into the earth at the edge of the village. She carried a toddler and her eyes were red-rimmed from crying.

Even from here, Britta could see the black halo about the child.

The little crowd of villagers parted to let the woman through, as though she was a lodestone pointed the wrong way and they were iron filings. Britta stood, drained of will, and watched her come. The woman's eyes were filled with demanding hope, the baby listless with fever. Now Britta could pick out the darkened, rotted foot.

"Heal my babe, Wicce." The woman's whole soul breathed out with her words.

Britta sucked air into her lungs. If ever there was a time when she should refuse her aid, this was it. The babe was dead. It would happen soon, too, perhaps before the night was out. She would fail. She and Karn would be stoned to death. But then, refusing might have the same result.

An old man, his white hair matted and thin, stepped forward. He wore a medallion worked in bronze, which showed an eye glaring balefully at the world. "You think that a stranger can heal your babe when I have told you that the devil claims him?" he quavered, pointing a bony finger at the mother. "You should have let me cut off that foot before it was too late."

"He would not reach manhood as a cripple," the mother whispered. She rounded on Britta. "Ranulf, let her heal my Aelder."

A great hulk of a man drew his bushy brows together and stared suspiciously at Karn and Britta. He must be Ranulf. "If you are a healer, how is it your slave limps, woman?" he growled.

The old man cackled in satisfaction and echoed, "Yes. How is it? How is it?"

Britta was afraid of the baby's blackened foot. But she needed time, and these people were like to fall upon them at any moment if she refused aid. She turned to Karn and saw him about to protest that he was not a slave.

"Unbelievers," she accused loudly. "It is only through my skill that this slave lives at all." She advanced on Karn and hissed between her teeth, "Not a word. Act like a slave." He glared at her. At least his eyes showed a bit of life. She pulled up his shirt and stood aside. The wound in his belly made the villagers mutter among themselves. Good, Britta thought. She reached for the leather thong that held his breeches. She could tell it took all he had to remain still as she pulled the leather down over his hip to show the angry, six-inch scar, half-healed. She turned back to the crowd. "There are others. He was a dead man. Now he only limps."

The villagers exchanged whispers as Karn retied his breeches with a scowl.

The mother of the baby cried, "I can see in her eyes that this woman can heal my child."

Ranulf sighed. "Work your potions, Wicce. I cannot deny her." The old man behind him screeched in rage. Ranulf put up a meaty hand and the howling stopped.

Britta knew she and Karn were trapped. Their only hope was that they could be away before the baby died. "Very well," she said, mustering her dignity. "We require bread, a round of cheese, and jerked venison before we go tonight."

"You will stay until your work is proved," Ranulf grated.

The old man cackled in victory. "If it dies, as die it must, the witch dies too, right, Ranulf?"

The leader only pressed his lips together. It was answer enough for Britta. She wanted to wail in dread. Instead she said, "I require light and shelter from the wind."

Over the mother's grateful incoherence, Britta followed Ranulf into the main hall. One villager pushed Karn down near the door to sit in the sere cold of the rising wind.

"I need my slave to assist me, please."

Ranulf nodded reluctantly, and two village men dragged Karn up and into the hall.

Britta directed that the smoldering fire should be stoked and instructed the mother to lay the babe on a trestle table. She gave her knife to Karn and gestured toward the fire. She could see him watchful, counting villagers, noting weapons, as he plunged it to the hilt in the hot coals.

While the knife heated, Britta emptied herself. She poured all the hope, all the fear, all her knowledge of foreordained failure into a little pot in the corner of her mind. She tried to remember how she had steeled herself against Wynn and her baby once at the beach. She would do the same now. Empty and closed, the little pots of her soul protected—that is how she would be. Her body moved mechanically, open-ing the pot of stime. She could still smell the green waving fronds picked so long ago, somewhere in the salve. Finally, she took the red-hot knife from the fire. She ordered two men to hold the child. Two women dragged the mother, screaming and crying, into the dying light outside.

The child looked unconscious. That was good. She could see the dread in the faces around her. They thought she would amputate, in spite of the mother's plea. Karn watched warily from the comer. Fenris peered in at the door. Closed and empty, she told herself. Protected.

The tiny foot demanded of her as wounds always did. Suddenly, Britta realized she was making a mistake. Closed and empty guaranteed her failure. It would take all she was to heal this babe. The gods would deny her, Jesu knew she was unworthy, but she must try.

She closed her eyes and clenched the hilt of her knife. She knew no chants, no formulas to call the power. She just concentrated on being. For a long moment she swayed in the firelight. When she opened her eyes, fear rolled across the faces around her. She raised the knife and slit the black, hard center of the baby's grotesquely swollen ankle. It cried weakly. She held a finger full of the gooey, fragrant stime salve aloft. Consciously, she upended all the pots of her soul she had secreted in her mind into that stime and rubbed it into the wound she had made.

The hard black knot was hot on her fingers* As she watched, the salve seemed to pulse with light. She heard a keening sound somewhere and realized it came from her own throat as she rocked back and forth in the firelight, gripping the tiny putrescent ankle. The heat from the salve seared her. The smell of stime filled her senses until she thought she would suffocate.

God, she wailed to herself. Gods, what is happening? Something surged out through her arms and down her fingers into the child. The blackness of the wound spiraled up and threatened to engulf her. It was not her at all who stood there keening, but something far more elemental, simpler and sure. Blackness swirled around the room and darkened the fire like smoke. The shouts of the villagers whirled in a storm of blackness, and the babe was shrieking too, until there was only the void.

Britta woke in the corner of the room with Karn holding her. Fenris licked her face. Concern drew Karn's brows together. Behind him, the villagers clustered. Someone wept in the background. As she looked up, she could see reservation in the Viking's, eyes. Was it fear?

"Britta, do you live?" he whispered.

"Of course I live," she snapped and sat up. The room swayed though, and she clutched his arm for support. Fenris arranged himself beside her. Several villagers stepped back a pace hastily.

"She is of the devil, Ranulf," the wild old man muttered. "And her slave is not mute." No one was listening to him. They all looked at Britta.

"Who cries?" Britta asked, suddenly fearful. She remembered only black, swirling mist.

"The mother cries," Ranulf said doubtfully, motioning the woman through the crowd. Britta's heart sank. The babe must have died. The mother, wildly weeping, stepped forward with her bundle wrapped in white flaxen cloth. White for burial!

Then she heard the smaller wail. The mother threw herself at Britta's feet.

"You are a saint," she sobbed. "I will worship you until the day I die."

With trembling hands, Britta bent to unwrap the babe. It cried heartily. She picked up the injured foot, wondering. The knife cut snaked over a normal-sized ankle, pink and softly bleeding under the gooey stime unguent. Slowly, Britta began to cry. She cried for the gift that was given through her, from whom she did not know. That gift had made this babe whole.

The two women wept together as the wondering village looked on. "She is sent from Jesu to save my Aelder," the woman cried.

"She is sent from the devil!" The gaunt old man's fringe

of long white hair made a glowing halo about his shining pate. "Mark my words, she is like the witch in the fens to the east!" He waived his arms. "She beguiles us with magic that she may eat our children, destroy our crops! This child is her changeling! Kill her and her slave and the babe, before it is too late."

There were mingled looks of fear and uncertainty among the plain faces in the hall. "It is true about the she-monster in the fens," a woman muttered. "My brother's wife is from there."

"I heard the witch eats all those who doubt her," a man in the back called.

Was this the wicce from whom her mother learned her craft? Britta shivered. These people were turning her miracle into an evil deed and she herself into a monster. Karn stepped up to her shoulder. Fenris growled low.

"I will importune you no further," she said as calmly as she could. She wiped her eyes and managed a shaky smile for the mother before she turned to the knot of people around them. "Only keep your promise of provisions. We will go."

"Where is your charity?" the mother of the baby accosted the room.

"She must be killed while she is weakened by her foul deed," the old healer screeched.

Ranulf held up a hand. "We are not so poor in spirit that we deny hospitality to one who has done us service." He dared any to say him nay. Some looked abashed, some doubtful; some still had fear writ plainly in their eyes. "They can stay in the old house by the woodpile."

Britta released the breath she hadn't known she held and turned to Karn. He looked at her warily. What happened to his confidence that she was a berserker? If even *he* was afraid of her, she did not know what she would do.

She sighed. Actually, she knew exactly what to do next. She patted Fenris's head for reassurance. Then she turned back to the babe and pulled open his blanket again. "I need some gut to sew the wound," she said quietly.

* * *

143

Karn fell into the small hut on his hands and knees, pushed from behind. His hip buckled as their bundle, fat with new provisions, and his crutch thudded beside him. Britta knelt beside Fenris on the straw-strewn floor, clutching him fiercely. The thump as the door was barred behind them sounded final. Ranulf was a cautious man.

Karn let his head drop to the straw as the shock of landing reverberated through him. A dull pain in his core radiated out to whatever wounds it could. As the echo of retreating footsteps and murmured voices died out, Karn rolled onto his back, his focus limited to breathing. It was some time before he noticed that the straw still smelled of summer sun. The air was dusty with chaff. He could smell sod, too. This was an unused storage shed, half buried in the earth. The dim light of the full moon came in through the cracks around the door and between the slats above the sod line, along with the wind. It would be cold in here tonight. With his returning senses, despair rolled back over him as well.

She had pitied him this day. That was the only possible reason she had taken him with her. And why not? Was he not pitiable? An impotent cripple without even the courage to take his own life. His thoughts wavered back to the moments on the beach before he had failed her. He could still feel her slight form curled against his side, the heat she raised in him. He had taken more beautiful women, more skilled, some willing and some unwilling. Yet today had been different. It was more intimate with Britta. She had known his body for weeks already. Did he not know what made her angry, what made her afraid? She knew what made him afraid, too. It had taken courage to tell him of her rape by Offa, her mother's death. He would never tell anyone what had happened to him. Perhaps he didn't have to tell. Britta already knew. Did that make her different? No matter. She had made it clear she did not want him. Even if she did, he could not satisfy her. All vestiges of what he had been were now gone.

He threw his good arm over his eyes, as if that would shut out his loss, and felt anger grow in him, unbidden. She had her magic, Loki take her, and needed nothing else. She should have left him at the beach. He would have done it had he been in her place. He wanted her to leave him. He repeated that thought over and over again. But some other voice inside asked why he'd followed her if that was true. He hated himself for his weakness. He hated her for her pity.

That thought brought him out of his cycle of despair. He heaved himself up on his elbow. She was crouched there in the corner, her knees hugged to her chest, one arm around the dog. What had happened in that hall? She had not been the berserker of battle tonight. Tonight there had been no battle. A berserker he could understand, but her power seemed to come at any time. Was she truly a witch, Loki's daughter?

She raised her head from her knees. When she spoke her voice was cold, but underneath it shook. "If you touch me, I'll finish what you tried to do today." In the streaks of light from the moon he could see her knife blade gleam. Then her voice cracked. "I don't know what I have. But I won't chance losing it again, just because they locked us here together."

Karn's anger rose, all twisted up with the pain at his core. "I do not hunger for your pity," he rasped. "I have had a thousand women, more beautiful. Do not wait for my touch." He sank back into the straw, seething. He must find a way to use her. He had to get somewhere the Danir held sway. Haltr or no, getting home was the only hope, however bleak, left to him.

The thunder of hooves brought Britta up from slumber straight into a crouch, pieces of straw hanging from her hair. Her heart pounded beneath the squeal of pigs and the shouts of many men. She looked wildly about. Karn dragged himself from sleep as well. The crashing and whinnying seemed to surround them. Fenris whined low and circled inside their little hut. Slowly, Britta regained command of her senses. The sun streaming between the wooden slats striped the dim room with motes of light. Karn had a hunted look about him as the horses outside stamped to a standstill. She pulled Fenris to her to silence him.

"You there, are you in charge of this village?" a rough voice called. Britta jerked her head to glance at Karn. His eyes flickered in the shadows. He too knew Offa's voice. Had the bastard tracked them even here? Ranulf and his slighted healer would give them up without hesitation.

Ranulf's deep voice boomed over the clink of metal and stamping hooves. "I am thegn."

"Does this sty have any horses?" Offa sneered at Ranulf's pride. "We are for Edmund, and we will require some to spell our steeds."

Britta held her breath, but Karn crawled through the straw to the door. She waved him back frantically as Ranulf spoke stiffly. "Alas, we have no horses to yield to you, eorl."

Karn put his eye up to the crack at the door. Britta raised her hand to cover her mouth, perhaps to keep herself from screaming. They were trapped. Did this Offa never stop?

The hated voice boomed out again. "Then we will take whatever we might find useful."

Britta and Karn exchanged looks. Britta wondered if her nightmares were revealed as clearly in her own eyes as Karn's were in his. She looked around frantically. The tiny hut was little more than a roof over a square hole in the ground lined with planks. There was no bed box, no shelf in the rafters, no place to hide.

Karn dragged himself over to her through the straw. "Do magic, Britta. Call the gods."

Britta searched his face as though some alternative would be revealed there.

"Call them," Karn said, amid the growing commotion outside. "Fast."

Britta knelt in the middle of the floor, closed her eyes, and tried to think to whom she should pray. "God, your servant begs you for guidance." One couldn't ask to be rescued, could one? She tried to feel penitent. All she felt was frightened. She squeezed her eyes shut and pushed out toward God. If the old gods were the ones who worked inside her, would they forgive her for praying to their successor? Gods! She changed the focus of her prayers. *Smite down our enemies!* Tears came instead of any hint of power. She opened her eyes.

Karn looked alarmed. "Britta, what do you?"

"I do nothing," she whispered fiercely. "The magic won't come." She wanted to scream, but she didn't. "I know, I know we need it. But it won't come."

Karn said nothing. His eyes were smoky blue with fear. As he began to scramble back to the door, he turned to look at her. "Give me the knife. If I fail, I will kill you first."

Britta tossed him the knife, swallowing hard. She grabbed Fenris by the ruff. If they came, she could let him go. The surprise of a huge black dog thundering against the intruders might create a chance for Karn to use his knife. Or it might get Fenris killed.

Footsteps thudded in the soft turf outside the door. "I'll wager there are animals in here," a voice called back to others farther away, laughing. "Unless these people live like animals themselves." Karn and Britta heard the creak of the door before the blinding morning light came flooding into the tiny hut. Britta gasped as she put up one hand to shield her eyes. Karn's silhouette in front of her raised his knife. The mailed figure in the doorway stood immobile. Through her lashes, Britta could just make out the face of their discoverer.

It was Henewulf.

Karn lunged forward, but Britta was before him, still holding Fenris. She gripped Karn's shoulder with one hand and toppled him back. They sprawled in the straw at Henewulf's feet. The man had not moved. Britta looked up at him. Fenris whined in excitement and strained forward. Britta could feel Karn's chest heaving under her as he fingered the knife. Not yet, she pleaded silently. Would Henewulf consider her repaid by his delay of Offa in the faesten?

"Well?" a rough voice called. "What treasure have you found there?"

Henewulf chewed at his mustache. "Nothing," he called

out, still staring at Karn and Britta. "Not even a storeroom." He slammed the door, and the hut was striped in light and darkness once again.

Still Britta did not breathe.

"Then let's seize some of those chickens. They will make a succulent feast tonight," Henewulf's companion called, from farther away now.

Britta sucked in air like a newborn babe his first breath. Karn scrambled forward and put his eye to a crack. Footsteps and mutterings, laughter, all melted into the general melee of sound. The Viking wasted not a moment, but tested the door. Henewulf had left the bolt unshot. Karn pulled it open and peered out. Then he motioned Britta forward. She grabbed her bundle.

"You first," Karn whispered. He gave her a shove when she hesitated. "To the woodpile."

Britta crouched on the crunchy carpet of leaves on a wooded hill, a mile north of the village and Offa. Fenris sat near her as sentry, his tail curled around his feet. Her heartbeat returned to normal as they watched Offa and his band ride out of the village headed north and east. She glanced over at Karn, slumped against the bole of a great tree. His eyes were deeply circled; his breath still came in gasps. His skin was clammy with sweat. He should be in a bed box, with a clean flaxen shirt next to his skin, not stumbling across the late autumn countryside.

"Offa goes east," she said, heaving herself up. "He must not know which way we went."

Karn shook his head. "He was not for us. Did you not hear? He goes to the king."

"So he wasn't looking for us at all?" Britta considered.

"Chance," Karn breathed. He closed his eyes.

Britta walked over to where the land fell away from their hill, Fenris at her side. She could see a long way over the rolling wolds to the flat country beyond. Edmund was preparing for the Viking invasion. There would be no peace for anyone in Anglia. She herself would never have peace until

she knew what had flowed through her on the night the trees
fell, or what had saved that baby last night. Or what had
refused her today when she had asked for help. It was something outside herself, something she did not understand.
Even her mother never had that kind of power. She felt
frightened and alone. There was no one like her, no one to
guide her.

Her father would have told her to pray. She'd done that
before, or near enough, and gotten no answers. He would
have said to seek out one wiser than she was. Still, she
couldn't ask him. He was long dead. She knew of no other
Irish monks. She tried to remember those long afternoons
with him. Hadn't he spoken of an abbess? Ethelreda of Ely?
She couldn't quite remember. He had said the abbess was
strong of mind, even if she was Romish, named for that
famous saint who kept her virginity through twelve years of
marriage to a king, until he at last gave in and let her take
her vows. Maybe Britta should seek her out. At least an
abbess would be able to say whether the maddening inter-
mittent power was a gift from God.

But wait...there was another choice. What about the
Witch of the Fens the villagers spoke of? She might be the
same wicce who had taught her mother. Such a one might
also know what was happening to Britta. What matter if
some called her evil? Last night they had called Britta evil.

Abbess or Witch of the Fens? The magic of her mother
or the faith of her father?

"We need a horse," she announced. "I can steal one...."
She trailed off.

"Do we go north to Orkney?" Karn asked warily. Britta
sighed. She knew what he wanted. Orkney was under Viking
command.

"No," she said quietly, knowing that she dashed his hopes.
"We go east to find the Witch of the Fens." Expediency had
settled it. The witch was closer.

Chapter Ten

They were desperate for a horse. The shortening days and halting pace irritated Britta until her temper shortened, too. Karn did the best he could, but he was still weak. Britta's one attempt to steal a horse had almost got them killed. Who knew that those men would be armed?

Britta sat on her haunches by the crackling morning fire under bare elm trees, chewing her flat bread and munching an apple they'd got from the last village. She pulled her cloak tighter in the cold and waited for Karn to wake. The air around her was still and crisp. A thrush warbled among the red berries of a guelder rose. Expectancy hovered in the smoke of the fire.

She was looking straight at him when he stepped carefully out of the woods on the far side of the stream. He was a great bay horse, the color of newly turned earth over his belly, blending almost to black over his legs and head, into the midnight of his unkempt mane and tail. An irregular white blaze zigzagged down his nose. His eyes were liquid wariness as he bent his head to the water. A broken rope knotted round his neck spoke of a break to freedom.

Oh, horse, Britta prayed silently. Who brings you here today, just when we need you most? Slowly she rocked forward onto the balls of her feet. Her heart would break if he turned and ran. God wouldn't let that happen, would he? But God might. The gods might, too; they were notoriously fickle. None knew that better than she.

The horse watched her as he drank from the stream. She willed her muscles into a leisurely rise. Would he drink his fill and wheel away?

He raised his dripping nose and snorted. She waded into the stream. He shook his head. She froze, too late. He whirled in a cascade of leaves. No, she screamed silently. Don't go.

To her surprise, the great horse took only a step or two before he paused and bent his neck to look around at her. He shook his head, as if to clear it. *Dear one, thank you for stopping.* She realized she still held her half-eaten apple. Slowly she held it out to him. He tossed his; head and stood his ground. Britta did not move. The icy stream took her kirtle and spread it soddenly downstream. There! He made his decision. He blew his breath out his nose and took a step toward her, curious. Or maybe he liked apples.

"Come, my beauty," she murmured. Three steps. Now into the water. The great horse stretched out his neck. His lips caressed her palm as he mouthed the apple. His huge tongue moved the pieces smoothly to his great grinding teeth. There was a crunch, crunch, crunch, and it was gone except for the juicy dribble from his chin.

"Good boy," she crooned and held her hand out again, empty now. He bent his nose into her palm and snorted softly. The warmth of his breath shot through her. She could not help but move in toward his chest and lay her head on his shoulder. They stood in the shallow, icy water while she ran her hand over his hot flank. The earth seemed to flow up through his hooves and bone and sinew, right into her cheek.

"Hey," Karn called, sitting up. Britta jerked her attention up, and so did her companion. "A horse?" he asked in surprise. She felt the beast's nose stiffen and she patted the great neck to calm him, grimacing a warning at Karn.

"Did someone try to catch you when you wanted to be wild?" she asked the huge horse softly, fingering his rope. She walked through the stream toward Karn. Her new friend followed docilely. She did not know whom to thank, but she was sure this was a gift.

Karn looked amazed.

"Here is your horse," she said. "You ride today."

Midday tomorrow they would be in Thetford, Offa thought, as all across the hollow under the protection of the hills, men made a camp out of chaos. Wagons were pulled up. Horses whinnied as they were led out of their traces. Could that weakling Edmund meld his raucous and conniving thegns into an army? The threat of the Danes just might hold them together. Offa hoped not. He wanted that honor for himself. Offa hefted the saddle from his horse.

"Offa," Badenoth called. He dragged a wizened man with wild white hair streaming out from a bald pate. "See the healer I have brought you. I found him in that village yesterday."

"Healer?" Offa growled as he threw his saddle to the ground. "We could use a healer."

"You want the young red-haired healer, not me," the wretch called over his shoulder.

Offa swung around. "What?" He strode over to the pair. "What did you say about a red-haired healer?"

"Nothing," Badenoth apologized. "Just the ravings of a lunatic."

"She is more powerful than me," the old man babbled. "Take her to war, not an old man."

Offa grabbed the old man's other arm. "Where did you see her?"

"At the village. She healed a baby." Spittle formed at the corners of the old man's mouth. "Some said it was a miracle."

Raedwald appeared out of the maelstrom of men, drawn

by the words of the old healer, his mouth agape. "It can't be," he muttered as much to himself as Offa, fear etched on his face.

Offa held up a hand for silence and motioned Badenoth to let the old man go. "Did she have a Viking with her, this red-haired witch?" he asked slowly.

The old healer looked for some sign of how he should respond. "Well?" Offa challenged.

"No," the old man shook his head. "No Viking."

Offa stroked his beard. She could have left him, but somehow he didn't think so.

"She had only a slave who limped. She claimed to have cured him."

Offa's stomach dropped into the dirt. He waved blindly at Badenoth to remove the man.

"I won't believe it," Offa whispered to Raedwald, who had gone white, as Badenoth and his charge retreated. "We sent them straight to Hell." Offa jerked around to pick up his saddle.

Raedwald placed a hand on his shoulder. "No. It is two days' ride back there. Let it go."

"More like a night and a day if I ride through," Offa said between clenched teeth.

"They will not be there. They will have moved on."

Offa turned to Raedwald and gripped him by the shoulders. "We cannot leave this handmaid of Satan free. She defies me. My God and my honor demand her death."

"Yes, my lord," Raedwald soothed. "She and the Viking will both pay. But you have wanted the throne all your life. This is your best chance. You must to Thetford at the head of your troops, else they will look to Edmund as their leader."

Raedwald spoke truth. He couldn't leave Edmund a free field.

"You can find them again easily," Raedwald continued. "And when you are king in Edmund's stead, you will have all of Anglia at your back to take your revenge."

Offa wanted the release of skewering that red-haired witch

and her Viking lover on his shining blade. He could find them, but it might not be so easy to kill them. They had already escaped twice. He leaned on his horse, torn, his head in his hands. The horse sidled nervously. Raedwald reached to take the saddle off again.

Offa acquiesced and stood, shaking. "I will go to Thetford. But I will not forget them."

Karn sat dully on the horse's back, feeling the beast move under him. The rhythm of its sway coursed up through his groin. He watched Britta, her red-gold hair gleaming in the fading light as she walked ahead of him. Fenris trotted beside her. He still could not believe she had caught this horse, that it did her bidding. More evidence that the gods favored her.

Yet her gift was fickle. It had not worked with Offa at their door. He could not think why that Saxon who found them hadn't killed them. He didn't ask Britta about it. Perhaps she spread her favors as well as her herbs. To all but him, of course. He jerked his mind back to the horse.

It was a good horse, solid bone and powerful haunches. He rode it because he didn't want to slow her down. The first day she had sat in front of him and held the reins. That had been torture; her straight back pressed against him, warm and near. She must have felt how it roused him, pressed as he was against her. Thor knew he couldn't finish what his body started, but his body wouldn't stop responding to her. When next they stopped for water, she got on behind him. That was worse. Her breasts pressed up against his back. At least she couldn't feel him harden against her. But she couldn't hold the reins from there. He smiled grimly. That didn't suit Britta.

So now she walked and led the horse. He rode, a symbol of his weakness. She kept them from starving with her herbs and her skill. He took the fruits of her labor. It chafed him more than the rope she used to tie him in her little house. He was adrift except for the direction Britta set him. Only the horse allowed him to keep up. Now if it could but make him a warrior again.

He thought about that.

If you could ride a horse into battle, you could rain blows upon your enemies, swinging your axe from above. What matter that his hip be crippled if he had the four swift legs of a horse to carry him? But you could not sit a horse in the heat of battle. At the first blow you would be on the ground, at the mercy of your enemies. Horses were used to ride swiftly to battle, to surprise the enemy before they were ready. Battles were fought hand-to-hand on the ground. But...

To war on horseback you would need a point of purchase, somewhere to brace yourself. Knees? Not enough. Karn peered down. It was the feet one needed braced, to stand in the saddle for powerful blows, to twist and attack those at your side or behind. Could loops hung from the saddle tree brace a man? Perhaps by pressing your feet down against the straps...

Karn's mind raced. *You would be faster than your enemies.* It would take a good horseman to move his horse in the fray of battle. And a good horse. But he could see it. He could practically feel it. The possibilities coursed through him.

There was still the problem of his shoulder. His grip was weak. His shoulder creaked to a stop as he lifted his arm. But it was better than it had been. With constant work and his plan to give him hope, the thing seemed possible. His will hardened. He would get back the strength in his shoulder. He would replace the limp with the strength and speed of this horse.

Karn looked around at the liquid light of the setting sun, how it made the bare tree branches glow with fire. He was on fire, too. He imagined himself on a fine horse, leading a fearless band of Danir mounted on horses, too. They darted and slashed down at their foes. Bright blood flowed. In his mind Karn raised Mail-biter, and the skull he cleaved belonged to Offa. Karn watched his enemy's eyes fill with blood before Offa crashed to the ground. Karn closed his eyes and savored that. Then he opened them with new purpose.

"Britta," he wanted to shout, "a horse will make me a warrior again." He didn't. He reached down and patted the fine bay neck of the animal between his legs. "I will name you Thorn, in tribute to the god who will make me warrior once again," he whispered in its twitching ear. He must find a place to make his saddle, work and rest and grow strong. Perhaps these fens would answer. He would get back what strength the gods would grant him. He would be one with this horse, a fusion of animal and man, berserker at his own will, not at the gods' whim. Only then would he tell Britta his dream. Then she could not pity him.

Exhausted as he was, he urged the horse to a trot and hung on as it passed Britta. He looked down at her with new fire in his heart. She would see.

"Britta," Karn said as he tore off a piece of dried venison with his teeth the next morning. "What are these fens?" Fenris sat at his feet, staring at the venison.

Britta walked up from washing in the stream, tying her girdle. She was not sure she liked the new Karn. His eyes gleamed from his drawn face even when he was exhausted. He had demanded that they push on yesterday until the light was totally gone.

"Swamps, in places," she answered brusquely. "Wastelands."

"That is bad," Karn murmured. He flipped half his venison to Fenris, who snapped it out of the air. "No dry places? Places where a horse can run?"

"There are islands of hard ground." Britta sat beside the small fire and warmed her hands. "The biggest one is the Isle of Ely. Monks have built retreats on most of them."

"What are monks?"

"Uh...Monks, priests, churches? You understand?" He looked blank. "Lindisfarne," she finally said dryly. Lindisfame was the first monastery sacked by the Vikings on the north coast.

"Oh, Lindisfarne," he nodded. "Kirks. Monks. Do you go to these dry islands?"

Britta's shook her head. "The witch would live in the heart of the swamps, I think."

Karn looked disappointed. He gazed speculatively at the horse, nibbling grass nearby. She wondered what he was thinking. At last he looked at her with apparent effort and said, "I need a knife, Britta. Not a good knife, but a knife. Can you trade for this?"

It hurt him to ask her for anything. "I can try," she said shortly. "I'll have to find someone truly needy and hope I can help with what I have left." Her herbs required replenishing.

There was one who still needed her herbs. "Go down to the stream and wash your wounds," she commanded as she rose to gather their meager things. Out of the corner of her eye she could see his rebellious look. She turned and raised her brows. "Unless you want to rot from within just when your strength is coming back."

At that, he swallowed his words and pushed past her down to the stream.

Three days later they came to the edge of the fens. The ground grew soggy on the little trail. The smell of vegetation rotting into peat hung in the air. The land itself flattened and the sky stretched big above it. Trees, mainly blackthorn and hawthorn, hugged the edges of the meres and swamps. Rushes poked up in ragged bunches from a few inches of brackish water.

Britta stopped when the trail west faded into the boggy soil and the reeds. The horse Karn rode stopped behind her. Fenris stood in the mucky trail, one foot raised unhappily. "This is it," she announced. A crossing trail went north and south. "Can you see anything from up there?" Britta saw only reeds, clouds racing across the sky, and a whirl of birds ascending to the north.

157

"Water," Karn announced. "North, a lake. Reeds. Is this fens?"

"Yes. They protect Suthfolc from our greedy neighbors, since no army can cross them."

"Your witch cannot live here, Britta. No one lives here."

"There are places like that mere where the water is deep and clear. There are fish and wildfowl here aplenty, so my mother always said," Britta returned, her tone defensive. "And there are villages at the edge; not many, but a few. People can live here."

"Your witch *is* monster, if she lives here," Karn muttered.

"Your English is getting much better," Britta observed. She had been suspicious about it for several days now. "How do you know words I have not taught you?"

"I remember." Karn glanced away.

"You remember? Have you been in Anglia before?" she pressed.

He seemed uncomfortable. He cleared his throat. "Saxons in my village in Denmark."

Britta started another question but snapped her mouth shut as she realized why Saxons would be in a Viking village. They were slaves. She turned her back on him and tightened her lips. He was an uncivilized beast; a ruthless raider violating lands not his own, taking slaves from her own kind. Saxons took Saxon slaves as well, but that was different.

"Thank you for reminding me why we hate the Vikings."

She took the trail to the south. Let him follow her or not as he would.

The broken walls of the huts leaned crazily into the setting sun. Britta, Fenris, Karn, and Thorn approached what once had been a village. Britta hesitated near the outskirts and drew her cloak around her against the late November chill. Birds flapped into the air as Fenris trotted into the circle of houses, their cries echoing eerily in the emptiness of twilight.

"Abandoned," she whispered.

Karn nodded. Five or six houses sank into the soft earth,

their walls broken, roofs fallen. The smell of moss and rotted wood was pervasive. Behind the village stretched the fen itself.

"Who builds his house on earth he cannot trust?" Karn asked no one in particular.

"A high tide from the sea must have raised the water level and flooded them out," Britta said. "Or some river changed its course. The land is so flat, the rivers can hardly push their way to the sea. They find new ways when the old clog with mud."

Karn pointed south. "Why did they not build there, where the land is harder?"

Britta turned and saw a raised and whitish pan of soil where the river left its load of lime. The lime flats stretched away west along the course of the long-ago river.

Karn dismounted from his horse and hobbled toward the deserted village on his crutch. One house, apart from the rest, was skewed but still standing.

Britta followed absently. The mysterious villagers had only needed to move a hundred yards or so when their houses began to sink. Suddenly she saw rude crosses leaning drunkenly at the far end of the village. "Maybe they had an outbreak of fen ague," she called to Karn. "They wanted to leave this place. I'll wager they moved west along the course of the lime."

Karn stuck his head inside the door of the little house. "Wood floor," he muttered. "To keep out damp."

Britta picked up a loom weight left behind in the grass outside the door, once brightly painted. The blues and oranges were flaked and faint now. Karn came out of the house and peered at its roof. The wind had pulled at the dead gray rushes, leaving holes gaping to the elements. He looked out at the fens. "Many rushes here," he said, "for the roof."

"What do you talk about?" Britta shuddered in the cold. It would be dark soon. "Let's go." She whistled for Fenris, who had splashed into the water after birds. "Fenris, come! The bottom is treacherous," she shouted.

Karn turned toward her, his eyes serious. "I stay here, Britta."

Britta frowned. "The village won't be far. I can trade some healing for food."

"I can ride Thorn there," Karn said, pointing to the lime flats. "No riding in the swamp."

"We can trade the horse for something else, now that we are here," Britta said impatiently. "You want an axe or a sword, don't you?" He had been so excited about the knife she got him at the last village, she thought weapons were her best inducement.

He shook his head slowly. "I stay here," he repeated. Regret was written on his face.

"Oh, well enough. One night won't hurt." Britta hated herself for giving in, but he seemed determined. She turned to see why Fenris hadn't yet answered her call.

"Not one night, Britta," Karn insisted, his voice low. "I stay the winter."

Britta turned slowly as she realized what he was saying. His eyes lit with some internal fire she did not recognize. He reached out a hand, palm up. His brows rose in question. She lifted her chin. "I am going on to search for the Witch of the Fens," she threatened.

He nodded. The hand dropped to his side.

So this was it, Britta thought, startled. She was not leaving him on some beach, weak and afraid. No, he had abandoned her. And he had known he was going to do this for some time, perhaps even since she found the horse. She could see it in his eyes.

Unless he had thought she would give up her own quest. Britta snorted her derision. "May your gods go with you, Karn. You will need them in this forsaken place." He looked doubtfully toward the horse. She bristled. Why should Karn have the horse that she had found? But she didn't have it in her. He needed the horse more than she did.

She willed icy fen water to course through her veins. "Come, Fenris," she snapped, and walked off into the twilight without looking back.

"Gods go with you also, Britta," drifted faintly after her. "I pray we meet again."

"Go to the tree and turn north. What kind of directions are those?" Britta asked Fenris. "The fens give you no mark of your progress and the fog obscures even the direction of the sun." For all she knew, she could have been traveling in circles for hours. All vestiges of the path had long since disappeared. Even the straggling hummocks she was following had all but vanished. The hazy light softened into a veil of fog, dimming as the afternoon wore down toward fearful twilight.

The village she'd found late last night had been named Stowa. Half the villages she knew had *stow* somewhere in their name, she thought with disgust. It meant "place." The villagers' meager directions to the Witch of the Fens were accompanied with dire warnings that she ate babies, made the dirt itself burn in summer, and prophesied from visions in the fire. This last had given Britta hope. Surely here was someone who might teach her about the magic.

All day Britta had been preoccupied with thoughts of Karn. Every time she recalled the way he'd left her, anger made her stomach churn. He wouldn't last a week without her. When the Saxons found him, he was a dead man. She vowed again and again to think no more of him.

Perhaps her failure to keep that vow was how she lost her way. "Even the birds are quiet," Britta whispered to Fenris, looking around. He stared up at her balefully, challenging her to get them out of this uncomfortable situation. They both stood in six inches of water, sodden through and shivering. Britta's arms were scratched and cut from the razor-edged leaves of the sedge. Her fear bubbled up like the gas of rotting reeds. The way back to the village was no more certain than the way forward. She peered into the thickening fog, where clumps of rushes loomed like crouching animals. "Hold your courage, Britta," she muttered and started forward as though she knew the way. Fenris dogged her heels hopefully.

Her wet kirtle dragged at her strength as she plodded through the brackish water. What god made a land so foul? Several times she fell to her knees, and twice an unsuspecting step brought water to her waist. The fog reduced the world to a small circle where their splashing echoed. Her senses were muffled, as though by a shroud of wet new wool, not yet spun. What she would not give for a fire and some dry clothes! She realized only slowly that she and Fenris might well die out here, wandering about in these godforsaken fens until they starved or froze. She had tried calling on her magic several times—to no avail, of course. It never came when she needed it.

So she gave herself to the marshes and let her steps go where they would. Her world contracted to sodden clothes, dull hunger, and the next step. Fenris picked his way in her wake.

In her dazed state, she began to hear something, something low and caressing rising from the fens themselves. It was a buzz, like the whir of insects on a summer's day, or a hum, as of a song. Sometimes the hum called to her. Sometimes it grew sharper, as if in warning, and she changed direction. It dawned on her that she was using that low sound to guide her steps. She could not wonder, though. Wondering might make the humming cease and it seemed her only hope, a slender link with purpose, whether hers or another, larger intent she did not know.

"Who do you think you are?" The screech almost sent Britta straight out of her skin. Fenris barked his surprise. Her own yelp was strangled in her throat. Who could be here in this wasteland of water, mud, and clumps of sedge mottled brown and green in the deepening twilight.

"Who will you become?" the voice cawed again. Hope surged. Who could this be but the very one she had come so far to see? Still Britta couldn't pinpoint the voice. It was like the calls of the countless birds that wheeled above the marshes, coming from everywhere and nowhere.

"I mean no harm," she returned in a soothing voice. "I look for a great wicce."

"What do you want? Everyone wants something," the voice said. But it didn't shriek.

"Are you the wicce?" Britta asked. "I want only to learn."

The silence stretched. Finally, the sedge right in front of Britta parted. At first she was not certain what she saw was a face. It looked like brown leaves in the dim light, wrinkled and creased, with slitted eyes and a slash of a mouth. The face adorned a stooped and wizened creature the color of mud from head to toe, including a gray-brown robe and stringy hair, so old that its sex was indeterminate. Was this the great wicce who taught her mother?

A piercing cackle cracked the silence. Fenris barked sharply and Britta tried to still him. "Learn what?" the witch asked after she had contained her mirth. "What I am, you can't learn."

Britta swallowed. This was not a monster, she told herself firmly, but simply a woman so old as to look like a different kind of creature altogether. "I want to learn to control the magic."

The witch went very still. The silence stretched, and Britta was afraid to break it. "You must first have it." The witch's glare was baleful. "Do you have it?"

Britta nodded slowly. "Or rather, it has me. Please teach me.

The witch looked from Fenris to Britta, speculation and a certain slyness in the mud-brown eyes. "You can be more useful than I thought."

Britta fingered Fenris's muddy fur for comfort. She felt the low growl in his throat. Steady, she thought, for both of them. She was about to say something, anything to break that calculating stare, when right before her eyes, the witch took a step back and melted into the fens.

"Where did she go, Fenris?" Britta cried. Her only hope to learn the secrets of the magic inside her had just disappeared. Then she heard a cackle off through the mist ahead. In the darkening fog, she saw a brown lump that might be a stump, or might be the witch, a dozen yards away. She shared the feeling that made Fenris whine his protest at such sudden dislocation.

"Prove you have the magic. Follow me home," Britta heard, drifting over the mud and the sedge. Then the lump melted from view.

"God's breath, Fenris! Her magic serves her every day, not like Karn's berserker." Britta searched the sedge. "How can I follow when she moves like water through these fens?" If she could follow, what? This crone was no kindly teacher. She might as likely slit Britta's throat in the night and serve her as stew as teach her about magic. But there was magic here, for certain.

So Britta focused her attention on the humming of the fens and stepped after the witch, Fenris in her wake. She had no choice. She could not turn back now.

Offa stood at the rear of the hall and watched the milling thegns find their seats at the great tables as Edmund's pages pounded the wooden floor with their staves for quiet. The hall inside the fortress at Thetford was richly hung with tapestries. It exuded the mustiness of the dried rushes that rustled on the floor, the sweet stench of mead, the acrid tang of too many men, and smoke from the lamps that burned in their sconces. Meat roasted somewhere. There would be a feast shortly, and the charred haunches of hogs and hinds would join smoked fish and huge bowls of beans and cracked grain flavored with herbs and berries.

Offa purposely did not sit with the others. He wanted Edmund to feel his presence, know he had come only by his own choice. He did not pay tribute in return for the protection of the loose association of lords who did likewise, and therefore made up the kingdom of Anglia. No, Offa brought the loyalty of many thegns and his own base of power. All the east of Suthfolc followed his lead. His men were trained fighters whom he paid to keep, not some hastily assembled rabble like the other contingents. Alone among the thegns here, his forces were a rival for Edmund's royal guard. That made him dangerous, and both knew it.

Slowly, Offa let his eyes circle until they lighted upon the one who claimed Anglia. The word *king* did not come easily, applied to Edmund. The man dressed like a king, certainly. Edmund's robe was the finest blue, his tunic edged with tapestry braid woven of gold threads. The rings on his hands and the gold chain and medallion hanging nearly to his waist were so heavy, they looked to weigh him down. But that was just the problem, to Offa's mind. Edmund was possessed of weak, watery blue eyes, a slight figure, and a sparse beard. He was a weakling, a whining babe who mewled about his health. A king should be a warrior. A warrior would never seek out sickness, as Edmund seemed to do. The two mages who physicked him stood like specters behind him.

Yet one could not underestimate Edmund. He was wily. How else had he gotten the throne from his brother? How else did he keep it? His cousin was dead these three years; his uncle had a hunting accident last fall. He used the prophecy and Delan's royal guard to keep his throne.

Offa saw several of Delan's men ranged around the room, hard-eyed and watchful. Their prowess in battle was legendary. As victors, they showed no mercy. But was their loyalty to Edmund or to Delan? Offa was betting on Delan. Darkly handsome, the commander stood behind Edmund. In all the room he was the only man Offa knew was as worthy of challenging Edmund as was he himself. Yet the man did not. He was Frankish, and he knew as well as Offa and Edmund that the Anglian thegns would not unite behind a foreigner. He must work through Edmund, and therefore Offa had to best Delan as well as Edmund, if he wanted Edmund's place.

Then there was the prophecy. Edmund was nominally Christian, but Offa knew the king believed what convenience dictated. A wicce, years ago, had prophesied he would die of a lung ailment; he would not be killed in battle or by a rival for the throne. That gave his enemies pause. But it gave Edmund pause, too. After that prophecy, his need of healers grew. He worried about his health constantly. Offa thought that was silly. Witches were Satan's children, and the Devil's promise could never be trusted. Edmund might die of sickness…but he might also die in battle.

Still, how to wrest the crown away? This war with the Danes might be Offa's chance to step into the circle of light. If he could shine in battle, he could win others to his side. But Edmund would not step aside and leave Offa to rule by acclaim. Offa needed a misstep, an opportunity. Perhaps Delan himself could be used against the king.

Edmund's reedy voice broke over the raucous thegns as they raised their drinking horns. "Great thegns, you gather with me to decide the fate of Anglia," Edmund called out. "Barbarians have taken Cent. They control the north. Like a vise, they press in to crush our homeland."

There were muttered curses through the crowd of men.

"If we stand together," Edmund cried, "we cannot fall."

The thegns lifted their horns as they shouted assent.

"Yet we cannot be too certain of our victory," Edmund continued. "We must crush the barbarians for all time, so our horses, our silver, and our women are safe from their marauding ships each summer. Let them go elsewhere for easy gain, to the coast of Gaul or to the Baltic Sea."

Again the hall rang with shouts. Offa grew wary.

"What mean you, we cannot be too certain of our victory?" he called out.

Edmund bristled at his lack of deference. "I mean, less-than-courteous eorl, that we require allies." A nervous muttering coursed through the throng.

"I have sent messengers to Mercia, to Northumbria, and to Wessex. We must fight together to break the Viking horde that masses before us."

There was dead silence in the hall. The old distrust among the seven kingdoms hung in the air almost as palpably as smoke from the sconces. Offa did not want allies for Anglia until he was securely on its throne, else he would do naught but collect rivals for Edmund's rule.

"Do we truly need help from the likes of Mercia and Wessex?" Offa's voice broke the silence. "We of Anglia are more than a match for this Viking scum. Only a month past, my men cut down the best they had to offer and burnt their bodies. We are sufficient to the job at hand."

Edmund stared about the great hall, gauging the mood of his subjects before he answered. Offa glanced about, too. They distrusted outsiders, but the thegns were not ready to speak out against their king. Edmund and Offa came to the same conclusion.

"You question your king's actions?" Edmund piped, sure of himself. "We stand together or fall to the Viking savages. I, your king, seek allies. That should be enough for you."

Offa seethed at the dismissal. He took two breaths. This move might be used against Edmund. Maybe God had shown him a way to the power he craved. Edmund smiled. How Offa hated that smile. *Well, smile away, puny king. Smile until you see another sitting on your throne.*

"Long live the king." He raised his horn, downed the mead, and strode from the hall.

Chapter Eleven

Karn sat in the doorway of his leaning house and cut the willow sticks for the door of the eel trap he held in his lap. He felt dull and hungry. Without Britta the whole of the Saxon island pressed in on him. He was alone against everyone he was like to meet. He bound the supple wands of his trap with rushes at the comers, the slats so narrow that a nice, fat eel could not escape. He would set it in shallow water, baited with a precious piece of fish he had speared. Later he and Thorn would begin their work on the lime plateau. He must get on with his plan.

Even as Britta was no doubt getting on with her plan. He wondered if she had found her witch, and whether the woman had explained Britta to herself. And whether that was good or bad.

He pushed himself up, the lattice square of his trap complete. He would likely never know whether Britta found her witch. He'd promised himself to find her again when he was whole—he dared not think why—but it had been a futile promise. He was not like to be whole ever again.

He limped off toward the deep water, carrying his empty trap.

Danegeld

*   *   *

Britta fell into the tall grass at the edge of the dooryard surrounding a small brown hut made of bundled rushes. Smoke wafted out into the night through the doorway. That meant there was a fire inside. But she could not walk another step. Fenris lay panting beside her.

"You don't know as much as you might," she heard the cracked voice say above her. A gnarled hand set a bowl in front of her that smelled of cold fish stew. "But you'll do."

The witch turned on her heel and disappeared into the hovel. Britta heaved herself up and reached, shaking, for the bowl. She scooped some morsels of fish into her hand to feed Fenris. He sniffed, hesitant. He was probably right. Who knew if this was poisoned? But Fenris lapped at last. Britta gave a mental shrug and drained the bowl. What matter did it make? She would live or not; this was her destiny. She lay back down in the grass, just for a moment, to gather her strength.

Sometime later she woke, her limbs stiff with cold in spite of the fact that Fenris had curled beside her to share warmth. Red firelight flickered out from the hide that covered the hut's door. That drew Britta to her feet. The mud coating on her kirtle cracked as she rose.

"Come, Fenris," she whispered.

As she pulled aside the hide, Britta saw the old woman sitting by the fire. She looked like a demon from hell, a thousand wrinkles lit from below. The hut itself was no less strange. Desiccated, dusty herbs hung, unused, from the ceiling. Everywhere Britta looked, the skins and heads of small shrews, hedgehogs, foxes, and birds stared with empty eye sockets from the wood rafters or the rush walls. The stench of curing hides was overpowering. Bits of metal were also pressed into the walls, shiny in the dim light, and shards of cloudy glass. The place, was horrific, choked with death. Britta shuddered. If Karn was here, they would exchange glances and know what each thought of such a house.

"I suppose you want more food," the ancient muttered bitterly. She stirred a pot.

"Please," Britta agreed, certain she did not want to look inside.

The witch glared at Fenris. "I never bargained for the dog."

"He won't be any trouble," Britta assured her.

The old woman grunted in disgust. "He eats out of your portion. If he gets in my way, he ends on the wall." A glimmer like greed grew in her black eyes. "He has a fine coat."

Britta dared not glance up at the hides above her. "As you say, he is not part of the bargain." She invested her words with as much purpose as she dared and pulled Fenris close.

The old woman cackled, revealing yellowed and uneven teeth. "We shall see." Then she poked one gnarled finger at Britta's bundle. "What's in there? Anything Wydda wants?"

Britta knelt to untie the muddy bundle and tried to remember if her mother had ever told her that her teacher's name was Wydda. "A bowl," she said, fumbling it out.

"Good," the witch muttered. "You won't use mine. What else?"

"A spoon." Britta hardly got the word out before Wydda grabbed the shiny metal.

"A spoon? A spoon?" The utensil disappeared under the folds of her robe as the witch fondled it in some kind of ecstasy. Britta watched as she put it carefully in a heap of other unrecognizable metal objects and turned back to Britta, her eyes now glowing. "What else?"

"No more metal," Britta apologized, hoping that the witch did not see her knife in its sheath at her girdle. Wydda's features wrenched themselves into a frown. "I have some herbal remedies." Britta hesitated. "I think you taught my mother." Wydda was certainly old enough.

The witch eyed her closely. "Those I taught do not have daughters."

A flush crept up Britta's neck and infused her cheeks. "Her name was Edith."

The witch peered at Britta. "I can see her in you. So she disobeyed and lost her magic."

Britta nodded, ashamed as always of her role in stealing

her mother's magic. The old woman grinned in a ghastly parody of glee. "She was not untalented. You might do nicely." Her glee turned into a scowl. "You don't follow in her lustful footsteps, do you?"

Britta swallowed hard and shook her head. She couldn't tell Wydda about Offa, or about what almost happened with Karn, else the old woman would never agree to teach her.

Wydda nodded. "Good. If ever you give yourself to a man willingly, there is no magic."

Ah, that was why the magic had not disappeared after Offa raped her. She had not given herself willingly. Already she learned from this woman! Britta reached for her bowl. She would have to eat with her fingers, since obviously spoons were too precious to use for eating.

"Not so fast, girl," the witch barked. "There is something else in that pack."

Britta snatched back her hand. Her father's Bible. Not that.

"What you have is Wydda's, if you want to learn from Wydda," the old crone hissed.

With shaking hands, Britta unwrapped the great book. Its tooled leather cover glowed in the firelight. With great effort, Britta did not clutch it to her breast. Instead, she held it out.

The witch peered at it. "A book? What use have I for a book?"

Slowly Britta drew the book back to cover her heart. "A Bible," she whispered.

Wydda snorted derisively. "Put it away. What I know has nothing to do with that book."

"Then you'll teach me?" Britta's thoughts leapt past the implied agreement eagerly. "Tell me how you controlled your magic enough to move through the swamps."

Again the sly look came across the face of the witch. "You must prove you have the power, girl. I teach not everyone who comes this way."

Britta looked around the dreadful hut, shot through with death, strewn with garbage. Even the herbs had long ago lost their potency. What would proving herself entail? She controlled her imagination with difficulty. It didn't matter. Wydda could teach her. She must try.

Britta watched Wydda tear at a piece of jerked meat with fingers like talons. "What magic do you have?" Wydda cackled. "Yes. One with magic is most useful to Wydda."

Under the stare of all those hollow eye sockets, Britta edged closer to the fire. "I don't really know what kind it is," she began uncertainly.

Wydda threw up her hands. "Don't know? Stupid girl! Do you transform? Do you heal? Do you have foresight? Can you speak with animals? Do have power over the elements? What?"

Britta shrank in the face of this onslaught. "Well, most of those..."

The witch went motionless. Britta could hear her breath hiss in and out. "Tell me."

Britta sucked in the foul air. She told about the halo of blackness that foretold death, and how the trees fell and the wind blew when she was angry with Offa, about healing the baby and the visions in fire that came true. Wydda was silent, her face a wrinkled mask.

"Talking to animals?" Britta mused. "Well, there was a horse who came to me...I don't turn into a beast..." She smiled painfully. "A friend of mine did call me a berserker once, but he only meant that I seem possessed when the power is on me." She trailed off.

Wydda looked thoughtful. At last she nodded. "To use one such as you, I need time. Do you have the courage to stay a while?" She appeared to think. "You seek knowledge. Then knowledge will keep you here." Her eyes raised to Britta. "You have learned one secret already. The power does not live in you beyond the time you spread your legs for a man." The old woman's eyes hardened. "Here is another. How old am I?"

Britta thought quickly. This was a test. Wydda was ancient, that was sure. She had taught Britta's own mother. Perhaps she was even older than a woman of her appearance might be. "Seventy-five," she whispered. That was older than anyone she had ever known. To her surprise, a cackle bubbled up from Wydda's lips that slowly increased until it shook her body and she began to cough and hack.

Britta knew she had failed. Was she even older?

At last Wydda caught her breath and leaned forward, her eyes glowing. "Thirty," she hissed. "The one you see is thirty. That is the secret of our magic. It saps us of the juice of life."

Britta's eyes darted over the white straw of the woman's hair, the net of deep wrinkles on the skin that sagged from her bones hinting of the skeleton within. The horror of it seeped up through the ground of the hut's dirt floor, making her breath come fast, her heart knock against her skeleton. Wydda could not be thirty. Sixty or eighty or a hundred. But not thirty.

Wydda pointed a bony finger at Britta's horror, tears of laughter rolling down her cheeks.

Britta turned away blindly and pushed aside the hide to stumble out into the night.

Reeds arched over Britta protectively as she crouched in a thicket of sedge. She had done with sobbing and rocking herself, her cloak clutched around her to substitute for the comfort of a mother's arms. Wydda couldn't be the one who taught her mother if she was only thirty. Yet the wicce had remembered Edith. Perhaps that had been a lie. Britta didn't know what to think.

Magic had exacted a terrible price from Wydda. That Britta could not escape. It must be evil, she thought dully. If it was something natural, it would not be such a punishment to have it. Her own bouts with magic had been exhilarating, generating only feelings of connection and oneness with an unseen world—but that was temptation talking! Who would not be tempted to recreate that marvelous feeling? Why else had she come to Wydda, but to learn to reproduce that connection to the world? Such a wonderful feeling must be a sin, a sin with a terrible price.

A rustling in the sedge interrupted her reflection. Had

Wydda searched her out? Or was it some dire creature of the fens? She had not long to wait, for the noise rustled straight toward her. Her heart was in her mouth by the time Fenris's black nose poked through the sedge leaves.

"Oh, Fenris." She sighed and gathered him into her arms. "This place is dangerous." His warm, damp tongue caressed her ear. She had harbored such hope! Magic was to be her way to certainty, to peace. Now it only frightened her. That hut, with its hides and bits of twisted metal, proved it was evil. She longed to talk to Karn about it. But she was not likely to see him again.

Fenris leaned against her. The stars above peeked through streaming clouds. The night air dampened the subtle smell of rot. What they needed was a fire. She gathered dead leaves from the clumps of sedge around her. With flint and stone from the bag at her waist, she set about coaxing a flame from the dank pile. When it crackled, she made a pad of rushes to protect herself from the cold ground and settled in to wait, for what she did not know. Perhaps for courage to leave the fens, or for an answer to the riddle of magic.

The night grew darker. The fens murmured with the sound of insects and small creatures. Sleep eluded her, though Fenris dozed nearby. Britta stared at the glowing coals.

Perhaps she did doze, that half-sleep that only seemed like waking. When the tiny flames leapt out of the coals into a sheet of flame that enveloped her senses, Britta felt a surge of fear.

"Gods," she cried out, "do you torment me?" There was no response, only the flame: orange, red, blue, dancing all around her until there was no escape. She gulped for air. Figures slowly appeared in the fire. She saw a young man, richly dressed. A sword with jeweled hilt hung at his side, and about his head there was a circlet of gold. Many others, shadowed, stood behind him. Only his face was clear. It was a handsome face, truthful, with a sense of purpose. His beard was blond, a young man's beard. He shouted at someone unseen. Where was the flame? All her visions had been in fire, of fire. There it was. A brazier in a stand burned bright.

As she watched, the young man swung around, shouting to the crowd. The tip of his sword toppled the brazier. Fiery coals rained down upon him. Flames leapt up his rich cloak. They capered up his back while he still shouted, unawares. The shadowy figures closed in around him. She could almost hear their cries of warning as they beat at the flames. The young man screamed, his whole side enveloped now in fire, his face engulfed. The flames were quenched, but it was too late. He'd been burned so badly he would surely die.

In the vision she stood on the brink of death herself. She could feel it, though she did not know how or why. Her view moved toward the young man. The shadows parted. Scraps of burned fabric mingled with the charred flesh of his arm. His face was burned, unrecognizable. Still she moved closer, down and down until she knew she knelt beside him. Her own white hands reached out. *Don't touch that flesh!* But she was powerless to stop the vision. She saw herself put her hands straight on the blackened, bubbling crust of skin.

The young king's form dimmed. When her sight cleared, the flesh under her fingers was pink as a new babe's buttocks, though the scorched fabric of his tunic still clung to it. He looked at her in astonishment and with fear. The danger to her had not abated—increased, rather, if her senses did not betray her—but she no longer cared. Something important had changed, but the vision didn't tell her what.

The illusion faded, leaving only the small crackling fire in the fens.

Britta sat next to Fenris, gasping. She was torn between relief that it was gone and simple shock. What did it mean? The answer welled up inside her, almost before she could ask the question. Healing was the goodness in the magic. It was her place to heal that king. It would be important to the world. *She* would be important.

But there was a cost. She had felt the danger. But there had been danger in the vision of Deofric burning. Yet she'd lived. She had seen herself burned as a witch. Would she die? Before or after she had healed a king? She did not know. Would healing him cost her youth, as it cost Wydda? It did not matter. Her vision said she *would* heal, no matter what the cost. Was another choice even possible? She couldn't choose not to have the visions.

She piled more rushes on the fire and drew close to Fenris, who slept as though the world had not just changed forever. But it had; Britta knew her way now.

She looked up from the flicker of her fire, so faint and vulnerable now that the magic was gone, to the cold stars in their black bed. God, or the gods, coerced her. The flames of the vision had seared her clean. She had connected for one blinding moment to something larger than herself. And she knew, sin or no, no matter what the cost, she would pursue that connection. Tomorrow she would go back to Wydda. For better or worse, Wydda could teach her how to find that connection again and ride it as Karn rode the horse she had called from who knew where. That was her future.

Karn sweated even though the air was cold as he pulled Thorn to a walk. The horse had broken a sweat, too. Enough for today. He swung his left elbow in widening circles until he felt the pain as he walked Thorn cool. He had gotten stronger. He could work for an hour at a time, and his arm had more range of movement each day.

He had drawn out his design for a saddle on the damp earth with a stick again and again until it was burned into his brain. Two weeks ago he and Thorn had dragged home an old hawthorn stump for the saddle tree. Already his knife had outlined the structure. Soon he would carve it to completion. He must pad it with something, even sacrificing the cloth of his cloak if he could find nothing else, so that it would sit on Thorn's back comfortably. Now he needed leather for straps strong and thick enough to stand the weight of a man. He could trade his knife for leather in the Saxon village. But there was always some reason to put off his expedition. Would they not know he was a Dane? He would end dead or enslaved. He could not be strong without a saddle, nor could he get a saddle without contacting the Saxons; he was doomed.

The lonely life here in the fens was not so bad, he told himself. He lived simply, on waterfowl and fish, the juicy lower stems and roots of reeds, the eels he caught in his trap. If there was no one to remark on his progress, it was something he had better get used to. After all, he was like never to see her again. And she was the only one who could assuage his loneliness. She was the only one who might understand.

He rode Thorn to the deep water he had found north of the huts, along a soggy trail. Here the water was fit to drink. When he lowered himself down, his knees buckled with fatigue. Karn ground his teeth in frustration. He wanted faster progress. Weeks of work and he was still nowhere near his goal. He might never again be a warrior. Worse, his failure with Britta at the beach haunted him. Even if he regained his strength, he would not be the man he'd been.

The sky boiled with snow clouds. All would freeze tonight. The shallower places in the fens would become pathways of ice. If he carved himself some wooden runners, he could work his hip by skating, as he had as a child in…Denmark. Once he thought there was no place for him in Denmark, since he had no land. Now he had no place anywhere.

He crouched beside Thorn and turned up a fistftil of the damp earth. It was good soil, richer than any but the best farms at home. If only it was not so cursed wet, it would support a hundred farms. He gazed out across the flat landscape. A farm here would be fit only for fish.

He opened the gate to the pasture at the edge of the village he had fenced in with wood from the leaning halls. Thorn stepped in and began to graze. Karn tried to imagine Britta bending over some cauldron, stirring a witch's brew, but he could not. She always came to his mind as he had seen her on her island, coming up the trail from the pool with wet hair, or carrying fragrant armloads of herbs in from the meadow, the sun making her red braids glow like fire.

He put those thoughts aside, as he always did. They were

for naught if he had lost his ability to please a woman. He would think of nothing but Thorn and his saddle. He would work to regain a warrior's strength. Until he was a man again, any dreams of Britta were just that—dreams.

Edmund turned from watching the panoply of troops in the courtyard below and paced the stone floor of his bedchamber until he had worn a path through the rushes. In the background a boy laid out the clothes Edmund had selected for the day. His clerk rustled several scrolls at a table near the window while his two physicians stood nervously just inside the door.

"You two are worse than useless to me!" he hissed.

The mages exchanged uneasy glances. The taller was a venerable graybeard who often stroked his long whiskers in order to look wise. Edmund had once thought he was just that. The younger was still older than Edmund himself, and broader in beam than his cohort. They had attended the king for half a year. Long enough to reveal their ignorance.

"My dear King Edmund," the younger one, Ibn Refandi, began unctuously. "The ways of healing are not always pleasant."

"If you are referring to that noxious brew you have me take each morning, I heartily agree," Edmund spat. "If only it healed."

"But see how much energy you have, my king," the other, Hassan Ghaffari by name, soothed. "You pace like a tiger."

"You have never seen a tiger," Edmund accused, rounding on them. "I doubt you come from the 'mysterious east' at all."

The two healers looked even more uncomfortable. "If there were more specific complaints," the old one began.

"Complaints?" Edmund fairly shouted. "I have a thousand complaints! I cannot eat a succulent roast and wash it down with mead but pain shoots through my chest. In winter the sharp air makes me cough. Smoke in the hall assaults me at my weakest point." He paced forward to shout into their faces. "Each complaint could end in my lungs!" he shrilled.

The physicians leaned back without actually retreating. Edmund paced away, disgusted with their fear.

"And what do I ask of you?" he continued sullenly. "Merely the cure of which you claimed you were capable." The page and his clerk were quiet in the background, hoping not to attract attention. "What shall I do with you, who lied so about your talents?"

The two mages seemed to hold their breath. Let them squirm. Edmund had felt this disappointment before, too many times. That witch who'd prophesied his death had cursed him with knowledge. Knowing that his health could fail at any moment was like a sword in his side.

How he loved that rush of belief when he first found new hope of escape! Each new healer, each new certain cure, excited him. But they had all been shams. It didn't mean the healer he craved did not exist, only that he had not found the one. This time, though, his disappointment was fraught with a bit of panic. There had been so many failures. There were threads of gray at his temples. He needed to find a cure soon.

The worry that welled inside him became a shout of rage. "You two will pay!" But as he worked up to retribution for his fears, the door opened on the captain of his guard— Delan, himself. He bowed as though his king did not look like a thundercloud, not too low, a perfect expression of one who knew his own worth and chose to use it in another's service.

"My king, excuse the interruption," he said in a deep baritone that was hardly apologetic. "But my audience is more pressing than usual, and the business is your own." Edmund could not help but admire the way Delan trod a delicate line between service and obedience.

Edmund picked up his sword in its scabbard where it lay across the bed waiting to grace his person. The weapon slipped from its sheath with a slithering, metallic sound.

"What, another bout of squabbles between the eorls?" Edmund asked sourly. He let the sword pull him forward and thrust itself in Ibn Refandi's belly. So fast did it move, Refendi had no time to protest. He could only gurgle as blood welled up over his lips and he sank to his knees. His older partner was not so silent. Ghaffari screamed, then collapsed, gibbering at Edmund's feet, as Refandi slowly slid off the skewer.

"Give me another chance to heal you!" Ghaffari screamed, backing away.

"But I have given you half a year. Haven't I, Delan?" Edmund asked, his voice soft.

"Nearly seven months," Delan said smoothly, removing his leather gauntlets.

"No more chances," Edmund hissed as his bloodstained sword thrust itself into Hassan's stomach. The old man shook his head, protesting weakly. Edmund could see the light dying in his eyes. He twisted the sword and pulled it up once, twice, the weight of the old man now full upon it. How must the last moments of life feel? Edmund willed the life force that drained from the dying man into his own body. The husk of the mage crumpled to the floor.

Edmund looked up. The page and the clerk were frozen in horror. Not Delan; he moved coolly to open the door.

"Guards, remove this refuse," he called, then nodded for the clerk to leave.

Edmund found himself shaking. He could hardly re-sheathe his sword. But he noted that the clerk took his orders as easily from Delan as from his master's mouth. He eyed Delan narrowly and motioned to the boy to bring his robes. Let Delan not think that he was important enough to inter-rupt the king's dressing. "What is it that cries out for my attention?"

"Offa is finding some support among the thegns now that the contingent from Northumbria has arrived. If Mercia and Wessex also send men, Offa may use the jealousies between these men as an excuse to challenge you."

"You never did like the idea of inviting the other kings to support us," Edmund remarked. He pulled a shirt down over his tight-fitting breeches.

"We can rout these Danes without help." Delan did not

bother to mince words. Perhaps that was one reason Edmund gave him every freedom.

"True," he answered. "But if my allies don't witness my victory, how will I turn it to advantage? When I lead Mercian thegns and West Saxon eorls and Northumbrians into battle, their victory is my victory, their loyalties mine. I want them to see me as the savior of the whole island. If I save it, it belongs to me, does it not?"

"Aye, if you can keep these allies together. But Offa waits only for passions to rise to turn the Anglian thegns against you."

Edmund frowned as he shrugged himself into a heavy woolen tunic of purest red. He moved to the window, where the shutters were thrown back to let in the cold, bright day. The gates of the faesten were open. Outside, for miles around, armies camped. More than three thousand men, all bent on destroying the invaders. Soon there would be twice that number, if the kingdoms all answered his call. The little village between the faesten and the river could not support so many troops. They would have to begin foraging in the countryside. "What do you recommend we do?" he asked over his shoulder.

Delan was unusually silent. "That is harder," he said after a moment. "Offa's death would not endear you to the thegns who follow him."

"I cannot move against him without some excuse," Edmund agreed. Through the open gates he could see a column of men snaking off into the distance. Sun glinted on pikes and armor. In the lead was a man who held the rampant lion flag of Mercia.

"If he moves openly against the allies you can have him executed to keep the peace," Delan growled.

"What, would I take the part of foreigners against my own? You shock me. No, when the fights break out, I shall take Offa's part. But time is on our side. He will make some misstep before the Danes attack in spring." The Mercian column wound its way into the compound. Knots of men formed whispering clusters in the corners of the yard. Edmund did not have to hear their muttering to know what was said. The Mercians looked uneasily about them as the leaders exchanged greetings.

"Offa could cause much trouble during the winter, my king," Delan pointed out.

Edmund turned abruptly from the window and lifted over his head the heavy silver chain held out by the page. "Then I suggest your troops keep the peace."

Delan's face darkened. His bow was merely a nod. "As you command, my king."

"Don't look so dire, friend," Edmund chided as he put his arm about the other's far more massive shoulders. "The prize is an entire island kingdom guarded by the sea, and wealth beyond your dreams and mine. And I can dream of wealth. A prize like this is worth risk."

"You dream far into the future, King," Delan said. "I work in today."

"Then we were meant for each other," Edmund said airily. Delan's hand thumbed the metal door latch, but Edmund called him back. "Captain, I have not dismissed you." He could see how that rankled Delan. "Where are the Viking hordes?" he asked as he turned to the boy who held his slippers.

"They gather near Offa's fortress at Dunford. They scour the countryside for horses."

"How many, man? How many?"

"Those at Dunford are but a thousand as yet. But some are still in Cent."

"This battle is won, and easily, if we can but hold our forces taut."

"Let us not underestimate the fighting heart of our enemy."

"Fie, numbers are numbers. And whose fighting heart matches that of a man defending his home?"

Delan did not answer. He merely nodded, obviously waiting to take his leave.

Edmund turned and waved his hand in disgust. "Oh, go then, if you are so impatient." As the door closed, he turned to gaze after the man thoughtfully. The narrow bridge toward his goal was slippery, and death by a lung ailment lurked in the chasm below. Offa wanted his throne. Delan wanted it, too. Any of his allies would like to grab his place. And there were the Danes.

Edmund needed to live. He wanted to be king of all the island. Which reminded him, he needed to find a new healer.

Chapter Twelve

Britta stood in the doorway of the hut, defeat like bile in her throat. Wydda sat rocking in front of her peat fire, her eyes closed, singing under her breath. Magic spells or merely an old woman's mutterings? "The traps are empty again," Britta apologized. She shook her hands to warm them after plunging them into icy water.

"You are hardly worth your keep." Wydda grunted and opened one eye. "I suppose you don't know any other way to get food." Britta could practically hear the wicce's bones creak as she used her stick to push herself upright. "I have to do everything myself. No help for Wydda, none at all."

"I have set the traps again. I am sure that tomorrow..."

"Tomorrow. Tomorrow." Wydda pushed past Britta and out through the hanging hide in the doorway. "No doubt you wait for Jesus to make fishes and loaves and wine."

Britta followed, puzzled.

Wydda made her way across the dooryard into the sedge. She knelt on the frozen mud beside the river not far from the hut. There were no traps here. Eyes closed, she swayed rhythmically on her knees, her breath rasping. Then she put her hands onto the ice at the edge of the river channel, palms down. The fens were silent. No wind rustled through the sedge, no birds called.

Britta found she was holding her breath. The fens waited. She waited. For what? For Wydda to come to her senses, Britta thought grimly.

Suddenly she noticed that the ice was melting where Wydda touched it. Not slowly, either. The witch gasped, as if in pain, and made a keening cry. Holes formed as though someone had built two fires on the ice. Wydda's hands began to glow. They trembled and shook as they reddened. Now she held them over black water that lapped at the gaping hole in the ice. It was a foot, now almost two feet wide. Britta was enthralled. Here was magic! But for what?

Wydda sat back with difficulty. She whimpered in pain as she scooped the air with her hands and brought them in to her withered breasts. What was she doing?

The hole in the ice came alive. The black water began to froth. From that seething confusion a silver, shiny fish flapped out of the water, then another and another, showering over Wydda, twisting onto the frozen mud. It seemed to rain, a fountain of fish.

Britta gasped, and then began to laugh. Fish squirmed everywhere. Magic!

Wydda pushed her hands away and the silver shower stopped. The water ceased to froth. Britta heard a bird calling and wind rising through the sedge. Wydda bent, gasping. Her face was gray, her lips almost blue. She coughed and sputtered as Britta hovered over her, wondering if Wydda would live to show her the secrets of the power she had just seen. At last Wydda put out a jerky claw and grabbed a handful of Britta's kirtle to pull herself up with a hacking sob.

"Never wait for Jesus," she whispered hoarsely, then turned and stumbled past Britta.

Britta stared after her in wonder. To have such control of your powers!

"Don't forget the fish." The witch gave a hacking cough that bent her double.

Britta knelt and scooped the flopping fish into her skirts until she could carry no more. The others she pushed back into the water. The hole in the ice was already shrinking. Taking up her skirt, she scurried after Wydda.

Inside the hut, Britta spilled the fish into a pot. The old crone lay in her bed box, staring into space. For a horrible moment Britta thought she was dead. She hovered, afraid to touch the gnarled wrist to check for the pulse that might not be there. It would be too cruel for the woman to die before she had revealed her secrets. Ashamed at such a thought, Britta hastily knelt beside the old woman. She was jealous. She had been trying for weeks to produce a hint of magic, and Wydda produced magic whenever she wanted. She touched Wydda's hand.

"Is that what you wanted to see?" Wydda's flat dark eyes opened slowly.

Britta saw pain and fear and shuddered herself. What could a woman who did what Wydda had just done possibly be afraid of?

"Your turn. There is no longer much time," Wydda said. Her voice was tenuous.

Britta felt the coming failure overwhelm her. "I can't," she wailed. "You know that."

"You have not told me the truth," Wydda accused. She sounded tired, very tired.

"I have, I swear to you." Britta tried to keep the note of desperation out of her voice.

Wydda studied her. "If you have the magic, there must be something wrong in the way you call it, some lapse, or some unworthiness. Are you unspoiled?"

"What?"

"Have you lain with a man?"

Britta swallowed hard. All her guilt and failure washed over her. Tears sprang to her eyes. "When I was fifteen, I was raped," Britta stammered.

Wydda stared into the coals, pondering. "But you have had the power since then?"

"Yes. Yes, many times."

The wicce chewed her ancient lips. "If you didn't spend your lust on it...You might still do." She glanced up at Britta. "I must think on this." Wydda closed her eyes again and seemed to sleep, leaving Britta to watch over her, trapped in her own fear. She had not dared confess her lust with Karn on the beach. Still, later she had healed the babe! Had she lost her power?

When Wydda woke in the late afternoon, Britta sat staring at her from the far side of a tiny fire. The witch stirred and groaned and finally sat with difficulty. Her gaze darted about the dim interior until it lighted upon Britta, silent and still. "Listen, girl," she commanded. "Now is time to make the magic, if you have it."

"I don't know if I can anymore," Britta stammered. "Since I am not a virgin..."

Wydda made her tortured way to sit opposite Britta. She lowered herself with a groan. When she was settled, she leaned forward in the dim light. "You must have it." The burning peat put up a single flame and a tiny tendril of smoke between them, as tenuous as Britta's confidence. As she watched, the flame died, leaving only the curling smoke.

"Rape has made you tight." Wydda nodded to herself. "Tell me how you have been trying to bring the power to you. Tell Wydda."

"I...I concentrate," Britta said. "But I do it with all my soul, I swear! I will the gods, or the one God, or whoever it is who has the power, to send it to me."

"I thought so." Wydda shook her head in disgust. "Stupid, stupid child."

Britta's spirit sank. "I don't know to whom to pray. Is that it? I don't have faith?"

"You have no need of faith. What you need is openness, and cunning!" Wydda showed more energy than she had since the fountain of fish.

"Cunning?" Britta turned the word over, as though she had never heard it.

"You go about it all wrong," Wydda complained. "Wrong, wrong, wrong. You must not try. Put away will. Open what you are to be used. Then listen. That is how you draw the power."

Britta thought back. Mostly the connection just came. It gripped her and took her where it would. Except the time with the babe. Then she had consciously put her doubts and fears into some part of her mind she could not touch and opened herself. Then the magic had taken her and worked through her. But she had not controlled it. She glanced up from where she had been staring at the smoking clump of peat to see Wydda waiting.

"That *is* how it happens, isn't it? Wydda knows."

"Yes," Britta said. "At least, that was how it happened once."

The witch nodded slowly. "When you get it, you don't know what to do with it, do you?"

"No." The word held all Britta's longing, all her fear of failure.

"Then listen to Wydda. For this you came to the fens. Only this." She leaned forward, and her eyes glowed with some opaque desire of her own. "You must drain yourself of will. You must open. And you must listen for the power coming. If you have the gift, it will come, become you. You become it. Wait until you are almost one, then unpack the little bag of will you have been hiding in a corner, and grab the power and jerk it toward what you want it to do for you." She rocked back and cracked her lips in a horrible, toothless grin. "That is the secret."

It sounded so…commonplace. Not at all what she imagined. Britta shook herself. No doubt why she had been so dreadfully unsuccessful. *Shed your illusions, Britta. They are all you have to lose.* Without another word, she closed her eyes and willed her body to relax. She pictured her will wafting out her nostrils with her breath.

"Tell me," Wydda whispered, as though from a distance. "What will the magic do?"

Britta found herself uninterested in responding; she was listening, though for what she did not know. At first all she could hear was her breathing, slow and regular. All she could see was the changing pattern of blood on the inside of her eyelids. The wind sighed outside.

"What will you do?" came to her from far away. "So I will know when you have done it."

"Fire," she whispered to herself, not knowing even if she spoke, for the wind was truly howling now. She could hear it rushing toward her, like a storm off the sea. It would blow right through her, waft her away, she was so empty. She would be lost.

But she was not afraid. All she wanted, all she lived for, was about to happen, or not. This was the moment that could give her life meaning, whatever that meaning was.

She leaned into the wind. She opened herself and felt it blow through her. Connection, sweet connection! It was a kind of ecstasy. She was the wind and it was her, and all she wanted was to have that connection go on forever, even if it meant that she was lost.

But she wanted to master the wind. She remembered now. She wanted its power. Wydda had told her how to get it. What had the wicce said? With the wind rushing in her ears, she couldn't think. If she couldn't think she would be lost. With a shriek of effort she reached out with her mind and grabbed the wind and pushed it toward the smoldering peat.

Agony shot through her body and mind. The wind was a blast from hell that burned her to her bones. She opened her eyes with a snap as the connection broke, realized she was shrieking. "My God," she wailed.

Pain coursed through her and she collapsed to the floor. Through it, Britta could see the flames leaping up toward the rush roof of Wydda's hut. Wydda herself was dancing crazily around the fire, beating at it with her cloak, to little effect. The grotesque eye sockets of the pelts lining the walls stared out, mocking her. That was all Britta knew as the pain pushed her down toward darkness.

She was dreaming. Her dream was strange. She could see herself across the fire, lying on the wooden floor, looking small and dirty. It was disturbing, to see oneself from outside. Something was wrong. Fear began to grow inside her. She saw herself jerk in her sleep and cry out. What was happening here? Something was happening.

With a shout, Britta fought her way out of sleep and sat bolt upright, gasping and sweating. Fire flickered over the hanging hides and glinted in the metal. She looked around wildly. Wydda stood across the hut. She looked disoriented, too, for a moment. Then she sat down and smiled in a self-satisfied way. "How are you?" she asked.

"There was so much pain," Britta murmured.

"You can master pain. Did I not tell you there was a cost?"

"Then, I did magic?" Britta asked, putting aside her nightmarish fears.

"Oh, yes," Wydda sighed. "You'll do nicely."

Offa leaned against the pole in the sparsely furnished tent outside the gates of the faesten. He would have thought that the younger brother of the King of Wessex would travel with more accoutrements. Young men loved pomp. But young as he was, this one lived like a soldier. This callow youth had been leading an army almost since he could hold a sword. Offa lifted his mean horn in salute. "Do your men long for battle, Alfred, as mine do?"

The handsome young man sighed. "They grow more restless daily. I could wish there was more love between Wessex and the Anglians."

"Ah," Offa agreed. "Our king does not help with that."

The young prince looked up, wary. "He pays more heed to his healers than his thegns."

"You wonder if he is the one to lead an army?" Offa asked, matching Alfred with a feigned hesitation of his own.

"The Danish threat is clear. We need a strong leader."

"We will rout the Danes." Alfred waved away the danger. "They are a rabble, not a third our size, from what our spies have told us. But what comes when the Danes are routed? Our kingdoms cannot continue bickering over land and wasting time in fruitless slaughter."

Offa picked his way carefully. "I, too, long for peace. An alliance, perhaps, between two strong rulers could achieve that."

Alfred rubbed his fringe of blond beard. "Between two kings who were kindred souls."

Rise to the bait, my fine young trout, Offa thought. "I see your problem. Edmund does not seem a kindred soul *with your brother.*"

The young man looked abashed, as Offa knew he would. "The responsibilities of a king are great." Alfred rose and paced the tent. "Even my brother does not see that. There is no learning in the land. Not even priests can read the holy texts or write in Latin. We have only the old runes now. There is no history of our people. How are we to make our future unless we can pass our experience down through the generations?"

"You long for immortality, my lord, as do I." *Reading and writing are a waste of time, boy.* Still, he could use Alfred's impulse to his gain. "You seek it through words. I find it in religion. And in building. My stone churches will last a thousand years." He did not mention that building monuments to God was a way to redeem his bloody past as well.

"Churches are important," Alfred agreed, eyes glowing. "We also need safety from attack, a strong army, and a system of faestens on our coast. We need order, a way of passing property from father to son. And we need a life of the mind. I want to give people a better life."

Listening, Offa found himself thinking the young man might actually be up to a war for peace. "Together, what could Wessex and Anglia not do?" he asked. "They could unite the island. There would be peace, room for your grand plans. Too bad it is Edmund who holds the Anglian throne."

Alfred sighed. Offa held his tongue. Finally the young royal looked up. Offa turned instinctively away and filled his drinking horn again; such guilelessness should not see cunning in his face.

"You understand me better than my own thegns," Alfred said slowly. "None realizes the importance of learning to our future, to the piety of the people, to our very relationship with our God." He paused uncomfortably. "I hear them whispering about me."

"Aye?" Offa nodded, raising his drinking horn and downing a healthy gulp of mead. "A man with a vision is a man apart."

The young prince smiled. "Perhaps we are both 'men apart,' Offa."

"Perhaps we are, Alfred." Grinning, he raised his horn to clang it against the goblet of a most naive young prince.

Karn returned from fishing to his hut in the abandoned village wondering about his Danish friends. They were somewhere in Anglia now, camped with Ivar the Boneless, waiting for spring. Good thing they could not see him now, limping home to a creaky hut in this muddy land. Bursting out of the reeds into the circle of leaning halls, he found with a start that his hut was occupied. A girl with blond braids peered out of his doorway with frightened eyes.

"You stay away from us," she called.

Karn froze. The girl was not alone. A shadowy figure moved inside his hut. Though he had not gone to the village, it had evidently come to him. He fingered his knife and wished it were a sword. He wished, too, that he had not let the blonde see him limp.

"You are in my house," he challenged, hoping she would not hear the Dane in his voice.

She looked taken aback. "Nobody lives here anymore."

"I do." He limped forward. As he drew closer he could see she had been crying.

"You cannot throw us out; Egbert is hurt. We have nowhere else to go to escape Cedric."

Karn motioned her out of the hut with his knife and leaned
against the door while he peered inside. A man was just
visible, holding the partially cloth-bound stump of his hand.
He moaned. *By the gods, what am I to do with this pair?
And more importantly, who will follow in their wake?* But
he could not let the man bleed to death. "You girl, blow up
the fire and I will sear his wound," he said gruffly. He would
be a poor substitute for Britta.

Karn worked over the man for a long time in the dim hut.
He cauterized the stump with a hot knife and pulled the skin
together for stitching. The girl could not watch, and the man
himself soon fainted, so he worked alone. When he had finished, he came out to see that the girl had charred some of
his fish for the midday meal.

"Will he live?" she asked in a small voice.

"I see worse in battle and they live today."

"Thank you," she said simply.

He wanted to ask her who Cedric was and why he had
done this thing to the man in the hut. Instead, he saw the
fulfillment of his fears: Three Saxons stood on the limestone
flat above them.

There was a time when that would have seemed good
odds. Thor, how he wished for a sword!

"Hild," came the cry from one of the men. Out of the
corner of his eye, Karn could see the girl swing around. Then
she stilled herself. That meant she wasn't certain if they
came as friend or foe. Unlike Karn. He was most certain
they were foe, or soon would be.

They started down off the ridge, the one who had cried
out running ahead. The other two swung their axes up to a
ready position. They had seen him. Karn gathered himself
in quiet readiness. If death was to come, at least he faced it
on his feet, knife in hand.

"Hild, I knew you must have come here," the man called.
The silver rings on his neck and arms proved him a man of
substance. His head was gray, but his body was hard and

muscled, his shoulders and forearms immense. They signaled that he worked the forge. He was a smith by trade. He passed Karn without acknowledgment and stood before the girl. The tension between the two held them rigid, oblivious of all. The two who followed the smith were not so careless. They faced Karn, arms at the ready.

The smith swallowed hard as he looked at the girl. "Is Egbert here?" he asked hoarsely.

"And where else would he be, except with his beloved?" Hild asked, an edge of defiance in her voice. "If you had stood for Egbert, Father..." Her voice broke. "If you believed me..."

"I do believe you, child. But Cedric is my thegn. A man lives by his loyalty to his thegn."

"Egbert almost died by it," Hild cried. "And I, Father? Would you have stood by and let him make me into a harlot for his own use?"

The smith just stood there, the iron of his body suddenly melting away, leaving him boneless and bereft. "You are right, child. I don't know that you will ever forgive me." Hild threw herself on his shoulder and collapsed in tears.

"Walther," one of the watchful ones cried. "There is time for this later. Look here."

Karn fingered his knife, his muscles tensed in readiness.

Hild's father turned with her still in his arms. All three Saxons stared at Karn. Surely they would see he was Viking. If this was the fight that ended in his death, so be it.

"Who are you and what are you doing here?" the smith challenged.

Hild stepped between them. "He is the kind stranger who tended Egbert when there was no one else to do it, Father. Would you cut a man down unfairly?"

The other two Saxons exchanged uneasy glances. Walther looked at Karn and then back to his daughter until finally he made a choice. He held out his hand in greeting. Karn watched the others. After a long moment of indecision their axes lowered. Karn turned to look warily at the man who offered friendship. Was this a barbarian trick? It would be an insult to refuse Walther's hand. A wise man would bide his time before declaring himself an enemy. Karn took the strong hand with his good one and nodded curtly.

The older man glanced at Karn's half-made saddle, his newly thatched roof, and the crutch that leaned in the doorway. "Is Egbert inside?" he asked, gesturing to the hut.

Karn grunted in the affirmative.

Without apparent concern, Walther pushed into the hut, his daughter beside him.

Karn backed away to lean against a wall, watching the two other Saxons. They muttered together, with sideways glances at him. Karn's way was not yet clear. They would fall upon him in an instant if they thought he posed a danger.

"You have done what you could," Walther said quietly when finally he emerged. "He is feverish. Will he live?" He addressed Karn directly.

Knowing the significance of that, Karn nodded. Walther's eyes were used to grading iron. They saw through to the distrust, the weakness, and even the lost warrior heart of him. Karn didn't want this man to know so much.

At last the smith shrugged. "Snurri, Frith, we stay the night here. Go and find what the fens will give us for dinner.

Snurri glared at Karn before turning to lope out of the village. Frith trailed in his wake.

"Hild, set some peat to drying. We will sit at the fire out here." Walther eyed Karn. "And you, will you not sit and talk with me before you decide whether or not to use that seax?"

With a start, Karn looked down to see that he still gripped his knife with white knuckles. Over a single Saxon he might prevail....Of course, this one was the strongest of the lot in spite of his age. Could he surprise the man with a knife in his belly? If he stayed his hand, the two others would return shortly. If he turned and left, where could he go where there would not be other Saxons? This was as good a place to face his fate as any. Uneasily, he put the knife in the waist of his breeches. He watched Hild pile chunks of peat to dry beside the fire.

Walther nodded. "We will go back tomorrow, child," he said to Hild.

Trembling, she stood. "I will never return to that village when Cedric works his will upon you."

Walther reached out and touched her shoulder. "He will not hurt you; I will see to that."

"You may say that, Father, but you can be sure of no such thing. He accused Egbert of stealing because he wants me, and none of you said him nay." Her voice was fraught with accusation. "We will stay here, thank you."

"You cannot stay here," Walther appealed in a low voice. "How will you live? Egbert has only one hand. Come back to the village. It is the way of our people to submit to their thegn."

Hild looked frightened beneath her determination, but she only knelt to tend her fire.

The four men sat around the fire in front of Karn's hut in the dark, picking their teeth with the points of their knives. Sparks flickered up into the blackness. "You have not said three words, stranger," Walther remarked. "We know not your lineage or your home. Tell us."

Karn knew he could not avoid speech forever. He would have to trust to their ignorance. "It lies to the north," he growled. His accent screamed that he was Dane.

"I thought so." Walther nodded. "Do you come from a line of warriors?"

Walther had likely guessed that because of Karn's obvious wound. He shook his head. "Farmers."

"Why are you not at home with a plough in your hand?" Snurri asked suspiciously.

"Brothers," Karn said. "No land for me."

"Younger son." Frith nodded. "It is a hard thing."

"What are you doing here?" Snurri pressed.

Karn looked at him steadily. "I look for land," he said. He'd meant it to be a lie. Had he not refused land in a dozen places already? But as he said it, he knew it was true. The love of land was bred into his bones from his father's loins. He had gone Viking because there was nothing for him in Denmark, but he wanted land where he could live in peace with men he knew and trusted, not among barbarians where every day brought conflict.

Snurri snorted. "There's no land you would want here. We grow some vegetables, but mostly we are fishermen. We get our living from the fens."

Karn nodded, then added, "I would not live under your thegn."

Walther's face grew dark. "He judges for his own benefit, not ours."

"What about your *law?*" It was a Danish word. "I know not the word in your tongue. 'Law' means rules a thegn cannot break."

"Is the thegn subject to this law in your land?" Snurri asked, curious.

"All are subject," Karn said.

"What happens if someone breaks it?"

"The law judges."

"How is the law decided?" Frith sounded suspicious.

"Law is not decided," Karn said carefully. "It is all the... the judgments. Is this a word?" When he saw nods, he continued. "The judgments from before-times."

"So," Walther murmured. "Taken together, they tell you how you must judge today."

"Are you not loyal to your thegn?" Snurri asked after a moment.

"To die for your jarl is all honor," Karn said slowly. "But law is more."

Snurri snorted in disbelief. Frith shook his head.

"We could use that in our village, that law," Walther said pensively as he gazed into the fire. "But I am thinking Cedric would not like it overmuch."

Britta screamed as the pain hit her and fell to her knees. She was so tired. Was it only two weeks she had been practicing magic under Wydda's watchful eye? She rolled in the dirt outside the hut as the fire in the dooryard leapt up. The kettle boiled and hissed. Wydda clapped her hands in glee. Neither of them bargained for the rushing wind that rose across the fens and almost knocked Wydda to her knees. The sedge bent flat as the wind whistled and tore at it.

I can't control it, Britta thought, panicked. The wind slapped tiny water droplets across her face like a whiplash. *I can't just boil water. I can't just light the fire. No, the world must uncoil all its power for me, even when I don't want it to.* "Stop," she screamed into the wind. Britta felt herself succumbing to the now familiar unconsciousness, always plagued by dreams. Fear ripped at her mind. The unconsciousness had become worse than the pain. As she fell into the darkness, she saw Wydda get to her knees, a glowing light in her eyes.

The dream was always the same. Britta saw herself as though she were someone else. Each time was longer. Each time she struggled to wake as though her life depended upon it. This time, the dream was more real. She was awake, yet still she looked upon herself from outside. The wind died, the kettle hissed. She saw her own eyes looking at her, curious. Why would they look like that? She felt confused and looked down.

What she saw chilled her to her bones. Old bones. She saw Wydda's ragged robes, Wydda's hands. She cried out, hoping she would wake, and put those wrinkled horrors to her face only to feel Wydda's desiccated skin, her thin lips. "What is happening?" she cried to herself across the clearing. A sly look was the only reply. Her breath wheezed out of old lungs, her joints ached. Inside her was the banked fire of a life whose coals glowed only feebly. She felt a black core of disease in her womb. It would soon consume her. She saw it all. She was Britta, in Wydda's body. The soul in Britta's body was Wydda. That was what Wydda had wanted all along.

No, she thought. Then with greater force, *"No."* The earth vibrated beneath her gnarled feet. The young, sly eyes across from her grew uncertain. You have the body, Britta thought, but my magic is more powerful. And I say, "No." The earth slanted away at her command. Water from the river coursed toward the hut. "You will not have my body," she shouted. The rocks in the fire's circle cracked and split. The young body's eyes shone with Wydda's fear as the water sloshed around her.

The Britta inside Wydda's crust put out her withered hands and shook the younger woman's shoulders. "I'll shake you loose!" she shouted. The waters from the river, set loose across the land, rose. The young woman put her hands around Britta's now-aged throat and squeezed. Britta couldn't get her breath. Perhaps Wydda's body was too weak to shake the witch loose before she herself died. But then, the physical act of shaking wasn't important. She raised her head and howled. "Get out!" Her life was almost gone from the younger woman's strong hands. Pain wrenched her body, just like the pain of bending magic to her will in the last weeks.

Britta felt her brain rattle in her head as the old woman shook her. "I'll shake you loose," the withered lips whispered. But the words died away as the old hands dropped helpless to her side. She was back, back in the body that was her birthright, and she was choking the witch.

"You don't understand," the crone croaked. "I'll die."

Britta unbent her fingers from the withered neck. "I know. I felt it," she said. The earth no longer sank. The waters of the fens sank into the peaty earth where the fire warmed it.

"They were never dreams," Britta said. "You weakened me to take my body for yourself. You wanted to be young again." She had a dreadful thought. Wydda wasn't thirty. She hadn't taught her mother. "Is this the first time, or is that body one you stole as well?"

"You will find out," the old witch cawed. "When you can't keep from working the magic. When magic drains the life from you. Then you will judge old Wydda fairly. You, too, will look for a young shell. You can use anyone, but if you find one with the gift, you can claim her powers. And you will do as I have done." Tears coursed down the hag's ruined cheeks.

A great sigh shuddered through Britta. "I will go now. There is nothing for me here."

"And condemn me to death?" Wydda half-pleaded, half-accused.

"As you would have done to me," she whispered.

"You can't," Wydda gasped as she sank to the muddy earth.

Britta got her bag. "Fenris!" She was startled by the wail that issued from her throat. Wydda's weakening sobs echoed around her. *I am killing her, as surely as I go.* But a darkness at her center stifled all compassion. Fenris burst through the rustling bush. Britta turned without a backward glance, and Wydda's sobs grew fainter as she struck out across the frozen fens.

Chapter Thirteen

Walther did not have a chance to decide whether to return to the village the following morning. Cedric came crashing over the limestone plateau with three warriors, all on horseback, before the three Saxons had the sleep fairly rubbed from their eyes. At least Karn assumed it was Cedric. Who else would look so angry? Karn pulled his knife and leaned against his hut. Hild hurried toward Egbert, hunched in front of the fire.

"She prefers that crippled stoat?" Karn heard Cedric rail. The thegn cantered into the open area between the abandoned huts and pulled up his whinnying horse before Hild and her maimed lover. Before any could act, Cedric drew his sword and raised it high, then clove the rising Egbert from shoulder to breastbone. Hild's shriek broke the silence as he fell.

Everyone erupted into action. Walther grabbed his daughter before she could throw herself on Cedric's leg. Cedric's horse shied and reared. "Monster," Hild wailed. Walther's friends shouted in horror. Even the three at Cedric's back looked dismayed, their horses churning nervously. Karn reached the edge of the group and slowed. He had eyes only for Cedric. The thegn was a big, blustery man, his complexion red. His brassy yellow hair blew about a puffy face in the wind off the fens. Not hard, Karn thought. He had gone a bit to seed out here in the fens, this thegn.

The bloodlust drained from Cedric's eyes as he sheathed his sword.

"You will pay the wergild for his death," Walther said through clenched teeth.

"To whom would I pay? He has no relatives, no wife," Cedric said pointedly. He looked around, taking in the pen for Thorn, the new-made roof on Karn's hut. "Who lives here?" he challenged. For a long moment the only sound was Hild's sobbing. "This is my land," he continued. "No one lives here but by my grace." Cedric's eyes fell on Karn. His hand leapt to the hilt of his sword instinctively. His horse stamped and snorted with the sudden movement, and his three followers circled warily. One drew his own weapon. "Who are you?" Cedric barked.

Karn made himself stand quietly. His knife remained at his side. The gods brought whatever came today. Once he would have been ready, but he was no longer the man he had been, in body or in spirit.

"No one," Karn said.

"You live in my village? You hide fugitives from me?" Cedric's eyes began to smolder with anger. "So you want to set up as thegn?" he asked. "Is that why they came to you?"

"They do as they do," Karn returned, knowing what would happen here. He considered his knife against Cedric's sword. A surprise lunge inside the reach of the thegn's weapon was his only chance. What chance was that? His sword arm did not yet have full range, nor anywhere near his former strength. His limp left him practically immobile.

Cedric did as Karn expected. Angrily, he swung his meaty shank over his horse's rump and hit the ground with his sword drawn. As he advanced on Karn, Walther and his Saxon friends melted to the side. Karn expected nothing else. What had Egbert felt as the sword clove to his heart? Karn fingered his knife. Cedric would see his limp soon enough. Fear gnawed at him. He would fail, as he had failed against Offa and his men. How could it be else?

"A sword against a knife, Cedric?" Walther shouted. "This hardly proves your prowess, any more than killing a man with one hand."

Cedric ground to a halt in front of Karn, his face purpling, and he half-turned to Walther. "Give him a sword," he barked to a pudgy follower. "I'll kill him just the same."

"No," Walther said clearly, before the sword could be offered. "I'll give him a sword." He strode to the pack he had-carried on his back last night and returned with a long, stiff package, carefully wrapped in oilskin. He carried it reverently past Hild, collapsed sobbing on Egbert's dead body, past a frowning Cedric, and proffered it to Karn.

Karn examined the smith's face and knew what was being offered. Whatever weapon this man had hoarded, he was offering Karn part of his past and all of his future. Still, it was a futile gesture. Karn couldn't win against Cedric and he didn't want the responsibility of defending anyone but himself. That was what he would be taking if he accepted this blade.

But the warrior in him saw something reflected in the smith's eyes. Was this not a weapon saved, but some primitive sword the smith had made? Slowly Karn reached out and unfolded the oilcloth. The gleam of polished metal winked up at him through the wrappings. As the cloth fell away, the shimmer of the blade pierced the air. Karn grasped the intricate hilt, almost against his will. There were no precious stones. This was a working weapon. But the swirl of the metal hilt glinted, bejeweled by the sweat of a man who had given some part of his life to make such a wonderful shank of steel. The strength that holding such a weapon gave a man raced up Karn's arm.

It would not be enough. *But the gods offer. How else explain the gift of this amazing weapon here in the trackless fens? I cannot turn away from the gods' challenge....*

He turned from Walther to Cedric. It was time.

Cedric sneered as Karn fingered Walther's sword and hefted it. "A sword does not make a man." He raised his own blade, longer than Karn's, and heavier. It would be nigh impossible to get inside its reach. "I own this village," Cedric shouted. "I own the fealty of its ceorls. And its wenches." Here he cast a fulminating look at Hild.

"Owning and leading are two different things, Cedric," Walther grunted behind Karn.

The Saxon faces in the semicircle watched the two combatants narrowly. Karn knew none but Walther supported him. They awaited the turn of events.

Cedric swung his sword with a sudden, piercing bellow, then he advanced in a single long stride. His sword came crashing down. Karn instinctively raised his right hand that should have held a shield—and almost lost an arm. At the last moment his warrior's instinct served him. He ducked and twisted. Cedric staggered as his sword buried itself in the peat. That stagger saved Karn.

Cedric righted himself. He had seen Karn's limp. His eyes gleamed in anticipation. "A coward," he shouted to his audience, "and a cripple. I'll make short work of this one." He strode forward. The flesh on his thighs shook with each step. He wielded his heavy weapon in two hands. Karn, too, must use two hands to lift his sword, but it was a shield only. He could not raise it far enough to return a swinging blow. He parried with a clang and stumbled back. Each blow sent pain coursing through his shoulder. With any other sword, he would be a corpse by now, but Walther's gift was amazing. Flexible and strong, it met the heavier blade with ringing defiance and sent the power of the blows echoing back up Cedric's arm.

Karn knew he could not last long. He conserved energy by forcing Cedric's sword to slip off his, to the side and down. The thegn had to then heave the heavy weapon up farther to strike again.

The Saxons who supported Cedric grunted their cheers. Walther and his friends were quiet. They, too, could see what would happen. Sweat streamed into Karn's eyes. The spongy earth sucked at his feet. His hip ached so, it might betray him. He gave ground again and again. What advantage did he have? Agility, once, before the limp. Cedric moved without a shred of grace. After years of fighting, how could he turn those to advantage when all he could do was parry and fall back? Even now, his arms began to tremble. It would not be long.

Then, through his exhaustion, Karn saw what might be a chance. Cedric had found a rhythm. Stride forward, raise sword, arcing blow, grunt of effort, louder as he tired. Then repeat. Too much rhythm in battle was a dangerous thing. Karn fell back yet again, just to make sure. Stay the course, he begged his screaming muscles.

As Cedric raised his blade, Karn did not turn his left side forward to let his sword protect him. Cedric's eyes gleamed. At the last moment, Karn pushed under the man's blow. He could not swing his sword, so he pointed it up. Cedric saw his mistake and saved himself by twisting away. Blood welled from the huge man's flank, but it was not a killing blow. He staggered. Karn pulled back. Cedric looked down in surprise at the blood seeping from his hip.

"Have done," Karn panted, his chest heaving. He leaned on his sword. "I am no thegn."

Cedric gave a scream of anger and stumbled forward, sword raised.

Karn felt the wonderful moment of coming metamorphosis. It was bloodlust rising. All thought ceased. He was transformed into a beast that worshipped killing. His sword, as he raised it with both hands, was part of him. A shout spiraled up from his lips. Cedric's sword raised high. Karn simply ran at him. Cedric's sword began to arc down, but Karn the Beast was there before it found its fleshy mark. He skewered his prey full on. Cedric's sword continued to fall. Some part of Karn felt it bite into his shoulder, but its force was gone. The man who held the sword was dead. Karn's borrowed weapon shivered in Cedric's abdomen and Karn howled.

Slowly, he came back to himself. His foe lay like a

slaughtered ox. The wonderful sword in his hand dripped blood onto the peat. The world was gray and white and windy. He looked around, feeling distant, as though coming back to a home known long ago and seeing that everything looked smaller than he remembered. Walther and his friends seemed stunned, Cedric's cronies confused. Hild knelt beside her dead lover with a puffy face and unseeing eyes. Slowly, Karn realized that Cedric's men were getting off their horses, swords in hand. His grip tightened on the hilt of his blade. As you would, yourself, he thought grimly.

Walther stepped forward. The world sharpened into focus once again.

"Stop, Grimbald," the smith said. "Let well enough alone."

"He was your thegn. You owed him fealty," Grimbald shouted. "Now I will repay his death with the death of his slayer." He started toward Karn.

Walther moved to stand in his path. "A thegn earns his men's loyalty." He spoke over Grimbald's shoulder to the other two who shuffled there, and to Snurri and Frith behind him. "Cedric had our loyalty as long as we could give it and long after he deserved it."

Frith took up a position behind Grimbald and the two others. "Who says that you deserve to avenge Cedric's death, Grimbald? Do you mean to be thegn?"

There were snickers, even among the two who followed him, and Grimbald reddened. After a long moment he sheathed his sword. "If you choose to follow this foreigner, take him as thegn," he shouted, then he motioned Cedric's other supporters back to their horses. "I will not stay in a village with no thegn. You'll be prey to any brigand coming through here. And when Edmund gets no taxes, he'll bring his troops and wipe the fens clean of you." He looked over at his companions. "I'm for finding a new master, men."

The other two shouted their agreement and started west with a whirl of stamping horses.

The group in front of the teetering halls was silent as the three horses thundered away.

206

They finally turned uneasy eyes toward Karn. He said nothing. Instead he put his hand up to the pain in the shoulder he could now feel. His hand came back sticky with blood. He turned toward his hut and started unsteadily toward the door.

Offa paced in front of the hall allotted to him, far from Edmund's central keep. He chafed under the king's show of power. Raedwald sat with his feet up on a bench and watched him fret.

"You have not enough to occupy you, Offa. You need to take your mind off the waiting."

"I thought by now the Mercian devils would have made more enemies than Satan," Offa raged. "Jesu knows I have sewn the seeds of discontent where I could."

"We all have." Raedwald sighed. "I encouraged a fight yesterday between one of Edmund's guard and a Mercian lout no better with a sword than a babe in arms."

"And?" Offa stopped to hear the results.

Raedwald shook his head. "Edmund's man struck him down. But the Mercian captain himself struck the first of his men to strike back, and Delan, too, held his men in check."

Offa turned back to his pacing, disgusted. "They hold the alliance together, no matter what we do. Edmund cannot unite the island," he spat. "It must be me!"

Raedwald felt obliged to add one final point. "Delan knows what we are doing." He cleared his throat. "He said he would be at your door if another fight broke out."

"I should just shove a sword in Edmund's belly, direct." Offa whirled like a cornered animal. He knew his second in command was lying low in the face of his volatile temper. He had to get out of this camp. "I should go back after that witch and the Viking."

"We have been through that a thousand times." Raedwald sighed. "You would come back to find that no one followed you. You are making progress here. That Northumbrian is ours."

Offa knew his friend was right. He imagined again what

he would do to the Viking when he caught him, and what he would do to the witch. It made his loins hard. But it did not help his temper. "Edmund is not man enough to lead other men! Can't they see that?"

"It is Delan who is the power here," Raedwald said. "Without the guard…"

Offa froze. Why had he not seen it before?

"What is it?" Raedwald asked hesitantly.

Offa felt his bitter smile crack his lips, dry from winter air. "We need everyone to see more clearly the weakling that Edmund is."

"What do you mean to do?"

"He has been looking for a healer ever since he killed those two foreign mages, has he not?" Offa felt the plan form in his mind.

"Yes." Raedwald's voice was laden with reservation. "But how does that help us?"

"We have a healer with us," Offa prompted.

"That crazy old man Badenoth picked up on the way?" Raedwald asked in amazement. "He barely has a head for weeds and small cures. He will never satisfy Edmund."

"Yet, if I seem to offer him up to Edmund's need, I gain in several ways." Offa stroked his beard, carefully smoothing it into its two forks. "First, I seem to all the world to support my king. Second, I allay suspicions sprouting too freely in Delan's breast. And,"—here Offa could not avoid gloating— "I am free to talk about Edmund's whining demands and fantasies. Ooooh," he chortled. "I will be so concerned. We all will. We will spread the stories of his imagined illness. We will thoughtfully discuss the cures our healer has suggested. Then will Edmund be revealed."

"That healer will not last long," Raedwald said doubtfully.

"When Edmund kills him for his failures, it will only make him seem more mad."

Raedwald raised his brows.

"Go find him." Offa grinned, still fingering his beard.

*　*　*

Karn sat, shirtless, on a crude bench in front of a hall in the new village, rinsing the cut on his shoulder with a bucket of water from the village well. The Saxons had overwhelmed him with their entreaties to join them, and after all, that was likely the only place Karn could find hardened leather for his saddle straps. Walther promised mead and meat and singing. It was long since Karn had heard the singing of sagas, though they would be Saxon songs.

His shoulder needed stitching. He wished Britta was here. He could almost feel the shock of her touch as he had felt it in her hut so many times, moving over his body more intimately than any caress. He sagged a bit. He was tired, that was all.

The Saxons, too, had become more thoughtful. He could see the mixed emotions in their eyes as they approached. They were glad to be rid of Cedric but fearful, not only of the future, but also of the foreigner who'd freed them. Karn held his shirt to his shoulder to staunch the bleeding and reached for Walther's wonderful sword. He stuck it, point first, into the soft earth, where it trembled like a living thing. Best it be close at hand.

"Who will act as thegn now?" Frith challenged. "You haven't answered that, Walther."

"Aye," the other said. "Who will pay our taxes? Who commands our loyalty in battle?"

"Is it you, Walther?" Snurri asked doubtfully. "Can a smith be thegn?"

"I am no thegn," Walther said with finality. He stared at Karn. "Well, foreigner, who will be thegn here?"

"You need no thegn," Karn said.

"We need a thegn to give our allegiance, if Edmund wars with the Viking scavengers," Frith said impatiently. "And for protection, Northerner."

"Protect yourselves," Karn replied gruffly. What would they say if they knew they asked advice even now of a Viking? "Fight where you want."

"We need a thegn," Walther insisted.

Karn did not like the way he saw Walther heading. He

did not want to lead these farmers. "The village can be soke," he said, trying to redirect the man's thoughts.

"A soke?" Walther asked, interested. "What is that?"

"A free village. No thegn. They pay tax, give men for battle."

Walther looked at Frith. "It wouldn't work," the latter decided.

"My people have many sokes," Karn returned. "Make a *thing*." No, that was a Norse word. "A council. A Witan. Elders make the law."

"Who sets the wergild to be paid when a man is slain?" Walther asked, considering.

"You set it together—for ceorl, for slave. You set the value of each man's trade."

Frith looked thoughtful. "What happens to the thegn's share?"

"Given to the soke," Karn said "to build a wall or dig a well."

"How much," Walther asked pointedly, "if the thegn doesn't set the price?"

"You decide," Karn said impatiently. "In my land each gives according to the land he tills. The land eight oxen plough in one day is a plough-land. Each plough-land gives one share."

"We call that a hide of land," Walther said, "or near enough." Karn could see that the smith, at least, was beginning to understand. "We must think on this." Then Walther came to himself and looked down at his daughter. Hild's eyes were glazed. "You need something to do, girl." He looked back at Karn, speculation in his eyes. "Why don't you tend our warrior's wound?"

Karn was about to make some gruff denial, but Walther interrupted him. "Accept Hild's help as a mark of our thanks and be gracious about it." He gave a rough grin as he pushed the girl forward. She seemed to see Karn for the first time. She knit her brows as she came to look under the bloody shirt he held to his shoulder.

He braced for the jolt of feeling as she touched his shoulder. It never came. She touched him, nothing more. Karn felt a small whisper of disappointment sigh out with his breath. Hild went into one of the houses to get a needle.

"We will prepare Egbert's body for burial," Walther said to Frith.

With a sense of relief that could not quite replace the forlorn emptiness inside her, Britta sighted the village she had stopped at just before finding the witch. All the way back across the frozen fen, she had grown in certainty. Magic was evil.

Wydda was evil, that was sure. Did the magic lure one into evil deeds? Perhaps already it had poisoned her. She and Fenris stumbled past the outer huts. Her gift was really a curse, meant to addict her to that feeling of oneness as it exacted its terrible cost. She didn't want it, wouldn't use it, wouldn't call the power, wouldn't heal, regardless of what the visions foretold.

Everyone seemed to be gathered at the far end of the town. She was too overwrought to care what they might be doing there. She bent over the well to haul up a bucket of water for Fenris and caught sight of her reflection in the dark pool below.

She jumped back and stood, trembling. Gods, no! It can't have started already! Surely it was a trick of the light, a reflection on the water—that was all. She took a deep breath and leaned over the well. There were her own green eyes. Her unbound hair stood out about her face, and a wide, white streak shimmered there like a mark of God.

This time she stepped back from her reflection slowly. It was a mark of shame, warning her that she could end like Wydda. "I will never use magic again," she whispered.

Fenris drooped by her side, his fur muddy and bedraggled. "Come on, old friend. You need a drink." Wearily, she hauled up a bucket of water, ignoring her reflection. Fenris lapped, but without his usual gusto. He was tired indeed. They needed food. Britta looked around. She had come away from Wydda's hut with nothing but Fenris and the bundle with her father's Bible in it. Even her herbs were spent. It will come to begging now, she thought.

She approached the crowd gathered down by the stream cautiously, knowing that they would distrust anyone who had returned from the Witch of the Fens, especially if they saw the streak of white in her hair. Fenris suddenly pricked his ears and darted away, barking. The crowd swirled and re-formed. What could they all be doing there?

Then the bodies parted and she saw Karn.

The thrill broke over Britta without her consent. How she wanted to tell him everything! His name was on her lips before she could think. "Karn," she called and started forward. Fenris was before her. He gave a bark and sped off to greet his friend with newfound strength.

Then the import of what she saw crashed in upon her. Karn, stripped to the waist, sat on a bench in the center of a knot of Saxons. He had gained weight since he had left her. He looked fit, though his muscular torso still bore red scars on his belly and shoulder. He stared up at the girl who bent over him. Who would not stare? She had a long blond braid, a beautiful profile. Her tiny hand plied a needle as she stitched at a fresh wound on top of the shoulder Britta had stitched once, too. Britta trembled to a stop, her stomach sinking somewhere near her knees.

Wagging his feathery tail furiously, Fenris threw himself at Karn.

The Viking half-stood, pulling the needle out of the woman's fingers. His hand strayed to Fenris's head as the dog leaped around him, but Karn's gaze never moved from Britta. He breathed her name. "What do you do here?"

Britta's throat was so full she could not speak. Karn pulled on Fenris's ears as the dog nuzzled him shamelessly. Had the beast no pride? The girl had been crying over Karn. Her eyes were red-rimmed. That gave Britta back her voice. "I thought you might need assistance," she said, struggling to appear unconcerned through her shame. She had stooped to call his name! "But I see I was not necessary. You have all the help you need."

At that moment two men approached with a lifeless corpse. Anger began to rise in Britta. No doubt Karn had challenged that poor dead man over the girl. "Returning to your old ways, Karn?" she asked sweetly, though she felt anything but. "I wonder that they tolerate you." The girl began to sob quietly, then pushed Karn back down and turned her attention to his wound. Britta was confused.

Karn finally found his tongue. He seemed hardly to notice the needle piercing his flesh. "Did you find your witch, Britta?" he asked.

"Yes." Disgust still warred with her anger when she realized what had risen in her breast at the sight of him. She had run forward like an eager girl. How stupid could she be?

Another silence stretched. "Did she tell you about your magic?" Karn asked finally.

"Oh, yes," she answered. "I know much more about it now."

"I am glad."

The villagers exchanged uneasy glances as the men laid down their burden.

"Are you not the healer who passed through several weeks ago?" the muscular old man asked.

Britta nodded. She could feel the streak of white in her hair.

"Perhaps you will stay to heal us, then," he said. "There are several in the village who can use your gift, and this warrior from the north as well."

Britta felt her voice break as she said, "I do not heal anymore." She wondered if she should pretend, for if she could not trade her skills for food and supplies, she might soon starve. She wanted only to be gone, slipping away into solitude as Wydda had.

Several murmured their protest. "She has been to the Witch of the Fens."

"Look at her. She did not have that streak when she was last here."

A woman sheltered her crying child. "How did she survive

the fens, except by magic?" A sign against the evil eye was made, and another.

Karn's voice cut through the murmuring. "I know this woman. She is not evil. You will stay, Britta," he said, looking at her closely. It sounded like a command. "You need rest."

The others certainly treated it like a command. The old man nodded. The murmuring stopped. The old man examined Karn, then said to Britta, "I will take you to a hut to rest."

"Fenris, come," Britta called as she turned to follow the old man. The dog paid scant attention. She had to call him thrice before he tore himself away from Karn. She welcomed her anger, that it might purge the shame. How could she have thought it would be any different? Was he not a Viking? He told her himself he'd had women in dozens of foreign lands.

"How dare you not come when I call?" she scolded Fenris. "He has you completely under his spell. I should never have taken a male pup. *He* just wants me to heal his shoulder. As if I would!" She hitched her pack over her shoulder. "Let his simpering beauty heal him." Her whispered tirade was short-lived. She wound down again to hollow depression.

The old man indicated a hut and opened the door for her. "Thank you," she murmured and went inside. To her surprise he followed her.

"I am Walther, smith in Stowa," the old man said. "Do you know our warrior?"

"Aye," Britta murmured. "I know him."

"He is a brave man." Walther looked somber. "He slew our thegn, but we are well rid of that one."

"He knows how to slay." Still she quailed to think of Karn facing an enemy in his depleted state. How had he prevailed? "Was that the man you prepared for burial?"

"No." Walter shook his head. "Alas, that one was a victim of our thegn's brutality."

That explained it. They were all grateful to Karn. He would no doubt like having Saxons grateful to him. "Your people are certainly trusting," Britta muttered as she pushed the tendrils of hair behind her ears, "to accept a stranger thus."

"He has good ideas," Walther said quietly. "I hope he will settle here and take a wife. We could learn from him. We could use his skill in fighting, too."

Britta could hardly concentrate after the phrase "Take a wife." Was a Viking likely to take a wife? She said slowly, "That one who stitched him looks a likely sort of wife."

Walther nodded. "My Hild. She could do worse."

Britta turned to the bed box, shutting off the conversation. She had no desire to hear more of the smith's plans for his daughter. For Karn.

When Walther had gone, though, she had no refuge from her thoughts and the churning in her stomach. She tried to braid her hair, but soon she began against her will to sob. Nothing was what she had planned. Magic was terrifying and evil. She was sore afraid she would lose her soul to it, tempted to use it and powerless to stop its horrible effect on her. Lord Jesu, let me not end like Wydda, she prayed. It would be best if she could take away temptation entirely. But how? Fenris nuzzled her to comfort her. "Oh, only friend," she whispered. "What am I to do?"

And then there were the disturbing feelings drenching her when she saw Karn today. They had surprised her, and yet were not a surprise. They had left her vulnerable to yet another disappointment. She tried not to think about it, but all she could feel was empty and forlorn.

Chapter Fourteen

Karn sat before the fire in the common as the afternoon waned, cleaning Walther's wonderful sword with a cloth. It would rain tonight. The Saxons were off burying Egbert and Cedric, but Karn's thoughts were filled with Britta. He'd been so overcome with joy to see her that words had failed him. But she was cold, sneering.

He knew why. She had found her magic. Now she had no room for kindness to a Viking. The marvel was that she had ever had kindness for him. Why had she healed him? He had never been certain. Now, strong with her magic, she must realize that she did not need an unmanned cripple. But he needed her.

She had been on his mind, through all those hours of loneliness on the flats. He could not remember a woman that had ever before possessed his mind like that, though he had oft possessed their bodies.

He shook himself. Britta made it clear that she would lose what was most precious to her if she gave herself to a man. With some wonder he realized that knowing how she felt, he would never think of taking her against her will. As though she were a Danish woman. And why not? Britta was worth five of any Danish women he knew.

He found himself studying the sky, its clouds that bunched and raced, thinking about the good soil, ruined. There was plenty here, if one could wrest it from the water. He had thought it a wasteland at first, but it was a good land. It was Britta's.

Wrest it from the water?—What this land needed was a dike to keep out the sluggish backwaters of the rivers that made the swamp—like that dike in Denmark. With a dike, he could have land here. The thought should have thrilled him—Thor knew that once he had wanted land of his own—but suddenly that alone wasn't good enough anymore.

"That sword was not so shiny straight from the fire." Walther's voice made Karn start.

He realized that he still wiped the blade long after it was clean. The steel gleamed in the wan afternoon light. Karn offered it to the smith. *"Thonc to thu,"* he growled. "It is a fine sword."

Walther shook his head. "You keep it," he said briskly. "It belongs in the hand of one who can use it as you used it today. You were one with the blade. I could see it."

Karn wavered. A man who owned a weapon like this was truly a master of his fate. "No," he managed. "This is too great a gift."

Walther chuckled. "A gift to us, too. We put the sword in the hands of the man who can best use it."

Slowly Karn laid the weapon in his lap. "I am not strong enough." He knew Walther had seen his scars. He had seen the battle, too. Karn had been no match for Cedric physically.

"You will grow stronger. The sword will wait. Use it to our gain."

This was a different bargain. They expected him to protect them. Did they not know his victory today belonged to the gods? He was half a man, not worthy of this weapon. And yet..."I am no Fafnir, to guard the world. I will leave when I must."

217

Walther shrugged. "Give it back when you go."

Karn caressed the ornately carved hilt. She was a temptress, this sword. He nodded in agreement, knowing that he could not hold up his end. But perhaps when he had his saddle…

Walther looked slyly at Karn. "Do not return to the old village, Karn. Leave your solitude. Perhaps you will even take a wife and settle down."

Karn shrugged. Once that might have seemed good, but now a dry dissatisfaction blew through him and turned the thought of settling here, in Britta's land, to dust.

Britta must have slept, for she woke to darkness. Voices echoed somewhere. Her stomach demanded food. Wearily, she pushed up from the strange bed box and ventured out into the night. She had nothing to trade. She would have to throw herself on the mercy of Stowa. Several of the huts had cook fires in them. Women ferried bowls to the large central hall, where firelight spilled out into the night through an open door. Male voices chorused in laughter inside. As Britta hesitated in the common area, one of the women spied her.

"I am Ethel," the woman announced as she swerved to where Britta stood.

Britta nodded. "My name is Britta. I have naught to trade for food—"

Ethel shook her head. "Karn says we are to provide for you. Come with me."

Britta swallowed her amazement. Karn would not be giving orders if they knew he was a Viking. How like him to order them about. He should try to order her about! Her flash of anger died almost as soon as it was born. He provided for her as she had once provided for him. She wasn't sure she liked to have their situations reversed.

A mist had settled on the village. The women talked about Karn as they moved about their cook fires. They retold the story of the battle. In the corner of the hut she ate her fare in silence. There were dried peas and dried blackberries, fish

and roasted fowl. The village had produced a feast in cele-
bration of Karn's victory. When she could stand no more
talk of him, she wandered into the night with a bowl of
sweetened oats. Before she returned to the hut she decided
to find Fenris. She knew where he would be.

Cautiously she peered into the hall. Men sat on the
benches, voices raised in excited conversation. Women
moved quietly among them or sat in the shadows. Karn had
the place of honor near the firebox and Fenris, tongue lolling,
lay at his feet.

"Snurri claims this 'law' is not set by the thegn," one of
the men was saying.

Karn nodded. "All can say the law. Each consents to be
bound by it."

"Aye, until the judgment goes against him." There were
chuckles around the circle.

Karn nodded. "But then it is too late," he cautioned.

His language had improved since she had seen him last,
Britta thought. Only Fenris saw her step into a darkened
corner, and he got up to come to her side. She stroked his
head even as she called him "little traitor." As she settled
herself, the group asked Karn question after question about
how his people lived. With a start she realized that they were
asking his advice.

"But who decides what work is undertaken?" one asked.
"The elders that you spoke of?"

Karn shook his head and tried again. "You do. When most
agree, that is the way."

"We could not do it," another they called Frith announced
fearfully.

"You do it now," Karn said. "Each speaks. The elders
speak, too, and if you choose your elders well, their words
are powerful. In the end, one asks each in turn what they
would do."

"Does everyone agree?" Walther asked, incredulous.

Karn chuckled. "No. But everyone agrees that what most
want, all will do."

"And if they do not?"

"They leave the village," Karn said simply.

"I begin to see this thing." Walther rubbed his beard.

"You are an elder born." Karn smiled only with his eyes, as Britta had seen him do so many times. No, she thought, suddenly. Walther is not an elder born. But you are.

Then it was Karn's turn to ask a question. "Do you not farm here? The land is rich."

"What is land today is water tomorrow," Frith explained. "Farming is not our way."

"Peat is a farmer's friend. You have much peat," Karn said. "Can you build a...dike?"

"There is an old dike, not far from here," Walther said. "It was built by the men from the south who ruled and left so long ago that none remember. But it was breached. The water has its way with us. That is the 'law' of the fens."

Karn nodded. But he looked thoughtful.

Britta watched Hild move around the room until she came to Karn and filled his drinking horn. She saw with an ache the soft smile the blonde reserved for him.

With the new round of mead, the singing began. They took turns completing sections of the story, since they had no scald. They sang of Eider and the Rhinemaidens from the time before the people came to the great island. When the song came round to Karn he held up his hands and shook his head, and it passed by him. But when it was done, Walther gestured to Karn.

"Sing one in your own language," Walther offered. Karn seemed to consider. Don't, thought Britta. If they know you are Viking, they will slay you. But to her dismay, he took another long gulp of mead and began to sing in a rumbling bass. Britta could pick out names of gods and some of the Danish words she had heard Karn use, "thing" and "skirt" and "skill," "knife" and "folk," others. She looked anxiously around to see if any of the villagers recognized the language. Apparently not. Who this far inland had heard the language of the Vikings? So it was not the sense of the words, but the power and expression of the song that held them. The thrill of a battle and the wonder at the gifts given by the gods to the victors came through. It was not a long saga. He knew it could not hold them long, but when it was done the men raised their horns and shouted. Britta felt her eyes fill. She must stay to see no more of this. Stumbling to her feet, she groped her way to the door. She had best leave the warmth of the hall and get to her bed box, cold as that was like to be.

The frosty mist and darkness seeped into her as she stumbled blindly toward the hut allotted to her—no magic to transform her, no island to protect her, no comforting isolation from caring anymore. Why had she ever opened herself to such pain? She cursed the day she had seen the Viking ships in her cove. From that moment all her hard-won peace was shattered.

"Britta," came a deep rumble from behind her. She should have stopped and turned. Instead, she ran to the hut looming ahead of her in the fog and threw herself onto the bed box.

"Britta." The voice was soft. She turned to see his form filling the doorway. The last embers from the firebox gave his features a warmth that warred with the bleak ice in her heart. "What hurts you, Britta?"

"Go back to your new friends," she snapped. That would keep him away.

He hesitated, then limped inside. Don't come nearer, she thought, but she didn't trust herself to say it. He threw more peat on the fire until it blazed up. Then, to her horror, he sat next to her. She pushed herself into a corner, hugging her knees to her breasts.

"Your magic does not give you happiness, Britta?" he asked.

How dare he be so gentle? Her eyes filled. And he, he moved in and gathered her into his arms, even though she shook her head at him.

"Tell me," he said and held her against his body. She tried to pull away, but she ended in putting her arms about his neck and wetting his jerkin with tears. Sobs took her. He stroked her hair and rocked her as though she were a babe.

She could not help but take comfort in the smell of him, the hardness of his arm under rough flax, and the muscles of his chest under leather.

"Tell me?" he asked when she had begun to breathe again.

"It is evil," she said brokenly. "The witch was evil. The magic sucks you dry when you use it. And the feeling when it comes is so wonderful that you want it desperately. You are tempted always to use it and so it sucks the life from you. That's what it did to Wydda. She tried to steal my body because hers was old before its time, and I pushed her out and left her to die. And I know I'll be tempted to use it. I had a vision where I healed a king. So I *must* use it. But I don't want that, not anymore." She looked up at him.

A sad softness crept into his eyes. His words came with difficulty. "We do not choose our path always. If you had a vision—"

"No! I won't believe we have no choice." The walls of the hut seemed to close in on her.

"When the Norns weave your fate, the gods choose for you."

"I want life to be simple, Karn." She drank in his features in the flickering light.

He nodded. "I, too."

She hesitated. What did he mean by simple? She blurted what had been in her thoughts since the moment she saw him today. "Will you take Hild to wife?"

He raised his brows and settled her more comfortably in his arms. "That child? No."

Of course, he was a Viking. Britta swallowed hard. Vikings did not think of wiving. That didn't mean he wouldn't have Hild. Vikings took their pleasure where they chose. The feel of his hand stroking her shoulders was almost like pain, but not.

He stopped abruptly, almost jerked his hand away.

A familiar feeling started somewhere in her loins. It was like the time at the beach. Britta blinked. A wonderful answer to her dilemma occurred to her. She wondered she had not thought of it before. She had need of putting magic out of her reach forever. He was a Viking, who did what Vikings did, and did not think of wiving. She breathed slowly, so that she wouldn't gasp with the simplicity of it.

Could he do it? He couldn't that day at the beach. But then he had been exhausted and sick. He was better now. Still, if he doubted himself...*Would,* he do it, with Hild fresh in his mind? She could only depend upon his Viking nature. She was at hand and Hild was not. And what of her? Her own doubts swirled about her. Would it be a violation, bringing nightmares of Offa? Would Karn force her as he had tried to do at the beach? Could she bear it, just to be rid of the dreadful power that put her very soul in danger? Other women seemed to bear it pretty well. She had heard them joke and laugh about bedding their men, as though they wanted it. At the least, if she needed to be rid of magic, who better to help her than a friend? Karn was that. Other than Fenris, perhaps her only friend.

She looked up at his face and saw confusion in his eyes. It surprised her to realize that she had been thinking of him, longing to be with him, for weeks. It had started even on Deofric. She saw the world in terms of Karn, wanting to know what he would think, wanting to share her thoughts with him. Was there a chance that lying with this man would not be what she most feared? In her dream on Deofric touching him had made her wet between her thighs, and it had seemed very right. And on the beach, had she not wanted him to take her before her fear overcame all? The thrill of fear tickling at her mind had a companion curiosity. Her gaze moved over his face, drinking in the familiar hard planes, the soft lips. She wanted to make love tonight to Karn for many reasons. Afterwards, he could go back to Hild. She pushed the stab of pain aside. She would have had what she required of him.

Required. Something in her body began to require, as it had on the beach.

Karn's eyes glowed with the intensity she'd felt in him from the first moment she saw him. "Britta," he protested as she reached to his cheek. He flinched as her fingertips traced the outline of his beard. She turned her head up to kiss the pulse of his blood in his throat, softly.

"Britta," he breathed. "You know not what you begin."

"I know." She ran her hand beneath his jerkin and felt his nipple harden under his shirt.

"Your magic…" It was a plea, a protest.

"I toss it to the wind," she whispered, "gladly. It is not for me."

"I should not believe you," he said. But his arms enfolded her in a crushing embrace and he kissed her upturned mouth with a fierceness that did not frighten, but enflamed her.

That feeling of being lost in the physical engulfed her. She did not need to explore his loins to know they would be hard and needy. He touched her breast softly in contrast to his fierce embrace, and she felt her own nipple harden under his thumb. The memory of Offa and his men wafted up out of the past. She felt a contraction start in her belly somewhere. "I want this," she told herself silently. "I want this, and Offa will not rob me of it." She opened her mouth deliberately to Karn's and touched his tongue with her own. So intimate. But not as intimate as her hands had once been with the flesh of him. She would take back from Offa one more thing that he had stolen from her. This was not Offa, but Karn, whom she had known forever, touched forever, wanted forever. She pressed her breasts against him, felt him tighten his grip on her arms. She would once have called his passion barbaric.

His hands moved over her body as he explored her mouth. She should tell him how much she wanted this, wanted him, but she had no breath. Thought melted into immediate sensation. He, in his turn, pressed her lips apart and searched her mouth with his tongue. It was not a violation. It was done sweetly, tenderly, as though he cared for more than just their need.

But then he startled her by pulling back. She reached for him, but the look of doubt in his eyes kept her from touching him. "I do not know if I…" His voice drained away.

She shook her head to hush him, her hands trembling just

inches from his shoulders. "No ghosts for either of us. Let us have only you and me here tonight, Karn."

Doubt turned to pain. He wrenched his head away. "I am not the man you need."

She had to stop the cycle, starting here, or they would end as they had at the beach. She gripped his shoulders. "Look at me."

He pressed his fine, full lips together and brought his head around, his eyes darting over her face. "It is me, only me," she said simply. "And there is all the time in the world." She managed a smile, though it felt tentative; then her glance failed and she stared at her hands on his shoulders. She was trying to reassure him when she wasn't sure herself. But she couldn't let courage fail either of them now. She ran her hands down his arms to take his hands. In the firelight her fingertips moved lightly over his palms. She took one hand and lifted it to her lips, kissing the lines that some said held his fate. Her eyes were only for his hand. Her tongue caressed the calluses, up the fingers. She sucked gently at his forefinger and raised her eyes to his. Her patience was rewarded by a smoldering look. He shook his head, but at the same time he took his finger from her mouth and ran his hand around her neck as he leaned close. She kissed his cheek, his beard, his earlobe, felt his hand on her neck tighten, his lips begin to demand her mouth. Yes, she thought. *Yes.*

As he pulled back, she smiled up at him, and this time the smile was strong. She could see it echo in his eyes. She pulled the shirt from his breeches and over his head. He loosed the brooch that held her cloak. His fingers worked at her girdle, while she touched the scars on his shoulder in the firelight. She traced the vessel that fed the muscle of his biceps, the ligament that bound his shoulder. She had stitched them together once. Now there was skin so soft, so smooth....

Then he had her naked in the firelight. She straddled the rough leather of his breeches and felt the hardness in his loins. Yes, she wanted to shout. She was impatient for his nakedness. She knew his body perhaps better than he did himself. Her hands moved over the ridged muscles of his back, as he held her buttocks with both hands and drank her in with his eyes. She touched his throat where his lifeblood beat, ran her fingers over the planes of his chest, crinkly with their dusting of hair. Her face buried in his neck, she kissed his satin skin. His scent would haunt her all her days. His groan vibrated in his chest. It was not one of pain. She smiled.

Sitting up, she pulled the leather strips from her braids as his hands explored her ribs, cupped her breasts, touched her nipples. She shook out her hair. It floated about her head in wavy red clouds the color of the fire. She could see the one streak of white smoke. Fire without, fire within, she thought, and turned the focus of her hands back to Karn.

Suddenly he stiffened. He gripped her shoulders and his eyes grew truly fierce.

"Is this Danegeld, Britta?" She didn't understand. He almost shook her. "Do you give your body as the price to make the magic go away? Would any man do for you tonight?"

Pain crumpled her face for an instant. That was part of it. But telling that would hurt him. And it was not the whole truth. "I have wanted this for a long time." That, at least, was true.

As though he was released, he rolled her to her back and pressed her into the furs with his body. Her fingers plucked at the tie of his breeches and he discarded them. She saw that he had no need to worry now that he would not be fully a man. Still she didn't find his most male parts frightening. She was only glad he wanted her, she thought, as thought became harder for her. He pressed against her. Not Hild, not any of the other thousand women he'd had. He wanted her. She ran her hands over his buttocks, the hard muscles of his thighs, pulling him in that she might feel him along all of her body.

To part her knees was natural. She thought she knew what would happen next, but instead he rolled over to lie beside her. He cradled her head and kissed her while he stroked her inner thighs. She shivered. The longing was so intense, it seemed almost like pain, an aching in her loins only Karn could stop. He bent and laved one nipple with his tongue, absorbing all her attention, so that his touch on her most female parts surprised her.

"Let me show you what the Frankish women taught me," he whispered.

She should have been jealous, but there was no time for that. A flash of pleasure jolted her senses down to one very concentrated point of light. He touched her in ways that she could not have imagined possible, until she arched into his kisses and moaned into his mouth. Only then did he lie between her legs. She spread them eagerly and he filled her, slowly, inch by inch. She gasped. This was what she wanted. How had she denied it for so long? As he moved within her, she thought she would melt. Instead, she pressed against him, point and counterpoint, faster as he moved faster, panting, wanting, until that was all she had room for: want.

The moment, when it came, was a revelation. Her cries were echoed shortly by Karn's groan as he arched above, pulsing within her. Slowly she subsided into soft yips of pleasure. Karn lowered himself to one side carefully and examined her face with concern.

"I have been wrong," she said softly, hardly able to muster her thoughts. His beard was rough on her fingertips. "My fear robbed me of this pleasure all these years."

Karn smiled. "And mine nearly robbed us of tonight."

"But we were not robbed, by anyone." She grinned, feeling more whole than she could say. "I liked that."

He fondled her breast. "Ah, but wait until I show you what the Saracen women know…."

"You will kill me." She chuckled, oddly lighthearted. "When can we start?"

"Not for a moment, I fear." But he didn't fear, not anymore. She could see it in his eyes.

"Then tell me, if I must wait, who are these Saracen women?" she asked in mock jealousy.

"They live to the south, where skies are hot. They follow the one God of Islam." He rolled onto his back and she nestled against his scarred shoulder.

"You have been far," she mused. "I thought that Vikings only raped and pillaged. How is it you took time to learn from women?"

He looked uneasy. "I learned many things, not just love."

"I want to know about love."

"A man should not speak of such things with a woman."

"He may do them but not speak of them, is that it?" she asked, concealing her smile.

"You know my meaning, Britta. But I see I will have no peace unless I talk to you of other women." He settled her better against him. "If you will know, it is sometimes not so pleasing to a man to couple where there is no joy for both."

"I'll wager those dark-eyed Saracens found coupling with you pleasant, Viking. If their bodies were not freely given, they would not have taught you their ways of love."

"How did you know they were dark-eyed?"

"Did you not say their sun was hot? Travelers from hot lands have dark eyes and olive skin," she chided. She cared not a whit for the women in his past, but the women who might still be in his future nagged at her. She forced a laugh and shook her head. It was then that she saw Fenris. The dog looked at them seriously, head cocked. "Don't worry that I groan," she assured him. "I know you have done the same as we have done this night, many times."

"Does he have a bitch dog?"

"He is like you," she chided. "He has them everywhere. He had many in Dunford, and I saw him only this afternoon, sniffing after one in Stowa."

"He is not like me now, then," Karn said, and moved a stray lock of hair off her forehead.

Britta hesitated. She dared not ask him what he meant. "Until you need Hild to sew your shoulder," she mocked, and turned her head away.

He raised himself on his elbow and pulled her toward him fiercely. "Is that what you think? he growled, his eyes blazing. "You think a Viking does not know the path to loyalty?"

She must be careful here. "I know a Viking has seen many women, many things. I know he craves adventure and glory. There is no glory in Stowa. There are no Saracen women here."

His grip on her slackened. "There is no law that a Dane goes always Viking."

"Isn't that what you want?" she whispered. It took all her courage.

A look of pain came across his face. His eyes went somewhere far away. He took a breath. "I want to feel whole."

She nodded and smoothed his brow with one finger. "You felt whole to me tonight."

His eyes returned. She saw them smile as he bent his lips to hers and brushed them lightly. Then he gripped her again and pressed his mouth to hers, searching for something.

Her hands moved over his back. It might be time to find out what the Saracen women knew.

Chapter Fifteen

Britta woke in the hazy light of morning, lying in the crook of Karn's arm. The scent of him, of what they had done together, filled her senses. The air outside was winter cold, but under the furs it was warm. She never wanted to move again. But as sleep fled her mind, she began to take stock. The magic was gone. She had seen to that last night. She had no regrets. But what now?

Karn's face above her was relaxed in sleep, his long, light lashes brushing his cheeks. He looked remote, as sleepers did. She was afraid to wake him. Perhaps the distance would linger in his eyes. After all, he was a Viking. What mattered bedding a woman to him?

It mattered to her though. And Britta realized that it might matter to her more than she had ever imagined. She had lost everything by it, and realized what there was to gain. Her own carefully cultivated defenses were completely gone. She was open and vulnerable to the world because she wanted this Viking. It wasn't just the alchemy of the body that he had shown her last night, though that was magical enough. He had shown her that what made him man could meld with what made her woman and form something new entire.

Dangerous ground, Britta, she told herself sternly. But it was too late to turn back. She was adrift in uncertain footing just like the fenland.

She saw him fluttering to wakefulness and wanted to ease him back to sleep. Too late. He fixed her with his azure eyes, lazy now with sleepiness, and smiled. Those full lips that belied the hard planes of his face curved up sensuously. She let a smile free, but it was tremulous. She must not let him see that she had been his, body and soul, last night. That was yet too perilous. He gathered her into his side and she sighed in contentment before she could stop.

"Good morning," he rumbled in her ear. One hand crossed to stroke her waist and hip.

She looked up at him, not knowing what to say.

His finger ruffled her lashes. *"Groenneygr,"* he whispered.

"Green-eyed?" she asked, startled.

He only nodded, smiling with his eyes and touched her hair, *"Raudhaerdth."* She looked askance at him. He ran his finger over her nose and cheeks. *"Freknottr."*

"Are you talking about my freckles?" she asked, half-outraged.

The smile that accompanied the nod touched his lips now. "It is not time that you learned Danish words, too, Britta?"

She was taken aback. Then she nodded. She owed that to him. It seemed that Danish words were not so different. Yet it had always been he who had to ask for words. Learning Danish would be another sign that she had given up the sureness of her isolation.

Suddenly she wasn't certain she had courage enough to do it. She rose to her elbow self-consciously. "The others will be breaking their fast."

He pulled her back to warmth. "Let them." Cupping her breast, he kissed her hair. All on its own, her hand stole across his belly. She encountered there the evidence of his awakening.

"There is another fast that we can break," he murmured.

She had to chuckle, realizing he had every intent of distracting her from her fear, and that he knew the one sure way to do it. "You Vikings are insatiable. I might have known."

"Are you sore, Britta?" he asked. "I wanted that your first time was only pleasure."

He meant her first time after Offa. "I don't think I could have stood any more pleasure," she reassured him. He had turned into Karn—delightfully Karn and not a Viking—sometime since he woke. "And no, I am not sore."

"Good," he whispered and stroked her hip. She felt the juices rise in her. She was potent and strong. She could afford to learn some Danish. They turned to each other at the same moment. She lifted her chin to find those miraculous lips. Who knew how long this would last? She would take whatever time he would give.

Karn sat on Thorn's back and steadied the great dark horse's nervous sidling. "Skittish, are you?" He patted the glossy neck. The air was cold, the clouds racing in the sky, but the winter would soon sheathe its fangs. Even now the snow was wetter, the mud returning. The land could imagine spring again. It was not enough time.

He pushed Thorn forward with his calves and thrust his feet down into the leather slings. Through painful trials he had learned that by pushing his heels down, he had the best chance of staying in the saddle.

Karn leaned to swing his heavy hawthorn stick at a bush pushing its way up through the bleak white soil, but he leaned too far and was forced to tug at the reins to right himself. Thorn went up on his haunches, and Karn, as in an oft-repeated dream, slowly tumbled off. Thorn neighed in protest. Karn let go of the reins as he landed with a grunt. How could muddy lime be so hard?

He got his breath and staggered up. Loki at work! Thorn shook his head accusingly some twenty feet away. The straps were a fine idea, Karn knew. His weakness made him fail. He trudged over to his horse and gathered up the reins.

"Once more, my friend," he whispered. "You are my only chance, Britta's, too." He pushed himself into the saddle again. "We will be man-animal, like a berserker, only always."

Spring would bring the Danir, looking for Edmund. He dared not think what would happen if Britta was still in Stowa when the Danir routed the Angles and raged across the land. He must take her away soon. Could he ask Britta to abandon her people? How could he not? He sighed. Before he could approach her, he must be ready. He could not go back to the Danir until he was a warrior again. Britta had given him back part of himself. The rest was up to him.

He needed to be warrior, too, to confront Ulf. He imagined the satisfaction of Walther's wonderful sword slicing into Ulf's flesh. His hand caressed its hilt, safe in its scabbard. But Ulf's face was not the one that haunted Karn's dreams. That honor was reserved for Offa. He would be banished only by vengeance—and that was not likely to happen this side of the Underworld.

Karn worked until he could no more. He and Thorn picked their way back to the village along the narrow path that was the only stable footing. He patted the horse's neck and got nodding and blowing in return. There was one nagging problem with his plan: How could he abandon Stowa when he had debts? The sword, the leather, a hut, help from all of them. His debts were many. Walther was a good man. In all the ways that counted, so were all the villagers, Saxons though they be. He had no way to repay them. His overwhelming debt to Britta he could never pay, of course. He would only spend his life trying, if she would let him.

Edmund kicked the old man's lifeless form. "This healer Offa gives me is worse than ludicrous." He felt the old hollowness return. Could no one push back the prophesy?

"You are well rid of him, my king," Delan said as he glanced at the body. "But not for his lack of talent. He has been supplying Offa with details of your most private concerns."

233

"Do not assume I am stupid, Delan. I did not discuss our plans in front of him."

Delan waited for privacy. The guards came in, stone-faced, and dragged the body toward the door. Edmund poured himself a goblet of mead and watched Delan. He was scheming again. Best let him know he'd never rule without Edmund, find a way to neutralize his ambition.

The door closed. "Offa tells of your concern for your health, my king. He makes it seem…" Edmund watched Delan search for a suitable word. "Unmanly," he finally dared.

"What?" Edmund shouted, rising. Let his anger do his work. He dashed the mead into the fireplace with a sizzle and flung the goblet away. It clattered on the wooden floor. "What matter if I seek healers? Others forget the prophecy. Is it unmanly to have a king who may not be killed in battle?" The pitch of his voice rose and he controlled it. "Mercia or Wessex cannot say as much."

Delan tried to deflect his anger. "We must deal with Offa."

Edmund smiled. Ah, here it was. Delan wanted to eliminate a rival. Fine. "Well, what's to do?"

"We cannot execute him here even on spurious charges," Delan said. "Send him on some mission, rid the camp of his plotting. Then, when he is far away…" He let the words hang.

Edmund paced thoughtfully. Did he want Offa dead? The man was trouble. But so was Delan.

"Offa's men tell of a red-haired witch with amazing powers, somewhere in the fens."

Edmund jerked around. "She has true power?" he asked eagerly, all hollowness gone.

"It is rumored that the Abbess of Ely also searches for her. She must have something."

"The witch who prophesied I could not die in battle was of the fens." Excitement rose in Edmund's gut. There was yet hope. "Could it be her after all these years? I must have her."

"And so you shall, my king. Send Offa to bring her. You kill two birds."

"You must not kill him before he finds my healer," Edmund ordered. Delan's priorities would not be his. Afterward, Offa could be sacrificed without another thought.

"No, no," Delan soothed. "If an accident befalls him on his way back here—perhaps some Viking raiders will intercept him, where no one can see—still will your healer be spared, to be found by one of your loyal guard. Offa's mission will be completed after his death. So sad."

"His thegns will be suspicious," Edmund muttered.

"With no proof that it was you and no eyes to see what really happened, they will lay their loyalty where it will do them the most good."

Edmund rubbed his hands together. "He can collect silver for Danegeld on his journey."

"The only problem," Delan said, "is to ensure that Offa will do your bidding. He might kill your healer, or he might ride to Mercia or Wessex to pour poison into the ears of the kings. He might play spoiler if he sees you have bested him."

Edmund waved Delan's concerns away. "I will see to his loyalty."

The captain looked wary. He examined his king's face for a moment too long before he spun and left the room. Edmund's heart swelled. A healer!

Britta sang as she went for water from the deep hole that served Stowa. Fenris lurked in the sedge and dashed after some small prey. "Drink, *drekka;* fish, *fiskr;* people, *folk;* fowl, *fugl;* seax, *knife;* like, *likr;* kiss, *kyssa.*" She practiced her Danish words. She could not help but smile. That smile broadened as she met Hild coming back from the river with her own heavy yoke.

How had she had ever bemoaned the loss of her solitude on Deofric? She had never felt so much that she belonged. She bent to the pool and filled the buckets on her yoke. She and Karn were welcomed in the village, for the sake of her healing and for Karn's experience. At night around the fire he taught Walther and Snurri and Frith and their wives about the law. Yes, wives as well. It seemed that in his homeland women could inherit wealth and run their own farms. They could leave property as they chose. Britta liked that part. So did the women of Stowa. It was clear that Karn could lead this village, if he cared to do it.

Fenris rustled into sight again. His prey must have escaped.

Would Karn stay? True, he could not stay away from her or she from him. He came early to the bed box where Britta waited eagerly each night, and they were often last to rise in the morning. The entire village teased them about their slothful habits. What those Saracen women knew! She was still amazed that she had found completion in this barbarian. On Deofric she had thought the dreadful word, Viking, said all she would ever need to know about him. Now she rather thought she would like to spend a lifetime finding out who he was. But a lifetime would not be granted to her. In some ways Britta dreaded Karn's returning strength. It signaled the time when he would go back to his people. When he talked about them he could not keep the longing from his voice. So Britta didn't think about lifetimes. She tried to think about todays. She whistled for Fenris and turned back to the village. Karn might be back from the plateau.

"Offa." Edmund welcomed him as he slapped the fork-bearded thegn across the shoulders. "Thank you for coming so quickly."

Offa frowned at the obedience implied. "What is your will, Lord?" Offa tried for civility.

"I hope you can help me." Edmund motioned him to sit at a table where a decanter of elderberry wine waited. "I must choose who leads our forces into battle against the Danes."

Offa's eyes widened before he could feign indifference.

"It is a position that will have much glory attached to it." Edmund turned and looked slyly back. "I see by your reaction that you thought it would go to Delan. Delan thinks so, too." He grew thoughtful. "You know I have no male relatives, not since my uncle died so sadly. I want to choose who will follow me, rather than have it thrust upon me."

Offa speculated furiously. Was Edmund offering him public preferment over Delan? Edmund could not abandon Delan without sacrificing the power of the guard.

The king seemed to read his thoughts. "As a matter of fact, though he has the guard, Delan will never find loyalty from the eorls and their thegns. He is, after all, a foreigner."

Offa nodded and tried to keep his face expressionless.

"Now, who to trust with this position of strength?" Edmund eyed Offa up and down.

Isn't that always the problem? Offa thought.

"So, I give you a mission. If you do my bidding, you lead the battle against the Danes."

"Delan still commands the guard." Offa wanted to do no one's bidding.

"Yes, that is a problem, is it not?" Edmund poured out two chalices of wine.

"Does Delan know your intentions?" Offa asked with some curiosity.

"He will. He's very bright, you know." The king smiled and sipped his wine.

Offa kept his face bland while he thought. The sovereign was pitting him and his captain against each other. Make both strong and they would fight for position, instead of trying to unseat their king. Yet how could he refuse the glory of leading the army? It was the prominence he coveted.

"What is this mission?" he grunted.

"There is a red-haired witch I want, a healer, somewhere in the fens."

Offa's chalice sloshed wine.

"I want you to find her and bring her to me."

Offa almost shuddered in anticipation. Edmund granted him a way to the throne if he would but do what he himself most wanted. He got up abruptly. "I shall start tomorrow morning, King."

"Good." Edmund did not mask his eagerness. "You must

go quickly. The Abbess of Ely also searches for her, no doubt to bend the girl's power to the will of the Church. *I must have her.*"

The Abbess of Ely? Offa stared at the chalice he still gripped. This healer was of the devil, not God. He could not let her pollute the Church. But he mustn't tell Edmund she was evil.

Offa turned and strode from the room, leaving his king gaping after him. He wanted not to bring the witch whole to Edmund but to destroy her evil utterly. But now she was worth more to him alive. A pretty problem. Still, that was for later. First he had to find the witch before the Abbess of Ely did.

Karn swung his oak stick in a figure of eight over Thorn's neck, sat back in his saddle and wheeled about. The trick was in the balance, not in the straps alone. Over time, he had learned to guide Thorn by shifting his weight, pressing to the outside around the turns, changing direction by looking where he wanted to go and pushing with the opposite hip. He spent less time on his back in the mud now. That was progress.

He leaned over and cut at the bush that stood in for an enemy, then righted himself and circled Thorn. A moment of triumph coursed through him. He might be a better fighter than he had ever been, so long as he did not have to dismount. Soon it would be time to return to the Danir. His bowels filled with dread at the thought of asking Britta to come with him.

Karn spun Thorn back toward Stowa along the island of lime, angry with himself for the confusion circling his belly. He dreamed of introducing his new saddle design to Ivar, and seeing respect in those old eyes. And he dreamed of introducing Britta to his father in Denmark. But the tugs that drew him away from his plan were almost physical. The land practically reached up to grab him, trying to convince him to stay, to build a dike, to take the earth away from the water and repay the village in arable land to support them as the watery fens never had. He was being torn between two futures, both of which were fraught with danger.

Karn turned Thorn's head into the brake of hawthorn and blackthorn scrub trees that pushed their roots into drier soil next to a mere about a quarter mile from the village. He could hear the ringing of Walther's hammer on iron, the happy shriek of children at their games. These were joined suddenly by a cry intended to wreak terror in the hearts of Saxons, and the thundering of hooves. It was a cry he knew only too well. Karn pulled Thorn to a halt in the trees. Shouted calls to arms in Saxon drifted out of the village and down around the Danish battle cries.

"Saxon dogs!" he heard a man bellow in the language he would have killed to hear yesterday. "Die where you stand," and "Crush them in the name of Thor."

Not here, you fools! Not now!

Karn's breast heaved as he imagined Britta's red hair bloodied. He urged Thorn on. He wasn't ready in mind or body for this. As he came out of the trees, he saw them, striding through the village toward the livestock pen. The Vikings' mounts were left to wheel and cluster at the edge of the halls. There were ten Danir, more than enough to overmatch the village. Frantically, he raked his eyes over the huts and the clearing as Thorn galloped along the narrow trail. Britta was nowhere to be seen. The village men scurried out of doorways with axes made for chopping wood, not people, and their hoes. Women grasped at children's hands and raced for the huts.

Karn drew Walther's sword. He drove Thorn in among the melee. He had to defend the horse pen. That would get the Danes' attention. Let Thorn not shy or Karn would fall and never live to mount again. Fenris yelped somewhere. Britta must be near.

"Stop," he yelled in Danish. "Stop, you fools." One Dane was about to cut down a woman in his path. Karn leaned down and slapped him with the flat of his sword, then righted himself and turned back. The man was down but not hurt. The look of shock on the Dane's face as he stumbled up to see his attacker on horseback gave Karn a grim satisfaction.

Walther came out of the smithy hut with a sword in each hand. He tossed one to Snurri, who caught it awkwardly. "Stop this!" Karn bellowed again above the screams.

"Get him!" one of the Danes shouted, pointing. It must be the leader. That was an order if he ever heard one. Karn did not have time to glance his way. He kicked out at one of the Northmen who charged at his side. The man sprawled in the mud. Karn turned back toward the pen and drove forward. The leader stood between him and the pen, his sword held low, with both hands. He meant to kill Thorn.

From the Dane spread-eagled in the mud came a single shouted word, "Karn!" But Karn's attention was riveted on the leader. It was Ulf.

Rage boiled up from his belly and formed itself into a shout. "Betrayer!" he screamed in Danish as Ulf charged forward. Recognition flowered in the man's face, bloodlust just behind it. Karn jerked Thorn to the side and pressed forward. The horse surged past Ulf, who wheeled and swung. Karn deflected the blow with his sword.

"Karn! It's Karn!" he heard someone yell. Metal clanged as Snurri and Walther defended themselves. Karn rode down a man who had Hild by the hair. She went down with him, then scrambled up and started toward the fens. Karn wheeled back to Ulf.

His foe staggered forward through the mud, intent on Karn. But two Danir came up from behind to stay his sword arm. Karn recognized his friends, Jael and Bjorn the Bear-Hearted.

"It is Karn, you fool," Jael cried.

"Karn!" Bjorn stood just outside the reach of his sword. "We thought you were dead."

Karn glared at Ulf, his sight veiled by the red of his anger. Slowly his vision cleared. The clank of swords died away as all stopped in wonderment that here among the Saxons was a Viking. There was no sign that he was Dane. Indeed, he looked remarkably Saxon.

I am not fighting for them, Karn wanted to shout. But wasn't that just what he was doing? The Saxons wondered why they had never realized what he was, as they heard their strange friend address their assailants in their own language.

It was Karn who broke the silence. He still stared at Ulf. "Find your horses elsewhere," he said in Norse. Without taking his eyes from Ulf, he said in Saxon, "Put down your weapons. They will not harm you if you yield."

"What, take orders from one of them?" Karn recognized Snurri's Saxon tongue.

"You and I must settle," Karn said to Ulf through gritted teeth, "for your treachery."

"If there is treachery, it comes from one who fights against his own," Ulf sneered. "Perhaps we should cut you down, along with your new kind."

"If there is to be a settlement," Jael said, "let it be before Ivar." Karn saw him glance at the others. Karn backed Thorn around to stand with his tail almost pressed against the main hall. Swords were fingered on both sides, but no one could decide who would fight whom.

"What say you, Kara?" Walther called. "Do you join your fellows against us?"

"Be still and you may come out with all your limbs," Karn growled.

"He sides with our enemies. Let him share their fate." Ulf hefted his sword.

Thorn stamped and nodded nervously. Karn looked in challenge at Ulf and felt the smallest smile spill over his lips. "One to one?" he asked, knowing he was no match for Ulf once he dismounted. It didn't matter. He would die seeking vengeance.

"A traitor's blood would make a fine drink for my sword," Ulf barked and dropped into a fighting crouch, but he looked uneasy at the prospect of hand-to-hand combat with Karn. He did not yet know his advantage. "Still, a traitor does not deserve to die in honorable combat." He looked around for support. He found it in some eyes. "Ask him where his brave brothers are," Ulf called. "Betrayed them to the Saxons, by

Thor." The Danir shifted uneasily from foot to foot.

Karn was goaded beyond endurance. "Betrayed into odds we could not best by you, Ulf," he shouted. "You scouted the coast. You knew that Saxon fort was upriver from the church."

"And how is it that you live," Ulf taunted, "if the odds were so great?"

Karn felt the eyes around the circle turn to him. "I was not honored with death," he mumbled. He wished he sounded bold, defiant.

"So we find you living happily among those who killed your fellows, leagues from the site of your battle?"

"Tell us, Karn," Jael urged. "Tell how it came to be, that we may silence this jackal."

Karn despised the fact that he must defend himself from Ulf's untruths. Yet how else could it seem to his friends, finding him among the Saxons? Them, at least, he owed some explanation. "A woman found me," he growled. "She brought me inland while I healed." He did not say that, even though he had healed enough to live, he had not healed enough to fight again.

"Why did you not fight your way back to the coast?" Ulf jeered.

It was at that moment that Britta ran into the village. She did not hesitate, but came to stand by Thorn's side, just touching Karn's knee. She did not look at the Saxons. She did not say a word. She just arranged herself with Karn against whatever enemies would come.

"Ah, I see," Ulf sneered. Karn saw Jael and Bjorn look at each other. "You betrayed your men for a she-bitch Saxon." Ulf raised his sword. "We should fall on you and draw your entrails out for all to see." He did not seem eager to move without the others, though.

"Let Ivar and Halfdan decide the truth of the matter," Jael called out.

"Aye," Bjorn added. "We have enough horses. Let us return to camp."

Karn could feel the nods as much as see them. Ulf looked

nervous; then he nodded brusquely. "I agree. If this traitor can tear himself from his new people, let him come. If not, we fall on him where he stands and kill him—kill them all."

Karn was thinking fast. He must get the Danir out of the village and away from Britta. He had seen himself taking her back to the Viking camp on his own. He had not bargained for them finding him here, with all the traitorous implications. If he was ever to gain acceptance by his fellows for himself and for Britta, he must have Ivar's confidence. He thought he knew a way to prove to Ivar what Ulf had done. That, and the new kind of saddle he brought might gain him acceptance, in spite of the fact that he was haltr. But Britta must be kept safe from Ulf's revenge.

"The Saxons are spared," he said. "I owe them." He could feel Britta's questions.

"Since you beg for them, they keep their lives, but not their horses," Ulf sneered. Several Danir moved toward the pen where the village's four horses circled nervously.

Walther hefted his sword. "Don't," Karn said in Saxon, resignation in his voice. "You have your women and your lives. Your horses are forfeit."

Under the resentful eyes of the Saxon men and the wailing of their women, the Danir broke into two uneasy groups, those who clustered about Karn and those who went to Ulf. Norse filled the air, but it had a fractious undertone. Thurmak added the horses to one of his strings.

"I must go with them, Britta," Karn murmured. "If I fight him here and lose, he will kill the entire village."

"Then let him go," she said, looking up, her green eyes desperate. "Do not fight at all."

"He will force a fight. He must kill me, since I know his lies. And I must kill him for his betrayal." He could not bring himself to tell her of his hope to be accepted once again, to take her with him to live among his people. "I return in a week, no more." He touched her hand on his knee, then clasped it strongly. "I must do this, Britta."

She looked betrayed and then resigned.

"A week," he said again and wheeled Thorn to join the

Danir as they trailed out of the village with their strings of horses. He did not look back at Walther and the other Saxons he had saved this day from death. He did not belong to them. He dared not look back at Britta. His own people thought him traitor; he did not belong to the Danir either. But he had hope.

Ulf's contingent and Karn's faction rode back toward Ivar's camp. Ulf and the six who followed him rode out in front, leaving Karn and his friends to bring up the rear. Several in each group led strings of horses—perhaps five or six in each. Karn should have felt jubilant, but he felt only uneasy, even with his friends.

"The way you wheeled among us," Jael said, excited. "I never thought a horse could be such an advantage in battle." They took the path that Karn and Britta had traveled so long ago.

"How did you stay on?" Bjorn asked.

"These straps." Karn pointed to the loops hanging from his saddle. "We all can do it."

"We would need to protect the horse from swords and spears," Jael observed.

"I thought of that," Karn agreed. "Chain mail, just like a man, I think."

The others nodded. Karn began to dread the time when they dismounted for the evening. Then all would know his weakness. He remembered the derision heaped upon a man in his village who'd had his hamstring cut in battle when all thought he should have died. Karn himself had joined in the fun. Oh, he knew how they would react to a haltr. He had reacted so himself.

Forcibly, he turned his thoughts away. "How is it Ulf leads your party?" he asked.

Jael hesitated. "He is Ivar's favorite, Karn. He is trusted."

"I think he positions himself to succeed Ivar," Thurmak grumbled.

"He was successful, once I was gone," Karn said bitterly. Still, he had hope. He had been thinking about Ulf's treachery for months. "To know of that Saxon fortress, Ulf must have gone ashore. But not alone. Four or five others know about the Saxon fort. I will seek them out. They can prove Ulf's treachery." He couldn't change the fact that he had lived when his men had died. He couldn't change his limp. Yet with Ulf dishonored, and when Ivar and Halfdan understood what horses could do for them in battle, it was just possible they might accept Karn, haltr or no.

Jael said quietly. "I am there before you, Karn. I sought them out in Cent, when you did not return. They all stood by Ulf. But of course they would—they were his chosen few."

"We shall see if they still want to lie after I have talked to them," Karn growled.

"You will have to seek them in Valhalla," Jael returned. "All but one are dead in Cent or at the Saxon fort by the shore."

"You captured the fortress where the island was?" Karn could feel his face flush with...with what? Rage? Shame? The need for revenge?

"Most had gone to support Edmund." Thurmak jerked the rope that pointed the horses.

Karn let out his breath. Offa had not been there. There was still a chance, however slight, that the theyn could die at his hands. "Where is the one of Ulf's party who lives?"

Jael pointed ahead to a man younger than Karn, a hulking mass of muscle. Just who Karn would have expected Ulf to take on as acolyte. "Erik Eriksson."

Karn's blood quickened in his veins. He set his teeth grimly. "I shall speak to him."

Jael nodded. "We will speak to him together."

Bjorn waited impatiently through this exchange. He seemed to be bursting with questions of his own. "What I want to know, Karn, is how you survived among these vile Saxon dogs."

Karn felt uneasy answering questions about "vile Saxon dogs." "No Danir had been so far inland. They did not know me for Dane. I remembered a little Saxon from the slaves in my father's house. The woman who healed me taught me more."

"This woman, she was Saxon?" Thurmak asked, incredulous.

Karn nodded. It did seem incredible that Britta should have saved him.

"Ah, she could not resist that strong Danish pillar." Bjorn laughed. "Even wounded, Karn exerts his power over women. Was she sweet as she writhed under you, my friend?"

Karn did not answer. He could never explain that it was not like that with Britta. The others took his silence for modesty and laughed again.

"It must have been bad, exiled alone among your enemies," Jael finally said.

Karn said only, "I thought I might never see you three again, that is sure."

"Are they slaves to their priests?" Thurmak asked.

"Do they eat their children?" Bjorn added.

"They are men," Karn replied simply. "They struggle for a living. They look to have their daughters marry well. They want fair treatment from their lords." He paused. "They want what men want." He had not answered one question that must be in their minds. It was a question he could not avoid. Why had he fought for them?

After a long pause he said, "I owed them. They took me in, gave me a sword." The Danir would understand that. A man owed for a sword. "They gave me leather for my saddle, and leather is precious in the fens." Karn forced himself to look at their faces, so he would know if they understood. Jael did. Thurmak looked thoughtful. Bjorn the Bear-hearted shook his head.

"Still, it must have been horrible," he muttered.

Karn said nothing. It had not been all horrible, not in Stowa anyway, not with Britta.

Jael looked at Karn with speculation in his eyes.

"And this swamp!" Thurmak gestured to the fens. "It is like the end of the world."

Karn nodded. "But the soil is the richest I have seen."

"All I want is rich land of my own," Jael sighed. "And here it is wasted by water."

"After we have crushed these Saxons, those of us who want to stay will take what land we want," Thurmak reminded them. "We will find land as rich as this, and not fouled by water."

"And fight every day of our lives to keep it," Jael muttered. "I just want to farm in peace, when my days going viking are over. Maybe feel a Saxon wife writhe under me in pleasure." He smiled slyly at Karn. "Maybe that one with the blond braids in that village you defended, Karn."

Bjorn snorted. "Our older brothers got the only peaceful land at home in Denmark. Our only way to land is the ship and the sword, to fight the barbarians to keep it."

"I think there is another way," Karn offered cautiously. "If we built dikes to take the land from the water, the Saxons would not begrudge us what was never theirs." He drew blank stares. His friends thought Loki had claimed him. He rushed on. "Building a dike needs strong backs only, and we have those. For our work we gain rich land and peace to farm it."

"Building a dike is complicated," Thurmak protested.

"Then Karn is your man," Jael laughed. "Remember, it was he who organized the supply lines and directed the digging of the trenches for the siege at Rouen."

"Saxons will share whert we have killed every one, and not before," Bjorn protested.

"There will be no peace if we kill their kin, that is sure," Karn said slowly. "But if we come in peace to reclaim the land and share what we reclaim, then perhaps." Suddenly what had been too wild to propose to Walther had been spoken to his Danish brothers. Spoken, it seemed possible. Jael got a faraway look. Thurmak scanned the water and the sedge that lined the path doubtfully. Bjorn began to smile.

"After we have fought by Ivar's side..." Thurmak paused.

They were all thinking the same thing. If Ivar and Halfdan

raged over the land and killed the Saxons, their hope of peaceful neighbors was gone.

"Perhaps the main force will not come so far inland," he finished lamely.

The hollowness knew no bounds. There were no tears. Britta's loss was too large for that. She sat with Fenris in the hawthorn and bracken a quarter mile or so from the village. Night was coming on and she was cold, but she couldn't bear to sit by the fires in the village and hear them berating Karn. How much better it would have been to never know him at all! She would still be on her island, alone, a mussel unopened to the world, and content to be so.

He had promised to return. She tugged at Fenris's ears absently, as Karn had used to do. She didn't believe it. He'd said so to make parting easier. But only one of two things could happen: Either that awful barbarian who led the Vikings would kill him in combat or in treachery, or his friends would defend him. She did not need her few words of Danish to see the welcoming looks, hear the way they called his name in gladness. They were his people. He would stay with them. They would paint her as a savage. They would laugh at him for wanting to return to her. He would put it off for a day, while they feasted. Then two days, so that Thorn could gain strength. Soon he would be lost to her.

She wasn't sure which was worse, to know he couldn't return or that he didn't care to.

The twilight shortened rapidly. Britta rose to go back to the village. She was startled when a small man materialized out of the brake. He was dressed in a brown robe, and his head was tonsured. Fenris barked at him, and he peered fearfully into the trees.

She stood up and grabbed Fenris's ruff. "It's all right," she called. "Fenris has appointed himself the village guardian."

The little monk's eyes grew large. He darted forward, examining her closely with nervous gestures. He must see the white streak in her hair. She put up her hand self-consciously to restrain a way ward tendril behind her ear.

The monk glanced warily about and motioned with his hand, then he approached.

"Do you seek shelter?" she asked. "You will find welcome here, I make no doubt."

The little man was still examining her. His chin receded decidedly, and his ears were over large, but he looked a kindly sort. Finally he turned to Fenris. "Is this your dog?" he asked.

Britta thought the answer self-evident. "Of course." But perhaps he thought Fenris a wolf.

The monk sighed in apparent self-satisfaction. "I have been looking for you."

"Me?" she asked, incredulous.

"I think so. Was it you who healed the baby in the village by the coast?"

Oh, dear. She didn't want it about that she was a healer. The sick and the lame would hound her everywhere. "I don't heal anymore. That is all gone," she hastened to disappoint him.

"But it was you?" he pressed. "And you who caused the storm to rage on Deofric Island?"

She nodded. "But you can't expect—"

She never got to finish her sentence; she was grabbed from behind and whirled around. A massive man, also in monk's robes, had her by the shoulders. She struggled wildly.

The little monk shouted, "Don't hurt her, Brother Ilwith," as he jumped up and down.

Fenris darted in with snapping jaws. The huge man howled in pain. "Get him off me, Alphonse," he shrieked. But he did not let Britta go.

The one called Alphonse began hitting at Fenris with a walking stick.

"Bind her hands," the hulking one growled. "We carry her."

"The abbess wants her whole," Alphonse shrieked. He kept Fenris at bay with his stick.

The large one tried to imprison both her fists in one of his and bring her hands behind her. She clawed at his face as she tried to twist free. "You are no help at all, Alphonse." He grabbed the cudgel from the smaller man. Britta bent to bite his arm, but she couldn't stop the cudgel's descent. Her head exploded in a flash of light, followed straight on by blackness.

Karn hung back as the others led their horses toward the stream. Though light was failing fast, Ulf watched him from some yards away, and Karn could see the hatred in his eyes. He clenched his teeth. There was no putting it off unless he wanted to sleep sitting on Thorn. He swung his leg over the saddle and thudded to the ground. He took Thorn's reins and limped toward the stream, his eyes meeting no one's. He did not have to look. He knew what he would see in their faces. He did what he could to straighten his gait, but it didn't help. He knew it wouldn't.

"I see the battle that left your fellows dead still took its toll," Ulf called.

Karn gritted his teeth and kept walking. Those already at the stream moved their horses aside to let him in. They gave him too wide a berth.

"No wonder Karn wanted Ivar and Halfdan to decide our little feud. It could not be a challenge, one on one. That becomes clear."

Karn took a breath and let it out slowly as Thorn lowered his velvet nose to the water.

"How is it you are still alive?" Ulf sneered. "You have not answered that."

"I owe you no answers, Ulf," Karn growled. "The will of the gods is beyond our ken. As for who owes for those fine warriors, you sent them against odds you knew and we did not."

"I knew nothing," Ulf sneered. "And no one will listen to one such as you."

Karn felt his breath begin to come heavily.

Jael came up beside him. "He wants to get your sword in

your hand before you put the case to Ivar." Karn saw his friend hesitate before he laid a hand on his shoulder. Even Jael was ashamed.

But Karn could not let Ulf go unchallenged. Now is not the time, his mind shouted, even as he called, "Erik Eriksson. You know the truth of it. Tell us whether Ulf knew there was a Saxon fort just up the gorge from that stone church."

The enormous young man reddened. Unsure of himself, he reached for his sword. Karn saw Ulf's eyes narrow and glance between Karn and Jael, Bjorn and Thurmak. Ulf now knew that someone had gone to the trouble to find out who had been in his little scouting party. Karn realized too late that by his accusation he had damned his friends.

"We only sailed by," Eric mumbled, eyes darting between Ulf and Karn.

"I have some advice, Erik Eriksson," Jael said. "I would speak the truth now, and publicly. Your secret puts you in danger. You are the last alive who went ashore with Ulf."

But the boy was too weak-minded to stand against Ulf. Karn could see, even if Erik survived to testify before Ivar and Halfdan, he would lie. Ulf was respected. Karn was but a cripple who should never have survived his men's brave death, found fighting to defend Saxons from Danish swords. Even his own friends now pitied him. Despite his idea about the saddle, they shunned him. How had he imagined anything would erase their distaste of weakness?

"I have no case to put in front of Ivar," Karn breathed as much to himself as Jael. "That boy will not stand against Ulf. And no one else can prove what he knew."

"What other choice do you have?" Jael asked gently.

"My sword will prove the truth," Karn barked. Bjorn and Thurmak ranged themselves beside Jael. The pity in their eyes raked his pride: they thought he would lose. But better to go to Valhalla with a sword in one's hand than with a supplication to Ivar on one's lips. He drew his sword.

Ulf's eyes lit, as he knew what Karn would do. A small smile curved his narrow lips.

Karn lifted Walther's blade. He must not let his enemy

see that his sword arm was not yet fully healed. His blood was cold in his veins, but his hand was steady. "Let us prove the truth now, Ulf," he called.

His foe stepped forward. The other Danir moved back, held their horses' heads. "Do you challenge me, Karn?" Ulf asked. He made no move toward his sword. Instead his smile grew.

"I challenge you." *Not only for my dead men, but for my limp and for what Off a did and for the months of pain and for the fact that I will never belong with my people again, the way it was before.* He dropped to a crouch and gripped Walther's sword.

Ulf shook his head slowly, amusement and regret large on his face. "I cannot fight a cripple, Karn. What would my brothers say if I cut down a defenseless man?"

Karn felt the words like a blow. Was he reduced to begging for the right to die beneath Ulf's sword? "Are you a coward, that you refuse to fight?" he croaked.

"I have no need to prove my warrior's heart." Kindness dripped from Ulf's lips. "If you have a grievance, go to Ivar and Halfdan. That is the only way for one such as you."

"I will *make* you fight me," Karn said, his voice rising in frustration and anger.

Ulf held up his hands, palm forward. "You cannot make me fight a cripple."

Karn's breath came fast. The horror of his situation blurred his vision. He could feel his sword arm begin to shake. Not fight him? Ulf would not fight? He felt a hand on his arm and turned to see Jael's silent supplication, as devastating as all the rest combined. Slowly he lowered his sword. The strength drained out of him as he saw sympathy or derision in every eye.

He had nothing left. He turned, half-blinded by a veil of emotion, and grabbed Thorn's reins. Pulling Thorn behind him, he pushed his way through the circle of Danir. The tip of Walther's marvelous sword dragged in the dirt. As the twilight deepened into dark and cold, he stumbled away from all his hopes into the night.

Chapter Sixteen

Karn staggered through the low brush in the gathering darkness with Thorn in tow, not caring where he went. He was more alone than he had ever been. How had he thought he could ever regain a place of respect? They would always despise him as haltr, and he would never accept a place on those terms. He was adrift, belonging nowhere.

The moon rose and with it a piercing wind. At last he crashed through the reeds into the spongy earth that signaled the edge of the fens. The give beneath his feet was comforting. His steps slowed. But the crashing sound did not stop. By the time he realized what the noise was, it was almost too late. Thorn sidled and snorted. Karn half-turned.

Erik Eriksson broke out of the sedge and rammed his shoulder into Karn's belly. Karn grunted and fell back, the weight knocking the wind from his lungs. Thorn reared and squealed, the reins jerked from Karn's hands. The two Danir rolled together in the mud as Thorn wheeled into the darkness. Karn pushed up on his assailant's chin. His lungs screamed. Erik rolled aside. Karn heaved in a great breath and reached for his sword, but already Erik's axe swung forward, glinting in the moonlight. Karn rolled to his left.

His foe tried to stop the heavy weapon, but it buried its head in the mud. Karn fumbled with his sword as he struggled to his knees. Erik pulled at his axe handle, spewing rage. Karn staggered to his feet. How could a cripple defend himself against a healthy young Dane? The bile of hopelessness rose in his throat. Why not let it end here, a voice whispered. Die in combat.

Erik's axe jerked from the mud with a sucking sound, and he rounded on Karn with a crow of triumph. Karn did not move. The wind whipped their hair and tore at the sedge leaves. He waited. The tip of Walther's sword touched the ground. Now, thought Karn, as Erik raised his axe. Karn's breath was surprisingly steady. He could see it in the cold air. Erik charged.

At the last moment, Walther's sword seemed to move of its own accord. The tip raised just enough to deflect Erik's axe. The brute screamed in rage and prepared to strike again.

Karn tried to wait, but his easy end was not to be. Erik's expression changed to surprise as his skull was split by an axe blade. Showered with blood, Erik's own weapon faltered and fell from limp hands. He sagged to the side, revealing Bjorn, still gripping the handle of his axe. He let Erik fall, then wrenched it from his skull.

Karn stared. What was Bjorn doing here? Ulf must have sent Erik, but would have forbidden Karn's friends to interfere. Which meant Bjorn had sacrificed a great deal to come. Karn didn't deserve it. He searched for signs of pity in Bjorn's eyes, but found only the thrill of battle.

"My life is yours, poor as it is," Karn growled.

Bjorn's chest heaved. "A man who attacks from behind as Erik, did deserves to be killed from behind."

Karn smiled in spite of himself. "A sentiment worthy of the Norns."

Bjorn stepped up and clapped Karn on the back. "You acquitted yourself well."

Karn contracted inside. "I'm alive."

Renewed crashing in the sedge alerted the two that they

would soon have company. Karn lifted his sword. He must fully engage in any fight at Bjorn's side, no matter how hopeless he might feel himself; he owed his friend that. But it was Jael and Thurmak who stumbled into the little clearing, pulling their horses. Blood trickled from Jael's temple and Thurmak's sword was covered in gore from his enemies and his own sliced arm.

"We thought you dead," Jael panted. He spared only a glance for Eriksson.

"I thought so, too," Karn said. "What of you?"

"Ulf and his wolves set upon us when we wanted to go after you."

Thurmak grinned. "Good odds."

"Dead?" Bjorn asked softly.

"All but Ulf," Jael spat. "He turned tail at the first sign that the battle was not with him."

"You should have gone after him," Karn argued.

"We thought of you and Bjorn," Jael said. "We made our choice."

Karn considered what Ulf's escape would mean. He would tell Ivar and Halfdan that they were all traitors. He and his friends were all exiled now. Karn felt a weight descend upon his shoulders.

"What of the other horses?" he asked quietly.

"Ulf took both strings." Thurmak's voice was gruff. "There are some strays about."

Jael peered into the dark, and Karn could see despair setting in. His friends saw the fens as a horrible land, forsaken by the gods and brimming with the enemy. They couldn't see it as he did. He sighed. Everything had changed. He no longer had the luxury of giving up. He shifted his weariness until it was almost bearable. Denmark was lost to them. There was only one alternative. "Let us find what horses we can. I know a ruined village where we can get out of the wind."

Britta had been locked in the tiny cell alone for three days. They had taken her kirtle and given her instead the rough white wool robe of a novice nun. No one brought her food, though the monk who had brought her here, Brother Alphonse, gave her water. The stone walls radiated cold, but she wasn't hungry anymore. She just felt light-headed and frightened. The only things in the room were a chamber pot and a wide wooden bench. If she sat back against the stone wall it made her even colder, so she huddled cross-legged and hugged her knees to keep warm.

Why had they imprisoned her? This might be a monastery, but God seemed far away, at least from her. She was totally in someone else's power. It was a feeling she had sworn she would avoid at all costs since that day five years before when she had been helpless under Offa's rutting weight. She missed Karn. Oh, gods, how she wanted the comfort of his arms. The fact that he did not even know she was gone, that he would have no idea where she was, even if he did return to the village, sunk her spirits further.

Even the solace of Fenris's company was denied her. The monks took him away, though the one called Brother Alphonse promised to keep him safe. Fenris had followed the monks when they'd captured her. When she'd come to her senses, her knife was gone and they were keeping the dog at bay by throwing stones. Brother Alphonse had only prevented the hulking Ilwith from luring Fenris into the range of his cudgel by announcing that the abbess wanted the beast unharmed, too.

That was the first time she knew that for some reason the Abbess of Ely had ordered her abduction. But why? And why had she not yet even seen this mysterious abbess?

As the sun rose on the third day, she tried to pray for deliverance from her enemies. After some consideration, she recited from Psalms. The words had been engraved on her heart, though the vellum pages of her father's Bible were lost to her now. " 'The sun shall not smote thee by day or the moon by night'," she murmured. Would prayers to God protect her from God's disciples?

At last Brother Alphonse came and announced that the abbess wished to see her. She had to find out what the abbess wanted before she could escape this dreadful place—of that she was sure. But as she wound her way behind him through the warrens of the monastery, her fear grew. The place was deathly quiet, at least until they passed a courtyard, and the crack of a whip startled her. She glimpsed monks, their robes hanging about their waists, flagellating themselves as they murmured supplications to God. They didn't look up as she passed, locked as they were in some twisted relationship with the Almighty that did not allow any sense but pain. Such intensity frightened her. Alphonse hurried her along.

He took her to a huge, cold room with winter sunlight streaming in through stone arches open to the air. There were rich tapestries and wonderful rugs and heavy wood furniture with carving such as she had never seen. Alphonse gestured for her to kneel on the hard stone floor.

Into the room came an old man or an old woman, Britta couldn't tell. Like Wydda, the only quality left to the figure was age. It wore a fine white wool robe and red leather shoes made with consummate skill. On the head was a close-fitting red leather cap that outlined the ears. Alphonse came to stand before it.

"Do you know who I am?" an ancient voice almost whispered.

Britta shook her head. "Many apologies, no."

"I am the Abbess of Ely. You will address me as Mother." The voice was flat and sure. "I want to ask you some questions." It paused. "Your answers will reveal you to me, girl, no matter that you try to hide behind lies. Do you understand?"

"Yes, Mother," she managed, as her insides turned to jelly. She had come to the abbess at last. And the sinking feeling in her stomach told her that she would be no gladder of that fact then she was about going to Wydda. She clasped her hands in front of her tightly. What did this woman want? Most important, how could she make the abbess let her go?

"You claim to heal." It sounded like an indictment.

So that was it! She thought Britta claimed the power of

God. And falsely, too, by her tone. "I don't claim anything," she replied.

The abbess pursed her lips and her face crinkled into a whorl. "The facts, girl. Who have you healed and of what? Don't lie. Alphonse has talked with many who are under your spell."

Britta could feel danger in the air. Was it better to say she had never healed? But that was a lie. And the abbess had obviously heard something of her. Ah, but the abbess was a woman of God! She had no doubt spent her life looking for evidence of God's presence in the world. No matter what she said, the abbess, in her soul, would want to believe that Britta healed and that the power of healing was sent by God. That had to be the way out of this place: to give the abbess what she craved and tell her that the healing was a miracle. But Britta had no proof she had ever healed, and no demonstrations were possible now that she had lain with Karn. How could she give the abbess what she wanted?

The abbess's stare bored into her. "Answer, girl."

Confusion washed over Britta. "I don't know what to say," she began.

"Tell truth, and God will forgive you."

Britta wasn't certain of that. "I don't know what the truth is, Mother."

"Do you confess some healing has occurred?"

Britta was trapped. "Yes," she stuttered. "I healed, but... not anymore." She looked for evidence that the abbess was eager to see it as a sign from God, but she could find none.

The abbess paced the room and fingered her beads. At last she turned and smiled. Her old face cracked into a thousand wrinkles. "Tell me about the healing itself, child. When did you first know that you could heal?"

Britta sensed that if there was a way to freedom, it lay in telling the truth, just as the abbess suggested. She could tell the abbess what had gone before and satisfy her need for miracles. What point was there in keeping Britta imprisoned when the magic was now gone?

"I am not sure when it started," she began, searching the

abbess's face. "I might have healed my mother, but I was interrupted and she died." The guilt surged up, making her flush and look away. It was all she could do to continue. "During the dry spell on the island," she whispered, "I think it was there. The herbs could not have given Syffa a child when her hair was already gray. Karn should have died, too. I see that now. When I felt the wrongness in his wounds, that was the healing. The first time I was sure was with the babe with the blackened foot. He had the halo of death, yet he was healed…." She trailed off.

The abbess looked startled, then she smiled again. "And did you feel the power of God working through you when you healed?"

How could Britta answer that? "Some power…I wasn't sure at first." The abbess would be disappointed in that answer. "I felt the power most surely when I had the first vision."

"You had visions?" the abbess asked. Her smile seemed pasted on. "What visions were these? Of archangels, or of the Mother of our Lord?"

"Well, no." Britta cleared her throat. "They were scenes, really. Some of them have come true, like the fire on the Island…." Again she trailed off. This was not proof of God's work.

"You must share these visions with me," the abbess said softly. "Yes, and you must demonstrate your healing powers.

"But I can't, not anymore." Perhaps it wouldn't matter if the abbess didn't believe her about the healing. What interest would the woman have when she realized the power was gone? Britta saw the abbess's eyebrows rise. "I gave it up." That should end this questioning.

"Gave it up?" the abbess snapped. "What do you mean?"

Britta didn't know how to say what she had done. At least not to an abbess. But she had to answer something. "I gave up the life of a healer and took up the life of a woman."

Comprehension dawned in the old nun's eyes. "You gave

up the gift of God for fornication?" She was incredulous, shocked.

The words pierced Britta like a knife. Her bliss with Karn seemed hollow and selfish phrased in such a way. The vision of healing the king...she had given that up. How could she explain? The abbess's eyes burned into her and seemed to see her weakness.

"You don't understand," Britta stuttered. "It wasn't just healing. That part was fine. But I brought the storms when I got angry once. I made trees fall in the forest. What if I became evil, like Wydda?" She broke off. Tears coursed down her cheeks. "I had to give it up."

The abbess's black eyes went opaque. "Wydda," she breathed. "You went to Wydda?"

Britta couldn't think. Did the abbess know the witch? "I went to see if she could teach me about magic. I thought this was magic then."

"Magic and witches." The abbess's voice was very calm.

"Not magic," Britta explained hastily. She had made a mistake. The abbess was a woman of the Church. Her fingers strayed nervously to the white streak in her hair. "It wasn't magic, or at least...I don't know what it was. But I couldn't control it. And when the power was on me, it felt so right, I might have done anything to keep on doing it, things like Wydda did. Was it wrong to remove temptation?"

The abbess stood perfectly still with her hands folded before her, looking out of the window over the fields and workshops of Ely. Finally she turned back to Britta. Her eyes were hard. "One must know one's enemy. We will talk again, woman." She clapped her hands sharply, and two nuns appeared. "Take her to her cell. Let her think about her sins."

As Britta struggled to her feet, confused, the woman turned her back. "But I don't heal anymore," she protested in vain. The abbess didn't answer.

Karn stood up over the pile of peat he had cut the morning after he and his friends arrived at the abandoned village. The time he had lived here by himself seemed like a dream. He looked out across the lopsided halls toward the dawn. The clouds were palest pink and gray like his breath in the cold. Ice edged the water, but spring was on its way. Birds whirled up out of the sedge. He would have to ask Britta their names. The fens were beautiful and rich. Their wealth lay in the soil and the birds and the fish. This land and Britta—these sustained him. The plan formed in the cold last night echoed in his head. Anyone would say he was a crazy man.

Eleven horses crowded into Thorn's pen now. They were critical to his plan. As were his friends. As was Britta. How would he ever make Jael and Bjorn and Thurmak see what he saw in the fens? But they had no choice now. He ran his hands over his eyes and tried to erase his guilt. *I dragged them into my own underworld. I am cast out, now so are they.*

Yet he had made a plan. It had risen up out of the land that called to him. Soon he would see Britta again. He held to that thought as he squeezed the peat block he had cut in one hand and felt the spongy texture of the soil. He would tell his friends about the old dike. With four strong backs, they could repair it. That was his hope. It was his friends' hope now, too.

That first interview with the abbess was only the beginning of Britta's ordeal. Fevered thoughts swirled in her head. The emptiness in her belly left her weak and unsure of herself. It began to go wrong when she admitted she had lain with Karn. How could she have called it magic, and told about Wydda? The abbess must believe Britta was evil. Which started another round of doubt. Was what she had done with Karn wrong? Selfish or wise? Evil? Confused? She could not answer.

And if ever she was granted another audience with the abbess, how would she get the woman to let her go? The abbess would look for guidance to the scriptures, to the life of Jesus. Perhaps that was the key. Britta turned over what she knew and found herself surprised.

Jesus had something in common with her. Was Jesus not the ultimate healer? He had raised Lazarus from the dead. Certainly he knew the future when he told his disciples that Peter would betray him. She could not compare herself to Jesus, of course. But the Bible said he was a man like any other. She was sure, at least, that Jesus was not evil. Had Jesus ever loved a woman? The way that she loved Karn, that is? It was heresy to even think it.

Actually, if there was one relevant lesson in Jesus's life, it was His miracles themselves. They had not been done for His benefit. Jesus had done His Father's will, not His own. When He was faced with death on the cross, he did no miracles to save himself. He'd waited for God's will, hard as that was, even when he cried out in frustration, "My Father, why hast thou forsaken me?" No, whatever Jesus had, He had not forced it. He'd let God's will work through him.

Was it forcing magic for her own benefit that drained Wydda so? Was that why Britta had felt no pain when she'd let the magic heal that babe's foot, when the trees had fallen? She'd been tired, yes, but there had been no pain. Britta began to think she glimpsed the truth of the thing...now that it was gone. But none of it would help her out of her cell.

Karn and his friends rode into Stowa warily the next day, leading six horses. Karn looked for Britta, but the village seemed deserted. At last Walther and Snurri and Frith appeared. The Smith carried a sword. The others had their farmer's axes at the ready. Karn motioned his party to stop.

"We come with gifts, Walther," Karn called. "Horses. Two times what you lost."

"You are Viking," Snurri accused. "There is no place for you here."

Hild peeked out of her father's hut. Other faces peered out from hiding places around the village. Britta was nowhere to be seen. He could feel his friends behind him fingering their swords. He had warned them this morning not to start a fight, no matter what provocation.

"Did I fight with Danes against you?" Karn challenged. Snurri looked uncertain. "I could have cut you down, but I did not." Walther's brow furrowed, but they were not won.

"Why are you not with your kith now?" Walther asked.

Karn decided he must reveal a part of the truth. He moved Thorn forward slowly, alone. "They did not want me, Walther, when they saw I lived with Saxons. They tried to kill me. My friends saved me. Now they are outlaws, too."

"Do not believe him, Walther," Snurri barked. "He will kill us in our beds."

"Take the horses, Walther. We want only to drain some land and plant. We can go to another place. But I would be here."

"Why?" Walther asked suspiciously. "Why would you be here?"

"You said there is a broken dike near here. We can make it hold the water back. There can be land for us." Karn glanced back at his friends, who could not understand what was being said. Bjorn held his axe ready. Thurmak palmed the hilt of his sword.

"That dike has been breached for as long as anyone can remember," Frith snorted.

Karn drew himself up. "We will make the dike new. It will be called Karn's Dike. To pay my debt, I give you these horses, and I will share the land we take from the water."

Walther lowered his weapon. "You owe us nothing, Karn. You treated us fairly. You freed us from Cedric and taught us to become a free soke. I do not believe you can make this dike. But the gift of the horses shows your good intentions." He motioned Snurri to take the string of horses from Bjorn, then he and the other men huddled in conference.

Karn glanced back at his friends' anxious faces. They had not wanted to come here. But what choice was there? They could not live unnoticed in the middle of Saxon land. Bjorn would not give up his oval brooches, and their weapons had the sinuous carving of the Dane in their hilt. They knew little Saxon. No, they reeked of Dane, unlike Karn when he had first arrived, clothed by Britta and without so much as a knife from his past. Stowa had a dike ready made, if they could fill the breaches. Here was a smith to make their tools, and folk to trade with. And here there had once been trust. A man could not work and watch his back at the same time.

Walther came to stand in front of Karn. "Keep your friends in line and you can stay. The first time they fight, or steal, or take one of our women, we will kill you where you sleep."

Karn nodded curtly. He did not say that his friends would consider four Danes to fifteen ill-armed Saxon villagers easy odds. Instead he said, "We will need spades, Walther, and picks from your forge. We pay you for them with a silver armband." He dismounted and motioned the others to put the horses in the pen.

Hild came into the open. Karn asked her the question first in his mind. "Where is Britta?"

Hild's face fell. "She is gone."

"What do you mean, she is gone?" Karn exploded.

"I know not." She shrugged. "She disappeared with her dog right after you left."

Karn felt the anger drain away from him, leaving a familiar feeling of despair. She had not waited for him, had not believed he would return. Perhaps if he had told her that he went to prove his good name and make sure they had a place of safety in the coming chaos…But he had been afraid she would never agree to live among the Danir. He'd hurt her and she had run.

Nothing mattered, not being warrior once again, not building the dike, not getting land of his own, nothing. She was not here to share it with him. He looked around the village, panicked. Someone must know where she had gone. He shoved past Hild and went in search of her father.

Karn trudged into the village late, tired to his bones. It was cold—the kind of cold that only the last, damp freeze of winter could be. No one knew where Britta was, though Walther thought she would return. It was possible. He had spent that day laying out how to use what was left of the old dike, where they would build, and how. But his mind was elsewhere. This should have been a joyous time, working beside his brothers to earn what they had craved all their lives, but it meant nothing. He knew what he had to do but not where to start.

Jael appeared from Walther's hut to greet him. Hild handed Jael a mead horn, and he gestured with it invitingly. "Come in, you madman, and share Walther's generosity." He glanced sidelong at Hild. "Ginfaest?" he asked, trying out the Saxon word.

She blushed and nodded.

Karn shook his head and spoke in Danish. "Jael, can you follow our plans alone?"

Jael grew serious. "Why?"

"I must find what I have lost." He leaned his tools against the hut, then walked away.

Jael followed. "Where will you look?"

Karn stopped in his tracks. That was the problem. Crisscrossing the fens to get news of her might mean he would miss her altogether. He turned back to Jael, thinking hard. One might know where Britta was, no matter how far she had strayed. "I go to the Witch of the Fens," he said, striding back past Jael to Walther's hut. He was going to need directions.

Britta stared at Brother Alphonse as he put down the water bowl. She was too clearheaded, between the bouts of confusion. The clearness was a symptom of her hunger. It had been so many days. "Wait," she called as he turned to go. Here was a source of information.

He turned back, nervous. He didn't want to speak to her. That was clear.

"What does the abbess want of me?" she asked. "I don't heal anymore, I told her that. There is no proof that I ever healed at all. You know that."

Alphonse looked sad. "They all say you have the power. I talked to them—the woman with the baby, Henewulf who got a son, all of them. Some say you are a saint, others a witch."

"But does the abbess want me to have the power?"

"I do," he said. His brown eyes burned. "To find a saint would be a great thing."

"Not for her."

He hesitated, then shook his head. "Even now you have a cult of followers who believe in you—perhaps more than in the true Church."

"She thinks I'm evil because I went to the Witch of the Fens."

Alphonse began to pace the cell. "I told her that you read the Bible, that you could recite large passages. She only wondered where a peasant girl learned to read."

"My father was an Irish monk," Britta answered.

"Oh, dear," Alphonse mourned. "Don't tell her that. The abbess hates the Irish church." He turned conspiratorially. "They disagree on the true date of Easter."

"There's nothing I can do? I told her why the healing is gone."

Alphonse nodded. "I heard. I don't think you understand. The abbess is named for Ethelreda, a saint who kept her virginity through twelve years of marriage to a king until he relented and let her take her vows. There is a reason that Ethelreda is her namesake."

Britta took a breath. The clearness was evaporating. "Not sympathetic to my choices."

"You are her opposite." Alphonse turned at the door. "And if she declares you a saint, you are above her." The words were ripped from him. "Too, she cannot let them think there is any power not of the Church. The old religion dies hard among the people. Nor can she make you a martyr. She must prove you are a fraud. Then, Heaven help you."

Chapter Seventeen

The boar charged Karn from the thickets of sedge. Almost too late, he lunged to the side. The boar scooted away as Karn went down, knife in hand, and slid out on the ice over a deeper channel of water. A loud crack split the winter air. The ice gave way in sickening slow motion. Freezing water gurgled up around him and closed over his head. The sluggish current took him. He looked up to see the light from the hole sliding away. He grabbed the ice at the edge of the hole. It broke away and he clutched at it again, frantically. With the edges still crumbling, he grabbed at the widening breach until he got his head up through it to air. Gasping, half from holding his breath, half from the shocking cold of the water, he edged around the hole to where the ice was thicker. Then he heaved himself up out of the water and laid the weight of his shoulders out across as much ice as he could manage, his legs hanging in the black, frigid pool. The ice creaked under him. He inched forward by gripping the sedge poking up out of the groaning ice until he slid over the thicker sections in shallow waters.

The boar was gone, frightened by the sight of its adversary

disappearing under the ice. It knew instinctively that a dip in that freezing water was death to living things.

Karn knelt on the ice, gasping, until he could push himself up. His sopping clothes dragged at him. He stumbled through the frozen fens, his way obscured by the fat wet flakes of the last spring snow. He couldn't go back to Stowa. He had to find the witch. The sedge all looked the same, the brakes of blackthorn, the occasional stump of a fen oak jutting out of the mud gave no landmark. Clouds obscured the sun and the anemic swirls of snow confused him.

Soon he was lost. He couldn't go back to the village if he wanted to. If there were a foot or two of snow, he would bury himself in it for warmth. The leather bag that carried his flints and fishing line was gone; the icy water had claimed it. No fire for him.

Karn willed himself to calm. He stripped off his clothes as they froze until he wore only his boots, his knife stuck in the lacing. His vision blurred. He wasn't cold anymore, but his feet were strangers to him in their numbness. Now he would never find Britta. The air seared his lungs, with heat or cold he couldn't tell. He stumbled, got his limbs under him, stumbled again.

The water had won. It was punishing him for his plan to reclaim the land from it. Freya, protector of those who worked the land had forsaken him, just as Thor had. He fell to his knees, wanting nothing more than to rest. He would close his eyes, just for a moment.

A cackle wakened him. "A man. A naked man for Wydda."

He opened his eyes a slit and found an old crone's gnarled face and bloodshot eyes just inches from his. He was too tired to be startled.

"Are you dead yet, man?" the crone asked. She did not wait for an answer but poked Karn with her stick. "Get up, get up, fine body, before you die."

Karn tried to brush away the stick with blockish hands, but the crone poked and prodded. "Up, man, there is a fire waiting at my hut."

"Go away," Karn croaked.

"No, no, no. Not gone yet. Get up. It is not far."

Karn was cross, under the haze that muddled his thoughts. What right had this old woman to order him about? But her stick was annoying and insistent. He would get up and make her eat that stick. Then he could rest. Somehow he got his frozen feet under him. She glided away.

"Follow, man. Not far, a few yards, no more." He stumbled after her. She was ahead, she was behind, prodding him. Why couldn't she let him rest?

"A man will do," the old woman muttered. "No magic, but easy and a chance at living." He didn't understand. He could only put one numb foot in front of another as she prodded him.

Karn woke slowly. His feet and his hands burned hot, pricked by a thousand needles. He had the same feeling of dislocation as when he woke in Britta's hut the first time. Where was he? He remembered little, except a dream about an old hag. He looked around, and his eyes grew wide. This was not like Britta's hut at all. Desiccated herbs hung above, and around him dead animal heads leered from the walls, along with bits of metal, glinting in the red firelight. Over the fire hunched the crone of his dreams. He tried to push himself up, but the needles became knives slashing up his hands and forearms. He collapsed back into the skins that covered him.

"Awake, man?" The old crone gave a satisfied, if almost toothless, grin. She limped over to tower above him and poked at his hands with bony fingers. He pulled his hands back protectively. "Frostbite," she announced.

He nodded. He had been frost-bitten before.

The old woman grinned toothlessly. "You'll get over it."

Karn raised himself to lean on his elbows and inspected his hands. They clenched, if painfully. Slowly he reached for the furs to uncover his feet. He knew full well what he might see. But when he threw back the wraps, his feet were only a bit mottled, purplish red.

"Not one black toe," the old crone cackled. "Warmed you slow, I did, and rubbed you with camphor." She crouched over him and pulled back his furs. She pointed to the snaking red scar over his shoulder. "Arm works?"

Karn eyed her warily. "I hold a sword." He knew where he was and who she was. There were no signs of Britta in the horrible hut. Still, the witch might know where she was.

She pointed to the wound at his hip. "Leg works?"

Karn took a sharp breath. "I limp," he said roughly.

The old woman let the furs fall back in disgust. "Damaged," she muttered. "Can't be helped. There isn't any other."

His nakedness under the fur made Karn feel vulnerable. "Where is my knife?"

"Where you can't hurt Wydda with it." She patted his shoulder with a withered hand.

Karn tried to suppress his uneasiness. This frail old woman couldn't hurt him, no matter what Britta thought about her. Had she not helped him, warmed him? Still, he hesitated to ask the question that consumed him. Britta had not left here on good terms. "When can I leave?"

She began to rock herself quietly. "Soon enough, Viking."

Karn started. She was the first to guess that he was Dane. She might well summon help against him. Perhaps she already had.

"Don't be a fool," she said, and cackled long. "Wydda doesn't mind, Viking. One warrior is like another. I have seen the killing, the hordes clashing. I have seen the ending of the world."

A thrill coursed through him. If she was a seer, she could see Britta. He had to keep her talking. "You have seen Ragnorok?"

An earthy chuckle came from the shadows behind the fire. "I know nothing of your gods, Viking. I know Edmund, King of the Angles. I see him through the clouds and mists—not clear, mind you, like *she* does." Here she seemed to snarl, but she recovered. "And I see your brethren."

"How does it end?" he breathed. "Do Danir best the Saxon

dogs? Do they kill Edmund?" It was a battle he would never be allowed to join.

The old woman studied him. "Fire burns in you for war. That would be a new feeling."

"How do you know Edmund, woman?"

"Edmund?" Wydda's face folded into a thousand wrinkles as she pursed her lips. She smiled slyly and refolded it. "Edmund wanted magic to promise him eternal life. Sent men to find me. Threatened me," she crooned. "I could have helped him, but Wydda does not do another's bidding. Even a king's." She settled into a lump of cloth in the shadows behind the fire. Only her pleated face was lit by the low flame. "Wydda told him that his fate could not be changed, but Wydda knew it." The eyes glowed with hatred. "He could not resist the knowing. I told him he would die of a lung ailment. It has pushed his desire for life almost unto madness. It always does." She looked up at Karn. "Now he lives in fear. It makes him small."

Karn shivered. No one should know what fate the Norns would weave them. "You are a great seer," he said, trying to flatter her. "You must be able to see anyone."

Wydda nodded, her lip curled. "What is it you want, man? Men are always wanting."

"A girl came here to find you, not long past," he began. "Her name was Britta." Karn hesitated as he said the name, as though it was a secret.

Wydda's eyes narrowed as she examined Karn. "Patterns," she muttered enigmatically. "We all connect in patterns." Again she smiled slyly to herself. "Fitting you should love her."

Karn started. "I know her." He did not want to admit to this one that he loved her.

"Know her?" the witch cackled. "There is knowing and *knowing*. You do not know her body. Of that I am sure."

Karn tried to mask his surprise. She did not know everything, this witch.

"You *have* lain with her," she said slowly. Then she cackled. "She gave it all up to lie with a broken warrior body?"

Guffaws wracked her body until she collapsed, coughing. When she recovered her breath, the witch hugged herself and began to rock. "Taught her. Tried to teach her." She gazed into the fire and seemed to forget about Karn. "That one had the magic, as even I don't." The witch raised her hand and the fire leapt up. Karn slitted his eyes against the brightness. It took all he had to remain still. "Fierce it was, about her. I had to go carefully. I almost had it, almost had it," the witch moaned. Karn dared to raise his gaze. The witch's rheumy old eyes were cold upon him. "I will never find another who has the power she had."

Karn clenched his teeth, as though that would keep his mind from caroming off the walls of this horrific hut. He had to make her tell him where Britta was. He dragged himself on his elbows toward the fire. "Where is she?" he growled. "I know you know where she is." He would choke it out of her, no matter that his hands burned.

"You hunger for her, Viking man." The witch crawled to meet him, until their faces almost touched. Her breath was rancid in his nostrils. "I would know these hungers." He could see the spittle snaking from the corner of her mouth. "I will help you find her. Find her together, we will, and make her pay for what she owes me." Suddenly she smiled. "Come, come closer to the fire, man. I want your limbs whole. There is not much time."

Karn wanted his limbs whole, too, and he wanted to get out of this hut. Still, she had said she would help him. He must keep his wits about him. He watched Wydda out of the corner of his eye as he made his way painfully toward the fire, dragging his furs.

Something woke Karn in the night. He reached for the knife that wasn't there. The fire had burned down to coals. He pulled himself from sleep and saw Wydda, bending over him, grinning. The light in her eyes was not reflected firelight. He pushed himself up, though his hands ached, and faced her.

"Oooooooh," she crooned. "Man-body. Softly now—no

fear." She reached out to touch his shoulder and he shivered. But he did not flinch away.

He could not. Her eyes fascinated. This woman knew things that no man knew. How had he thought her ugly? Knowledge made her beautiful, softened her wrinkles, made her gnarled joints supple and her caked hair shine. How had he not seen how infinitely attractive she was?

Wydda crawled closer, weaving her fingers through his hair, fondling the nape of his neck. "So easy," the wicce purred. "There is not much time. No fight. Just ease in."

Karn's vision blurred. He seemed to see himself from somewhere else. That was his own ear he whispered in, his hair running through his fingers. He was confused. Strength faded. His own blue eyes gazed back at him, and they were sly and evil. Gods, he yelled inside his mind, this is not clean, what happens here. It felt like what Offa did, some-how. Already he was weaker. He felt what it was to have one's body crumble toward the kind of death that every Vi-king feared, small and weak. The witch had done this. As he gazed into the sly blue eyes that used to be his own, he saw her triumph.

He would not go without a fight. Was he not warrior? He felt his frail chest heave as the familiar lust for battle came up through the withered belly, fueled by the will that still was his. "You will not have my body, crone," he whispered aloud. He saw himself as animal, berserker. He was sub-sumed in rage. His brain burned with a berserker's purity of purpose. The blue eyes in front of him wavered. The room trembled. Then he was back in the body that was strong. He saw the small, wailing crone before him and grabbed her by the neck. The needles in his feet and hands were forgotten as he stumbled up and shook her like a dog shakes a rat. "What foul deed did you mean to do?" he shouted, furious. "What gods do you serve?"

Wydda was past answering. Her head lolled. Something lifted from him—the comforting rage of the berserker, or perhaps her vile presence. The hut was empty around him. He dropped her as though she were a burning coal, and she folded into a little pile on the floor of the hut. Her muddy eyes stared up at him. Was this what she had tried to do to Britta?

Karn found himself shaking. She'd meant to steal his body. He was glad he had killed her. But how would he find Britta? He looked about the empty hut. He must find his knife. When the dawn came he would bury Wydda and help himself to her furs and her food while his feet healed enough to carry him back to the village. He prayed he would not need more than a day or two, and that the ice that made the fens passable would last.

Something was wrong in Stowa. Karn saw women weeping. Men talked in tight groups and children were nowhere to be seen. His friends emerged from the main hall. Thurmak had already half-drawn his sword.

"Walther, what?" Karn asked the smith. "Danir?"

Walther shook his head. "Saxons collecting Danegeld. Took all the silver we had."

Karn glanced around. One woman held her kirtle to her shoulder where a brooch of silver should have been. Walther's neck ring was gone, and Snurri's heavy bracelet. The village had not been rich, and they were poorer now. "Did they come for we Danir?" Karn asked, incredulous.

Walther shook his head. "They only took the silver. Your friends were out at the dike."

"Else we would have cloven their skulls," Bjorn spat.

"Why here?" Karn wondered aloud. The fenland was not a place for collecting wealth.

Walther sat heavily on a stool outside his smithy. "They were on their way to Ely looking for Britta." He sighed. "But the fork-bearded one still took time to take our silver."

The bottom dropped out of Karn's stomach. "They wanted Britta?" he repeated. "A Saxon with a forked beard?" He gathered himself. "What was his name?" There were many Saxons who parted their beard.

"Offa, they called him," Snurri said as he wandered up, rubbing his bare wrists.

Karn closed his eyes. "Britta is in this place, this Ely?" He tried to gather his wits.

"Offa thinks so. He says the whole countryside waits for the Abbess of Ely to declare her a saint." Walther put out a hand to steady him, but Karn broke away at an uneven run for the pen that held the horses. He grabbed his saddle and pushed through the gate.

"Where are you going?" Walther and Jael cried in unison, but in two different languages.

Karn had no time for questions. "Where is this Ely?" he snapped. He threw a bridle over Thorn's head as the other horses jostled around him.

"Due south," Walther answered. "You cannot get there before them and you are no match for their number."

"He is after her because she helped me. I cannot let her pay for that," Karn said in Danish to Jael. His friend and Walther exchanged looks. Both knew it was no use to argue, and Karn was glad. That would save time. "I need some jerky, Walther. How many days?"

"Two," the smith said, and motioned Hild into their hut. "Go east to the limestone plateau and follow it south as far as it will go, then strike southwest."

Karn swung himself into the saddle. Thorn snorted. "Stay out of trouble until I return," he called over his shoulder to Jael in Danish. "They will not hurt you if you keep to yourself." He smiled grimly. "Without me to translate, your Saxon might improve." Hild came rushing up and handed him a hastily tied bundle.

"As though you have been here to translate." Jael shook his head. But he motioned Karn to go. "You will not be satisfied until you have found this Saxon woman. Who can deny you?"

Karn drew Walther's wonderful sword half out of its scabbard. "I must take this with me, Walther," he said curtly, then spun Thorn's head to the south. "But I will return it if I can."

*   *   *

275

They had most of a day upon him. That thought would not be banished as he rode, pushing his horse onward. They had come in the morning, and he had started almost as the sun was setting. But they would stop to rest and he would not. The moon was high and lit his way through thin, streaming clouds. He stuck to the limestone plateaus.

The vision of Britta, taken by Offa, drove Karn on. The magic that might protect her was gone because she had lain with him. He gritted his teeth and pushed Thorn through hawthorn trees, black skeletons in the night. She had courage, Britta. She was going to be declared a Christian saint. Though she had fallen to Offa when she was but a girl, now she rose from the ashes of her suffering to rebuild her life. Karn's breath came in gasps. In that they were the same. Somewhere in the last months he had found the will to go on, even after what Offa did. He'd almost lost that when Ulf laughed at him. He'd almost lost it when Britta left. But he had not. And now he knew where she was. He could be of service to her. Ulf would not have the last word. Britta would.

Yet if she was declared a saint, she was lost to him. That cut at his heart. No matter. What mattered was that he saved her from Offa and that she got what she wanted.

Karn rubbed Thorn's neck and felt the lather there. He swung down off the saddle and pulled the horse behind him. It was close to dawn. His long trek had cost him precious strength. He flexed fingers and toes. They were still returning to life.

As he limped ahead, the image of Offa danced before his eyes almost as often as Britta's face. How he would like to meet the thegn here, now, and use Walther's sword to cleave his skull! But he was not strong enough to best him. He knew that. Britta must be saved by stealth, not strength. Offa would have to wait. Now, Thorn, he thought, comes our real test. We push on, though our strength wanes.

Alphonse came again to get Britta. He was joined by several monks, who formed a cordon around her as she stumbled out of her cell into the growing gloom of late afternoon. Britta's periods of clarity were gone. It had been so many days. She had only seen the abbess that once. What could the woman want of her? What could she say to gain her freedom?

The little band moved toward the great wooden gates across the abbey courtyard. She could hardly believe her good fortune. They were going to let her go! Brother Ilwith drew back the gates' great bolt. Britta imagined herself melting into the crowd she could hear outside and escaping to the fens. She looked around for Fenris. How could she go without the dog? Brother Alphonse stood forlornly nearby.

"Please bring Fenris to me," she begged as Ilwith opened the great gates. "You promised you would keep him safe." Brother Alphonse looked as though he might say something, then stopped himself and hurried away.

Britta stared longingly at the gap in the gates, widening toward freedom. Crowds milled everywhere. As they saw her little group, shouts arose. She couldn't make them out. The motion of the crowd, the noise, the rank smell of so many people so close about her, made her senses reel. Her escort pushed through the crowd. Some faces seemed angry as they yelled, some just excited. A ragged peasant woman reached to touch her robe and was pushed back by the monks around her. Then they were through the crowd.

A huge pole loomed ahead of her in the square. The faggots heaped about it struck her like a blow. Her knees gave way and she sank to the ground. There would be no freedom today. Tears welled as the monks pulled her to her feet and dragged her forward. This was her vision, coming true. How could she not have guessed? Fear sat on her chest and choked her thoughts.

Fire. What was it like to die in fire? She had never considered it, even when she was running through the burning forest on Deofric. Now she could practically feel the flames lick her limbs, burn her flesh, consume her.

The monks around her parted. The abbess, in her finest scarlet cloak, stood on a small platform. One of the monks grabbed Britta's arm and hauled her up to kneel before the woman.

The ancient nun raised her arm straight above her head, and the crowd hushed. At last she lowered her hand to her side. "You come here before us claiming sainthood," she intoned in a voice that carried over the silent square.

Britta trembled. It didn't matter what she said. Her vision had shown her that. She could deny sainthood; she could deny the gift she once had; she could acknowledge it and say it was magic; she could say it was all a lie and beg forgiveness—it would not matter, for all roads led to the stake.

"Before we declare that you have the power of God running in your veins, we require proof." A murmur of excitement rippled across the crowd. "I will set you a test to make a miracle." Britta looked up into the abbess's stony face and knew it was useless to plead. This was what Alphonse meant when he said that the abbess would prove her a fraud. "If you prove your divine powers, I will declare you a saint. If you do not, you pay for your sin." Those cold eyes held no pity. Britta thought she would faint and dropped her head. "If you are a saint," the abbess continued, "God will meet any test I set for you."

Britta knew she would pass no test today. She had seen herself in flames.

"Since you say you can heal," said the abbess clearly, "do it." Her hand moved out from the folds of her cloak, holding a large knife, gleaming and sharp. The crowd muttered. "I will subject none of those under my care to your wiles,"— her voice rang out over the silent square—"so you will heal me." She held out the palm of her left hand where all could see and calmly drew the knife across it. A bloody stripe appeared. The crowd gasped.

Britta shook her head. *I can't heal anyone anymore.* The crowd held its breath.

The abbess loomed above Britta and held out her bloody hand. "Heal it," she commanded. "Or I will know what to do with you." The crowd fell silent in expectation.

Britta stared at the hand in horror. Blood dripped onto the platform, onto her own kirtle. The abbess was not going to move until she healed that cut. And she couldn't!

"Please, Mother," she sobbed and took the abbess's other hand in her own. She could not bear to touch the bleeding hand. "Please, let me go." She was talking not only to the woman in front of her, but to the woman who had told her all her life she was to blame. She pressed the hand to her forehead as blood ran down the abbess's other wrist. "Let me go. I can do nothing."

And she felt nothing, except that the abbess's hand was cold. Not cold in the ordinary sense. Britta raised her head and looked at the old flesh. Her fingers moved over the dry, papery skin. No, Britta thought slowly. No, it was a coldness from deep inside the old nun. Cold and...barren. She was barren. Life could never spring from those loins. She had never parted her legs in lust, never allowed herself to crave beauty, never wept in joy, never loved another, never loved God, not really. Never. Britta felt the dark, hard center of this woman and knew that for the abbess, there would never be magic in the world, or miracles.

Britta opened her eyes and stared up into the abbess's small dark pupils. "It is too late to heal you," she said clearly, almost against her will. Their eyes locked them together. Britta slowly pulled herself upright using the abbess's red robe, stained darker now with streaks of blood, until they stood face to face. Still the other didn't move. Britta saw a kind of horror growing in her. "Your wound is here," she breathed, and touched the withered breast. "You cannot love, not even your God, and no magic but your own can heal you."

Britta looked out over the crowd, and her voice rang with a power beyond her starved body's strength. "She is not a bad woman." Britta shook her head. "But she lusts for power. That is why she and Ilwith smothered the old abbess all those years ago."

Ilwith moved out of the gasping crowd, a look of dull

surprise on his face. People stepped back from him in distaste.

"The old abbess was almost dead anyway," Britta continued as she turned. "But she might have named another successor, and you were already old. You couldn't wait for another to die."

The abbess's mouth formed a silent *O*. The crowd began to murmur. Ilwith looked panicky. A moan escaped the abbess that grew into a shriek. She pushed Britta away, who fell to the floor. "To the stake," she shouted, her voice trembling. "She is an impostor, an impostor, I tell you! She will say any lie to save herself."

The monks around the platform leapt up and jerked Britta to her feet. The crowd seemed confused, not sure of what they had heard. Several echoed the abbess. "Burn her!" The horror of the charred stake threatened her sanity. Already several monks held burning brands aloft.

Behind her, she heard Ilwith's terrified voice. "Mother, Mother, how could she know that?" he called up to the platform. "That was years before she was born."

The abbess strode forward and hissed, "Quiet, you fool!"

The crowd buzzed. "Then it's true?" someone called out.

The abbess was shaken, but she recovered. She looked out over the amassed townfolk of Ely and said, with all the authority of her scarlet robes, "I am abbess here, chosen by God. I have the power, granted by God, to declare saints, and to execute His justice on sinners. I tell you that this woman lies. She is a fraud, and I will execute her for that sin."

Some in the crowd rebelled. "This isn't right," one shouted. But another yelled, "If she's innocent, God will save her." They milled about nervously, unsure what to do. Whatever they did wouldn't matter. Britta began to feel distant. Maybe this was what happened to people who were about to die in pain. Maybe this was how they bore it. They just went away. Britta felt herself fading away from the crowd and the stake and the abbess. Her only sorrow was that she would not see Karn again, or Fenris. Movement caught her eye. Brother Alphonse held her dog, leaping in joy to see her, at the edge of the crowd. Hold him tight, Brother Alphonse, she thought sadly.

The last rays of the sun broke through the cloud, lighting the square like a benediction. Monks pushed her up on the uneven piles of wood. Her hands no longer trembled. They looked translucent, skin spread over bone and blood and sinew. I can see exactly how God made me, she thought, if it was God who had. Perhaps it would be Satan who welcomed her soul.

They tied ropes across her chest and hips. She laid her translucent hands across her breast. The abbess strode over to stand in front of the stake. She had worked herself into a frenzy. "Abomination!" she cried. "She admitted she is not a virgin. Aldheim tells us that a virgin is as gold and a married woman is but silver. She was not even married! The Lord does not work through soiled vessels. Impure!" The abbess pointed to her with one long finger. Spittle formed at the corners of her mouth. "She used the gifts of Heaven for her own ends!"

Britta smiled. The abbess might be describing herself with that last accusation. Britta had seen that in her soul. It didn't matter. She accepted. What would come would come.

"Burn her!" the abbess wailed, and pointed to the monks with brands. They lowered the burning torches and the flames leapt up. Britta should have been sobbing, begging for mercy, screaming to God to save her soul. But she didn't. She just stared into the fire. It was fearful but familiar. She had stared into fire before, and the fire had told her its secrets. "Tell me the secret of death," she murmured, "and what lies beyond."

The heat beat at her. Flames jumped up near her feet. She watched dispassionately and waited. There they were, figures in the flames. A fortress. Where was the other flame? She always saw the next fire. There it was. Men lined parapets, arms raised, holding burning javelins. Huge pots tipped over the palisades and spilt their oil. In the melee below the gates Karn fought for his life. The smoking oil splashed him as they pushed a cart carrying a log up to the gates. Then the javelins rained down. Karn disappeared, engulfed in the terrible blaze. Screams of the burning men ate at her mind. She shut her eyes. "I won't see this," she shrieked silently.

But there was no choice. She could hear the burning men, smell the burnt flesh. "Karn!" she howled. The vision wavered in smoke and dust. The gates of the fortress opened. More flaming men came running out, screaming, until they fell to their knees, their faces melting as they pitched forward, finally silent. But they continued to burn. Inside her there lurked a strange anticipation, an incipient feeling of triumph. That sickened her more surely than the horrible deaths she beheld. She would cause this fire that ate men alive. She was sure of that. And she would consider it a triumph.

"Karn," she cried, needing him, knowing that he was nowhere near. A familiar freshening wind sighed somewhere, making tattered rags of the flames at her feet. Tears poured down her face. "Karn," she sobbed. The power had come when she wasn't looking. She felt it coursing through her. What was it doing here, when she had used her love for Karn to banish it? Gods, she prayed, God! What is happening? The strength of the energy inside her, outside her, frightened her. Yet it felt so right, so true. The power coursed up through her until her cry became a shriek of ecstasy. She stretched out her white, translucent hands in supplication, whether to God or to Karn she couldn't say.

Her palms bled brightly, a little welling fountain in each hand. Britta's scream turned to a whimper. The flames were at her knees. Heat scorched her robe. The square grew silent but for the crackling of the flames. The abbess, the crowd, all stood frozen. Then the muttering began.

"The wounds of Christ," Brother Alphonse called, louder than the rest.

The abbess slowly lowered her finger of accusation. All through the crowd a new word coursed and grew. "Stigmata."

Chapter Eighteen

Britta sipped her bowl of soup cautiously. Her stomach still rebelled if she tried to eat too much. She held the bowl in both hands; the wounds had closed as miraculously as they had opened. All that remained of the stigmata were blushing circles in each palm. Brother Alphonse watched her with anxious eyes, unlike Fenris, who lay at her feet, his tongue lolling fatuously. The monk had made him a collar of braided leather in the last two days, and the dog looked positively domesticated.

"But what will they do with her?" Britta asked Alphonse. "I could not bear it if she came to grief through my doing."

"It was of her own doing," the monk reminded her. "Her own and Ilwith's."

"Still, she is the abbess," Britta murmured and sipped again. She must gain strength faster. She had to get back to Stowa. Against all odds, Karn might have returned. What if he did not find her there? She had to warn him of what she had seen in her vision. It had prophesied death in front of fortress gates, splashed with hot oil and immolated by burning arrows. *Almost certain death.* After all, she had not died at the stake. She held on to that.

Alphonse hesitated. "The Bishop of Lincoln comes to declare a new abbess, Holy One."

Britta saw the look on his face. "Do not have those thoughts, Brother," she cautioned. "And don't call me Holy One."

"But you would make an ideal abbess," Alphonse protested.

Britta thought quickly. "One thing the abbess said was true: An abbess must be pure."

"Whosoever the Lord our God has blessed with his powers and with the sign of his presence, she is anointed in the eyes of the Church," Alphonse intoned. "A life of prayer and meditation will focus your powers and your holiness."

Britta sighed and sipped her soup. She could not seem to escape this power. Why had it remained, even though she lay with Karn? Her mother, the abbess, Wydda, all were wrong. The power didn't require virginity. She had never felt less like a saint. Saints did not feel triumph when they caused men's deaths, as she had in her vision at the stake. The stigmata were a manifestation of her surroundings, not a sign of holiness. A life of meditation in a cell like the one in which she had spent the last weeks had never been less attractive.

"You should be the abbott, Brother Alphonse." She sighed. "You have true faith."

He began to protest, when a great commotion issued from the cloister courtyard. A monk burst into the cell, bowing hastily.

"What is it, Brother?" Alphonse asked, annoyed. He had become the acknowledged leader here because of his connection with Britta.

"Warriors at the gate, Brother. They will not be denied."

"Very well, I will see them." He turned to Britta. "Rest, Holy One. I shall return."

"Don't call me that," Britta protested hopelessly. Brother Alphonse and his compatriots might become as insistent upon her remaining here as the abbess had been.

The monk had hardly risen before the clatter of horses'

hooves was heard in the courtyard, along with shouts of "Where is she?" Britta jerked her gaze to Brother Alphonse.

Alphonse darted down the corridor of the cloister shouting, "What do you mean by this?" Shouts and curses drowned at his protests.

"We want the witch for Edmund."

Fenris began to bark. Britta stumbled to the doorway, her palms suddenly wet with sweat. Offa, mounted on a huge charger, clattered down the cloister, scanning the cells as he went. When he saw her, he let out a roar of discovery. Britta froze in terror. Offa? Here? Now? She thought she had left the thegn and all his memories behind. He pulled up his horse, as though uncertain. For a moment, they just stared at each other. Belatedly, she tore her eyes away and turned to run. As if galvanized by her terror, Offa urged his horse forward. He leaned over his saddle and scooped her up across the horse's withers, as though she were a dried autumn leaf. Fenris barked crazily and leaped at the horse. It shied and whinnied.

"No," she screamed as the horse righted itself and leapt out into the courtyard through the arch of the cloisters. Above her, Offa wheeled the horse back toward Alphonse.

"Did the abbess declare her a saint?" Offa shouted.

"Unhand her," the monk shrieked.

"Is she a saint?" Offa roared.

"The bishop will declare her," Alphonse stuttered. "God blessed her with stigmata."

Britta couldn't see Offa's reaction. The clatter of hooves and a blur of color filled her senses.

"Away," Offa shouted. The crowd of horses and men trampled the abbey's carefully tended gardens as they made for the now broken gates. She could feel Offa's fist at the rope around her waist. Somewhere Fenris barked. She turned and saw that Brother Alphonse had him by the collar. Then they were out the abbey gates and into the wet afternoon, and she was a prisoner of the one she feared most in the world.

* * *

As Karn heaved himself off Thorn just outside the gates of the abbey, his knees almost buckled with fatigue. A stake stood in the center of the open area, charred and ominous.

He looked around frantically. Was Offa already here? He must find Britta. He dared not think about the stake. They were going to declare Britta a saint, weren't they? The villagers he had stopped to ask could talk of nothing else. But in his gut, he did not trust priests of this new religion to know true worth. The gates to the abbey stood asunder and, inside, milling about, monks wept and rent their clothes. It boded ill.

"You, priest!" As he led Thorn inside the gates, he accosted the first monk he saw and turned the man toward him roughly. "Where is the red-haired woman?"

The monk turned up despairing eyes. "You seek the Holy One?"

"I want Britta," Karn shouted at him.

The monk began to blubber. "You are too late, too late."

Karn's stomach sank into his boots. "Tell me, man," he commanded and shook the monk so hard, the man couldn't hold his head up. In the distance he heard barking. With great effort, he stopped. "What are you called?" he asked, willing his voice calm.

"Alphonse," the monk managed. "Brother Alphonse."

The barking suddenly registered with Karn. He knew it. "Brother Alphonse, where is the red-haired girl?" He gritted his teeth in order not to shout. His restraint was rewarded.

"They took her," Alphonse sobbed. "They took the Holy One."

Not death at the stake. Karn took a breath. But Offa had arrived before him. "It was the fork-bearded one," he said.

Alphonse nodded.

Karn nodded, too, deliberately. He sucked air into his lungs. He knew his course. "Which way? Which way ride?" The language was not right, but he didn't care.

Alphonse pointed northeast. "They took her to Edmund, to the king," he whimpered.

Karn ran to gather Thorn. "Let the dog loose," he called

as he swung into the saddle. Fenris had heard his voice. He would find his way. And Karn could wait for nothing now.

Britta felt Offa's hand at her waist like a brand, holding her to the saddle in front of him. Eleven warriors and an extra horse picked their way carefully through the treacherous fens that surrounded Ely to the northeast. The past rose up to swallow her like the dark sea of despair that had engulfed her after Offa raped her. Only the fact that his act was likely to be repeated when they stopped for the night roused her to action. So she tried to call the power. She willed herself empty, but nothing happened. No sighing wind. No swelling feeling of completeness. Nothing. She clutched at her sanity as her panic grew. Maybe the magic was gone after all. Then what of the stigmata? What of the vision of Karn? She willed her mind to quiet. Wydda taught her to call it. Why couldn't she call it now? Too weak? Because she had renounced it? Because she had realized that the good never called it for themselves? Maybe she was meant to go with Offa to Edmund. After all, she'd had the vision of healing a king.

Stop, she told herself sharply, before you go mad. The power might be there or not. She could not call it now. That was all she knew for certain.

Their first stop was at a pool of clear water. The wind was rising. Ragged clouds chased each other east, the way they rode. Offa threw himself off his horse and landed with a thud. Britta stared at him with furrowed brows, wary.

"Be careful, Offa," Raedwald muttered as he dismounted. He cast uneasy eyes at the turbulent sky. "Remember the island."

"Get down," Offa ordered. He made no move to help.

Britta heaved herself from the horse and nearly fell when her legs would not support her. As she pushed herself up, she studied the hated, hardened face. What emotions flickered there? Hatred. He wanted to hurt her. But something else, too.

Raedwald whispered, "If you kill a saint, there is not enough stone to buy forgiveness."

Offa grabbed her hands, turning them palm up. She could feel him quiver at the rosy circles left by the stigmata. "You are the only one who ever bested me. Are you are a saint?" he asked. His voice shook with intensity.

She managed to raise her chin but said nothing. Everyone wanted her to explain herself. It was the one thing she couldn't do. "If I say I am not, will you kill me?"

He gripped her hands until she thought her bones would break. "You have power. The entire countryside talks of it. You could use it to my gain, I think. But I must know where it comes from. Saint or Satan's tool," he growled. "One or the other."

"Maybe neither," she managed, feeling lost.

An ugly look crossed Offa's face. "You can't be neither. And saint would be sure."

Raedwald came up and broke the moment. "Don't take a chance. Whatever she is, Offa, we bring her to Thetford. She is the key to your future. Remember that."

"She is. But how?" Offa seemed to shake himself. "By giving her to Edmund? By keeping her myself?" He paused. "Why have you not raised your power against us?"

Britta dared not let them know she couldn't call her magic. "I go to Edmund willingly. It is my destiny to heal a king."

Offa grunted. "Or maybe to kill him." He looked confused. The others had begun to cluster around. Britta saw a friendly face with a sense of relief. It was Henewulf.

"See she doesn't wander away, Henewulf," Offa ordered. He turned to the maps that Raedwald spread against a hawthorn tree. "First we must best Delan. He will come after us."

Henewulf smiled at Britta reassuringly. She glanced around at the others. As she caught one warrior's eyes, he made the sign against evil. Another eyed the storm clouds nervously. Good.

"I am glad to see you," she whispered to Henewulf.

He shook his head. "Don't be. You are for Edmund, Wicce. He may be the death of you."

No one made a move to touch Britta that night, afraid either of her or of Edmund. She lay on a horse blanket wrapped in a fur, in the center of a whorl of Saxons. Offa had roped her wrist to his. Her senses filled with the smell of horses and men and smoke from the fire. She tried to comfort herself by thinking of Karn, but then her vision of his danger at the fortress would rise and any peace was gone. Confusion and cataclysm loomed ahead—deaths she'd cause, perhaps Karn's. She slept only in exhausted snatches.

The next morning they rode east toward the coast, not north. Offa was trying to outwit someone named Delan by swinging wide toward the Viking horde on the way back to Thetford. Britta was still weak from her ordeal. She sat a feisty young horse that Offa led with difficulty.

In mid-morning a figure on horseback appeared, outlined against the sky at the top of a low rise. A great black wolf shape loped by his side. It was Karn, and he had Fenris with him. Her stomach wrenched, whether in joy or dread she could not tell.

"Look, Offa," Raedwald pointed as he rode up beside his leader.

"I see him," Offa grunted.

"Delan?" Raedwald asked quietly.

"Delan will send more than one man." They considered silently.

"Do you think it is the Viking she stole from you?"

Offa barked a laugh. "Maybe. I can get part of my revenge. Edmund has no use for that one."

Britta said nothing, her heart bursting with conflicting emotions. Karn had come for her. But was he not one step closer to the flaming arrows, too? Her young mount sidled under her nervously, and she held to the saddle.

"Shall I send men after him?" Raedwald asked.

"And chase him over Christendom? We have something he wants. He will come to us and we will kill him, oh so slowly." Offa turned to Britta. "Did you partake of pagan cock? That doesn't sound saintly."

"How many saints have you known?" she snapped.

"Perhaps he scouts for the Vikings," Raedwald interrupted.

If Karn came for her, they would cut him down. Her fear made her bold. "Whether I am witch or saint, I will not brook you raising your hand against him."

"If he comes for you, we have no choice." Offa's smile was as frightening as Britta remembered. He drew his horse next to hers. "I see you more clearly now. Everything about you belies the saint. Could not the devil produce stigmata?"

"What would you have me tell you? Either answer might be a lie."

Offa nodded slowly. "I was never unsure before today. Even if you are the devil, still I cannot see whether to ally with Edmund or with you. You lead me away from my true path, witch."

Karn disappeared from the rise of the hill behind Offa. "I am not your ally," Britta muttered.

"I must think what must be done." Offa's eyes were hard.

Britta wondered if Karn had shown himself to reassure her. She wished she felt reassured.

Karn waited until the moon was set. Darkness served his purpose. He would never get Britta away with so many enemies surrounding her. He left Thorn tied to an oak tree and unsheathed Walther's sword from its scabbard. It was time to even the odds. He tied Fenris by the collar to a tree. He did not want over-eager help tonight.

He slithered down from the hillside toward the dying coals of the Saxon fire. There was only one sentry. *Foolish.* On the flat, he placed one booted foot in front of another carefully, moving through the trees downwind from the camp. The sentry circled the far perimeter about thirty paces away. Karn slowed his breathing and rested his gaze on Britta, sleeping in the circle of Saxons. She was tied to Offa. No slipping in to steal her away. She looked thin and drawn. *Thor, let their fear protect her.* They would not know she had given up her magic, he told himself. As the sentry stalked past Karn's hiding place, he darted in and ran him through. He let the body fall softly to the ground, but the gurgling death throes woke the others. A cry of alarm broke the night. Karn stuck his sword in another Saxon belly and drew away.

He heard Britta cry out. "Henewulf!"

The Saxons were up and after him. He was forced to turn and half-limp, half-lope back into the trees. He darted left and lay flat in the lee of a fallen elm as they crashed through the underbrush around him, shouting and cursing. After long moments he scrambled back up the rocky slope, not down the draw as they assumed.

Soon he stood next to Thorn, hushing Fenris to quiet. He could hear the clatter of scree sliding down the slope below. One Saxon had not been fooled, but Karn did not draw his sword. Instead he let loose the rope that held Fenris. The dog shot down the slope, a blacker shadow in the night. Karn did not need to see what happened. He heard the snarling, the cry that crumbled into gurgling. Three, he thought. There were still eight, counting Offa. He could not risk Britta by striking when he was sure to fail. He did not know their destination. Would he have time to carve them down to a number he might manage before he must risk all, including Britta herself?

Britta knelt over Henewulf in the dark hour before dawn. It was not dark enough to hide the black halo that circled him. Karn's sword had done its work well. The Saxons broke camp, their angry mutterings against the Viking filling their mouths with futile bile. Britta struggled for breath as she lifted Henewulf's head into her lap. "I'm sorry," she choked.

His eyes flickered about before they fixed on her face. "Not your fault," he murmured.

That was a lie. She was the reason Karn had killed him, unknowing though it was. This man's soul was on her list of debts, just like her mother's was. "Don't speak," she said. "Save your strength." That was useless now, of course.

"I am immortal." The whispered words forced her to lean close. "My Edgar lives on."

Tears welled in Britta's eyes. "He is strong, you said."

"He is your gift to me." The words were ashes in the rising dawn wind, barely there.

She could not deny it. It would be denying him his only solace. She nodded. "A fine legacy you leave," she whispered.

His lips under his mustaches curved up and froze there as the light died in his eyes. Britta clenched her lashes shut over her tears.

"Leave him," Offa shouted as he mounted his horse. The sky behind him pearled at the horizon. Rough hands grabbed Britta up, away from Henewulf. It didn't matter. He was gone.

Karn watched the tiny party, now only three other than Offa and Britta, hurry across the plain toward the heaving mass of Saxons encamped around the fortress just outside the little town below. His shout of rage broke through the midday air. At four to one, he had resolved to take his chances, but he had missed his opportunity: Offa had made it to safety. Britta was lost. He'd had three days, yet he had not won her freedom. Those Saxons had not slept in two nights. Still, he'd managed to kill four more.

It was not enough. His heart felt as though it might burst. Britta rode into Hel's domain with Offa himself, and he was powerless to rescue her! He watched them pick their way through the encampment as they moved toward the open gates. It would take an army to breach these fortress walls once they closed upon her.

He knew an army, he thought grimly. He turned Thorn's head south and called to Fenris. There was but one hope to rescue Britta now, but it might cost him his life to procure it.

Britta watched the small figure on horseback and the dog disappear from the rise on the hill behind her. The hope that flickered under her fear of the future evaporated along with Karn. She longed to be with him, but she had to be here in this fortress. That feeling had been growing stronger with each passing hour. She had entered a tunnel or a cave, a dark place where anything might happen. She might emerge into the light again or not, but the world at the end of the tunnel would be like nowhere she had known before.

She turned away from the empty horizon and gazed with horror at the thousands of soldiers surging about her in the camp outside the gates of the fortress. They lounged by fires. They shouted and threw dice. They sharpened swords and curried horses. They filled the streets of the little village she could see next to the river. The melee of men was more frightening by far than the storm she had once raised.

She had not one friend among them. She could not blame Karn for killing Henewulf. He had been trying to free her from Offa. Yet the only one who wished her well was now gone. He had not deserved to be paid so for saving their lives. Despair welled like bile into her throat. "Deserving" seemed to have nothing to do with the world at all.

"Well, Witch," Offa growled. "I brought you safe to Edmund in spite of your pagan lover, in spite of Delan himself. Now we will see whether you or Edmund is my answer."

A darkly handsome man rode with a troop of perhaps twenty men in from the west.

"Delan," Offa shouted in mock surprise. "Were you sent on a mission by Edmund as well?"

The man turned his horse toward them, glowering. "How is it you come from the east?" he asked between clenched teeth as he drew close.

"The better to reach here in one piece with my charge." Offa laughed grimly.

"Your journey looks to have been difficult," Delan said, glancing behind Offa to where only Raedwald, Badenoth, and one other warrior now straggled behind.

"I expected worse," Offa returned.

Delan's eyes narrowed and turned toward Britta for the first time. She was acutely aware of her novice's rough wool robe, dirty with days of traveling. "May your gift reveal the worth of its giver," he sneered and jerked his horse toward the palisades.

Offa turned to Britta. "If you disappoint Edmund, he will kill you," he said. "If he tries, I suppose you will kill him. Either way, I win. If you live, then will we talk about an alliance."

Britta swallowed hard. "I will do what is meant to be done." Offa kicked his steed forward viciously and motioned for his small troop to follow him.

The gates loomed above her as she and Offa's party rode through. Soldiers and wagons teemed through them. The fortress of her vision. It was these gates that she saw broken asunder, belching fire and human torches. It was from these walls that flaming arrows were loosed upon Karn. She stared ahead, her mind alive with carnage no one else could see.

Offa jerked her horse forward and she came to herself. The central living quarters loomed above. Three floors, there must be. There were several towers that stretched even higher, like the bell tower in the church at Dunford, except made of wood. Men in rich dress as well as warriors moved in and out through great carved doors.

Delan threw his reins to a waiting boy and dashed into the gloom of the interior.

"Whispering to Edmund against me," Offa growled into his beard. "Bastard whoreson."

Britta worked herself into a fever of anticipation. She would know Edmund's face anywhere. It had been burned into her memory from her vision in the fens. Could she still heal him? Above her, great shutters banged open and a slight man in a red cloak leaned out.

"Is that her, Offa?" he screeched.

"Aye, I have brought her."

Britta watched in shock as he rubbed his hands together greedily and motioned them up. She looked around in bewilderment as Offa lifted her off the horse and grabbed her arm. This screeching scarecrow bore no resemblance to the regal young man she had healed in her dream. "Is that Edmund?" she whispered.

"Aye." One of the men behind her chuckled. "A fact you will live to regret, I'll wager."

"Not for long," another called. "I give her two days." Raucous laughter echoed all around.

"How many healers has Edmund killed so far?"

"Three, this winter."

They are trying to make me afraid. Britta sucked in a huge breath to fend off fear. But their tactics had already worked.

Offa guided her into the dark hall. "Your moment of truth approaches, Witch."

Britta gathered herself as she and Offa climbed the stairs to where Edmund waited. There was no escape from what would happen here, whatever it was. He was not the one she'd healed in her vision, but he wanted healing—Offa made that clear. She might have magic, might not, but her skill with herbs had not deserted her. She would try to heal him, because she needed time. She and all inside the fortress hurtled toward the death by fire she had seen in her vision. Yet she felt sure she must wait for something, for the fire, for the Danes, for Karn to return. She didn't know which.

At the top of the stairs, they emerged into an audience room bathed in light from open shutters in contrast to the dark below. Britta could feel Offa behind her, a dour menace. Delan was there. The king whirled and eyed her almost hungrily, dwelling on her streaked hair. Should she bow? Kneel? In the end she decided to do neither, though she could see bowed heads on either side. Instead she drew herself up and examined the King of Anglia.

"Well?" he asked sharply. "What do you see, Healer?" he barked.

What to say? She could hardly tell him that she saw a weak chin, a mouth too used to pouting, a sallow skin, to be sure, but not a diseased one. He was thin, wiry rather than sickly, with an inward look to his eyes, a cruel subtlety that could not please.

"I see a king, liege." She inclined her head slightly.

"Do you not want to examine me?" he whined. "I have craved a healer for so long."

Britta glanced once at Offa and saw his plain disapproval of Edmund in his eyes. You walk a dangerous road, old enemy, she thought. It was the same road she walked herself. She motioned Edmund to a chair. "If you will allow it, Liege," she said. No, that would never do. She must sound more in control than that. "Though, of course, it is not strictly necessary."

"Not necessary to examine me?" He sank into his padded chair. "That is a marvel, sure."

He wants to believe. Britta felt his forehead. She rolled up his eyelids and looked into the pupils. "What is it that troubles you, Liege?"

"Meat and mead give me pains in my chest," he complained. "Smoke makes me cough. It is my lungs that worry me. It is prophesied that I will die of a lung ailment."

"Do you bring up phlegm?"

He cleared his throat self-consciously. She saw him decide to lie. "Yes, yes, I do." Others exchanged knowing looks.

"Does breathing give you pain?" she asked, still nursing hope somewhere.

"Most horribly. I suffer more than anyone can know."

"I know exactly how much you suffer, Liege." Britta kept her voice neutral.

He smiled, then looked uncertain. "Well, then, what do you prescribe?" he asked irritably.

Now her goose was cooked, she thought forlornly. There was nothing wrong with him. He was one of those twisted souls who imagined illnesses, whether from fear or a desire for attention, it really didn't matter. How could she cure what was not wrong?

She must buy time, even if the cure was not real. "Your minion—" Here she gestured back toward Offa. How it would gall him to hear himself called that! Britta repeated it with relish. "Your minion took me suddenly from the monastery where I prayed and studied. He did not bring my herbs or my books. I have nothing here to cure you with."

Edmund lowered his brows and glared, first at Offa, then at her. "Can you do nothing without these paltry herbs?" he barked. His demeanor had suddenly turned ominous. His other, murdered healers had no doubt seen just such a look before their demise. She plunged on.

"They are the catalysts, without which my greater magic does not start its work," she amended. "Let me but go out on the hillsides, newly greening, and I will find burdock and chamomile, woodbine and rue growing aplenty after the wet winter. I can make a decoction of these and infuse it with my powers. Your cure is certain."

Britta held her breath. She was alone against Edmund. Offa would welcome the king killing her. Delan wanted her failure to discredit Offa. Edmund himself was no better than a sulky snake, waiting to bite. But she had a plan. She wanted none of the herbs she had named. What she needed to find was valerian root, and plenty of it.

"Oh, very well." Edmund waved a hand. "Delan, take her wherever she wants to go."

Britta had delayed as long as she could. The decoction had been completed long ago. She allowed the fire she tended in the yard to burn down for the last time in the early mist of pre-dawn. She alone was awake, except for the sleepy sentries at the gates. Edmund had sent messengers to gauge her progress on the half-hour until she had informed one that to disturb her concentration was to diminish the power of her potion. Indeed, the power of this potion was the question. She had reduced the tea made from the valerian roots she had gathered until it was as strong as she had ever produced. Would it be enough?

All during the night, Karn and the magic filled her mind until they were intertwined. It was when she'd rescued Karn from Offa that the magic had started again in earnest. He'd got inside her protection and had drawn her out until she was open to the world. In the end she had lain with Karn for love, all protection gone. And the magic, which should have been banished, wasn't. Wydda and the abbess and her mother, all had only a glimpse of the power. One didn't keep it by hoarding your virginity, but by opening yourself to the world, no matter the pain. True power could not be used. No, you had to go the way it wanted to go, even when you couldn't see where the magic tended. Was that what she was doing now? She didn't know. What she saw ahead was death and flames and destruction, for Karn, for herself, for her people. She should be hopeless. Yet she waited for something. Something was going to happen, if she could but last.

She stood up, her joints creaking. She was bone-tired. The camp around her began to stir. She was in the world now, all right. Her island was gone. The protection of not caring, gone. Her magic came and went as it pleased. She didn't even have a knife. But she would not trade her love for Karn for any security, even if she never saw him again.

She lifted the heavy pot from the tripod that held it over the dying fire and poured the tea, thick with bits of root, through a sieve and into the last of several clay jars lined up beside the coals. She would not wait for Edmund to summon her. Picking up the first of the jars, she turned toward the carved doors of the king's living quarters. It was time to take the initiative.

"Summon the king?" the sleepy guard asked incredulously.

"Summon the king," Britta repeated firmly. The man looked as though he was about to faint at the very thought. "Or stand aside." When he hesitated, she swept him away with a wave of her hand. He backed away as though he thought her mad.

She pushed open the door to Edmund's chamber and walked in. In the dim light leaking through the closed shutters, she could see him in the great bed with posts like beams, piled high with embroidered coverlets and laid with furs across his feet. He stirred sleepily at her entrance.

"King Edmund," she called softly. "Wake to your cure."

He started and pushed himself up. She stared with all the intensity she could muster and stalked over to sit beside him. Her wild red hair brushed his thigh. "Your sickness has its root not in your body but in your dreams," she whispered sinuously. "It is your dreams that we must cure. You have nightmares?" What tyrant who killed healers would not?

He looked uneasy. "Well, then," she continued, "I will cure your body by curing your dreams." She poured from her clay jar into a goblet set on a table by his bed. "Two cups of this and my magic"—she paused dramatically— "and you are cured."

She held out the goblet to him. He stared, wide-eyed, at it, then raised his eyes to hers. She did not blink. Finally he clutched at the vessel and drank it down in greedy gulps. She smiled as she poured him another. *Drink, sulky snake. Drink, and dream for as long as you can.*

Chapter Nineteen

Karn walked into the Viking camp as the mist began to lift. He was acutely conscious of his limp. The sentry who first hailed him now led Thorn and hefted Walther's wonderful sword in admiration. Karn could feel those who recognized him draw back in disgust. Muttered epithets from some hung in the air as he passed. Those he had known well were simply wary. They had not reconciled Ulf's stories with their experience of him. Still, there were no welcoming grins.

He touched Fenris's fur and drew comfort from the connection to Britta he found there. Their winding progress through the camp seemed endless until they came around a clump of elm trees. Offa's fortress loomed above.

Karn's courage dropped through the pit of his belly. What was the shame his fellow Danir might heap on him compared to his horrible secret? His step faltered. He had walked far back along the path of living, almost from the brink of soullessness. But now shame broke through all the barriers he had so carefully erected. How could one such as he face down Ivar the Boneless?

They wended their way up to the captured fortress. The

great gates stood open. Danir streamed through in both directions. Karn's stomach churned as he realized that the sword at his back prodded him toward the very hall where Offa had raped and tortured him. He could not face his accusers there, in that hall! Fenris melted into the surrounding activity rather than enter such a confined space, leaving Karn utterly alone.

As they bent through the hall door, his knees trembled. He could not let Ivar see him thus. His vision adjusted to the dimness. The irregular dark patches that stained the floor transfixed him. He either looked away now from these marks of his shame or he would never look away. Thor, give me strength, he prayed without hope. Thor had turned away from him that night. It had been Britta who aided him, not Thor. Britta. He swallowed hard. And Britta needed him.

He took a long breath and jerked his gaze toward the end of the hall, where a crowd of men stood. They sputtered into silence, staring at him. Ivar sat on a huge rough chair as though it were a throne. His brother Halfdan stood at his side, mead horn in hand.

"So, our wayward warrior has returned," Ivar said. His face betrayed that he had heard Ulf's stories. Did he believe them?

Karn scanned the crowd for Ulf and did not see him. That was bad. He had counted on provoking Ulf to expose himself and his lies. That left Karn trying to counter what was half-true. He straightened himself and limped forward, trying to think only of Britta. "As you see, First Jarl." Every eye observed the limp. Some looked away, some grimaced.

"What brings you here?" Halfdan asked. Was he sneering?

"I come to join the battle. I require revenge on those who have taken from me what I hold to my heart." He would never win over Halfdan, but Ivar had trusted him for nearly twenty years. Yet surely Ivar could see his shame and unworthiness.

The jarl looked vaguely uneasy. "There may be no battle to join, by the gods. Has Loki sent you here to mock us?"

Karn didn't understand. "I have always served Thor—and

the bold brothers." A general hubbub of protest rose against him.

Halfdan inserted himself. "How does it serve us to betray your men to death and join the Saxons against us?" Karn saw Ivar rest a restraining hand on his sibling's arm.

"I am not a traitor, First Jarls," Karn said with as much conviction as he could muster. "Only bring Ulf forward and let him face me. You will decide who is the traitor. Or let us fight, my hand to his, and let blood decide the truth." Karn felt his need for satisfaction bloom like an ember firing up in his belly. Ivar could make Ulf fight whether Karn was crippled or not.

"Ulf is gone inland," Ivar said. "I decide who is traitor." Halfdan glared at his brother, but he went to sit on a bench by the wall. Karn was Ivar's man. Ivar would be his judge.

Karn felt the ember in his gut turn to ashes. Britta could not wait for Ulf to scout or maraud. He must counter now what these men believed. But how, when he had only words at his disposal? "I bow to your will, First Jarl," he said, gritting his teeth.

A murmur rippled through the Danish warriors. Ivar was famous as a lawgiver, stern and just. If Ivar ruled against him, his blood would flow within the hour, no doubt in the blood eagle, unless Ivar could think of some death more painful. Not one pair of eyes in the crowd looked on him with favor. Ulf had done his work well.

"First, there is the matter of the cowardice that betrayed your band to death," Ivar began.

It was not a good beginning. Karn must wrest control of the story from Ulf, his absent accuser. He drew himself up and said, "Do you want my saga, Ivar?" There were cries of protest from the men. Karn had to shout to make himself heard. "Or are you closed to truth?" The voices faded. No one challenged Ivar as he sat in judgment. A bold move was the only one left to Karn. He could see that he had stung Ivar, who prided himself on his sagacity. Ivar's brows descended ominously, but he pointed one oddly bent finger at Karn to signal his agreement.

"You sent me, O great Jarl, here to the village by the beach. Wealth was my task, though my men and I longed for the Whale Road, to follow you south into glorious battle against the Cents. Still, we followed your Word Path to plunder. Remember with me that it was Ulf who showed us the stones piled high to their one God, the kirk. Ulf asked you to give my band the honor of gutting it. An easy target, Ulf said. But this fortress where we stand was close, as Woden has shown in his wisdom, and Saxon warriors ten times our number avenged the kirk. Battle bright, they rained on us. Casks of courage spent your Danir: Saxon-slayers five-fold. Side by side they slew for themselves and for the honor of their kinsmen. Swords bit mail. Valkyrie swooped down to take our fallen, soaked in Saxon blood. Not one stood at the end of the day."

"Not one?" Ivar asked. Anticipation leapt from man to man around the hall.

Karn paused before he could go on. He could not tell the whole story. "The Valkyrie passed me by that day." Here he lifted his head. "It may be that they saved me for another day." He must answer one other, unspoken question. "The barbarians spent their wrath on me, to leave the haltr one you see. Yet the plans of the bold brothers were sealed behind my lips, else the full strength of the Saxons would have greeted your dragons at the shore."

The room erupted in clamoring questions. Ivar raised his hand for silence. "I will do the questioning here. What has this fortress to do with Ulf?" Ivar asked with narrowed eyes.

"Ulf scouted down this coast last summer," Karn pressed. "He knew this fortress. With me dead, he would supplant me in your heart, that he might take your place when the Valkyrie come for you at last." The jarls, including Ivar, considered. "He stands in your heart now."

"You race too fast to the battle, Karn," Ivar admonished, almost privately. "You know not where my heart stands. Can you prove what you say?" This was his chance to make his point.

"No," Karn admitted. "But why is that? Ulf's companions

when he saw the fortress could prove my tale. Do any of Ulf's scouting party yet live?"

The men exchanged uneasy glances all around.

"You killed Erik Eriksson," one blurted. "He was the last."

"I had not that honor," Karn corrected. "Bjorn the Bear-hearted clove his skull as Erik attacked me from behind." There were several knowing grins. Halfdan actually chortled as he drained his horn of mead. "I wanted him alive," Karn insisted. "He was the last who could prove my sooth. Ulf sent him against me. Thus, did not Ulf kill him?" Kara examined Ivar carefully and caught a flicker of agreement there. Ivar had his own suspicions of Ulf. Karn could feel it.

"Do you deny you lived among Saxons?" Ivar changed the direction of the inquiry.

"A Saxon woman healed me."

"Why would such a one heal a Dane?" one of the other asked sharply.

Karn examined this question, as he had so many times before. He shifted his weight to his good hip. "She has a gift from the gods. She could not help herself." He saw their skepticism.

"And later?" Ivar asked, pressing.

How to explain about later? The truth was his hope, and Britta's. At least enough truth to give him pain. "I could not return to you haltr. I knew how it would be." He took a breath. "I learned to ride and hold a sword, so I might return sea-strong and battle-ready."

"Ulf saw you living easy among them."

"He told truth there," Karn agreed. "They are humble folk in the fens, stout and true."

"You speak of Saxons?" one of the men asked in amazement.

Karn bridled. "They did not know me for a Dane. They treated me kindly and learned law." He saw questioning looks around the circle. They did not believe Saxons could learn civilized ways. "One gave me a fine weapon." Here he pointed to Walther's sword in the sentry's hand. "I owe a debt. If that makes me traitor, so be it. A man with honor knows honor in others."

A murmur, this time of surprise, ran around the hall. The gift of a sword was a great one. Several moved to examine the finely wrought hilt.

"Why have you returned now?" Ivar asked. The frown had grown thoughtful.

"It is spring. You will ride into battle against the one who built this fortress, who killed my warriors wild. I want to ride with you, for my revenge and theirs." He did not mention Britta.

"You, fight with us?" another of the men sneered amid a general noise of protest.

"You bring a haltr body only to our cause?" Ivar asked.

Karn wondered if the soft tone mocked him. "I bring a way of riding into battle. I made a saddle a warrior can fight from. With the horse, I am stronger in combat than I was before. I can teach others to make that saddle, train them to ride it." There, he had given his gift.

Halfdan rose to his feet and waved his hand impatiently. "Horses are for the pursuit of an enemy, surprise. They are not an advantage once the battle begins." The derisive murmuring among the other Danir showed they agreed.

He felt himself failing. They thought him a traitor, a cripple. How could he shove this army toward Britta and Offa? He tried to master his sense of desperation. In truth, he had half-expected to meet the Danes on the road. Why were they not already on the move? He stabbed in the dark. "Do you know where your enemies lie, and how many they are?"

Ivar glanced at Halfdan. Karn could tell he had struck a nerve because of the restless muttering among the men. This must have been what they were discussing when he entered.

"Our spies come back dead on their horses or not at all." Ivar admitted. "We know they are camped to the north. But we know not the size of their force, or the exact location."

"I know these things," Karn announced. Let their need outweigh their distrust.

305

"Don't believe him, Ivar." Halfdan advanced to stand behind his brother.

"You take the word of a traitor?" The outcry was general. "He leads us into a trap."

Karn raised his voice. "A trap, but not of my making, for they number three times your force and more."

The throng grew silent.

"Worse, they are encamped around a fortress, larger and stronger than this one. Edmund will take refuge inside and bide, even if you slay the army that surrounds it."

Ivar nodded thoughtfully, then he glanced sharply at Karn. "I trusted you once, more than the others," he accused. This was the hurt that balanced his doubts of Ulf. "Why should I believe you now?" This was the question that must be answered, the price that must be paid.

Karn shook his head, then finally shrugged. "For the years of faithful service that speak against Ulf's easy words. Because you know I held you close to my heart. How else will you move against the Saxons? I know you, Ivar. You will risk the truth of my words for the taste of victory." He wished he felt as certain as he sounded. He hoped Ivar could not see the hollowness at his center. He hoped, too, that Ivar would stand against his brother's obvious opinion.

Ivar grew more thoughtful as the silent crowd waited for his ruling. "What of Jael, Bjorn, and Thurmak?" he asked. "Did you bend them to your Saxon ways?"

"Ulf cursed them when they stood for me. They did not leave you willingly," Karn vowed. "Were they here they could vouchsafe the truth of my words."

"But they are not."

"Neither is Ulf."

Ivar had traded for as much time as he could. He pounded the arms of the chair to signify his decision. "You will lead us to the Saxons," he barked. "The outcome of the battle will decide your fate. If there is an ambush, you will be the first to die." Halfdan met Ivar's steady gaze and finally shrugged his shoulders.

"When can we start?" Karn sighed with breath he did not know he held.

"Tomorrow," Ivar said, rising. "We have much to do."

Though Vikings moved fast, it would still be two more days before they reached the fortress. Four days since he left her. Could Britta survive Offa for four days?

But Ivar was not done. "You two." He motioned to two of the jarls. "Show our found friend a place to camp, and watch that nothing may befall him before he fulfils his trial with us."

Karn pressed down a protest. Was he a prisoner here? Well, he would use those guards for information. There was yet one piece of unfinished business he dared not transact with Ivar. He held out his hand for Walther's sword. The sentry looked to Ivar, who nodded. With obvious reluctance the man handed over the gleaming weapon.

"Where is Ulf, that he is not here today?" Karn asked, as, flanked by the two Danir, he strode back out into the morning. "I must yet have satisfaction for his lies."

"You missed him, and he you." The younger of the two smirked. Karn remembered him now. His name was Gamall. "I would call it luck for you, since you are no match."

"Think you he will be back before tomorrow?" Karn asked. They threaded their way through the busy camp as shouted orders echoed in the damp coastal air.

Gamall shook his head and pointed to a small campfire. Fenris came dashing up with the half-charred carcass of a rabbit he had stolen. "Ulf and a party of warriors seek you in the Saxon village where he found you. They left four days ago. He will not be back before we leave."

Karn tried to steady his breathing. His mind's eye painted the Danir, led by Ulf, descending on the village. Ulf would kill everyone when he did not find Karn. Worse, whatever would happen had happened already. He was too late to save his friends. Deliberately, he sat cross-legged on the winter's leaves in front of the smoldering dregs of the fire. He pressed his lips together, as though that would suppress the pain. The three Vikings could fight. Perhaps they were not all

307

dead. He wanted to go to them, but he could not. His two guards arranged themselves nearby. Karn watched Fenris set to his meal.

"You and I are for Britta, dog. No matter the cost."

Britta sat at the open window, watching the sun set. There was a clatter on the stairs behind her. She turned to see Delan burst through the door. His face went dead, betraying nothing. Now it began. She was silent, merely lifting her brows in inquiry.

"Where is the king, Witch?" Delan asked softly.

"He sleeps, as I said this morning," Britta replied.

"Aye, as you said this morning," Delan agreed. "But still he sleeps."

"It is his dreams that cause his turbulent health." She must make him believe her. "I am curing his mind." She rose and stared at Delan, unblinking.

"Are you?" he asked. He sounded as though he really wanted to know.

She nodded and smiled serenely. "I will give you back a king who can lead you. Do you want him healed? The thegns depend upon you to control his unpredictability. You like that."

Delan started, as though he had been struck. "You know nothing of these things, girl."

Britta smiled.

Delan glared at her for a long moment, then turned upon his heel.

Britta let out the breath she had been holding and turned to her pot of valerian potion. She had never made a decoction this effective. How long could she keep Edmund unconscious, and Delan and the others at bay? Only so long would she live.

The next morning it rained. Karn mounted Thorn in the early light. The Danish camp was a hive of activity as the Danir got ready to move out. Horses stamped in the mud. Wagons left deep ruts as they rumbled down the hill loaded with supplies. They would arrive at Thetford long after the battle was decided. The smell of wet leather and wet horsehide permeated the air. There were shouts and clatter everywhere. Even so, Karn's ears picked one shout out of the din.

"Are you on the move, brothers? Are we for Edmund?" It was Ulf.

Karn swung Thorn around to search the chaos. There he was, at the head of ten hardened warriors. "Stay where you are, brothers," Karn snapped out through the din to the warriors behind Ulf. Several drew their swords when they recognized him. "Ulf and I have a reckoning."

Ulf looked up, startled. "You! How did you get here?"

Karn rode Thorn forward. "I came to tell Ivar of his enemies and to join the battle."

A scowl disfigured Ulf's handsome face, his white-blond hair dripping from his ride through the rain. "You are a lame traitor," he sneered. "No one would let you share our victory."

Karn's brain raced. He wanted this fight. But if he lost, he was no good to Britta.

Behind him, Gamall shouted his greeting. "Ulf! This one has been saying that you betrayed his band for your own gain."

His foe's troop muttered. Ulf's own scowl deepened. "I thought to find you consorting with our enemies and dispatch you," he said tightly. "It is a shame you were not there."

Karn refused to think about his friends in Stowa. "I am here." He watched Ulf's nostrils flare as he tried to control his anger. Karn realized that Ulf had no choice but to fight now—he had hoped to dispatch Karn far from Ivar, but he could not afford to let Karn counteract his lies here in the Danish camp. They would fight. The only way to Britta lay through Ulf. The Danir near them backed into a makeshift circle around them. They, too, knew what would happen.

"Both name each other traitors," one of them said. He was an older man Karn knew but slightly. He strode out between the horses. "I am Dag. Will you settle it?"

"Men, does he deserve a fight?" Ulf asked those around

him. "Cut down like a dog for his treason, maybe, not honored with combat." Several of his men moved up beside him.

Dag stepped close, his left hand resting lightly on his sword. "If truth be known, it will be known hand to hand," he said into the relative quiet. The crowd continued to gather members from the surrounding surge of Danir. "Will you settle it?" he repeated.

Karn saw Ulf abandon the help of his supporters with a grin, wave them back. He thought Karn an easily vanquished foe. He was probably right. He had almost been a match for Karn in the days when Karn was whole. Now he would be faster, stronger, more mobile.

Ulf leapt from his horse and fingered his sword. "I *will* settle it," he barked impatiently.

Karn would have to give up Thorn to fight Ulf. A shiver of fear shot through him, as much for Britta as for himself. He dared not fail. He raised his bad leg with care and dropped to the ground. "*I* will settle it," he returned grimly.

Ulf gave a greasy smile and drew his sword. He slapped the flat of the blade against his open palm with a dull *thwack*. The rain lightened to a heavy mist. Still, both combatants dripped.

Fenris wove his way through the crowd. Karn grabbed his ruff. He could feel the rumble in the dog's throat, though he could not hear it. Britta would never forgive him if Fenris was hurt.

"Gamall," he called, "take the dog." Gamall grunted with the ignominy of his assignment, but he dragged Fenris backward to the circle, the dog protesting with yips and whines. Karn threw Thorn's bridle to another Dane and turned to face Ulf.

Ulf lowered himself into a battle crouch.

Karn looked down at Walther's wonderful sword. The blade balanced with heavy certainty in his grip. The Saxon carving glinted in a determined sunray that illuminated what would be their killing ground. It may be that you avenge your maker this day, he told the sword silently, or are forfeit to his killer. He moved into position as Ulf smirked. He did not try to hide his limp. Underestimate me, Ulf, he thought. His best chance was that his foe brought his character as well as his skill to the fight. Ulf was cocky by nature and not a patient man. Those traits might work for Karn, if he could live to take advantage of them.

Even before Karn took his battle stance, Ulf lunged in, sword held high. The clanging parry sounded flat as the mist closed in again. A shout went up around the circle. Ulf was a fury of blows, fierce and sure. Karn staggered into position just in time to turn each back. He tried not to see the crowd, hear their shouting, feel the rain. He must connect his fighting instinct to the sword and let it do its work without distraction.

Ulf was relentless. Yet he could not find a place where he did not meet Walther's sword. The opponents slipped and slid on the muddy ground. Ulf struck a blow to Karn's shoulder. It crashed and slithered along the metal as it cut his borrowed mail shirt. Karn went down into the mud. Blood welled from his upper arm. From his knees he struck away Ulf's sword and scrambled up.

The clangs and the shiver of steel went on. Ulf grew angry as his first energy flagged. He had to choose his blows. Frustration welled up in his eyes. A little longer, strength, hold a little longer, Karn thought, as the shock of Ulf's blows made his arm tremble.

Then it happened. Karn saw the decision flash across his enemy's face. Ulf would not wait for Karn to fail. He lunged in. He pushed Karn's sword back upon him with brute strength.

Everything came back to Karn with a rush. Ulf shrieked frustration and malice not an inch from his face, only just louder than the shouts of the men around him. Droplets of water ran down their swords, making rivulets across the muddy hands that gripped the hilts. Karn smiled. He let Ulf's sword slide off his. The scrape of metal on metal rang out. Raindrops sprayed from the sword points. Ulf lurched, off-balance. Karn used that instant to heave himself to the right. His own sword circled and took Ulf's with it, slithering along its length. The circling continued. Karn was behind Ulf. He sliced down across the back of Ulf's legs and spun to face him again.

Ulf cried out and leaned over, hands on his knees. Blood dripped from the slashed leather across the back of his thighs where Karn's sword had struck deep.

"Equal footing now," Karn gasped. Ulf's groan became a shriek of rage as he straightened up and limped into the fray. He slashed this way and that, spending strength without heed. Karn knew Ulf would weaken fast. As he waned, Karn began to plumb his own small reserve of energy. Now it was Karn who gritted his teeth and swung his sword, ignoring his slashed shoulder. He could see fear in his enemy's eyes. He let the revelation of Ulf's fear fuel him.

Ulf fell back as blood streamed from his thighs. Muscle was cut. As Karn watched, Ulf became increasingly hobbled. Good; he had cut at least some tendon, too. A backhanded blow to Ulf's off shoulder drove him to his knees. Ulf thrust upward, straight for Karn's belly, but Karn met steel with steel. He pressed his parry, just as Ulf had done, then again he pushed Ulf's sword out and around in a swinging circle. This time Ulf's sword catapulted from his weakened grip to land on the ground ten feet away. Silence fell over the crowd.

Karn stood back, chest heaving, and hefted Walther's sword. He could deal the killing blow. Triumph coursed through him, then soured. Would he allow Ulf to die in combat? Send him to the Valkyrie for his treachery? He searched Ulf's expectant face. Ulf waited for death with Norse courage, looking Karn in the eyes. Karn felt his burning intensity sigh away. His knees almost buckled. He used Walther's sword to prop himself up as his breath rasped in the silence.

"Finish him," Dag hissed.

"No," Karn panted. "He refused to fight me once. Now I refuse to finish him." He leaned against his sword and looked around at the Danir. "Let him pay as I do for his

312

treachery." Karn let his voice rise. "Let him limp himself back to manhood if he can."

"You cannot shame me thus," Ulf screeched. He tried to get to his feet, but one leg gave way and he fell heavily into the mud.

Ulf's supporters grumbled. Karn looked at Dag. "My victory proves my words."

Dag looked around the circle, challenging. "The gods declare the truth today."

Karn did not wait to see if any would try to avenge Ulf. He staggered back to Thorn and shoved himself up into the saddle with trembling legs.

"Are we ready to move?" he asked.

Already the wagons rolled down the muddy road toward the north. Troops were strung out across the hills and riding hard. "Make haste or miss our glory," Dag shouted.

Karn spurred ahead.

"You cannot do this to me," Ulf cried from where he lay in the mud. Men around the circle turned and scrambled for their horses. Gamall freed Fenris and leapt into his own saddle.

One by one, Danir turned their horses toward the northwest. Even Ulf's supporters made their choice. Not one looked at Ulf as he began to gibber after them. "Traitors, all of you!"

Ulf's shrieks echoing after him, Karn turned Thorn's head toward Thetford and Britta.

Chapter Twenty

Britta poured the last drops of her valerian tea into a goblet. This was the third day she had been feeding Edmund her potion. He would wake soon, groggy, and she might buy one final day. After that, who knew? She set down the cup and stared out at the camp, beginning to stir. She needed more time. She felt it. Perhaps escape was possible, or there was some deed to do before she died. She didn't know what the feeling meant and there were no visions, hard as she had stared into the fire in Edmund's room these last days.

Dejected, she took her goblet past the two guards outside Edmund's door. They had grown used to her, but she was not allowed to leave. That was Delan at work.

Edmund's pinched and sour features floated on his pillows. Even sleep was unable to soften them to kindness. Was this her king? It did not take wise eyes to see he was a bad leader. A thought flitted though her: Edmund was in her power. Was she meant to kill him? She pushed the impulse away. She could not kill in cold blood. Leaving Wydda to die had been close enough. Besides, after Edmund, who would rule? Gods protect the land from Offa! Was Delan a better leader? She paced uneasily beside the bed, waiting for Edmund to wake. Of all those she knew, only a Viking with bright blue eyes and a limp was made of the stuff to lead a people. Courage arid generosity together, an iron will and a large heart. That was what it took.

A noise outside stopped her in midstride, and she whirled to see Delan standing in the doorway, his face contorted in a scowl. "Enough of treating Edmund's dreams, Witch."

It was what she had feared. "His case is difficult. You know how unsettled he is."

"This treatment bodes not well for Edmund," Delan insisted.

"Did he not drink eagerly?" Britta's calm was feigned. Edmund stirred behind her.

"Aye, and that has stayed my hand too long," Delan growled. "The men now wonder where he is. And that enflames rebellious curs like Offa."

Britta turned to offer Edmund the goblet. Would Delan stop her if Edmund reached for it?

Delan jerked her around, and the goblet clattered to the floor. The last of the tea was sucked up by the thirsty wood of the floor. A day, a whole day lost!

Britta raised her eyes to Delan's, angry now. "Look what you have done." Her voice rose.

"It's for the best," he returned briskly, picking up the goblet.

"We'll see what Edmund has to say when he hears of it." She was casting for straws. When Edmund woke with a bad head and three days gone, he would likely kill her then and there unless she could give his spite another direction.

"He'll thank me for saving him from the likes of you," Delan snarled.

"Have you saved me, then?" a sleepy voice behind them piped. Britta jerked her head around to see the king blinking peevishly. "Saved me from whom?"

Offa could hear Edmund's anger all the way down in the forecourt of the fortress.

"Well, he isn't dead," Raedwald remarked glumly. "I thought that witch of yours might kill him." Their fire was built in a corner of the yard, close to the outside wall. In all the bustle of the camp, there was yet some privacy here.

Offa shook his head. "One possibility gone."

"Would you have allied with the devil's daughter if she had killed Edmund for you?"

"You are sure she is not a saint?" Anger choked Offa's voice. He wished he was sure.

Raedwald looked surprised. "It was you who said she could not be a saint if she worshipped at some Viking's pagan cock."

Offa rose from where he crouched by the fire and began to pace. He pushed the uncomfortable doubts away. "If she has power, I want to bend it to my purpose. I don't care what kind it is. If she won't submit her power to me, then I can't afford to let her live."

"She has power. We saw it together." Raedwald's voice was steady and practical. "But if you bend the devil's power to your purpose, you risk your soul."

Offa ran his hands through his beard. Why was this so damned difficult? He did not suffer doubt willingly.

"I don't think she will serve you. And I don't think you can best her," Raedwald added.

"I am not sure I can either." The words were torn from Offa's throat. The witch had got under his skin and he could not reach the itch to scratch it. "Maybe Edmund will kill her."

"Aye." Raedwald began to chuckle softly. He put his hand on Offa's shoulder and pointed. There, across the yard, the red-haired witch was being dragged down the stairs between two of Delan's men. She looked small and frightened. "Let Edmund brave the storms."

Offa was sure of nothing at the moment. He couldn't remember ever having felt this way.

The door of the stockade slammed shut with a solid thunk behind Britta as she picked herself up from her hands and knees. She would not live another night. The bare earth floor of the tiny cell smelled of sweat and urine. The slatted window let in bars of light but not fresh air. She had failed. The only reason Edmund had not killed her immediately upon waking was that his queasy stomach overcame him. One could not kill with one's head between one's knees.

She could not die yet. The urgency twisting her gut was for more than herself, but she didn't know what it meant, what she should do. Her neighbor felon pounded on the wall behind her head, shouting some lewd challenge. She could think only of Karn. He would know what to do, what her premonitions meant. No, it was more than that. It was Karn for whom she waited. The certainty welled up inside her like a fount of cool water. It was her vision of death trying to come true. How could that be reassuring?

Offa's face appeared at the slats in the door. Britta scrambled into the corner, as far away from him as she could get. "Witch," he hissed. "Edmund is your enemy. He will kill you."

Britta said nothing. She clutched her knees. Everyone was her enemy now.

"Join with me against him," Offa commanded. "Kill or be killed."

"I just want to be left alone," she choked.

"Too late for that," Offa growled. "Save yourself and submit your power to me. I will rule the island. Riches and power will be mine, and yours."

"I don't want either," she said, her voice failing. Was he offering her an alliance? "I don't serve your ends or Edmund's."

Offa clenched his teeth. "You bend your will to mine or you will die. I will enjoy watching you meet your fate," he said. "Or, when Edmund tries to take his revenge, I will enjoy your killing him. Which is it?"

"You don't understand," she sobbed. "It isn't up to me."

Offa's face suffused with anger. "You have the power. I have seen it. The monks saw it. The people talk of it across the land. Witch or saint, I want that power—enough to risk my soul."

"Would that I could give it to you," Britta whispered.

"Think on what I said," Offa warned. "You will have to make a choice."

His face disappeared, leaving Britta feeling small and helpless.

Offa was right; Edmund would kill her before Karn came, before her vision of fire and horror could come to pass. She put her head down on her knees. She was lost. Karn was lost, and something more was lost, though she could not explain what, even to herself.

Offa leaned near the door in Edmund's large audience hall, drumming his fingers on the wood of the wall. It would be good to have escape near at hand if what he thought might happen here actually came to pass. He was wound to a fever pitch. All his hopes would be realized or dashed here tonight. Edmund sat on the huge carved chair that served as his throne. He looked to be in a foul temper. He touched his head petulantly from time to time. The torches in the room kept at bay the deepening dusk and lit the company of thegns and princes. The son of the King of Mercia and his crowd muttered in the corner. He wore his circlet to indicate his royal standing, as did the young sapling sent by Wessex. Alfred of Wessex drew near and whispered to Offa.

"Why have we been summoned so peremptorily?" he asked. He leaned against the wall between Offa and a large brazier that lit their corner with a pulsing, ruddy glow.

"Have you not heard the rumors?" Offa asked absently. "Men are saying the witch kept him in thrall. It is not only you and I who think he may be unfit to rule. He must prove himself tonight to all." He turned to Alfred. "If he does not, we are ready, are we not?"

Alfred grew thoughtful but said nothing.

Offa's loins churned. Edmund would punish the witch publicly tonight lest he be thought weak. If she killed him, Offa might have enough support among the thegns to claim the throne, though Delan would certainly challenge him. If she could not defend herself, she would be dead before they left the room. Offa was not sure which he wanted more.

Edmund motioned to one of his attendants, who thumped his staff upon the wooden floor until the whole room rang with the sound. The King clutched his head. "Stop that infernal banging," he screeched, as though it was the lad's own idea. Offa saw Edmund calm himself forcibly before he rose. "You come here tonight at my command," he began.

He reminds us that we do his bidding. Offa chafed at that thought. So did several others. Only Alfred, beside him, observed the scene in a cool and studied manner.

"You are here to witness my action against she who tried to poison me." He nodded to Delan, who turned and left the room.

"Will you punish the witch?" the Prince of Mercia called.

"In spite of her treachery, I rendered her sorcery powerless through force of will alone," Edmund announced. "Tonight she will give her life as proof of her submission."

Offa felt his member rise in anticipation.

At that moment Delan returned with two guards who dragged the red-haired witch between them. She stumbled as they hauled her up before Edmund. Her white robe was dirty, her red hair wild and tangled, its white streak shooting out from her forehead like a spray of lightning. She looked every inch the witch. Offa saw Edmund shiver. Delan fixed Edmund in an iron gaze as though to will him strength.

Edmund steadied himself and motioned to Delan. "Let her face my thegns to meet her fate. All will see her blood flow."

"Do not make it quick," Offa called, though he had meant to keep his own counsel.

There were calls of "Aye," and "A bit at a time."

Only Alfred of Wessex disagreed. "If she deserves to die for treason against you, my lord," he called, over the noise, "then make it a clean kill." The noise subsided. All turned to him, including the witch. "Do not degrade yourselves in torture," he finished.

"We each have our own ways of dispatching enemies,"

Edmund sneered. "She will be an example to others who might think to work against me."

The girl ignored the clamor for blood that rose around her. She wavered on her feet in the flickering light, staring at Alfred. She reached out one hand, transfixed. The assembly fell silent.

"It is you," she whispered to him. "From my vision in the fens." She moved forward toward Alfred and Offa, almost floating. Somehow none dared stop her. She did not seem to see Offa, but touched the Wessex prince's jawline with one finger. "I thought it was Edmund, but it is you."

Alfred was frozen, captured by her eyes. Offa himself could not move. "Will it happen as I saw it?" she asked as the thegns hung on every word. "I don't know..." She trailed off. "It will happen if it wants to happen." What did she mean?

Edmund was the first to break the spell. He rose and drew his sword from its scabbard in a slithering, metallic promise of violence. He strode forward and took the witch by the hair, driving her to her knees, then dragged her to the center of the room where all could see. Offa was glad. He wanted some distance when she got angry.

"Witch," Edmund threatened. His sword pierced her robe at the thigh and ripped a screeching tear in it. A red line appeared in her flesh, but her green eyes looked up and through him, calm somehow. Offa held his breath. Edmund raised his sword.

From beside Offa, a shout of protest broke the moment. "You mustn't kill her!" Alfred cried. Edmund turned slowly. Alfred lunged forward. His sword jostled the brazier next to him. "She has had a vision!" The brazier spilled fire as it toppled. Coals showered everywhere. Offa leapt back to avoid them, but they found purchase in Alfred's cloak. Flames leapt up his back. In a moment, they engulfed him. Shouts caromed around the hall, but all were paralyzed, Offa most of all. Not four feet from him, Alfred dropped to the floor and screamed, rolling in a vain attempt to smother the licking yellow fingers that devoured his clothing.

Offa looked around wildly. What to do? The witch rose and stumbled toward the burning figure, groaning. All drew back as she knelt and stared into the flames that covered him. Her moans circled up to match his screams.

Her shriek seemed to free the thegns. Delan pushed Offa aside, whirled his cloak from off his back, and threw it over Alfred. Shown the way, several of the others did likewise. They fell to work smothering the flames. At last the figure on the floor lay still. The flames were gone, but the tattered cloak smoked. The thegns rocked back on their heels and stared at each other with stricken eyes. The horror of the sudden immolation was too shocking to be truth.

No one paid much attention to the witch, no one except Offa. He heard her moaning as she rocked herself. "I saw it all," she keened.

The thegns looked up at the King, then at Offa and Delan. No one wanted to see what lay beneath that smoking cloak. Edmund nodded to Delan, who took a breath and pulled back the mantle. His jerky movements betrayed his dread.

Offa gasped with the others as the charred arm and the blackened face were revealed. Fully half Alfred's body was burned. He was a dead man, even if he yet breathed. If he died not in the next moments, still slowly would he rot to the same end.

Only the witch had not gasped at Alfred's horrible visage. She was streaming tears. "Black halo. Too late," she murmured over and over again.

"Get her out of here." Delan gestured to the guards hovering nearby.

No one moved. The witch reached out toward the charred flesh with one white hand, crying silently. Who would touch something once human that now looked like a haunch of venison left too long on the spit? As he stared at Alfred, Offa was forced to face the fact that he himself was mortal, blood and bone, vulnerable to any accident of the flesh.

Offa held his breath. The witch was wracked by sobs. It looked as if she would touch Alfred against her own will. Then, in the last seconds, she did not hesitate, but laid her hand full on the bubbled flesh showing through the burnt shreds of cloth.

"Ahhh," Offa sighed, an echo of others in the room. She sighed as well and closed her eyes, sobbing no more. A kind of rapture spread across her features. She jerked and gasped for breath, yet a slow smile curved her lips. They parted softly, as though she forgot herself in the arms of a lover at the moment of ecstasy. Offa was fascinated.

So he didn't really see the miracle. He saw her open her eyes and give a knowing smile Offa thought was meant for him. When he could tear his eyes from her, he saw Alfred smiling in return. The whispering among the thegns whirled up into a roar. Alfred's arm was whole and pink. His cheek glowed with health. Offa was light-headed from the shock. Several in the room staggered back. There were cries of "Miracle," and "The gods speak through her."

She had the power. Oh, such power. Offa's loins burned. He *must* have it.

"It can't be," Delan muttered. "She is an impostor. She didn't heal the king."

But she was not an impostor. Offa knew that, though others might try to deny it later.

"Why could you not heal me?" Edmund whined into the din of comment.

She tried to stand and stumbled, weak, but none would touch her. With a supreme effort, she stood without support, swaying. Her eyes were still far away. Several thegns steadied Alfred as he, too, struggled to his feet, looking at his arm in sheer amazement, feeling his cheek.

"Because there is nothing wrong with you, Edmund, though there soon will be." The words burst from her like a babe nine months and more. What did she mean? She looked around the room, examining the rafters, the drinking horns set upon a sideboard, the rugs, as though she had never seen such things. Then she began to probe the faces of the thegns, frozen now again and staring at her. She looked exhausted, yet her eyes glowed with an inner light. Her glance passed over Offa as though she did not recognize him.

"You will die, Edmund, in the coming battle," she said after a moment. "They will declare you a saint." Her voice gained certainty. "The Danes will triumph here. Their sons will mingle with your daughters to build a strong race. You cannot do it alone, yet they cannot either.

"This boy"—here she managed a smile again for Alfred—"will vanquish the Danes, in his turn, and he will be called Alfred the Great. He will bring the island together, Dane and Saxon, to make a people who will sing songs remembered through time. Their language will be spoken in kingdoms we cannot yet ken." Her voice rang through the silence of the hall. "The island will be called England and its sons will roam the world from sunrise to sunset and change it forever."

She shuddered and sagged toward the sideboard. Offa's hands had gone clammy with cold sweat. Had she prophesied the future? The others thought so. How could they not, when she had performed a miracle as prelude? Edmund sagged on his sword hilt, his death foretold. The thegns turned to Alfred, seeing him in a new light. He had been saved to do great things.

And what of himself? She said nothing of him. A thousand questions caromed off the empty spot in his belly. "Witch," Offa croaked as he advanced on her. "What of me? Do I rule after Edmund? Do people remember my name?" He could not keep the need from his voice.

The girl looked up at him, still dazed, and shook her head. "I didn't see you."

"What of my churches?" He wanted to shake her. "Those will stand."

"I saw no churches." She paused. "Wait...I saw the church at Dunford fall into the sea."

"This is a miracle." Delan declared his religious leaning as he moved to support her.

Offa felt the room recede. She dismissed him thus? The void inside him filled with a gut-churning rage. He drew his sword. A howl escaped between clenched teeth as he lunged for her.

Delan must have heard him, for as he whirled his sword was ready. "What do you do, churl?" he growled as their steel met. Offa couldn't see for the red film that descended over all. He screamed and cut at Delan again and again. He must get to the witch! Delan backed in a circle, keeping the witch behind him.

"Devil," Offa realized he was yelling. Now he stood between the Frank and the door. He was about to lunge in for another stroke when he was knocked to the side by a great blow. He staggered and turned to face the new enemy. But it was the great door that had hit him as it swung wide. A muddied man stumbled through. Offa wavered, confused.

"My Lord King," the man gasped as every gaze turned on him. His face was streaked with sweat and mud; his chest heaved. Dazed, he went down on one knee, lowering his eyes.

"How dare you crash in like this?" Edmund began, his anger cycling up.

Offa felt the red haze receding, leaving him beached and dry.

"What is it, man?" Delan demanded.

"Vikings," the man breathed, grateful to deliver his message. "They are on the move."

Offa looked around the room. The thegns were shocked into silence. That for which they waited so eagerly came at last. But now all was changed by the prophecy. He turned to the witch.

Her eyes still held the tragedy of knowledge as she said, "It begins." A palpable shudder coursed through seasoned warrior and new-bearded youth alike. Even Offa felt a chill.

Delan turned fiercely to the sentry. "How many?"

"A third of our force, at most," the messenger said brokenly. "Or even a quarter."

The Vikings could not win, then. Could the witch be wrong? The room hummed with murmurs of satisfaction. Only the messenger did not seem comforted.

Edmund tried to take back command. "Let us make our

final preparations," he ordered. "This witch is obviously trying to frighten us."

Offa agreed. Of course she was in league with the Vikings. One in particular. That explained her prophecy. It was a trick to weaken them. His world came back into focus. "Remember your promise, Edmund," he called. "I have the leading of our forces."

Delan looked uncertainly at the witch. "Where did you encounter them, man?"

"By the village of Whitford, lord." the man answered.

"Good," Edmund interjected. "They are a full two days from here."

"But no, my king," the sentry stuttered. "We have hours, not days." The man fairly trembled. "They are riding, all of them, not marching orderly on foot. They spare not their horses or themselves. I fear they will be here before the dawn."

Barely time to deploy their thousands, Offa thought with a start. The Vikings might well come upon them in disarray. A ripple of uncertainty coursed through the room. Eyes turned back toward the witch. "What she says comes to pass," someone murmured.

"Are none saved?" another asked.

The girl shrugged. "I know no more than I have said."

An old thegn stepped to her side, half-pleading, half-threatening. "Range your powers with us, Witch, and crush our enemies."

She looked frightened. "I did not choose this magic today. It does what it will."

She would not bend her power to anyone, Offa realized, least of all him. That meant she must die. "Do you stray from your purpose, King?" he asked, his words twisting out of his clenched belly. Edmund could order Delan to step aside. "If she stands not with us, kill her."

"We cannot know she will not help us." Delan spoke to the thegns as well as to his king. "Killing her does not change the prophecy. But it takes away one possibility for the future." Delan glared back at Offa. Edmund had matched them well. He fingered his sword.

Before they could begin their battle again, Alfred stepped forward and clapped the messenger upon the shoulder. "You have satisfied your charge," he said. The room quieted as he surveyed it. "We should not kill the one who tells our fate. Her vision is a gift from God. And some may yet be saved. Let them find us as ready as may be." His eyes glittered in anticipation of the coming battle as they swept the room.

The tide turned against Offa. He could feel it. No one wanted to risk killing the witch. She might be their personal salvation, if not the army's.

"Offa commands the eastern flank, Delan the west. I will hold the fortress with the guard," Edmund ordered, obviously trying to reassert his control in this impossible situation. His face was white. The witch had prophesied his death, after all. "We must send for reinforcements. Who better to go than Alfred, who has been prophesied to live?"

That meant Edmund hoped to sit out a siege inside the fortress until Alfred could return. Offa looked at Delan and saw that Edmund had promised both of them sole leadership of the army. Both were now betrayed. It didn't matter. It would take all they had to win the day, and organization at the flanks would be weakest. Better Delan commanded half than that they lose.

The Frank hefted his sword, accepting the assignment. "I am for it, whether I live or meet you all in Hell," he said through clenched teeth. He took the witch's arm. As he strode out the door, the room erupted in a shout, and the thegns dashed after him. Edmund stalked in their wake, at the wrong end of the charge. Offa was left alone to contemplate the end of his dreams.

Delan left Britta in the stockade, this time with the door open.

"If the Vikings breach the wall somehow, pull the door shut." Then he was gone.

She gazed blankly at the walls of the stockade she had so

longed to escape scant hours before. How long before the men took their revenge against her prophecy when the battle turned against them? She noted dully that the door could not be barred from inside. This place would provide no protection. Her knees gave way and she crumpled to the floor.

The magic took her when it pleased. Didn't it? Or had she not, in the last moments, *wanted* to touch that boy king? The destruction she would cause now seemed inevitable. Tomorrow the Vikings would come. Karn would be with them. Her vision said she would help give her people over to the barbarian horde. Men would die. Flames obscured Karn's fate. She held her head in her hands and moaned. In spite of all, she wanted him to come. She wanted it from someplace so deep inside her that it could not be denied.

She tried to focus on the prophecy. Two peoples together. That was the greater good. In the fire that burned on Alfred she had seen it all—other fires down the ages, battles, great boats burning, cities aflame, all the violence, all the pain. But there had been another flame that coursed through all the mayhem, a small flame and steady, growing, a different kind of fire. In the end the destructive fires had been consumed in that one steady light. What did that mean?

Offa's face appeared at the stockade bars. Britta started and pushed herself back against the wall. "Don't think I have forgotten you, Witch," he said through gritted teeth. "If the Vikings win, as you predict, you'll have to deal with them. If I live, you'll deal with me."

He spit through the bars and jerked away. Slowly she wiped the gob of spittle from her hand, where it had landed on the pink mark of the stigmata. She couldn't think. She couldn't cry. She could only crouch there, listening to the clatter of metal and horses' hooves, the shouts of men around her. She didn't know what any of it meant. She only knew that there was fire ahead.

Chapter Twenty-one

Karn pulled Thorn up at the crest of the hill above the Saxon fortress. Thorn snorted his protest wearily. Fenris circled nervously at his feet. The pre-dawn sky boiled red with the coming sun and the threat of spring storms. Behind him two thousand Danish host rippled to a stop as well. The horses had got little rest, the men none.

Halfdan and Ivar came up beside Karn to look down across the plain to the Saxon fortress. A stream of peasants and their carts flowed out of the little village that lay to the northeast along the river. Edmund's forces seethed as they pushed into lines of defense.

"They have been warned," Ivar muttered. "That last scout got through."

"Did you count on that, Karn?" Halfdan asked.

Karn remained impassive. It was left to Ivar to say, "Karn led us here. He cut down more than one Saxon on the way. Though he strikes from a horse, still he strikes true." Ivar glanced at Karn, his eyes speculating. "Sometime when we have routed these Saxons, you will have to show me how you use your horse, Karn."

Karn had eyes only for the fortress down below, where Britta might still be alive. The rough gouge Ulf had inflicted across his upper arm ached. He pushed the pain down and pointed. "They have not yet manned their outer bulwarks. We can yet take them unprepared."

Halfdan examined the scene of frantic activity closely. "Aye," he muttered. "Let us lose no time." He turned and shouted to the throng behind him. "Take up your weapons!"

Cries of "Dismount and prepare!" echoed down the line. A shuffling thunder cascaded away as men got off their horses. Karn, too, dismounted. He opened a bulky pack tied to his saddle and shook out the chain mail he had laced together the final night at the Danish camp. He anchored it to Thorn's saddle and drew it round his breast. It would be heavy. That was bad when Thorn was tired. The horse had served him well; Karn would have liked to spare him. But everything must be sacrificed to reach Britta. He only hoped she was still alive.

"What are you doing?" one of the men near him asked with some contempt.

"Preparing for war, as you are." He reached down and patted Fenris. "You must stay back, friend," he muttered. Fenris had worked himself into a frenzy of excitement. His tongue dripped foam. His sides heaved. Karn poured some water from his leather water pouch into his own wooden bowl and tugged at Fenris to draw his attention.

"Drink, boy. You will have need of it." In spite of his excitement, the dog lapped at the bowl. He prepared, too. Karn rinsed his bowl and drank himself.

"We sweep in from the east and the west," Halfdan shouted. "They are least ready for us on their flanks. Then we move in to crush their center.

"Varnak," Ivar called out over the din. "You and yours will come from the west with me at the riverside, and Jellick, you are for Halfdan and the east."

Karn looked up from his preparations. He had done much thinking about this battle. "Unless we break through those gates today, we will sit here all summer while they starve."

Britta could not wait for that. He raised his voice for all to hear. Ivar and Halfdan knit their brows in disapproval. "A small force could punch up the middle with a battering ram."

"That would be suicide," one in the circle of Danir said clearly into the silence.

"The Saxons will be drawn from the center to support their flanks. It is possible." He must be there and ready at the gate. He knew that. Ivar and Halfdan were not yet convinced. "I will lead the charge to the gates. If we fail, what have you lost except a small band?"

Ivar looked at Halfdan, who nodded. "Forty and ten to pull a wagon for the ram."

"Who goes with Karn?" Ivar shouted. "Theirs may be the greatest glory of the day."

Karn did not turn to search the crowd. He fingered Fenris's ears. Shouts rose around him, and he felt movement. When he looked up, two score had stepped forward. Some were faces he knew. He nodded at them silently. Others he had never seen. One or two still looked doubtful.

"Do you follow a cripple, Thorvald?" one of the Danir shouted from the rear.

Karn looked at the uneasy faces around him and found one looking slightly shamed. "If I fall," Karn cried, "Thorvald leads in my stead. His will be the glory." He looked Thorvald resolutely in the eye and saw him steady. More Danes stepped out of the crowd to join them.

Karn turned to Ivar. A kind of blunt respect shone in the old jarl's face. "You know I must hang back while you press in from the sides," Karn said, "then thrust quickly down the center. Think you that I will turn and run?"

Ivar turned back toward the scene of the coming battle, then to Karn's new followers. "Kill him if he does."

Britta sat in the doorway of her stockade. Shouts echoed everywhere. Men ran in all directions. Alfred left with a small contingent to bring reinforcements, riding hard to the south. Offa and Delan had left the fortress hours before with two thousand men apiece. Edmund stayed inside the walls with five hundred of the guard. That left five hundred to defend the gates.

Edmund stomped up a ladder to the ledge running round the palisades where he could see the battle unfold below. He looked as nervous as a cornered animal, though he barked shrill orders to those about him. The great gates swung shut with a thud that struck Britta to the heart. She was locked away from Karn.

"Those with javelins, man the catwalk," Edmund shouted. "If the Vikings come near the gates, we rain death." He looked around. "Set some cauldrons to boil."

Britta laid her cheek against the rough bark of the stockade. Men rushed to start fires. Others brought jars of cooking oil from the storehouse or wheeled cranes into position for hoisting cauldrons up over the walls.

Edmund whispered to a young thegn, sandy-haired and light of beard, who glanced in her direction and started down the ladder. Britta watched as he loped across to her stockade.

"Come with me, Witch," he said cautiously. "The king wants you at the parapet."

He escorted her to the base of the ladder and motioned her up. Britta climbed slowly, as though to a scaffold. I don't want to see it happen, she thought, shaking her head rhythmically from side to side. I don't want to cause the death. I don't want to be anywhere near Edmund. And I don't want Karn to die.

Edmund himself pulled her up the last rung to the catwalk, a wild look in his eyes. "My best protection is your need to preserve your own hide," he rasped. He gripped her wrist and twisted her painfully to look over the edge of the palisades to the writhing mass below.

Out beyond the Saxon disarray, the Viking horde lined the hilltops. As she watched, they plunged down the hill, their bloodcurdling screams echoing across the plain.

Everything was converging on her, Edmund—the Vikings, the deaths of her people, the death of Karn, her own role in bringing all this about. "No," she moaned. No one listened. They were all transfixed by the sight of pure destruction descending upon them.

Karn held Thorn steady. The Danir divided into two streams headed east and west. Some chanted war songs, some prayed as they ran, some simply shouted to boil their blood. Everything he had ever wanted hung in the balance of this battle.

A tree trunk crashed behind him. His men would make quick work now stripping the branches. Thorvald directed several men to pile a cart with shields to protect the heads of those who pushed the rams. Still Karn waited. After about three-quarters of an hour, he saw what he'd been waiting for. Two organized Saxon phalanxes wheeled out from the center to right and left. They were deploying to support the flanks.

"Thorvald," he called. "I lead twenty to make a hole. You lead twenty to defend the rear. When we reach the gates, my men will weaken them with axes; yours will turn and fight. Then bring up the ram." Thorvald raised a hand to show he understood.

Karn grabbed Fenris's collar and led him to the cart. "I want you whole when I need you," he ordered. Fenris looked outraged. "Stay with the ram." He patted the floor of the wagon. Fenris leapt nimbly up while Karn tied him to the tongue then mounted Thorn.

"You ride a horse?" Thorvald asked, astonished. "You will fall at the first skirmish."

"Not with these," Karn said, setting his feet into the loops of leather hanging from the saddle. "Follow close and guard our rear." He looked down at the men around him as his voice rose. "Let the scalds sing our names to our sons and theirs. Victory will be laid at our feet today as tribute, or the Valkyrie will toast us in Valhalla tonight."

He drew Walther's wonderful sword. A Saxon sword to battle Saxons. He hefted it and felt its weight. All his fear washed out of him. He was empty, waiting for the bloodlust of battle to fill him. *Britta, I am coming.* A shout rose from his belly. His fifty answered his battle cry. All thought left him. He pointed his sword toward the gates behind the swirling Saxons and kicked Thorn forward. Fenris barked behind him. Karn heard the din distantly. He was strong, more than human, less. He was berserker. Thorn's hoofbeats throbbed in his loins as he thundered into the valley now ripe with the scent of blood.

Offa strode through the broken Saxon lines on the left flank like one possessed. Shrieks of rage or pain shrilled around him. Prophesy be damned, he thought fiercely as another Viking cur fell under his blows. Silent to conserve energy, he worked his way back toward the center with perhaps two hundred of those who had sense enough to know that the battle was being lost at the edges. Fresh forces defending the gates could still prevail, if they could be rallied.

"To the gates!" His voice carried out over the din and was echoed by others. "The center is the key." The day was yet his to be had. The kingdom would be his by acclaim. He felt the power surging through his arm as he pressed forward. Damn the witch and her prophecy!

Karn, astride Thorn, threw himself into the Saxon line. Conical helmets, chain mail, leather, all reeled together in the last wisps of morning mist, the cacophony of clanking metal and the cries of the dying. Thorn snorted and whinnied. His eyes rolled wildly as Karn drove him forward. His fellow Danir fell behind. Karn didn't care. They must break through quickly or it would not be long until they were drinking in Valhalla.

He stood in his saddle and slashed about him. A young Saxon, hardly bearded, looked up in sudden fear when he saw Karn looming over him. It was the last emotion he would ever have. Thrust down, slash to right, shove a hefty, red-faced Saxon with his left foot, steady Thorn, push forward. Karn's senses contracted into the moment, each new enemy, the next blow. Danish yells rose behind him. He glanced back and saw his band slicing their way toward him, amazement writ large on their faces at the trail of destruction he and Thorn left in their wake. The wagon with the ram rumbled in the rear, Fenris barking frantically.

"By the gods," Thorvald yelled. "If you live, teach me to fight from a horse."

Karn swung his sword to parry another Saxon blow. The bloodlust that filled him began to wane. Only six now dragged the cart. Fifteen or so defended. He kicked a Saxon away from his side and slashed the chest of another. They were still so far from the gates.

"Defend the ram!" Karn yelled. Danir struggled in to do it. He leaned to thrust his sword into a Saxon throat when he felt his arm take a glancing blow. He refused to look at the blood, but slashed the man's shoulder to the bone. Desperation welled into his mouth as bile. He grew tired, like the time at Dunford, but he toiled forward. He had to reach the gate.

Britta twisted in Edmund's grip to get a better look. "Let me go," she cried. Far below the parapet a rider pushed through the battle. Only one she knew would ride a horse. Could it be?

Edmund pulled her along the Parapet, shouting orders. "Be ready, but hold until the ram gets to the gates." The word spread. Edmund turned to look out over the palisades. Britta pressed herself against the rough wood palings. The figure below was obscured by the shadow of the fortress itself. It *must* be him. The sun rose above the walls.

"Karn," she shrieked in fear and joy. Fear prevailed. He was attacked on all sides. There were but a few who fought with him against the surging Saxons. He looked up to the source of her shout. She felt his gaze like a brand before he slashed to either side and pushed forward.

Edmund snatched her back from the parapet walls. "Do you salute a Viking?" His countenance darkened. He drew her close to his wiry body so that he could peer into her face. "Traitor! Is that why you prophesied our doom?" His voice grew sure. "It was all false!" He chuckled ominously. "You weaken our resolve to leave us easy prey for your demon lover and his hordes." He grabbed her neck, turning her head forcibly out toward the fray. "I am not afraid of your prophecies." With his other hand, Edmund drew out his knife. "You will see your lover skewered with my javelins before I slit your throat, traitor Witch."

Maybe she *was* a traitor. At that moment she would sacrifice the battle or her own life or Saxon sovereignty for one Viking. A sea of Saxons pressed in around Karn and Thorn. Tears spilled onto her cheeks. "No," she moaned softly, as though she could stave off the future.

Karn felt the drift of the battle shift toward the east. Something had happened. Thorn was too tired to be frightened by the noise and the smell of blood. Karn neared the end of his resources, but his arm still slashed. His band moved forward, inch by painful inch. The gates were near, if they could last. He chanced a look around and saw a clot of Saxons moving back in from the eastern flank to reinforce those at the gates. At their head was a face with a forked beard half-seen under his helmet. He would know Offa anywhere.

A sigh of panic whispered through him. A Saxon slashed at Thorn's head. Instinctively, he pulled Thorn backwards as the horse neighed wildly. Karn sidled up to the man and pushed him into another Dane's sword. Anger began to churn in his belly alongside the fear. Not again. Not this time! Offa and his troops pushed toward the ram. Karn pressed forward doggedly. The Danes' only chance was to open the gates before Offa could capture his ram.

Above him, Karn heard a high, clear voice, the only female voice for miles around. It called his name. He looked up to see the other face he would know anywhere. *Britta!* His eyes locked with hers for the briefest instant. He did not salute, but swung to the left with new purpose.

"Time grows short, Danes. To the gates!" He kicked Thorn ahead and dredged into his center to find new strength for his arm. Offa or no, Britta needed him at the gates.

* * *

Britta watched the battle in horror as Edmund crowed in her ear.

"Offa comes to defend the gate," the king cried. He seemed not to care what that meant about the battle at the flanks.

Britta, too, cared only for that piece of war unfolding below. Karn and his Danes had pushed almost to the gate, but the ram lagged behind. Fenris barked on the cart that held the ram. What was Karn thinking to bring her dog into battle?

"Ready the javelins," Edmund yelled. The cry reverberated along the parapet. A forest of javelins rose, clacking, in the morning sun. Many were wrapped with oiled rags.

"No," she said softly. Down in the courtyard, cranes hoisted cauldrons of boiling water and oil into place. It was her vision coming true—Karn engulfed in flame! The cauldrons inched above the parapet. She turned frantically back to the scene below her. "No!" Her voice rose.

"Oil," Edmund shouted. The cauldrons tipped forward. Oil splashed Karn and his men.

"You can't," she breathed. Everything was happening too fast.

"Light the brands," Edmund crowed. Javelins shared their deadly flame along the line.

Now her vision would burst into life. There was no way to stop it. She struggled wildly against Edmund's grip as she leaned over the parapet. Below, Offa's men pressed in on those who defended the ram. Didn't Karn know what the oil meant? *Get back from the gates!*

"Loose javelins," Edmund shouted.

"No!" she meant to scream. No sound escaped her throat. All the power of the scream went inward. Her choices fell like shattered light around her. She could draw the power and bend it to save Karn, regardless of the cost. But that would make her the cause of the destruction she had seen in her vision. Did she have a choice?

Offa pressed toward Karn. If the fire did not get him, Offa would. The Saxons on the ramparts hefted their spears. In another instant it would be too late to choose. She prayed for forbearance to Jesus, but it was Thor who answered her, as if she'd prayed for strength.

In that moment she was calm. Her soul was cold fire, but her mind was clear. History would make itself here. Her vision told her that she would be the conduit. She would call the power down because the world willed it, or the gods willed it, or the one God willed it. She cared not for the workings of the gods across the centuries. She cared for one man, a speck in the sweep of history. She knew what she would do. She knew what she would sacrifice. She didn't care.

She stood up straight, yanking Edmund with her. His hand is wound in my hair, she thought, to no particular purpose. She thrust her consciousness up and outward, ignoring the javelins raised above the churning bodies below. A thrumming echoed through the ground. It sounded like a thousand men, riding hard. Too soon for Alfred's reinforcements.

Come to me, she sang to the magic, a siren song. Open I am and ready for you. Come down from wherever you come, to me, a perfect chasuble. I make myself empty. Empty to be filled by you like a lover fills a woman. Like Kara filled me. Come and do what it is you are longing to do. Her palms tingled in expectancy. She saw the javelins loosed. They arced away.

The earth growled now, a grinding sound, louder than the cries below. It moved inexorably across the valley toward the fortress. Others around her, below her, looked about themselves for the source. Some of the javelins were away, piercing any armor in their path, lighting human torches. But not all were loosed. Men looked about in terror. Edmund shouted something in her ear. She turned slowly. Fear blossomed in his eyes. He unwound his hand from her hair frantically and backed away. A wind rose from somewhere and whipped her hair around her face like red serpents. Below her, some still fought, some screamed and burned. The rising wind flicked sparks from man to man. Kara would be a human torch at any moment.

She thrust her arms into the air, palms prickling with sensation. Not yet, she panted to herself. There was still more energy to come. She felt fuller with every passing second.

The grinding grew to a shriek, and the trembling in the earth erupted into jolts. The ground heaved like a shaken blanket. Men fell. Fire swept across the army below. Soldiers lurched in every direction as though they could run from the jerking ground. Britta screamed into the wind, still rising. The palisades squealed as the wooden timbers rubbed together. The stone under her feet bucked like a demented beast and men tumbled to the courtyard. The earth itself seemed to slosh and undulate. Edmund scrambled for the ladder as she grabbed for the tilting palisades.

Britta thought she would burst. The power was too strong to bend! The wind inside her screamed and shuddered. If she didn't act soon, there would be nothing left of her. She saw the fire roll over the place where she had last seen Karn. As she clung to the timbers of the wall, she shrieked, "Let Karn live and I will pay the cost!" But her voice was lost in the wind.

The palisades growled and ripped asunder. The catwalk twisted and broke. Edmund clung to the ladder as it heaved itself backwards. He landed with a thud on the rolling earth. Her joints were jolted with her senses, as though her body was being ripped apart as well as her mind. She was the center of total destruction. She couldn't see Karn. Her senses were filled with dust and burning bodies and screaming.

The huge wooden post she clung to cracked with a terrible screech. Britta was flung to what remained of the catwalk as it twisted away from the buckling wall. The splintered end bent down with her weight. She slid helplessly toward the broken hole. Then she was falling, the heaving earth rising to meet her. The breath slammed out of her body as the hard dirt hit her. Then the timbers of the fortress wall crashed down on top of her.

Karn raised his head, much as that hurt. The shaking had stopped, but life would never be the same if even the earth beneath one's feet could not be trusted. Around him, smoky dust rose from the ground. Bodies lay scattered everywhere. Men screamed in fear. Karn's leather jerkin was soaked with smoking oil under his chain mail. Yet somehow the fire from the javelins had not touched him. The cart, wheels at crazy angles, pointed a broken axle to opposite ends of the sky. Beyond the cart lay the huge log meant to get him into the fortress to save Britta. A man crushed under it still groaned.

Britta! He staggered up and leaned against the cart to quell his rebellious stomach. The gates were gone. They had crumbled with the wall into a flaming, twisted mass of wood and men. Britta had been standing above those gates. Gods, have you tricked me? Have you breached the fortress only to take away my reason for entering? He stooped for his sword. If she were in that flaming hell he would find her.

For that he needed Fenris. Why else had he brought the beast, but as a way to find her? He fingered the chewed end of the rope that had held the dog. "Fenris," he shouted. He glanced back at the fortress and saw the growing flames. Fenris was long gone.

Karn lurched toward the inferno of the fortress, struggling with the buckles of his chain shirt. He shed his oil-soaked clothing. Bare to the waist, he hefted his sword. But the Saxons who issued from the black billows of smoke were not interested in fighting. They screamed as they burned, or if they escaped the flames, they sought only safety from a world gone wild. Even one who wore a circlet of gold screamed in fright. If he was their king, he did not lead them.

Karn clambered over the broken stumps of the palisades, elbowing aside those who were climbing out. Inside, smoke seethed from licking flames in several places. Bodies lay everywhere. There must have been buildings here once, but they were only heaps of lumber now. Panic welled in his breast. She might be buried somewhere in this chaos.

"Britta," he screamed. He turned about helplessly, unable to see clearly through the growing smoke, then started as he felt a cold, wet sensation on his hand. It was Fenris, whimpering in fright, the rope, one end chewed and hanging, still tied about his neck. He knelt and took the dog in his arms, its black fur rough against his bare chest.

"You can find Britta," he whispered. "Britta."

He held Fenris's collar and began to crisscross the debris of the courtyard. Neither took notice of the stream of wounded and burned that staggered to the gates. The fires were growing hungrily. If they didn't find Britta soon, it would be too late for all of them.

Karn and Fenris clambered up the debris of the palisades. When the dog whined and nosed the wood, Karn stood paralyzed, hope and despair battling in his breast. Then he leaped off the pile, lest his added weight crush her. Fenris barked in a frenzy of excitement. Karn looked around, crazed. Fire licked at the pile of tumbled timbers. If she was under there…

Stooping, he peered into the darkness under the pile. He could just see the pale glow of a dirty white robe half-covered in debris and a spill of red hair. "Britta," he called through the din of shouts, the snap of fire burning toward them. There was no answer, no movement.

He swallowed hard. She was locked inside the heap as surely as a prison. He had to move the right piece of this wooden puzzle to avoid crushing her. What held that space around her? If he chose wrong, she would be crushed. His eyes tearing with smoke, he picked a beam and got his shoulder under it. Muscles straining, he managed to drag it to the side in two unsteady steps. The hole he created still wasn't big enough. He chose another, larger beam. "Gods give me strength," he prayed. It was command as much as supplication. He pushed up with his thighs.

Fenris whimpered behind him. Alerted, he searched his senses. The grinding began again. The whole pile groaned. Karn did not even stop to think. He shoved his shoulders inside the hole he'd just made, pushing roughly against the timbers. Even as he felt them quiver, he grabbed Britta's robe. The creaking became a roar. He jerked back with all his strength. A timber dealt him a crushing blow on his left shoulder as the pile collapsed.

They fell back together. The ground jerked and shimmied. Timbers bounced around them. When the earth quieted, Karn scrambled to his hands and knees, coughing with dust and smoke.

"Britta," he sputtered as Fenris came to nose her. Her face was ashen under the smudges of dirt. Hand trembling, he touched her throat. Her pulse beat back at him. He bit back triumph and pushed up her robe to feel her arms and legs. She was whole. Her God had protected her. He smoothed back her hair, saw the swelling bruise on her temple, the blood smeared in her hair. That was why she swooned. He lifted her into his arms. They were not yet safe.

"Fenris," he yelled. The ragged hole in the palisades he had come through was about to be engulfed in flame. It was the only way out.

Karn held Britta close and thanked Thor that the Saxons were too busy trying to survive to pay much attention to him as he limped toward the burning gates, Fenris in his wake. He tore the cloak from a body near the opening, then wrapped it about Britta and up over his own head and shoulders. Cradling her close, he stumbled toward the hole in the wall. Fenris was more nimble on four legs. The dog cleared the hole just before the flames engulfed it.

Karn paused before the solid wall of fire only for a moment. He filled his lungs and staggered through, crouched low. Even as they cleared the flames, he ripped the cloak from about them. It flapped away, afire. He laid Britta in the dirt in front of what had been the gates. Her robe smoked. He ran trembling hands over her face and shoulders. She wasn't burned. He pushed his fingers through his hair to see that he was not alight. Then he took her in his arms. "Britta."

Her green eyes opened slowly. They stared at him as though from far away. "Karn," she whispered. Fenris whined at her side and she raised a hand to him. He licked it gingerly.

"Don't talk," Karn said. "I will get you out of this place."

"I can walk," she said. Grimacing, she lifted her head, but thought better of it.

341

"You do not walk," he said. "Karn orders you now." She lay her head on his shoulder as he staggered to his feet.

They turned away from the gates toward a premonition of Ragnorok. Great crevices rent the earth. Scraps of burning wood floated in the wind over their heads like deadly orange and black insects. Carcasses stuffed the crevasses where they had fallen and been crushed in the grinding teeth of the earth. Others were strewn across the landscape, felled in battle or by the gods. Most of those who stood had forgotten about fighting. They roamed aimlessly, or talked fearfully in groups, looking for comfort. Some had begun to stream away from the battlefield as though they could outrun the shaking ground. The Danir seemed the better organized. Already several knots of his fellows herded Saxons toward the river.

Another ripple through the ground made men howl and throw themselves to the ground. Karn spread his legs and rode it out, cradling Britta against the shock.

Thorn galloped by, neighing, and wheeled in their direction. "Whoa, *fraendi,*" Karn called. The horse slowed to a trot, then stood, trembling, before them. Karn sidled in and collected his reins. "I know the ground should not shake." He dragged Thorn with them as they picked their way among the dead and the defeated, away from the fortress. Britta seemed to slip in and out of consciousness. Fenris trailed in their wake. Forced to circle a great crevasse that blocked his way, Karn was stopped by the sight of a forked beard half-buried in the earth's gaping wound. Offa. Blood smeared his face, but still he looked peaceful. Disappointment left Karn hollow as he stared into the hated face. The earth had taken the revenge that belonged to him.

Karn glanced up at the hill where the Danish raven pennant now fluttered in the distant sunshine, almost serene above the smoky hell of the battlefield. He limped toward it, using energy that should long ago have run out. There was still one barrier to Britta's safety.

Chapter Twenty-two

Britta leaned against Karn's bare chest as he stumbled through the wreckage of the battle, leading Thorn. Fenris stalked beside them through the chaos. The world was bathed in a red glow from the burning fortress behind them. Blood smeared her cheek. Karn's wounds whispered to her, but she could not answer. She was empty inside. She didn't turn that mighty force. If Karn was alive, it was because he was part of some plan. Whose plan, she didn't know. She held up one hand, wondering whether the power had made her old, like Wydda? It was only scratched and dirty.

Everywhere, Vikings gathered weapons into piles. From this moment her people were subjugated to the Norsemen. She couldn't mourn. It was the first step toward forging those people into the sons and daughters of the island she had seen generations hence.

Karn's arms trembled, yet she did not ask to be let down. It was right to be here, hearing his pulse throb in her ears. She was both far away and lost in the immediate. As they came up the rise, Britta saw archers surround a man bound to the bole of a gigantic tree. It was Edmund. Behind the

343

archers half a hundred Vikings milled into quiet.

"You cannot kill me." The king shook his head in pity. "I will die of a lung ailment."

The archers raised their bows. "A lung ailment!" Edmund screeched. Bowstrings trembled in the notch of their arrows, eager to send them on their way. His voice trailed off, as the horrible possibilities of that prediction roosted in his mind.

Whistling cut the air, then Edmund's shriek pierced the day. He sprouted arrows like a hedgehog as they nailed him to the tree. Britta could almost feel his lungs fill with blood. It welled out of his nose and mouth as the struggle for breath turned liquid within him. Then his head tipped to one side and his mouth slackened.

Britta exhaled. The Viking leaders turned away and the crowd began to disperse.

"I am sorry, Britta," Karn murmured. "Ivar and Halfdan must set their own upon the throne, whether he is Saxon or Dane."

Britta nodded. "Yes. That will be necessary." She saw two grizzled Vikings talking quietly to Delan through an interpreter. Perhaps the Frank would get his wish to rule, if only as a puppet king.

Karn stood, feet apart, holding Britta in his arms. Halfdan and Ivar broke away from the tall, dark captain. What Karn would do next would exile him from the Danir forever, and to no purpose. What he wanted most, he could not have. A woman who had such power coursing through her could have no thought for a man or the hearth fire. Britta was made for greater things. But he had to protect her. All saw her on the battlements with Edmund. All saw her raise her arms as the ground began to roll. The Danes would think her as much a leader of the Saxons as Edmund, and therefore just as much in need of killing.

The Vikings milled into a new crowd surrounding Karn and Britta. Karn steadied himself. It would not do to look weak. Ivar and Halfdan shouldered their way through the throng.

"The day is ours," Karn greeted them.

"I am not sure it belongs to us," Halfdan muttered. "We did not open those gates."

"I have done what I said I would do." Karn dared not allow them time to think. "I took you to the Saxons. I led the fight for the gate. I have proven my loyalty."

"It seems you had a reason to get inside those gates," Halfdan challenged, gesturing at Britta. "Some here say she called your name."

"She did. She is the one who healed me. And I claim her now, in front of all, and ask to hold the fens for the Danelaw." Karn put all the strength he had into his voice.

"You were brave." Ivar looked pensively at Britta. "No matter what brought you here."

"We should keep this witch and use her against our enemies," Halfdan urged his brother.

"If she is witch," Karn said to his countrymen, his eyes on Britta, "how would you hold her? Can you command one who commands the elements? Edmund could not, for his gates were breached." He glared around him at the battle-weary Danir.

"Then we must kill her to prevent her using her powers against us," Halfdan said.

Just what Karn feared. There was only one argument and that was their belief. "If she is witch, any action against her will be answered by the gods." At that moment the ground rippled gently under their feet. He looked down at Britta, but she shook her head. Karn thanked whatever god had made the earth roll. As he looked up, fear undulated around the circle.

Ivar decided, "She is yours." He grinned. "Keep her content at home, jarl of the fens."

Karn nodded once, whistled for Fenris, and turned quickly away, before the sons of Ragnar Lothbrok could take back the promise. He settled Britta more comfortably against his chest as he strode down the hill into the confusion of the battlefield. Some would say he had got what he wanted, Britta and the land. But neither was in Ivar's power to give. Only the Saxons could let him live in peace beside them. Only Britta could give him what he wanted most. But he feared she belonged to the magic now. He belonged nowhere and to no one.

Britta watched Karn pull a shirt foraged from the dead over his head. Wounds, some fresh, some older, marked his body, but she could do nothing for him. She had not even the supplies to stitch them. He grabbed the leather jerkin and the cloaks he had taken. The sun was heading for the horizon. They had rested, but still she was empty, and Karn looked exhausted.

"We must leave this place today, Britta." His eyes were serious, even sad, as he placed a cloak gently over her shoulders. "I will see you safely to Dunford, if you wish it."

The world closed in on Britta like the banging of a cell door. He would see her to Dunford? Did he not mean to stay with her? But how could it be otherwise? *No one can love a woman who causes the earth to quake.* She assumed he had once loved her, but she didn't even know that for sure. Shame surprised her. The time at Stowa was an interlude for him, like a thousand others on the Frankish coast, among the Saracens. She had forgotten he was a Viking. Her feelings for him clouded the meaning of the word barbarian until she was seduced into foolishness. He would be off as soon as he had disposed of her.

She managed to shake her head. "Not Dunford."

Karn looked uneasy. "You cannot stay here."

"Where do you go?" Did that question reveal too much of her soul to him?

The uneasiness in Karn's expression deepened. "To the fens, as fast as I may."

It was as good as any place. "I will go to Stowa," she whispered.

He nodded and lifted her to Thorn's back. Her mouth felt like carded wool. The nerves in her hands woke to stabbing life. Her future stretched bleakly ahead. When news of the earthquake spread, would she not be overwhelmed with supplicants for healing, kings wanting faestens breached, or predictions of the future? The magic itself might be gone, but that wouldn't stop the stories. Isolation in the fens or the life of a nun might be the only ways left to her.

Karn led Thorn forward. She was glad they were going to the fens. When he had left her, the sere landscape would match the spirit that remained to her, as it matched Wydda's spirit. Perhaps the fens needed a new witch.

Karn led Thorn and Britta between the carcasses at the edge of the killing ground, Fenris stalking behind them. He searched for the trail that ran southeast. He would do his duty by Britta, and by Stowa, but it would give him no joy. Perhaps nothing could, not anymore.

His thoughts were occupied thus darkly when a figure with a forked beard stepped out of a grove of trees to his left. Karn's head jerked up and he went still.

The moment was thrust upon him by the gods, gift or curse, whatever he would make it. He threw Thorn's reins to Britta, dimly registering her fear. Then he turned. It was him alone against all his fear, all his doubts of himself, and against Offa. Somehow the thegn had survived.

A slow grimace of satisfaction spread over Offa's face. Blood still smeared one side of his countenance, but otherwise he looked little the worse for his sojourn in the crevasse. He hefted his sword to get a better grip. Karn noted grimly that it was springy in his hand. Dread dug a pit in his belly. There was a time when he would have welcomed death in battle. But he could not leave Britta alone to face a victorious Offa. Another sickening uncertainty rolled through the ground like a wave. Shouts of fear echoed behind them.

Offa staggered forward. "I live, Witch, and you are spent."

"Beware the storms, Offa," Britta breathed.

The Saxon laughed, low in his throat. Karn remembered that laugh. "I thought of a proof for your sainthood, Witch.

347

Do you forgive what I did to you, to your father, your mother?"

Karn glanced up at her and saw her as Offa did, drained and fragile. Fenris nosed her foot tentatively, but she did not respond. Karn thought fear choked her.

"No," she whispered at last. "I do not forgive you."

Offa looked relieved. "Then you are not a saint. I will punish your defiance, both of you."

Karn lifted his sword. "You will try." Britta could not help him now. That was as it should be. Could he hamstring Offa as he had Ulf? He used both hands to draw sluggish circles with his sword point. He had no shield now, no chain mail, but it didn't matter. This could not be a battle of defense. Thor, he prayed, you abandoned me before. Yet I fought back from defeat. Does that not give me the right to call on you now? Give my arm strength!

Offa grinned as he saw that Kara must hold his sword with both hands. "Tired, Viking? I see your blood. This will be short work for a potent Saxon thegn."

Karn did not waste breath responding. He stood, stubbornly, waiting. He had not long to wait. Offa lunged in, his sword swinging in a deadly arc. Karn raised his own to parry. The force of the blow sent him staggering. The clang of steel rang in his ears.

Again Offa struck. Karn managed to parry and retreat to avoid the full force of the blow. It was just like fighting Cedric, with as much disparity of strength. But Offa was inventive, coming at Karn from all angles. Karn gave way, avoiding bodies as he stumbled backwards, hoping to save strength in case Offa left him an opening. But an opening did not come.

The thegn bared his teeth. "Soon, now, Viking," he panted. "But don't think I'll kill you."

Waste your breath, Karn thought. His own wind and strength were hard to find. He swung his blade out to get at Offa's legs as he had with Ulf, but his enemy parried easily.

"You'll pay for that." Offa's eyes gleamed. He redoubled his efforts. Retreating under the rain of blows, Karn stumbled over a corpse. He pushed himself up and rebuffed Offa's sword with his own. His legs would hardly hold him.

"Your old wounds betray you," Offa gasped. "Shoulder, wasn't it?" Clang and retreat. "And your hip?" Offa swung his blade in a circle and got inside Karn's guard. The point of Offa's sword ripped through his breeches over his hip. This man knew all his weaknesses. He was toying with Karn. Clang and stagger backward.

"You bled from your backside too," Offa sneered.

Karn tried not to let the old shame overwhelm him. Shame and fear were his enemies. Time was his enemy. He weakened with every blow. Thor had not heard his prayer. Anger began to grind up from his belly. Did it amuse the god to let this small-souled Saxon steal the joy of a whole body and his warrior's pride? Karn lurched forward and thrust his sword up under Offa's.

Offa leaped back. "Oh, ho, that brings a rise out of him," he gasped. "Does his member rise, too, at the memory of it?" He came at Karn straight on and bore him backwards yet again.

Anger and frustration burst their chains inside Karn. Offa would have him and Britta, too. He was not enough of a man to beat this barbarian hand to hand. He tried to push back anger; it would not restore his strength. He could not let it steal his wits. Offa came on again, his sword gleaming dully in the dusty light.

Wits. Wits! He let Offa's sword slide down his own, then stumbled over another carcass and went down. He had been praying to the wrong god. It was not Thor who could help him now but Loki. Only by one of Loki's tricks could he win. He got to his knees and held up his sword to protect his head from Offa's blows. Offa knew he had won. The metal rang again and again.

Loki, he prayed. Trickster. Your tricks are Little Magic. Lend me a little magic now. Offa leaned in on Karn's sword, using his strength to grind down the last of Karn's will. He pushed up against Offa's weight, his head down. Sweat dripped into his eyes. He could hardly see or breathe. His last stamina was giving way. Offa had won. I'm sorry, Britta, he thought.

Through the sweat he saw an axe, a Saxon weapon at his knees, its handle loose in a dead man's hand. But Karn had no strength to use it. Loki never uses strength, he heard a voice in his head say. He stared at the axe and then turned his face up toward Offa.

His foe's narrow eyes, so close to his own, gleamed in anticipation. The only way left to him was to risk all. He took in all the air he could grab with his lungs and abandoned strength. He let go of his sword. It spun off to his left. Offa's weight, leaning on the sword, took him forward and left as Karn rolled to the right. Offa fell beside him, a look of surprise on his hard face. Karn scooped up the axe in trembling hands. The other man hit the ground with a thud. Karn struggled back to his knees. He boosted the axe into the air, putting his hips into it to aid his shaky arms. The weapon arced up, aiming for Offa's back. His target rolled left. Karn panicked. This, his last blow, would miss his enemy. With a roar of effort he pushed the arc of the axe after Offa. Offa's sword came up.

It was too late. The weight of the axe head carried it down, as though it had a will of its own. It buried itself in Offa's skull between the eyes, their surprised look now frozen there forever.

Karn knelt, hands on his knees, trying to get enough air into his lungs. The Saxon's corpse twitched and twitched again, as it realized its death but slowly.

"Thank you, Loki," Karn whispered at last, "You taught me a truth."

When Kara had command of his body, he looked around for Britta. She had slid from Thorn's back to hold Fenris. Now she took a step in his direction, arms outstretched, but her legs could not hold her. She wavered and sat abruptly in the dirt some thirty feet away. He gathered up Walther's sword and half-crawled, half-stumbled to kneel beside her and take her in his arms. He just held her, pressing her head against his heaving chest. He could feel her trembling.

"I could not help you," she whispered.

"As well you could not," he answered, his throat full. "It was for me to finish."

She looked up at him. "I must not be a saint," she whispered. "I could not forgive him."

"We agree, Britta," Karn muttered. "I did not forgive either."

Britta felt Thorn's shoulders move under her as he walked behind Karn. The afternoon waned. Life without Karn stretched ahead bleakly. He did not look back at her. Fenris circled out to catch the scent of whatever had passed this way. Karn's wounds began to call louder, but there was nothing inside her to answer them. Offa was dead by Karn's hand. That should make her happy. Wasn't that what she had wanted all these years? It merely added to her emptiness.

The sun set, but still Karn pressed on, stumbling in exhaustion.

"Karn, stop. You need rest and so do I," she finally complained. "Why do you hurry?"

He looked up, his face drawn in the twilight. Insects sang in the new wet grass around them. "Ulf went with a party of Danir to Stowa looking for me."

He needn't say more. The only question was whether any in Stowa were left alive.

"Then ride with me." His wounds tugged at her insistently. They were getting worse.

"For a while." Once he would simply have boosted himself up behind her. Now he led Thorn to a rocky outcropping and clambered up awkwardly.

As he pulled her against him, she understood why. He burned with fever. Shocked at the heat, she turned to see eyes too bright. He would not look at her, but urged Thorn on.

The feel of him against her was a torment. The night deepened and the call of his wounds wound up into a howl that tore at her sanity. They must be festering already. She couldn't help him. She wasn't sure she would be able to help anyone ever again.

At last he sagged against her. She grabbed the reins and pulled Thorn up. Fenris whined at their feet, knowing something was wrong. Britta slipped to the ground and tugged at Karn. He slid off their horse and staggered heavily against her. She braced him up and looked around, panicked, then half-dragged him to a spot sheltered by some boulders in a grove of oaks.

He lay down with a groan. She scrambled around for pieces of wood and struck her flint with trembling hands. When fire leapt up, Britta dreaded what its light would reveal.

"I wanted this land," he said behind her, his voice thick with exhaustion. She turned slowly. The blackness on his wounds struck her like a fist.

She knelt and touched him. His fever burned her hand, even through his cloak. His wounds had soured into that kind of poison that raced through the body quickly. Fear pounded at her until she couldn't think. The one thing that could help him was gone. Was this her punishment for trying to wield magic? The blackness pulsed and grew until the firelight could not illuminate him. It pooled in his center, a knot of death.

Her eyes filled as she looked into his face. He knew it. "I can't bear it," she thought, and found she had whispered it aloud.

"Yes, you can," he said roughly, his breath rasping. "It is the way of the world."

Her stomach clenched. Not Karn! The magic had saved him for some reason. The world must need him. *She* needed him. She knew she must try, no matter how empty she felt.

She seized his knife and ripped his jerkin and the cloth of his shirt to reveal the jagged, festering wound in his shoulder, throbbing with blackness. It looked two days old and more. She sliced the bandage about his thigh. His breeches opened over a putrid gash that screamed at her. She prayed for the power to come as it had come before, in a rush that would make her faint. Rocking on her knees, her soul bare to the elements, she howled silently for it to come.

There was no rush. She felt only small. She couldn't think for the panic, for the shrieking of Karn's wounds. It wasn't coming! Sobs choked her as she rocked forward against his body. Without thinking, without hope, she placed one hand full on his thigh, the other on his shoulder.

A shock charged out through her palms. Her lips pulled into a grimace. Again and again her body jerked against his, as the power surged through her. At last, she collapsed against him, limp. She struggled erect and pulled her hands away. In the flickering light she could just make out a pink-skinned circle, the only evidence of the jagged rent in his shoulder. The muscles under the smooth skin of his thigh bunched and released as he blinked slowly into awareness.

He was healed, so much better than with her crude stitching long ago. The magic had been there all the time, lurking inside her, waiting for what it wanted to do.

A shuddering breath filled her lungs. Wait! She scrabbled at his clothing until she revealed the old scar on his hip, the jagged line on his other shoulder she remembered so well. Could she not mend her former lack? She almost crowed in satisfaction. He would be a cripple no longer! She placed her hands deliberately on those old wounds.

Nothing happened. She pressed her hands into his flesh, feeling the warmth, the shock of longing that touching him engendered, but no more. For long minutes she stayed that way, rocking gently back and forth, until she knew it was no use.

She opened her eyes. "The magic won't heal the old wounds," she whispered. Why would it save him but not make him whole?

He sat up with a grunt of effort and took her in his arms. "Would you change who I am?" There was a smile somewhere behind his eyes. "I am haltr now." He used the Danish word. "It is the price I paid to be who I am."

"Your Danegeld?" It hurt to think of what he had lost.

"No, Britta," he said, serious. "One chooses to pay Danegeld, to banish what one fears. But when what you fear comes back, the cost increases."

She looked at him, considering. "I see. You did not choose your wounds," she said. "But then it was Danegeld when you tried to pay with your life on the beach, to banish fear of what you had become."

He nodded. "As you paid to make your magic go away once." He fingered her hair.

She hesitated. "That was not the only reason I lay with you." Did he not know how she yearned for those days when they thought the magic gone? "But as you say, it didn't go away."

He let her go awkwardly. "The world's gain." Resignation echoed in those words.

"I don't care about the world." She shook her head.

He reached out to smooth her hair behind her ears, then thought better of it. "You would be a great teacher, Britta."

She breathed out sharply. "I don't want to be a teacher. I don't want to end like Wydda, or live a life of isolation like the abbess." What she wanted was impossible.

He looked down at his hands as though they didn't belong to him. The tension of not touching filled the air around them, until she thought neither would ever speak or move again. She had to say something, she told herself. But what was there to say?

Karn finally spoke, as though his words would choke him. "I know what I want."

Britta's gaze darted about his face. He wanted to go viking to lands where triumph and women and riches awaited. Say it, Britta urged silently. If you say it, I will be released.

His voice seemed torn from his throat. "I want...what I fought for, Britta I want you."

She stared at him, struggling to push down the elation that threatened her resolve. It didn't matter. He wanted her as she had been in Stowa, barren of magic, not as she was now.

"Hush," he said, and touched a finger to the tears on her cheeks. The shock of that touch started the sobs. "You don't have to say it. A woman with your power would not live in the fens with one who limps and tills the land."

She lifted her head. He thought *she* would not want him? "Oh, but I would," she hiccuped through her tears. "I brought down the faesten to save you, Karn, not for the future."

Karn gripped her arms as though he would shake her. She drew back, frightened at the intensity in his face. "You can't know what living with magic will be like," she faltered.

"You don't know either, Britta." He pressed her now. "You won't be abbess, you won't be Wydda. You will be you."

"I could not ask…"

"You can ask nothing I would not give. Did you not give me back my life?"

"I could not help but heal you," she whispered. She didn't want him to owe her.

"I did not mean the healing." His eyes burned blue. One callused hand touched her hair, then slipped behind her neck, asking gently, "I meant now, when you say you love me."

How had she ever thought his eyes icy? Her fingers traced the curve of his jaw before she could stop them. The touching she had so feared once bathed her in wholeness, like the magic at its best. His face clenched, as though in pain. He took her in his arms, so fiercely she couldn't breathe, and held her to his chest. His heart thudded in her ears, echoing her own. She turned up her face to kiss the hollow of his throat where his blood beat. His countenance softened as he bent to kiss her, but his lips pressed hers ruthlessly. It was a Viking's kiss and she returned it.

Anything could happen. He might leave her tomorrow. Magic might strike at any moment, or leave her dry and yearning. How could one know? Her arms encircled his neck. One couldn't keep the world out, as she had tried to do for so many years. One couldn't banish what one feared. It was the nature of courage to try to make life what you wanted, whether nothing about the future was certain or everything was foreordained.

"I'll try," she whispered, their lips so near she breathed his life and sent hers back to him.

He stood and helped her up. "We go to Stowa, to make the best of what we find."

Epilogue

Witch or saint—which? If the gods know, or the one God knows, neither has told me. I have decided it doesn't matter whether grace or magic runs in my veins. I can only open myself to the world's direction, no matter how fearful that is. Who gives that direction, I will never know.

The direction can seem contradictory. They made Edmund a saint though he didn't deserve it. The town known as Bury St. Edmund thrives on the coins of his pilgrims. All in the seven kingdoms who are free to give allegiance have named Alfred king. He deserves all his honor and more. The east of the island, under the Danish king, Guthrum, is now the Danelaw. Two kingdoms, but one people. For now they speak the same language, simple and strong. It happened quickly, as Saxon maid whispered to her Danish lover and Dane traded horses with his Saxon neighbor. People learned to adapt and that made them stronger, too.

You ask of Kara and me? The heartache, the adventure of our lives belongs to another song. Know only we returned to Stowa to find some dead, Saxon and Dane, and some living. Jael married Hild. Kara built a dike and knit Saxon and Viking together, in spite of their differences. Perhaps because of his suffering, Karn grew to be a wise leader. He named Walther's sword Friend of Freya, goddess of fertility and farmers. Karn never became a Christian, as other Norsemen did. He prays to Loki, to Freya, and sometimes even to Thor. He says it takes wisdom to practice the old religion. You decide whom to pray to and still that god might not help you. Our beliefs are not so different.

Fenris had many sons, each labeled my familiar. Thorn sired a long line of fine warrior horses that are Karn's pride. Ivar took the secret of Karn's stirrups to the Frankish coast, where the Norsemen there called Normans will bring it back to conquer those who did not understand.

The magic fades. Most cannot believe those wild deeds sung in the sagas are mine and Karn's. But I will listen to the world until it has no more use for me, unsure to the end.

Only in the sagas are we sure.

Made in the USA
Charleston, SC
13 October 2013